# The Red-Ribboned Letters

E. Philip Trapp

PHOENIX INTERNATIONAL, INC.
2003

07   06   05   04   03      5   4   3   2   1

Designed by John Coghlan

Inquiries should be addressed to:

**PHOENIX INTERNATIONAL, INC.**
1501 Stubblefield Road
Fayetteville, Arkansas 72703
Phone (479) 521-2204
www.phoenixbase.com


**Library of Congress Cataloging-in-Publication Data**

Trapp, E. Philip, 1923–
    The red-ribboned letters / E. Philip Trapp.
        p. cm.
    ISBN 0-9713470-3-4 (alk. paper)
    1. World War, 1939–1945—California—San Diego—Fiction. 2. United States. Navy—Officers—Fiction. 3. Hospitals, Naval and marine—Fiction. 4. San Diego (Calif.)—Fiction. I. Title.
    PS3620.R37R43 2003
    813'.6—dc21

                                                                2003012480

To the unsung heroes of WW II, the mothers, wives, and sweethearts who, in angst, made the tanks, ships, and planes, the engines of victory

In this documentary within a novel the love letters of Tally are true. None is excluded and each is presented in its entirety. Other than the changing of names to protect privacy, not a word was added or deleted to keep intact every nuance of thought and feeling of a young woman in love during a war that would take over fifty million lives.

The Red-Ribboned Letters

# The Meeting

San Diego, a seaport of such an even and gentle climate that the natives grumble whenever the mercury dips below 50 or climbs above 75, had a population of approximately 200,000 in the early years of the 1940s. With the outskirts mostly open country and the sea breezes steadily blowing in, the night howls of the coyotes could be distinctly heard in the heart of the city. Balboa Park, a fourteen-hundred-acre colossus constructed for the 1915 Exposition to celebrate the opening of the Panama Canal, the waterway that put San Diego on the map as America's first port of call on the Pacific, was the cultural center, its landmark and famous tourist attraction a world-class zoo.

The tragedy of Pearl Harbor directly affected many families in the old mission town as it was the home base of the destroyed fleet less than a year before. Reaction was swift. The bay soon bustled with activity in the forming of a new and much more powerful navy. Downtown at any hour was a sea of bell-bottom blue.

Times were tense and hectic. Skylights were painted black, and searchlights crossed the skies nightly looking for enemy planes. Plants ran three shifts to keep pace with war demands.

Hollywood's biggest stars led war-bond rallies. Wives and sweethearts flowed in and out of town in delirious greetings and teary farewells. War brides became the norm in the popular live-for-today philosophy. Sailors often proposed after the first dance in a town swept up in wartime hysteria.

Reality quickly began to take the romance out of the excitement. As the fighting increased, so did the gold stars on windows and the arrival of amputees and other severely injured to further crowd the military hospitals.

It was the transfer of her brother Ted, splattered with shrapnel in Guadalcanal, to the large navy hospital that brought twenty-one-year-old Tally Dugan to San Diego. She left her hometown of Denver in October of 1943, hitching a ride with a family friend, a truck driver, to be by Ted's side for the many surgeries yet to face him.

Tally had no sooner unloaded her luggage than she dashed to the hospital. When she stood at the door and saw him lying on the bed, one eye totally gone, part of his lower jaw missing, and a lip deformed, she was shocked. For a moment she thought she was in the wrong room. Could this be her brother, the strong, handsome youth who well could have posed as the poster marine for recruitment? She was told it would be bad but had not thought this bad.

She moved slowly up to his bed and lightly grasped his hand. "I love you, Ted," was all she could say. This was her first introduction to the cruelty of war and she wasn't prepared for it.

He looked up and made out her form. "Tally!" he gasped. There was a long pause. Then he mustered a weak smile. "What's a good-looking dish like you doing in a dump like this?"

Tally rallied her wits. "To flirt with my favorite marine. Might even pitch a tent for a few months if he acts decent."

"How in God's name did you get here?"

"Bummed a ride with Pat Wilson, who was running a load to the Coast. I'm staying with his cousin Ella until I find a place of my own."

Ted's body suddenly stiffened. A tear dropped on his cheek. He clenched a fist. "Lord, I didn't want you to see me like this. I'm a wreck. Don't know if I'll make it. Don't even know if I want to." He tapped his chest. "Still some scrap iron in it. Doc says I'm in for a slew of surgeries on the face alone." His breathing quickened. "The marriage, too, is dead in the water. Jenny was here, you know, repelled by what she saw. Is back home likely in conference with a lawyer at this moment. Can't blame her. God, what's the future? What can a man do with a broken body and a face that scares dogs and kids?" Starting to choke up, he stopped talking.

Tally gently squeezed his hand. "I know it'll be a long haul, but you'll make it. Got to. We need each other. You mean more to me than the rest of the family put together. So, however long it takes, I'm staying on. I think Jenny will stand by too. I saw her before I left and I can tell she still loves you." Tally slowly released her grip. "Look, I gotta go now. We just pulled in. Haven't even unpacked my toothbrush. Only wanted to pop in to let you know I'm in town and plan to stay. Tomorrow I'll be pounding the streets for a job and a place to live. But once I'm settled, I'll be checking in on you regularly." She moved to the door, turned, and blew him a kiss.

"Tally," Ted called out, "hell, I'm glad you came."

Out in the hall she leaned against the wall and softly sobbed.

Things fell rather quickly into place. Convair, a huge aircraft company—aeronautics and the military the lifeblood of San Diego since the first World War—had an opening in their Research and Development Division. Tally's artistic skills landed her a job on the swing shift in the engineering section. She met two other workers in the production department during a coffee break, Cindy and Debbie, who, it turned out, had recently rented a house and were looking for a compatible third roomie to ease expenses. They bonded instantly and arrangements were made for Tally to live at the "ranch," the pet name for the house because of a stable at the rear for Debbie's champion horse. The largest bedroom, with twin beds, would be shared by Tally and Cindy. Debbie would take the smaller second bedroom, and the third one would be reserved for overnight guests. The spacious living area with a fireplace would be a multipurpose room available for parties, entertaining friends, relaxing to music, and holding after-hours gab sessions.

Two other workers at the plant, Susan and Avis, though living elsewhere, became habitual visitors. The quintet, calling themselves the "Inner Circle," formed an intimate support group, balancing their work schedules with fun activities such as dances, picnics, horseback riding, tennis, swimming, dining out, and going to movies and concerts.

The war had dramatically altered lifestyles. Gas rationing now led to the popular use of car-pooling and public transportation. Whenever one hopped onto a streetcar, it was usually standing room only. Biking and horseback riding replaced weekend cruising in roadsters. The rumble-seat era was over. Rationing of food and clothing made ordinary shopping trips an adventure. Morale bent but never broke because everyone believed in the cause and had faith that right would prevail. All saw a better tomorrow, like the song said: There'll be love and laughter and peace ever after. Personal comforts were gladly sacrificed for national needs.

Soon after getting settled in, Tally and Cindy, in bed but not yet sandy-eyed, got into a chat begun by the picture of Dave, Cindy's beau, on her bed stand. "I've been admiring the photo," Tally said. "A very nice-looking guy. How'd you two meet?"

"It was in college before the war. I was a sophomore and he a senior. We were at the same party, but I hardly noticed him as he's not the flashy type. It did strike me though that he looked like Gary Cooper: tall, lanky, honest looking. He didn't mingle much with the girls. So, I was taken by surprise when he called a few days later and asked for a date. Now being very fond of Gary Cooper, I thought why not. We had a good time, went to dinner, saw a movie, *The Maltese Falcon* with Humphrey Bogart, and then went home. He was sweet but not exactly amorous. A week went by and no phone calls, so I figured it was all just a lark. I scratched him off my list."

"Then what happened?"

"A month later, mind you, a whole month later, he called and said he had two tickets to a Hoagy Carmichael concert. Well, who could resist that! I put him back on the list. It was a marvelous concert, we both loved it, and I would say it jump-started the relationship."

Tally laughed. "Love blossomed with the playing of 'Stardust.' Why not! It's a wonderful tune."

"It became our song," Cindy purred. She continued. "Before long, we were going steady, got dead serious, and kicked around the idea of getting married when I graduated. Then the war broke out. That put a hold on things. Well, to make a long story short, Dave got a commission, went to a training school, and ended up a line officer on the *Colorado*. I got to see him for several days in San Francisco before he shipped out. That night I cried myself to sleep, certain it would be a couple of years before I'd see him again." Cindy's eyes flashed. "You can bet when he sails back to port, I'll have a justice of the peace handcuffed to the dock! So that's my story. . . . Now how about you, Tally. How is it that a beautiful Maureen O'Hara hasn't a picture on her bed stand?"

"Guess Susan and I are two of a kind. Two frivolous floozies content to play the field."

"You don't fool me! There's more to it than that. Will the real Tally Dugan please speak up."

"You want the morbid details? Okay. But I swear, Cindy Gilligan, if you so much as leak any of it out, I'll deny it and accuse you of malicious gossip."

"Cross my heart and wish to die if I breathe a word."

Tally took a deep breath. "I've had two serious affairs. My first big pash was in high school. He was the football captain and I, being his girlfriend, was voted homecoming queen. We dated throughout our entire senior year, seemed to be perfectly suited, and everybody expected us to marry after graduation and live happily ever after, in the storied Hollywood ending. But when he proposed, a little voice inside of me raised a doubt. It baffled me. Why the doubt? I couldn't figure it out. He was loads of fun and popular with my friends. Could it be my broken-home complex?

You see, my parents divorced when I was young. I stayed with my mother, who was bitter about men, and we didn't get along very well. I don't know if that had anything to do with it, but as long as any doubts persisted, and they never went away, I couldn't in fairness to either of us accept. The news shocked everyone. My best girlfriend, Lois, thought I had slipped a cog." Tally let out a short laugh. "I can happily say his grief was short-lived. He quickly found a charming replacement, the wedding bells rang, and at last report they are living in a cozy white cottage with a rose garden."

"The second affair, pray tell."

"It happened about a year later. He was part of the town's old wealth, Ivy-League educated, well mannered, certainly one of the best catches in town. He took me to the finest places, treated me like royalty. If there ever was a rock of security, he was it, and he represented everything a girl could wish in a man: wealth, status, culture, the whole ball of wax.

"On this special occasion he took me to this very posh private club. With violins in the background he dined me on caviar, champagne, and quail under glass. Very heady for a simple working girl. Then, during crepes suzette he presented me with a small jeweled box. My eyes popped on opening it. I never saw a diamond so big or so brilliant. I dreaded to think what it must have set him back. Then suddenly, that little doubting voice rose again inside of me. I was in a terrible bind. I couldn't ignore it, yet to heed it would ruin a perfect evening. He sensed my turmoil and came to the rescue. Took the box and told me he was in no hurry for an answer, just wanted me to be aware of his devious plan and have time to run a character check. I thanked him profusely."

"You had to be plumb out of your mind," Cindy gasped.

"Exactly what my friend Lois said. She declared she knew no female more fickle this side of the Great Divide. I've begun to think she might be right. Maybe I was born with a loose wire that makes lasting intimacy impossible. One of nature's freaks destined to travel alone through life's long journey."

"Heavens to Betsy! Perish the thought! When Mr. Right comes along, that little voice will not spout a doubt."

"That's what I once thought. I'd know immediately. No waffling. Now I'm not so sure."

"Two strikes is not out, sweetie. Gads, it's three A.M. Let's get some sleep. We've got tennis tomorrow with Avis and Susan."

"Just one more thing, Cindy," Tally said softly, "I couldn't have wished for a better roomie. Good night."

Despite her busy schedule of work, play, and house chores, Tally visited Ted almost daily. She even signed up at the hospital for volunteer work, being a Girl Friday, reading to those without eyes, walking for those without legs, writing for those without hands. The volunteers were instructed to keep a cheerful front while interacting with the patients, but it often taxed Tally to the limit, especially when thinking of how much they've been cheated of life's normal activities. The good news with Ted was that although his progress was frustratingly slow, he had by the Christmas season got off the critical list. Between surgeries he often got passes to go to the ranch for short visits where he was warmly embraced as an honorary member.

A stir took place when Tally received an invitation to a New Year's Day cocktail party sponsored by the Research and Development Division of Convair at the Skyroom in the El Cortez Hotel. Being the only one of the Inner Circle in R&D, she was at first reluctant to attend. Cindy argued the case for it. "It gives you the chance to meet people, especially some VIPs who, I'm sure, will be there. Who knows what tall, dark, and handsome Robert Taylor may be lurking in the wings."

Tally tossed a sofa pillow at her. "You and your glamorous movie stars!" She tossed a second pillow. "And you and your boy-meet-girl fantasies!" She caught a returning pillow. "I want you to know, Miss Matchmaker, war is no setting for a sensible damsel to get herself entangled in an amour. But I'll concede you one point. I should get to know my fellow workers better. And," laughing, "it does give me a chance to wear my pretty pink cock-tail dress while it's still halfway in style."

It was a lovely party. Tally arrived looking festive in her pink chiffon dress and matching satin slippers on pencil-thin heels. She had fixed her dark auburn hair into a high upsweep. Eyes turned on her. She had intended on staying less than an hour, but when she glanced about the elegant room and saw champagne bubbling in stemmed crystal, caviar on silver trays, and people glowing in *bonhomie*, she adjusted her time frame.

After taking an offered glass, she eased her way to "Pops" Marley, her boss, chief engineer of the night crew, to pay her respects. He greeted her cordially and introduced her to Robert Graham, the person he was conversing with, a man in his late twenties, square chinned, square shouldered, and with the height to carry well his stocky frame. Tally noticed his pleasant smile and the fine cut of his suit. "Robert," Pops said, "is vice president of sales for one of our suppliers."

"I'm impressed," Tally responded, "to meet one who has climbed so fast."

"Don't be," Robert replied, blushing slightly. "We're just a small company lucky to be in the right place when Convair got its contract for the B-24 bomber."

Pops laughed. "Don't let Robert's modesty fool you. He sold us on his company against stiff competition to supply the key parts for our new fancy tricycle landing gears. This young man is a whiz at sales. He could sell furnaces in July in Death Valley!"

Detecting Robert's growing uneasiness at being the focus of praise, Tally brought relief in feigning the excuse that she best break away and meet her obligation to greet several people to whom she felt indebted. There was gratitude in his eyes as he expressed his pleasure in meeting her.

The waiters, attired in white vests and black bow ties, seemed to make it their mission to keep the glasses full. By the time Tally was ready to leave, shortly after another brief but pleasant chat with Robert, who had finally escaped the clutches of Pops, she had the rosy feeling she had slightly overreached her capacity. When she returned to the ranch, she plopped on the sofa, shoes off, to face Cindy and Debbie, all ears for a full report.

"Well," Tally said, unable to conceal a slight slur, "I'm glad you coaxed me into going, Cindy. The party was beautiful. The Skyroom was beautiful. The people were beautiful . . ."

"And," a smiling Cindy injected, "to pardon the interruption, I bet the champagne, too, was beautiful."

"Wooee! One of the waiters had a bead on me. The moment my glass was empty, he'd pounce. However," Tally giggled, "despite what flaws you critics may observe in my elocution, I assure you, I am in complete control of my faculties."

"Just the same," Debbie said, "I'm putting on some coffee."

"Did you meet anyone?" Cindy grilled.

"Of course. Bunches and bunches."

"That's not what I mean. Anyone special?"

"No Sir Galahad if that's what you mean. Pops did introduce me to a VIP, though. He was shy, modest, but rather cute. A vice president of something from one of our suppliers. Must be quite good to be a top executive and only in his twenties."

"What does he look like?"

"No Robert Taylor, but no Boris Karloff either. He has a nice smile and is soft-spoken. We didn't talk too long because he was getting embarrassed at the way Pops was fussing over him. So I eased away. I did chat again with him but I don't think women are too much on his mind. His head seems all on business."

Debbie returned with the coffee. She filled the cups, passed them, then raised hers. "Not champagne, my fellow musketeers, but to a happy New Year, anyway."

The winter flew by. It began as a major adjustment for Tally. It was her first winter without snow. No tobogganing, no ice skating, not even a snowman to build. But she soon discovered a new love. The ocean. She had never seen one before and she found a fascination in strolling along the shoreline and hearing the surf pounding the rocks. She had arrived in San Diego during its wettest time—most of its ten inches of annual precipitation fall between November and March. It enthralled her to walk in the rain and see the distant ocean turn into clouds of soft vapor, stirring her the same way as to walk in the falling snow and see the distant Rockies turn into clouds of soft cotton.

St. Patrick's Day, the harbinger of spring, suddenly loomed up on the calendar. Tally, Cindy, and Susan excitedly looked forward to being hostesses at the Irish Ball held at the historic Hotel del Coronado. Debbie had to pass because of an out-of-town horse show; and Avis, too, who was hobbling about on a sprained ankle suffered in a tennis match. So the trio, decked out in the color of the day, and looking every bit as Irish as the names of Dugan, Gilligan, and Rafferty would imply, boarded the ferry that crossed the bay to the peninsula of Coronado.

The dance committee outdid themselves in converting the Crown Room, a nineteenth-century architectural gem, into a leprechaun fantasyland. Green balloons hung from the fabulous chandeliers with papier-mâché elves peeping over and between them. Painted shamrocks on crepe paper decorated the paneled walls, and grinning leprechauns ornamented the tablecloths and napkins. The ball, after all, was to honor the boys about to head overseas, and the *Zeitgeist* dictated that no outlay was too extravagant for those preparing to go the last mile to defend our liberties.

The navy, as usual, arrived *en masse* and in high spirits. The girls were barely settled at their table displaying their pinned-on hostess badges when they were mobbed. Slower numbers moved to faster numbers, and then to the boogie beat, the latest craze. Tally, at ease with all tempos, was caught on a nonstop acrobatic track, the final phase finding herself flying from jitterbugger to jitterbugger, relief coming only when the band stopped to catch their own breath.

She slumped in her chair to join Cindy and Susan, who had returned earlier from the fray and were watching with amusement the gymnastics of the remaining few still in action. "If the band had gone on two more minutes," Tally gasped, "the paramedics would have had to cart me out."

"But you've got the beat down," Susan said. "I admire your stamina."

"Who taught you?" Cindy asked.

"No learning to it. It's just feeling and reacting and hoping there's rubber in the bones." Tally mopped her brow with a napkin. "But a small dose goes a long way. When you're bouncing from partner to partner like on a trampoline, it's a marathon. Believe me, I'm not budging until after intermission."

As she finished talking and as the band began reassembling, she heard a voice with a light brogue waft above the rumble of the room noises. "Would the fair colleen care to whirl with the likes of a Timothy O'Reilly?"

She looked back and up to stare into eyes as sparkling as the sapphire in her ring and a smile so warm as to run her mascara if she held her stare. A surge of adrenalin swept through her and instantly revived her weary body. "Well, begorra," she gushed, "indeed she might."

On the dance floor she nestled comfortably in his arms. He was just the right height and moved ever so lightly on his feet. The band began playing a Cole Porter medley, opening with the perennial favorite "Night and Day." "Shall we do the Dip?" he softly asked.

"Let us dip," she softly answered.

With his hand gently altering pressure on her back, she was able to anticipate his every move, be it a forward or a backward bend, a single or a double twirl, a short or a long dip. Her skirt would flare out when she spun. They glided as smoothly as skaters in an ice revue.

"Wonderful dancing with you," Tally bubbled as the long medley came to its end and intermission formally arrived. As she started to move toward her table, he took her arm and eased her instead toward the exit. Suddenly they were outside. "And where might we be going?" she asked, eyebrows slightly arching.

He pointed toward the north sky. "If the Rose of Erin must be shared, then let it be with the biggest Dipper of them all."

Tally heard the pitter-patter in her heart. The little voice inside of her, ordinarily the conscience of restraint, was the bellwether of revolt. Erin go Bragh, it cried, seize the moment and let the devil take hindmost! Whereupon Tally committed the cardinal sin of war: She deserted her post. With eyes fixed on the Great Bear, she flung forward a hand, the go-ahead to take off for the stars.

They locked fingers and bounded for the sea. She suddenly stopped short. "My purse! I left it at the table."

"Taken care of. Your most cooperative friends returned my signal. It's in safe hands."

"Timothy O'Reilly, you dog, you had this all preplanned. You are incorrigible!"

"Kidnapping, my dove, is not for bungling amateurs. Requires teamwork, especially when the quarry is so popular as to command a high ransom. But now that I've snatched you from the madding crowd, be of stout heart and face the perils. Let us fly."

And fly they did. At the shoreline, he paused, smiled, and above the rustle of the breakers softly sang several lines of "The Rose of Tralee."

> She was lovely and fair
> As the rose of the summer.
> Yet, twas not her beauty
> Alone that won me.

Oh, no, twas the truth
In her eye ever dawning
That made me love *Tally*
The Rose of Tralee.

Tally held the vision. A pale moon, indeed, was rising, not above the green mountain but above the beautiful green sea. She pressured his hand. "I love the ballad," she said.

They wandered leisurely along the shore, two blithe spirits, taking in the sights and smells and sounds of the ocean, oblivious to a world at war. He talked of his fascination of nature, marveling as much at the serenity of her sunsets as at the fury of her storms. Tally, in turn, raved on with her enchantment of the ocean, as awed with its dramatically changing moods as with its immensity.

They came upon a huge boulder jutting out toward the sea. Noting it had indentations, she insisted, in spite of her heels, that they scale it. "I'd remove my shoes," she said, "but a run in nylons these days is worse than ruining a heel."

They moved out on its flat top to its far edge and listened to the pounding of the tide on its hidden base. He slipped an arm around her waist. "This is no ordinary rock," he said with solemn gravity. "Hear the beat of its heart. It has a life and soul of its own. But, I must warn you, it is incredibly sensitive. If you should doubt any of this, it will surely die of heartbreak and decompose into a drab, commonplace rock."

"I believe," she said imitating his solemnity, "and may lightning strike me dead if I ever go back on my word."

The night's odyssey went on, two beings lost in the romance of a majestic sea and a starlit sky, and it might have gone on to daybreak had he not happened to glance at his watch. Taken aback at the flight of time, they headed toward the ferry, but being famished, they stopped first at an all-night cafe.

Tally, amused at the overattention of their teenage waitress, nudged him with her foot. "I do think the girl has a crush on you. Do you affect all women this way?"

He laughed. "Blame it on the shoulder bars. The lure of gold. But I think I can break the infatuation."

When the waitress returned with their order, he asked her if she knew much about amphibious warfare. She confessed but a little. "Well," he said, "I so happen to be a wave commander. Do you know what that is?"

"Not sure, sir."

"Well, a wave commander is one who is in charge of WAVES. WAVES, I'm sure you know, are the enlisted women in the navy."

"Yes, sir."

"It also so happens I'm on a very special assignment. I've been selected to train a hand-picked group of WAVES for a very daring mission. If you promise on a stack of Bibles not to tell a soul, I'll tell you what the mission's about."

Her wide eyes widened even more. "Oh, on a stack of Bibles, sir."

"Very well. There's a certain island in the Pacific that must be conquered if we have any hopes of winning the war. I can't tell you which one because only General MacArthur has that authority. That's how top secret it is."

"Yes, sir."

"Trouble is, the island's so well fortified that there's no way we can invade it and come out alive. Now lower your head so I can speak softly. The task for these selected WAVES is to row ashore dressed as nurses in a life raft and wave a white flag. They're to inform their captors they're from a hospital ship that sprung a leak and sunk. Now comes the ploy. In being taken prisoners of war, they sweetly volunteer to serve coffee to the gunners manning the beach. But when they take coffee to the gun emplacements, they silently kill the gunners. When all are dead, they raise the white flag, the cue for the marines who are waiting off shore to storm the beach and take the garrison."

She whispered softly, "But, sir, how do the WAVES kill silently?"

"With one blow from the back of the hand."

"How can they possibly do that?"

"I've taught them. See this innocent-looking hand? It can kill within two seconds. Now refill our coffee. Remember, if you mention a word, I'll be forced to put this hand into action."

"Yes sir. Not a word, sir. Right away, sir." She scurried away.

He smiled at Tally. "Doubt if she'll want to linger within a ten-foot-pole reach of me."

Tally kicked him lightly on the shin. "You're a devil, Ensign O'Reilly, hiding behind the mask of a choirboy."

On the ferry, as they sat facing the water, he draped an arm over her shoulder. "Have you ever noticed," he asked, "the narcissism of the stars? See how much brighter they shine on seeing their reflection in the water." She snuggled closer. She had never met anyone with thoughts quite like his. He ran his fingers lightly through her windblown tresses. "Love the mop. That's it! Mopsy. Thy newly christened name in honor of thy crowning glory." He then diddled with a handful of her auburn locks. "I can't believe it," he said, raising his voice in feigned surprise. "They say vanity is the soul of woman, yet I can't find one narcissistic hair." She twisted his ear.

The ranch was a good walking distance from the ferry landing. As they strolled, they talked of their next get-together, which they found could be no sooner than the following Sunday with the navy keeping him busy during the days and Convair keeping her busy at nights. On her back porch, where the door always remained unlocked, they scribbled addresses and phone numbers on scraps of paper.

He then suddenly kissed her, flashed a melting smile, and said perhaps she should know that Timothy O'Reilly is his name only on St. Pat's Day. The rest of the year he goes by Cory Zigler. He pressed a finger to her lips and added that before she contacts the bounty hunters to hunt down an Irish imposter in a navy getup, she should know that his mother did come from a hardy stock of potato pickers in old County Cork. Then, with an acrobatic leap from the porch, he was off and sprinting toward the dock.

Tally tiptoed into the house and, seeing lights still on in the living area, strided in to find the radio going and Cindy and Debbie penning letters. "I thought by now the two of you would be into dreamland."

"Still catching up on correspondence," Debbie replied.

"I'm also waiting to return something I think belongs to you," Cindy said, impishly waving Tally's purse.

"I know all about how it got in your possession. You know this makes you an accomplice."

"To what?"

"Aiding and abetting a deserter in times of war is an act punishable by death. So if I hang, you'll hang with me."

"Got good news. No crime's been reported. Susan and I covered for you. We told the chief hostess you had picked up the bug and had to leave early. She took it hook, line, and sinker. You're not only home scot-free but have her full sympathy."

Debbie broke in. "Tally, we're bursting with curiosity. Cindy's been raving about this dashing cavalier who's a cross between Rory Calhoun and Tyrone Power."

Tally laughed. "Wouldn't you know that would be Cindy's description."

"Well," Cindy said, "Susan totally agrees with me that you two made a beautiful couple on the dance floor. Now we want to know what he's like off the dance floor."

"Wonderful," Tally gushed. "We walked for miles, yet I'm not the least bit tired. It was such a perfect night: a full moon, bright stars, a light breeze but windy enough to muss up my hair." She laughed. "I've now got another name: Mopsy. Oh, he was so much fun . . . witty, full of laughs, a romanticist, a child of nature, and he likes sports. Above all that, he sings a beautiful tenor. He warmed the cockles of my heart with a couple of verses from 'The Rose of Tralee.' And wouldn't you know, the wit subbed Tally for Mary in the lyrics."

"There's a gleam in your eye," Debbie said. "When's the next date?"

"Next Sunday. Was the earliest time we could get together with our work schedules."

"One last question," Cindy whispered. "What about the little voice?"

Tally smiled. "All it said was to seize the moment. . . . I'm still too wound up to sleep so I think I'll join you two and dash off a letter to let him know I enjoyed the night. Oh, by the way, his real name is Cory Zigler. Timothy O'Reilly is what he goes by on St. Pat's Day."

With the sonorous voices of the Andrews Sisters on the radio setting the mood, Tally, with a light heart, let her pen flow:

March 18, 1944

My Mysterious One,
    Good morning to you! May it be a good day. Seems I'm constantly saying good morning—when I come home from work, when I go to bed, when I get up, all because of the crazy hours of the swing shift, which, in a crazy way, I don't mind.
    I'm really writing because I'm a mite contrite. Did I cause you to miss the two o'clock ferry? The next one's not until five, which would mean no sleep at all. If you can manage that, "Ensign O'Reilly," you're a much better "man" than I.
    Okay, I'm also writing because I had a wonderful time last night. There is something about the shoreline, the ferry, the waters which I love—the reflecting lights, the sound of the breakers. When they ration fun I think they need to take into consideration whom you're with and what you like to do. Incidentally, my shoes after such a workout were screaming for a bath and a good rubdown when I got home.

Yes, I'm also writing to let you know I don't normally let a fellow kiss me the first time out—especially when he uses a *nom de plume!* Mr. Zigler! It was pitch black and, I must say, you move awfully quick in the dark. Since you do have Irish eyes, an Irish smile, an Irish voice, and more than a touching acquaintance with the Blarney Stone, I think it's highly possible you may have an Irish mother. Therefore, I've held back, for the time being, of turning loose the bounty hunters.

Begorra, isn't it a life! The weeks fly by and before we know it they've been lived. So especially true this past year. In a way, the whole world is going too fast. But, won't you know, sure as I'm writing this, it'll drag forever this week.

I've had company writing tonight as roomies Cindy and Debbie are in a writing mood, too. At this late hour, we can usually get good music, soft and dreamy and sometimes classical on the radio, which is nice background for correspondence— that is, until it lulls you to sleep, which has just happened to my roomies. I'm talking about 3:00 A.M.

Being deserted with only the radio for company, lest I too should doze, I'll join the rest and say "bon soir" and sweet dreams. And, Cory, you too get some rest. I want you fresh and ready to rumba—or maybe I should say "dip"—with your latest dance partner. Till Sunday,

Mopsy

☆ ☆ ☆

At the Amphibious Training Center Cory was having a fitful day. With but a couple hours sleep and a hurried breakfast, he was out in a Higgins-type boat shortly after the crack of dawn bouncing up and down in a heavy surf gaining the skills of operating a landing craft. The classroom lectures were a thing of the past, and the men were now putting into practice what was taught. These boats turned out not to be as simple to master as it seemed when watching the instructor demonstrate. The effects of inhaling diesel fumes and tasting sea spray while holding a firm wheel were never mentioned. And it seemed one had to learn the hard way the importance of hitting the beach on the perpendicular. Even slight angle approaches can cause the stern to swing and the boat to beach on its side high and dry, a disaster called *broaching*. It then takes an army of hands and a liberal invoking of the Lord's name to overcome the resistance of the breakers and right the eight-ton boat.

Cory's struggles were further fraught with the persistent intrusion into consciousness of a bewitching auburn-haired colleen. The consequent breakdown in concentration had him doing such things as letting his boat drift into shallow waters and scrape jagged rocks. This would bring forth the wrath of the shore instructor: "God Almighty," he'd bellow through his foghorn, "you're wrecking another screw. Get your ass into deeper water." And a redfaced Cory, slamming gears into reverse, would do just that. It was to his great relief to finally hear the signal to secure boats for the day.

His buddy Scorch gave him the needle at dinner that evening. "Tell me more about this chick you met last night. She must be some number the way you screwed up today. Guess I should have gone dancing instead of guzzling beer with the guys."

"You blew that one, old friend. She had two other dolls with her who definitely would meet your criteria of pulchritude. But Mopsy—so named for her gorgeous mop of hair—stands in a class by herself. She dances like a nymph of the woods."

"Rave on, Macduff!"

"She's the genuine article. Doesn't put on the dog. She has the eyes of an angel but when they twinkle you can see devils dancing. We tramped the shoreline half the night, and she was as bouncy at the end as at the start. She even scaled a monster of a boulder in high heels. Now, how many chicks do you know who can do that? All in all, she's about a five-feet-five, one-hundred-and-fifteen-pound bundle of high-octane femininity."

"So when do you and Wonder Woman scale the heights again?"

"That's the rub. Not till Sunday. She's on the swing shift, which screws up the works. When I'm free, she's not."

"Changing the subject, the cannibals will be gathering at the Pit. Coming?"

"Not biting. Loftier principles have me holing in for the night."

"I believe," Scorch said as he rose to leave, "you're running a fever. Better see a doc."

Cory returned to the barracks, grabbed some writing paper, and propped himself up on his bunk. He let his mind drift to the night before, to the dance, to the moonlight walk, to the angel with the windblown tresses, and began writing:

March 18, 1944

Dear Mopsy,

The weirdest thing happened yesterday. You may not believe it, but sure as the name's O'Reilly, this is the way it was. After asphyxiating all day on boat fumes, I dragged the bones back to the barracks, dropped dead on my bunk, and had a dream.

I was at a dance, an Irish hop, and saw before m'eyes a blur of motion jigging on the head of a pin. "Who is this phantom of delight?" I asked the leprechaun next to me. "Why, an angel, m'lad," he said. "Don't you know that only angels can dance on the head of a pin?" She did have the look of an angel. "Might she dance with me?" I asked. He winked. "She might since angels are partial to pinheads."

The blue of my eyes met the green of hers. "Shall we?" I ventured. "Let's," she bravely replied. I marveled at how gracefully she floated over the polished pine. She was also clairvoyant, always a step ahead of my every move, never once letting heel mash foot. When the music stopped, the leprechaun whispered in my ear: "Take her outside, m'lad. Angels are also partial to starlight. It brightens their halos."

Out we went and what do you suppose happened? The portals of heaven opened, a meteor lit up the sky, and we saw harps strumming. Irish harps. But the wonders of the night had only begun.

We turned our eyes toward the sea (the open sea, blue and fresh and ever free) and, lo, rising from the waves was a gold carriage. The leprechaun had ordered Neptune's chariot. It whisked us over high breakers, jutting boulders, castles in the sand. When the dashing ride ended, well past the bewitching hour, and the angel poised to take wing, I stole a kiss, touching lips, ah, as soft and moist as a rose petal in morning dew.

The leprechaun consoled me in the afterpain of parting. "The dance is over," he said, "but be grateful, m'lad, because the luck of the Irish was with thee. Angels, you see, wear halos for protection. Your cherub lost hers in a puff of wind, so in presumptuously stealing a kiss, bound to raise a good angel's hackles, you escaped a deadly ray of white heat." He then up and vanished and, alas, the dream was over.

Now for the shocker. This morning I found a scrap of paper in my coat pocket. The name "Mopsy" was scrawled across the top and the day Sunday was underlined. What could this mean? Was there actually a dance? Did I really meet an angel? Did we truly walk under the stars? Did I honestly steal a kiss? When with an angel, who can tell what is real and what is a dream!

I now must confess to the crime of unlawful entry. I bribed my leprechaun friend with a four-leaf shamrock to sneak in and pilfer your box of halos while your eyes are fastened on this letter. I believe in giving Irish luck an extra boost.

On Sunday, Mopsy, be on the lookout for yet another gold carriage. This one, however, coming straight out of the Arabian Nights, has been booked by none other than . . .

Sinbad the Sailor

Conundrum

If an angel yesterday
Gave me a sweet hallo,
How can we possibly say
She had no halo?

"How the week is dragging on," Tally moaned, gabbing with Cindy in one of their usual bedtime chats. "Susan and I played tennis Monday, Avis and I took in a movie on Tuesday, the three of us went horseback riding on Wednesday, and in-between times I sandwiched in visits with Ted and other patients, and yet the week has moved at a snail's pace. Oh, me, still two whole days till Sunday."

Cindy laughed. "No question. The love bug's bitten you."

"Was doing okay until I got his letter. I had reasoned it out that I'd let myself get caught up in a will-o'-the-wisp. He'll soon be sailing the Seven Seas and that'll be the last I'll ever see of him. Then he writes, so witty and charming, and I'm right back in a dither, doing such things as misplacing my drawing instruments and bumping into water coolers. Buck, the worker sitting behind me, who has an uncanny way of reading my mind, has been giving me funny looks, like the kind one gives to one who should be institutionalized!"

"The magic of love," Cindy rhapsodized. "It makes time go all too fast when together and all too slow when apart. How well I know."

Smiling, Tally picked up the letter. "After building me up as an angel who's lost her halo, he ends his letter with a pun." She reads: "If an angel yesterday gave me a sweet hallo, how can we possibly say she has no halo?"

Cindy laughed and turned out her light. "Cory and Dave would get along fine. They both have the same kind of humor."

At long last Sunday came. Cory was due at ten A.M., but Tally was dressed and waiting fifteen minutes early. She was in a cotton red-and-white striped dress with a low neckline, short puffed-out sleeves, and a flared skirt for easy movement. A wide black leather belt accented her small waist and neatly defined her well-proportioned figure. She was barelegged and in tan leather loafers, ready for whatever jaunts Cory had in mind.

He arrived on the dot in his work grays, arms swinging. Seeing him coming from the window, she popped out the door to greet him on the steps. He clasped her hands, held her out at full length, took in her fresh beauty. "Ah, delightful in every way: no pompadour to tumble, no binding garment, no nylons to sprout runs. The all-American girl ready to romp and play, and that, Mopsy, is what we'll do—romp and play."

She laughed. "I thought I might be in for another vigorous workout. So, Wave Commander, which beach do we hit?"

"Please don't mention that subject for the rest of the day. It's been an excruciating week. Never saw a surf so agitated. It kept tossing us to and fro from dawn to dusk. But enough of the complaining. It's off to Balboa Park for us."

"My favorite playground," she bubbled.

Hand in hand, they strolled toward the park with Tally animatedly filling Cory in with her fun activities during the week. "Ah, the joy of being a civilian," he said, grinning, giving her a light whack on the bottom.

The first thing to catch their eye after they entered the park was the Casa del Prado Building. "Many of the social clubs use it for a meeting place," Tally commented. "The elaborate handwork on the exterior just blows me away. It must have taken a thousand artisans to do the carvings alone!"

"One reason why baroque died an early death," he replied.

They proceeded on to the Museum of Man and were fascinated at the display of artifacts depicting the early southwestern cultures. Observing the skilled handiwork prompted Cory to quip, "Makes one wonder if man has progressed or regressed."

They then stopped at the Museum of Art. Cory pointed at the statue of Velázquez on the ornate façade and said, "I've come to the conclusion, Mopsy, if it's one's dream to be a great painter, one should first select a Spanish mother and a Spanish father. I'd have to put Velázquez and Goya among the top-ten artists. . . .

I'm looking forward to what's inside. I understand the museum has a fine collection of Asian art."

"Painting is one of my hobbies, although I've only dabbled at it," Tally said ruefully. "Perhaps when this horrible war is over, I'll have time to get more serious about it."

They browsed for over an hour. She caught him more than once in rapt concentration. "You do love art, don't you?" she asked.

"I love beauty, Mopsy. Just imagine how much more beautiful the world would be if we had more artists than generals."

She squeezed his hand.

Being Sunday, the Park Band, a crowd favorite, was about to put on its weekly outdoor concert. Cory hustled up a couple of sandwiches and soft drinks, a box of popcorn for the pigeons, and found some sprawling space on the grass. She propped her head on his lap while nibbling and listening. From time to time he ran his fingers lightly through her hair. "It's a great day to be alive," he said. "It's a great day," she echoed.

The concert over, they took off, arms around waists, for the famous zoo. "One of my favorite fun places," Tally enthused. "The animals are precious. Did you know there are over three thousand residents here? They come from all over the world. The zoo also has the world's largest collection of parrots."

He laughed. "No need for a guide book with you around. Let's go see the apes so we can pay respects to our honorable ancestors. Do you suppose we descended from them or just sprouted out sideways?" She punched him lightly in the ribs.

They moseyed on till evening, gawking at the flamingos and other exotic creatures, laughing, joking, having a good time. He glanced at his watch. "No wonder I'm half-starved. It's seven o'clock. Let's grab a bite. Does seafood hit the spot?"

"Since coming down from the mountains, I can't get enough of it. And my tummy's growling, too."

They found an unpretentious eatery specializing in creole seafood and ordered a heaping platter of shrimp jambalaya with a beer chaser. Totally refueled and lighthearted as larks, they bounded for the shoreline.

"Now if you flap your arms, hop as you run, and caw like a seagull," Cory said, "one might land on your head and beg to be your pet." He charged off flapping and hopping and cawing, and Tally kept pace until both ran out of breath.

"Foiled again," he said. "Must not be mating season."

"The only bird that noticed us," Tally said dryly, "was the old duck sitting on the bench. He stared at us as though we had gone loco."

As their crazy frolicking went on, Cory showed amazement at Tally's energy. "You've got more get-up-and-go than monkeys on ginseng. How do you explain it?"

A twinkle appeared in her eye. "I grew up hiking in the Rockies. Was a tomboy until my voice changed. What about you? Nothing slow poky about you."

"Sports have kept me in fair shape. Coaches, you know, frown on smoking."

She drew close to him. "Good a shape as you're in, I know your day begins early, so maybe we should start back."

He gave her waist a light squeeze. "And shortchange the charm of the night and the joy of the company? The saints forbid! Let the breezes blow, let the hair swirl, let us romp, and let tomorrow take care of itself."

"Oh, Cory, one of the things I love about you is your philosophy of life. It comes out in so many ways. You're so upbeat. And it's infectious. You make me forget time, cares, the uncertainties of tomorrow. The world's in flames, yet you make everything seem possible, nothing impossible. . . . How do you do it?"

His blue eyes lit up. "It isn't all that complex. We have two choices: We can see the world as a beautiful place with splotches of ugliness or we can see the world as an ugly place with splotches of beauty. One view has us seeing roses in the rain, the other has us seeing the mud. Now, Mopsy, how would you have it?"

They arrived back at the ranch with little time to spare before the last ferry left for Coronado. He cradled her head in his arms. "One of the many endearing things about you, Mopsy, is your laugh. It's so full of warmth and cheer." He then kissed her good night, much longer this time. Tally gazed beyond his shoulder and saw the stars grow larger, the universe smaller. She felt if she reached out she could touch infinity.

He was suddenly out of her arms and dashing for the pier.

Tally entered the house, her emotions churning. Is this love? she asked herself. Yes, she had to be in love. She had never felt this way before. Her body was never more alive. Every sensation was more intense, every image more vivid. She pranced into the living area. No one was there. All were asleep. She sat by the window with the moonlight streaking through. She was bursting inside. She had to let her feelings out. Dare she tell them to Cory? He must know. Love is not easy to disguise. She picked up her pen and gave in fully to her aroused emotions.

March 24, 1944

Cory, My Darling,
    Forgive me for letting the heart move the pen. It dares be so bold. In the short wonderful time I've known you, it's letting me call you darling and letting me feel so natural in doing. You have turned topsy-turvy my once rational world.
    Yes, Sailor Sinbad, you've been gone the whole of ten minutes now, and I'm already impatiently awaiting the next arrival of the chariot. May the gods who control the clocks see to it that their hands move fast.
    Cory, you know what? There's something inside o'me that pounds hard and fast just at the thought of you. Could it be that's the way the heart thumps when one's falling in love?
    I always believed that the heart would instantly know when

the right fellow came around. Its voice would raise no questions, raise no doubts. So it's come to pass. When you hold me in your arms, the voice is still, telling me by its silence that it hasn't a doubt in the world.

I fear you shall be terribly tired reporting to duty today as I cheated you out of sleep again. Forgive me, I simply forget about time around you.

The day was truly fantastic, Cory, and one I shall never forget. Despite the cautious signals experience teaches us, I could not slow down the emotions from taking the turn they did. My brain kept warning me that it's an illusion, the reality being the one-way ticket for parts unknown, but my heart overruled my brain and love was all that mattered.

And so, on this our first anniversary, darling—one whole week—you have swept me off me feet and lifted me to that magical cloud where only angels and leprechauns play.

Yours with all my love,

Mopsy

# Ending Amphibious Training

"Why the long face?" Debbie inquired as she and Tally took the streetcar after work because Mr. Barker, the driver of the car pool, had reported in sick. "How can this be when only this afternoon you were all smiles telling us of the great time you had yesterday with Cory?"

"He called tonight to break our date for next Sunday. The darn navy pushed up their schedule so they have to go to sea this Wednesday for training exercises instead of next week. Means it'll be several weeks before I see him again. To ease my disappointment he promised to phone tomorrow at my coffee break."

"That's the blasted military for you," Debbie consoled. "These sudden changes in orders are getting to be routine for them."

Tally boiled water for a cup of tea on arriving home, fetched her writing materials, moved into the living area, and flicked on the radio to lighten her mood. Glen Miller's orchestra was playing "Moonlight Becomes You."

Oh, Cory, it sure does, she thought dreamily. How becoming you are in moonlight. What magic you weave over me! Not fair. You weave and then leave. But I love you all the same. And that's what I'm going to tell you. She began writing.

March 25, 1944

Darling,

Before slumber catches up with me, may this message catch up with you: I love you. How wonderful hearing your voice today! Did you have much trouble getting a line through to the plant? It can be exasperating at times.

There were several things I was tempted to say on the phone, but passed. Like the question: Why do you allow your face to pop up in front of my desk, causing me to make so many mistakes on the design I'm supposed to be drafting? A fellow worker, Buck, who sits behind me, overheard the tail end of our conversation and the word Roger. He said, playing the devil, "Natalia, you're impossible. You definitely told me his name was Cory." So I fell for the bait and gave him a short course in naval communication (he grinning all the while) instructing him that "Roger, Wilco, and Out" is the navy way of saying goodbye, a word, by the way, I'm in favor of taking out of the dictionary. I sometimes wish I sat behind Buck because he's uncanny on picking up what's special on my mind. But, darling, as long as it's you, so what? May the whole world know. So there, begorra!

With just one more day in the area for you, I look forward so much to hearing your voice again. Then begins the countdown: the minutes, the hours, the days that separate us because of the crazy navy insisting on exercises. I'm already beginning to love you so much that it hurts. . . . Yours ever,

Mopsy

Tally and Cindy did not budge until noon. They leisurely dressed, put on their faces, and ambled down to the kitchen, drawn by the smell of freshly perked coffee. Debbie, in the meantime, had already breakfasted, given Lash his daily workout, and was into her second cup of Maxwell House. "About time you two lazy bones stirred," she said. Then a bigger smile appeared on her face. "Oh, I nearly forgot. A package arrived this morning for you, Tally. It's on the kitchen counter."

"No return address," Tally mused. "Wonder who might have sent this." She opened it and let out a short shriek. "Look, look," she bubbled, and they all huddled over the kitchen table at a portrait photo of Cory in dress blues. The attached note said: In fear you might forget what I look like when I'm vacationing on a cruise.

Cindy gushed. "So handsome! Tyrone Power, make room." "Just gorgeous," Debbie raved. Tally picked up the photo and danced round the room, then laid it back on the table. "See how it catches the warmth of his smile and the blue of his eyes. I love it, I love it!"

Cindy shook the package. "Hey, there's something else in here. She dumped out a broach, a silver dove, on the table.

"Wouldn't you know," Tally cried out, "a peace dove. My prayer too. A world at peace. Oh, Cory you've made my day. I shall wear it and write everyday that you're on maneuvers."

Tally was still on her emotional high when Cory called that night, hardly letting him get a word in edgewise as she described her thrill in getting the picture and the pin. She then insisted he write often while at sea, and call her the moment he returns to the base. She babbled on, pausing long enough for him to squeeze in an "I love you, Mopsy," but before he could utter another word, she overwhelmed him with an "I love, love, love you too," at which point the phone disconnected.

Still wound up at bedtime, she stared long at his picture by her side before beginning her letter.

March 26, 1944

My Darling,

I thought today would never end, so much did I want to rush home, stare at your picture, and send by very special telepathy how much I love you. The picture truly captures your essence, the sparkle in your eyes and the warmth of your smile. I want you to know my roomies are goggle-eyed.

It was also wonderful hearing your voice tonight and know that even though I couldn't see you, there's not a thousand miles separating us—yet. I'm hoping with all my heart you'll be back within the couple of weeks that you're guessing. I'll just live each day hoping and praying it's fate's will.

How sweet of you, darling, to send me the pin, the peace dove, along with the pic. I know how much you crave for peace in this mad world. I'll be ever so proud to wear it—close over my heart always, which craves, too, in the worst possible way for peace to come again.

Today, we didn't get much accomplished as Cindy and I both slept until nearly noon. We rarely do that (do I detect skepticism) because so much has to be done during the day. Debbie, the third of us musketeers, rides Lash, her beautiful horse, nearly every day to keep him in training. You now have our complete household, except my brother Ted who is one of us whenever he can get a pass from the hospital. I shall go over to see him tomorrow as he is about to have another operation. Perhaps, I hadn't mentioned him to you. He's been in the hospital since October, wounded in Guadalcanal, and is the main reason I came to San Diego. They're having to reconstruct part of his face, including one eye which was destroyed. He was such a nice-looking guy, but, thank God, he's going to make it. His spirits are up; he's so happy to be back.

I'm working on getting some decent pictures for you. Don't despair, they will come.

In a few hours you'll be out to sea. My heart and love goes with you, darling, and I shall be waiting. Loving you,

Mopsy

Tally's spirits remained high throughout the next day. Susan, who had come in the morning to play tennis, oohed and aahed at the photo and told Tally if she ever grew tired of Cory, be sure to let her know first. The group in the car pool immediately noticed the peace dove and pestered for the story behind it. It also drew more than its share of comments at work.

Buck, playing the usual devil's advocate role, theatrically recoiled at the sight of the pin, knowing full well the gift-giver. "A peace dove from a man in uniform! A man paid by the military a peacenik! Treason, I say. Off with his head."

Tally again reacted to the bait. "I want you to know, Buck Wells, Cory is very patriotic. And he's upbeat. He's not against war, he's simply for peace."

Buck winked. "Women have the strangest logic. But, I want you to know that I, too, want peace. I hope it comes quickly because I'm tired of people looking at me and wondering why I'm not in uniform. They think I'm a draft dodger. Nobody suspects that I have a heart murmur."

"I for one don't think you're a draft dodger or have a heart murmur. I just think you flunked your mental exam. People possessed by the devil are rejected by the armed forces."

Buck grinned. "Touché."

At day's end, Tally, still riding high, hugged Cory's photo, and started another of her customary late-hour letters.

March 27, 1944

Cory Darling,

Top of the morning to you! Have I mentioned lately that I love you. In case I haven't, here goes: I Love You. You've been with me a bunch today, kinda hovering over my heart, flicking before me tantalizing memories and images: your blue eyes, your handsome smile, your curly black hair, your clever wit, your humorous way of seeing life, your love of the ocean. I could go on and on. I go all apart when looking at your picture. Geeminy, how easily and naturally it was to fall in love with you. . . . Hmmmmm.

Today we got up at eight o'clock, hardly of our own free will. The trashman chose this to be his house-cleaning day and, jeepers, he rattles cans louder than the milkman! I made a trip to the stables with Debbie, and trotted to the hospital to check on Ted. The day was shot. With car pool again cancelled for the day, we dashed to catch the "Special."

Oh, by the way, how would you like to go to the chilly beach with us tomorrow, if for nothing more than to keep me warm? Good! We're going to try to take some snaps so eventually I'll have some good ones to send you. I didn't have too much luck fishing among my souvenirs. In the photo I sent you yesterday, the dog's name is Butch. He belongs to a girlfriend in Denver.

Darling, do you realize you'll soon be gone almost a full 24 hours? Now by my calculations that's a mighty long time away, but the cold, heartless navy doesn't seem to much care.

Bedtime beckons and I'll be thinking of you as I fall asleep. Ever yours, my darling, with love and kisses.

Mopsy

"What a marvelous day it's been," Tally said as the musketeers, home from the car pool, plopped wearily into chairs. "For one thing, I had my very first swim in the ocean."

"A chilly one at that," Cindy said. She chortled. "But then I've been told a cold shower is what the doctor prescribes for the lovesick." She ducked a wad of paper Tally quickly balled up and fired.

"The beach house was darling and the luncheon was delicious," Debbie intervened. "We can thank Susan for our invitation. Barbara is a charming hostess."

"She is, indeed, delightful," Tally agreed. "Refined but not standoffish. Has Susan told you much about her?"

"Only that her father, a retired navy captain was forced back into active duty, and her mother, a former concert pianist, came from a distinguished family in the East. They sent Barbara to private schools and then to Sophie Newcomb College in New Orleans. The war was on when she graduated so she hired on at Convair. She wanted to be part of the war effort."

"I envy her," Tally said.

Cindy laughed. "With your good looks, Maureen O'Hara, why would you envy anybody?"

"Looks come and go. My brother Ted a good case in point. One moment full of handsomeness; the next, gone with the wind. The same can be said for wealth. Rich one moment, broke the next. But what Barbara's got is something that nobody can take away. Time only improves on it. I mean she has a charm and polish that only travel and education can give one, and it lasts a lifetime. She's a very privileged girl."

"But, then, so are we," Debbie said, "for having each other.

Now, if you two don't mind, I'm calling it a day. It's been a long one. Before you two stirred, I was out exercising Lash."

"I'm bushed, too," Cindy said.

"I'll douse the lights after I write a good-night note," Tally said. "Got another letter from Cory today. My sweetie must have written it right after boarding ship." She curled up in her favorite chair, and as the room emptied out, the scratch of her pen sounded rather loud:

March 28, 1944

Cory Darling,

This has been a full day but the best part was in receiving your letter. Sure and you have the Irish gift with words. I've read it a dozen times already. Each time it perks up the spirit. I'll always look to find roses in the rain because they'll remind me of you. How I'd love to meet your mother! Much of what comes out of you must have come from her. Do you suppose she'd give away any of her secrets?

The girls enjoy rubbing it in, watching me pore over your letters and moon over your picture; but, in truth, they're envious and drowning in curiosity, waiting for an update. Cindy and Susan think you're a pretty special person, even from the brief time they saw you at the dance.

We had a great time at the beach today, although a mite cool for swimming. One of the girls has a house off the beach so we spent most of our time there, including lunch. It was a fun-loving group.

No one was in much of a working mood tonight at the plant, for reasons other than mine I don't know. I and four fellows about me are designing a new plane seat. It's coming along on schedule, but what was a picnic was picking up on some of the unrelated discussion that went on! Hmmmm. I'm sure glad the boys in the navy don't let girls dominate their thoughts!!!

We had our snack out on the field to watch the planes come in. Being so dark, it was fascinating seeing them roll in over the bay. Then, on seeing the reflections on the water, I began wondering what you are doing and how things are going. Geeminy, I yearn to see you. Get back soon, Cory, I need you and love you and every fiber within me says it was meant to be. . . . Forever yours, darling,

Mopsy

☆ ☆ ☆

Day two at sea. Dinner was over and Cory and Scorch, sharing a stateroom, were plunked on chairs on the quarterdeck, Cory about to write Tally a letter.

"Some tub we're on!" Scorch complained. "Amazes me it still floats."

"She's a relic from World War I," Cory replied. "Yet the new transports are patterned after her. So what you learn will help later."

"I'm betting the skipper of this tub is also a relic of WWI. They must have dragged him out of mothballs to resurrect this ghost! Never saw a guy so drill happy. I'll be dreaming all night about fire drills, abandon-ship drills, air-attack drills, water-damage drills, you-name-it drills! What can come next?"

"Boat drills, old buddy. Now that the boat crews have been assigned, the word's out we start practicing boat operations tomorrow. We'll get the straight facts later tonight."

Scorch shifted his eyes to Cory's writing pad. "Don't tell me you're writing that chick again. The femme fatale's really got your number. Your testosterone level must be up in the red zone!"

"Ah, wait till you meet her, Scorch. She's packaged like nothing you've ever seen. And I don't mean just the tape measurements. . . . Now cut the rap. I want to get this letter off before the night session."

"What about the redhead from La Jolla?"

"What about her?"

"I don't believe this," Scorch muttered. He rose and headed for the stateroom as he saw Cory drifting into another world.

March 29, 1944

Mopsy Darling,

How great to relax! Been one of those days. Drills, drills, drills! Everything from fire to abandon-ship drills. "Faster," screams Simon Legree, a tough relic of WWI standing on the bridge, "seconds saved will save lives." (Provided ours aren't lost first!) Tomorrow it's raising-and-lowering boat drills, now that the crews have been formed. Please keep a good supply of liniment on hand, sweetheart.

Enough of boats, drills, and loud speakers. Time to get into the world of dreams, leprechauns, and you know who.

A question. What is this great attraction we have for the sea, Mopsy? The poets write freely on it. I never grow tired of Debussy's *La mer*. No music better captures its grandeur. Do you suppose we have a memory gene of our original home in our blood? Scientists tell us our blood has the same percent of salt as the sea. Is it coincidence? I prefer to think not. Let the final rites read salt to salt rather than dust to dust.

If all this be true, my ancestors must have drifted off on a glacier because the ones I know started life miles from the ocean. Most first saw the light of day in Buff Creek, a landlocked burg in mid-America. Guess I should tell you more about Buff Creek so you'll have more sympathy for my handicaps.

Buff Creek is a community isolated from the rest of civilization by cliffs and a deep gorge. A concrete bridge over the gorge is its only connection to the outside world. It's unique in other ways. Nobody is rich or poor—no mansions, no shacks. Settled by lace-curtain Micks and draft-dodging Krauts, it's now mostly a hodgepodge of Irish-Germans. Homogeneity comes in color (all white), in dress (all blue collars), in religion (all Catholic), in politics (all Democrats). Not many deviants lurking about on whom to practice prejudice. The depression hit folks fairly evenly. A can of beans got every kid into the Saturday afternoon movies.

Now, about the family. It's small. I've only an older sister, Kathleen. Bright but overly conscientious, she softened up the teachers to accept my weaker academic interests and let me concentrate on the more enjoyable noncurriculars without too great a price in the studies. Nice to have an attractive older sister leading classroom interference.

My Irish mother, with a teaching background, made travel a vital part of education. She would plan the family's annual vacation around a major historic city, thus cramming us full of culture from an early age.

My German father, secure in a government job, ran a democratic household in the sense that he was open to opinions, such as what color to paint the house, what model of car to buy, what breed of dog to have. Oddly enough, his own opinions usually prevailed, rejecting ours on suddenly discovered flaws in logic. So much for the ways of the family.

As I write I'm perched on the upper deck, facing west, taking in the beauty of the sunset. I've a suspicion that Sol, too, loves the sea. He's never more glorious than when closing out his day, the moment he sinks on a pillow of waves and spreads his rays of pink. Do you suppose this great ball of fire, too, has salt at the core?

What joy, Mopsy, it would be to have you in m'arms to witness the coming change of the guard—the round-faced cheeseman relieving the sun-burnt chariot driver. But I shall console myself with the thought that soon I shall be snuggling next to an angel under the canopy of the stars stealing kisses and worrying not, having bargained with the sea breezes to send her halo whirling off into the blue yonder.

Remember the French fairy tale of the Beauty and the Beast? The fair maiden's love for the beast turns the monster into a handsome prince and they live happily ever after. Well, if you love me with all your heart, m'beauty, who knows, you may see this sea turtle ending up in the mantle of a prince.

With that good thought, I bid thee sweet good night. I must get back to weaving on my magic carpet which will give the golden carriage a spell.

XXXXX Cory

It was not a good day to be out in a boat. The sea was spouting whitecaps and shooting sprays over the heads of the crews. More than one sailor was turning green in the bobbing LCVPs as the morning progressed. Lt. Gil Harvey, commander of the boat division, anxiously observing the scene on the bridge with the skipper next to him, finally said: "Sir, perhaps we should curtail the exercises until the sea calms down. I doubt if these kids are up to this."

"Hell no. What better way to test their mettle! We'll see what they're made of."

Out in his boat, Cory was giving encouragement to his coxswain, Rob Roy, an eighteen-year-old cracker from Georgia. For most of the morning they had been practicing aproaches to the ship from both the wind and lee sides. "You're getting your approach angles and speed much better," Cory praised.

"Thank you, sir."

"The trick, Rob Roy, is to adjust your speed to the elements and not reverse the engines too soon. It makes a big difference if you come in from the wind side or the lee. All a matter of speed and timing."

"Yes, sir."

Cory glanced toward the bridge. "We've got the sign to approach and be hoisted. Now put to work what you've learned. Do you feel up to it?"

"I'll give it a lick, sir. Sure wish we were coming in from the sheltered side." Cory patted him on the back.

As the boat was making its angle cut on the port side, Cory barked orders for boathand Hughes to standby for the hook and for boathand Baker to station himself on the stern with the boathook to keep the boat clear of the ship's hull. He then saw that Rob Roy was overshooting his mark. "Too fast and too close," he yelled.

Rob Roy slammed the engine into reverse just as a giant wave swept the stern. The sudden change of speed and the force of the wave sent Baker flying off the boat. He hit the hull with a sickening thud and fell limply back into the sea. "My God," Cory shouted, "he's heading for the screw." Flipping off his helmet, he dived into the drink between the limp form and the whirling blades. He felt a painful sting, too late realizing he had miscalculated the distance of the propeller as the boat had fishtailed. Then the screw suddenly stopped spinning. Rob Roy had the wits to cut the engine.

The crisis was over. Cory wrapped a line that was flung over the side round the unconscious Baker. He was quickly hauled onto the stern and lay face down, still breathing, water pouring out of his nose and mouth. Cory hoisted himself aboard and screamed: "Don't move him, he might have internal injuries."

Rob Roy restarted the diesel engine, recircled, and made a good approach this time. Cory and Hughes, working together, connected the iron hook to the iron ring in the well of the boat. The davit raised the boat to the deck railing where a small crowd had gathered, including the medics. Corpsmen gently lifted Baker on a stretcher and whisked him off to sickbay. Cory's bleeding arms caught the doc's attention, so he ordered him, too, over Cory's protests, to be taken to sickbay.

The crusty, leather-faced skipper, observing the action from high on the bridge, bellowed through his megaphone, "Good work, Mr. Zigler. Now hear this: All hands back to your stations. We have a war to fight."

When Scorch got aboard and got wind of the incident, he shot to the dispensary to find an alert Cory sitting up getting the final strips of bandages taped on his arms. Scorch was instantly relieved. He turned to the chief medic. "Think you'll have to amputate, doc?"

"He escaped the hatchet this time. Lots of nicks and scratches but nothing deep. He'll be on duty tomorrow and in a week he won't even show a scar. The really lucky one is Baker. A minute more and chances are he'd have drowned. Although he hit the hull like a wrecker ball, all the X-rays are negative."

Scorch looked at Cory's arms. "No wonder the boys topside are calling you Gash. You've got enough nicks to dull a razor. But how does it feel to be a hero?"

"Knock it off, dude. If it's a hero you're looking for, my vote goes to Rob Roy. If he hadn't had the smarts to cut the engine as soon as he did, I'd be mincemeat. The next time we're ashore I'm going to treat him to the biggest steak west of Texas!"

Doc finished putting on the last piece of tape. "Okay, out of here, both of you bums. I've got better things to do than hear more of your jabber."

God, thought Cory as he strolled out, how would Tally like dancing with a one-arm sailor!

☆ ☆ ☆

"Ah," Tally said to Cindy, "a glorious day it is, indeed. Tis Friday, the morning sun has brightened the room and a gourmet restaurant beckons." They were at their vanities putting on the accessories to their spiffy outfits in preparation for their weekly splurge on the town. "This was a great idea of yours," Tally said, "to get the Inner Circle together for a snazzy lunch. It's fun to dress up, and I'm especially looking forward to our going to the Skyroom at the El Cortez. Haven't been there since the cocktail party on New Year's when I was slightly under the influence."

"If we don't schedule in these sorts of things," Cindy replied, "we'll likely never do them, and we'll regret it later. Who knows how long we'll all be together? Changes take place so fast these days."

The group, looking chichi in their frills and satins, high heels, and bouffant hair styles, chitchatted gaily up the steep hill to the hotel, reveling in the charm of the season.

"Spring is my favorite time of the year," Tally gushed. "I love the dogwoods in bloom and the sweet smell of the lilacs."

"The gardens do come alive," Susan agreed.

"As does a young man's fancy for love," piped up Avis. "Which reminds me a letter from Mark is overdue. I do hope he's behaving himself in that wicked port of Norfolk."

Cindy sighed. "The tragedy of it all. Here we are dressed to the nines, in the prime of life, and our sweethearts are oceans away. War and love mix like vinegar and syrup."

"At least I have Lash," Debbie said with a wry smile. "The army hasn't as yet recruited horses."

"Well, not the entire horse," Avis quipped. They all laughed.

At the Skyroom the maitre d' seated them at a table overlooking the city, giving them a spectacular view. Susan, the native in the group, pointed to an area. "There's Old Town, all that San Diego was before the railroad came in late last century. We should eat sometime at the *La Casa de Bandini,* the former home of the town's richest and most influential citizen."

"Since we've gathered at a table fit for a king," Avis said, "let's order a feast fit for a king."

"Capital idea," said Debbie. "Being that this was Susan's choice, I propose she does the honors. We can then divvy up simply by dividing the horrendous check by five."

Tally and Cindy led the group in salaams.

Susan spoon-tapped her crystal to bring quiet to the table. "Chef Rafferty highly recommends to her fellow gourmands: shrimp cocktail, caesar salad, steak au poivre, and chocolate mousse for dessert. The tab for the royal feast may run as high as three bucks a head since we're into haute cuisine." Sighs concurred.

After the food arrived, the waiter brought a bottle of Beaujolais to the table. "Compliments of the gentleman in the far corner," he said.

"Will you believe it!" Tally gasped. "That's Robert Graham, the VIP I met at the New Year's Day party." He was lunching with two older well-dressed men. The girls waved and he waved back.

"He's nice looking," Cindy said.

Tally laughed. "Cindy Gilligan, when have you ever seen a man who wasn't?"

"If I had a pea on my plate," Cindy retorted, "it would now be in your eye, Tally Dugan. You're half-blind if you don't see a Spencer Tracy in him. . . . Twas mighty sweet of him to do this."

As they were leaving, Tally detoured by his table to thank him for the wine. He rose politely to his feet, introduced his companions, and then quietly commented that it was but a small recompense for her nimble wits on New Year's Day when Pops was on a toot.

A gracious gentleman, she thought as she rejoined her group. She rushed home, changed clothes, went to see Ted and other patients, and reported to work barely beating the punch-in clock.

Before commencing her last act of the day, Tally reread Cory's past letter to put her in the right writing mood.

March 29, 1944

My darling,

Tis Saturday morning and tis hard to realize another week's gone by the boards. Of course, the day is yet to be lived but it's always a relief knowing that the next day is Sunday, a day away from the grind. Honestly speaking, however, I do like my job, but I do look forward to the break.

As I look at your picture it makes me wish more than ever that you were here. Guess that's letting out a little secret that I'm missing you. Guess that's also suggesting that I'm a bit smitten with a certain Cory "O'Reilly" Zigler. Now that it's out of the bag, I recommend that you tell the admiral to halt the exercises as there are more important matters to attend to!

We girls usually get together once a week for a super spiffy lunch and Friday was the day. After putting on our best finery, hose and heels, we ambitiously strolled up the long hill to the El Cortez. Have you been up to its skyroom, darling? It's so beautiful.

I got a letter from Lois, a girlfriend in Denver, with whom I was intending to go to New York this summer. I've cancelled the trip. Traveling is becoming more and more a hassle these days, and besides, I've grown rather fond of California of late. Surprised?

Regardless of what this terrible war brings forth, Cory, I have it to thank for bringing you into my life. If the days ahead should prove painfully long, my comfort will come in the joy of knowing that having you in my heart will always make them bright. Yours forever,

Mopsy

"The good news," Debbie said to her roommates as they were having their after-breakfast coffee late Saturday morning, "is that I got notice to report to the day shift come Monday."

"Wonderful," Tally and Cindy exclaimed in unison.

"But the bad news is that I'll be asleep while the two of you are awake. Sunday will be our only full day together, and then on some of those I'll be off to horse shows."

"This also puts the kaput on the group's weekly lunches," Cindy said.

"But your evenings will be free and life will seem more normal again," Tally said cheerfully. "I can't wait to get the chance, although Pops isn't too encouraging. Anyhow, I'm happy for you. And we'll have plenty of time to compare notes. It's not like you're leaving the city."

"We're still the three musketeers," Debbie reaffirmed. She rose to her feet. "Guess what! Stable time for me. Lash must be chomping at the bit for his grooming and workout."

Later in the day Tally made her routine stop at the hospital. She found Ted a bit down. "Cheer up," she exhorted, "the docs are commenting on your good progress. They are seeing light at the end of the tunnel. They assure me that with a few more surgeries you'll be back to your old self. Not so for that sailor boy, not yet twenty, down the hall, who's going to be told he'll be a paraplegic. Think what a jolt that will be!"

"Okay, sis, I get the message. Stop complaining about a hole in the shoe when the guy next to you hasn't any shoes. Go on, take off and give him a pep talk. I'll feel better tomorrow."

The moment Tally walked into the sailor's room and saw the look on his face, she knew he had knowledge of the bad news. "Hi, Charlie," was all she felt safe to say, knowing that only yesterday he bubbled about getting back to the oil fields in Texas when he got his discharge.

Defiant tears welled in his eyes when he saw her. "I'm a Goddamn cripple," he blurted out. "I'll never walk again." He muttered another profanity under his breath.

"I know. I just got the word."

His voice cracked. "The butchers cut my nerves."

"But your pain was so unbearable. They had to do something."

"The bastards took away my life."

"The only other way they could control the pain would be to turn you into a zombie. They thought it best to keep your brain alive."

"I'd rather be dead."

"The brain is the most precious thing we have, Charlie. We're a vegetable without it. They can make you a brand-new set of legs."

"I don't want to talk about it."

She clasped his hand. "I understand. You're exhausted. I'll stop by the first of the week. Sleep will help."

Tally told Cindy about Charlie during their bedtime chat. "The severe nerve damage to the lower part of his spine happened during training exercises, the kind Cory is now doing. Charlie's not the first one to be badly injured in training. While Cory tends to make light of such matters because he's so well coordinated, which is definitely to his advantage, the frequency of these accidents still keeps my anxiety level high. I'm going to church tomorrow and I'll say a prayer for his safe return."

"I'll join you," Cindy said. "Our crazy work hours have made me miss out more than I should in my Sunday morning duties. Rout me out when you awaken." She turned out her bed lamp.

"I'll join you in dreamland after my letter to Cory."

March 30, 1944

Hi Darling,

Another week done and Sunday closing in. Golly, don't I wish you were! It's more than just a Sunday, it's our second anniversary! Two whole wonderful weeks of knowing you. To celebrate shall we go to the Auditorium in the evening to see the Ballet Russe? Or, perhaps, go dancing at the Marine Room or the Square. And then afterwards, a stroll in the sand along the bay to watch the surf roll in. This time I'll relieve myself of my hose! Now, should the opportunity arise, you could give me a lesson in bridge. I have a sneaking suspicion you are a whiz at the game. Playing at a penny a point calls for real confidence.

Geeminy, you've actually been gone less than a week and it's like ages. That's what love does. Makes time go at the speed of light when we're together and slow as eternity when we're apart.

Today was utterly mundane. A trip to the grocery with Cindy and a batch of ironing. Debbie's going on the day shift Monday so she's having a short weekend. She's entering Lash in the horse show tomorrow and we're pulling for her to take the cup again. With her new work schedule, we probably won't get the details until next weekend. Saturday night, once my favorite night, is beginning to lose some of its luster. You were right in saying so much of life is learning to live with change.

Cory, darling, gazing at your picture helps to melt away the frustration of absence. I see happiness and I can be happy in knowing you are.

I must get up early tomorrow because we're going to church, thinking it might not be a bad idea getting on God's good side these days! Is nine o'clock early? Probably not by your standards. Undoubtedly, you will have been up and at 'em several hours by then. Good night, dearest, I'll see you in my dreams.

All my love,

Mopsy

Tally shook her dead-to-the-world roommate. "Rise and shine, sleepyhead, if you have any hopes of making church on time. Tis nine o'clock."

They dressed, breakfasted on juice, cereal, toast, and coffee, and headed for the services at the First United Methodist, a modernistic oval-shaped church. Tally felt an inner tranquility as she walked down the red-carpeted central aisle and cast her eyes on the grand view beyond the oval window making up the center of the wall behind the altar. The feeling stayed with her until the end of the services when the names of those in uniform who had made the supreme sacrifice the past week were read aloud, a regular Sunday announcement since Pearl Harbor. The congregation then joined in prayer. Oh, Cory, Tally prayed, may God see fit to never have your name so read.

Afterward, Tally went to the hospital and found Ted in much better spirits. She had yet to mention Cory to him, waiting for the opportune moment, which she now judged had come.

"Ted," she said, her eyes sparkling, "there's something I've been dying to tell you, but I wanted the timing to be right. Are you ready? . . . I'm wildly, madly, crazily in love."

He stared at her incredulously. "Would you mind saying that again?"

"I'm in love with the most absolutely wonderful person in the whole wide world."

He stared even harder. "Have you gone off your rocker? Had a sunstroke? You, my kid sister, who once said that anyone falling in love in wartime has to have the IQ of a moron."

"I know, I know. But how was I to know that the heart can veto the brain?"

"I hope I have the strength to hear more."

"He's an ensign in the Amphibs. He's now on maneuvers that will end his training in Coronado. Then it's ship assignment and off into the Pacific. I met him at a dance on St. Pat's Day. He whisked me off at intermission. We walked the shoreline most of the night, and then dated all day and most of the night the following Sunday. With me on the swing shift, that was all the time we've had together."

"Two times together and you're head over heels in love?"

"Now don't get logical with me, Ted. He did phone a couple of times, and he does write the most beautiful letters. He is a poet, a philosopher, a nature lover . . . a wonderful dancer."

"I can't believe this!"

"He's so easy to be with. Oodles of fun. Witty. So much on the ball. And so upbeat. Something I wish you'd be. I'm sure he loves me, too. But, he's so talented I hope he doesn't find me dull."

"Tell me about his vices. Surely he has some."

Tally thought for a moment, then laughed. "He gambles. He told me he plays bridge at a penny a point."

Ted grinned. "Are you sure he's from this planet?"

"Remember, I've only been with him twice. As I get to know him more, I'm sure some foibles will pop up. He does have his share of the devil in him. Well, the truth is, I've never quite felt this way about anyone else before."

"To be serious, Tally, I hope you've found what you've been looking for." He opened his arms and gave her a hug. "The feeling, I know, is great, but tough times are ahead: months of separation, an escalating war, which he'll be in the thick of, and then a world afterward that no one can imagine."

"We can't stop living. The world's crazy now, but does it always have to be? Maybe what's happening now will fade away like a bad nightmare. Well, I've got things to do." She blew him a kiss. He shook his head as she bounded out of the room.

Tally and Cindy joined Avis and Susan for cocktails at the Skyroom and then the four of them went to the Auditorium to watch the Ballet Russe.

A happy Tally ended her day writing to Cory of the fun she had.

Sunday Night<br>
March 30, 1944

Darling,

Big Bonus! I'm writing two letters to you in one day. Must mean you're pretty special. Didn't know that, did you? The day has been full, starting with Cindy and I putting on our church-going attire, including gloves and hat, and attending services. I then dashed off to see Ted at the hospital.

I finally had to tell Ted all about you. Of course, what could I say? Not much. Only that you are fantastic, superb, titanic, colossal. Enough for him to conclude that you must be from another planet. He said he has never heard me carrying on like this—his down-to-earth sister who once made the declaration that war and romance don't mix.

Cindy and I met several girls in the skyroom tonight before going to the auditorium. It was a brilliantly clear night. Visibility extended for miles—but not as far as I wished, my darling. The ballet was spectacular, but now I'm more than ready to let my thoughts and dreams of you engulf me. Take special care of yourself for the one who loves you. . . . Yours ever,

Mopsy

"How strange it seems," Tally commented the next night, "to come home from work without Debbie in the car pool." She and Cindy were in their favorite chairs, relaxing to a Mozart concerto on the radio, about to write to their favorite sailors.

"What worries me," Cindy said, "is that what I think happened to Debbie is no isolated incident. It's a sign of what's coming. What I mean is that I believe we're in for some major cutbacks in jobs. Rumors are starting that some of the military contracts are not going to be renewed. Apparently, the military feels it has enough stuff to win the war."

"We're on soft money," Tally said, "so unless we can switch to the company's payroll, our jobs could be in jeopardy."

"I know some people are already checking the ads for jobs

THE RED-RIBBONED LETTERS

48

outside the war plants," Cindy replied. "I bet the swing shift will soon be eliminated. Those who aren't transferred to the other shifts will be getting the pink slip."

Tally sighed. "So we now have to worry about job security as well as the safety of our sweethearts." She picked up her pen. "I resolve to keep my anxieties to myself, not dump them on Cory, and always be upbeat when I write. He has stress enough managing those boats." She began her letter.

March 31, 1944

Cory Darling,

The last day of March, a new week, and what a wonderful start! I awoke this morning to find your letter on my pillow where Cindy had quietly placed it. What a grand feeling! Just about next to having you here to kiss me good morning. The sleep drained immediately from my eyes and was replaced by the love I hold for you. Hmmmm. Aren't I shameless the way I open my heart to you!

The letter, darling, was delightful as are all of them. I reread them to memory, melting like warmed butter before their charm. What colleen would not melt! I guess you know the very first one unlocked the door to my heart and thereafter reason went to the winds. The thought of being with you took precedence over all else in this whole wide world.

The calendar claims we haven't seen each other for over a week. Little does it know. Truth is, my darling, you've been with me every minute of every day—occupying both my waking and sleeping dreams.

I'm still floating on a cloud somewhere up yonder wondering if I shall ever come back to earth—and maybe not wanting to. Not wanting to for fear the reality I find might tell me I've been living a dream. Oh, I do so want everything to be right, which is love with no demand, no doubts, no conditions, no strings attached.

Since one is expected in crazy times to be a bit crazy, what one does or feels, I guess, shouldn't be harshly judged. I don't care what others may think, if what is done makes our love stronger. Now, if standing on my head would bring you home, let them stare as I walk on my hands down the street!

I love the snapshots, they're so much a part of you—almost like opening your letter and, presto, you're sealed inside. Hey, something for the dehydrators to work on. Hmmmm. On the other hand, I prefer you just as you are.

The hint that the ship will soon be laying anchor fills me with joy. I can't, can't, can't wait!

I, as part of my reserved nature, have been rather negligent in disclosing much of myself, so in fair play I shall return your short autobiography in kind.

From what I've been told—I can't clearly recollect—I was ushered in during a snowstorm in November. My father wanted a boy and in the cold plowed through the snow at 4:00 AM to discover a girl, but after a brief conference decided to keep her. So here I am, the middle of five children: an older sister and brother, and a younger sister and brother.

My parents separated when we were all quite young and I was put in the custody of my mother. I graduated from high school at sixteen, doing a little grade hopping, and have been more or less on my own since. I would have liked going to college but other priorities, maybe I should say necessities, came first. During the past few years I had the pleasure of rediscovering my father. He is a kind and loving person and I have grown very fond of him. After teaching school for years, he took up contracting and works in Denver, which I consider home most of the time. I've never been close to my mother. However, I have an aunt and uncle in Wichita whom I adore and often refer to as my folks. So, unlike you, darling, a product of a secure home, I have scattered roots.

You mentioned your Catholic upbringing, Cory. A good number of my friends are Catholic, but I actually know very little about Catholicism, having never been in a Catholic Church. I don't have strong religious opinions, being, I guess, a lukewarm Protestant, and respect everybody's right to their own beliefs. All I know is I want you happy, Cory, and would never block anything that would give it to you. My happiness rests in knowing you love me.

A strange thing happened at work today. A swarm of mosquitos suddenly rose from under my desk. The insects have declared war on me; mosquitos at work, ants at home. I'd prefer giving my blood to a better cause. But, I'll survive, darling. Nothing that sleep won't cure. And, of course, you will be very much in my dreams. Loving you ever,

Mopsy

It was the following night, or early the subsequent morning, depending on one's perspective, when Tally talked to Cindy. "You are right. Rumors were flying at work tonight that massive lay-offs can be expected. Pops tells us to stay cool. Says the vicissitudes of war can bring dramatic turnarounds."

Cindy nodded. "I agree. Rumors can drive one nuts. Let's not let ourselves get all worked up. I say we should put our minds on better thoughts. I'm going to write Dave about the fun we had today at the Coast Guard base. He'll be real envious that we got to see Kay Kyser, one of his fun people."

"I'm with you." Tally picked up her pen. "Today, I think, is the second of April. Dates get confusing when you arrive home from work the following day."

April 2, 1944

Cory Darling,

If you should happen upon a heart on the ocean blue, grab it, for it must be mine. It's gone astray and last reports have it wandering on coastal waters.

Up to now I'd have said it would have been impossible for me to have met someone and be as much in love as I am with you in the short time we've known each other. Begorra, it's incredible how quickly an outlook can change. My whole life's plan has flipflopped. I find myself totally submerged, helplessly bound, fully enslaved; yet, loving it, knowing this heart o'mine would rebel at any other thought. You must understand, Mr. Z, for the past five years I've been staunchly independent, have scrupulously avoided entanglements, and have stayed very much in control of my life. Just what did you put in my tea!

Today was a lazy, pleasant day, starting about 10:30. Cindy and I spent the rest of the morning experimenting with the camera of her boyfriend, a line officer on the *Colorado*. The type of film is also new and since we are no Edison's, the pictures may turn out a big flop. We had fun and if anything comes out in focus, I'll send it off to you.

Around noon we met the gang for lunch at the Skyroom and went out to the Coast Guard Base to hear Kay Kyser. We punched in for work one minute before the whistle blew.

But, the best part of the day, by far, was receiving your letter. How they always make my day!

Linda, one of the girls in our group at work, and I got into a rather interesting discussion. She began talking about a boyfriend, Dan, in the navy, so the conversation jumped back and forth between Dan and Cory. Then she slipped in a Pete, whom she is engaged to and who is now on one of the transports. It's supposedly coming into port soon, and she seems excited about it. Just where Dan fits into the story I'm not clear and just as soon not know as m'thinks some highfalutin two-timing is going on. Not for me! I shall wait faithfully and if necessary forever, for I have so much to wait for. I love you, Cory, for many reasons; but, perhaps, most of all for just being who you are, one of the sweetest guys to walk the earth.

I'm curled up in our big chair while writing, and it feels so good just to be home, to relax, and bring you close into my thoughts. A picture, they say, is worth a thousand words. I'm thinking that now as I sit with your picture on my lap and beautiful music playing in the background. Your smile comes more alive as I look at you. You can't guess how well I've come to know you. We spend so much time together.

I'm missing Debbie since she went on the day shift. Haven't seen her since last Saturday. Lash did take first place in the horse show, but since cups were not awarded, she ended up with another blue ribbon. Consolidated show comes next. She is certainly a marvel with horses, and, I might add, a most delightful roomie. I'm fortunate to have the roomies I have. Not only tons of fun, but hearts of gold. Cindy has just joined me in writing.

I now think of each passing day as bringing us 24 hours closer, and the thought eases the pain of separation. I look forward to every minute we can spend together, for I know, in the not too distant future you will be far away for a long, long time. Even so, you'll never be far away in my mind. I'll love you always.

Mopsy

"Dave!" Cindy shrieked. Tally, in the kitchen two rooms distant cleaning up the breakfast dishes, could hear the outcry even with the water running in the sink. She dashed into the living area to find Cindy on the phone shrieking short disjointed sentences for at least ten minutes before hanging up.

"That was Dave," she said breathlessly.

Tally smiled. "That much I gathered."

"The connection was terrible, but he's in Seattle. The ship's in dock, but he doesn't know for how long. I'm so excited. Just can't believe he's back in the states."

"What happened?"

"Never thought to ask."

"The ship must be in for repairs."

"I've got to get to Seattle."

"Maybe he can come here."

"Never thought to ask. Wonder if I can get leave. I'll resign if I can't."

"Slow down, Cindy. I'm sure things can work out without doing anything drastic. Give yourself some time to think out the situation. Dave will surely call again and have more facts. Just don't do anything rash."

Cindy was in a dither the rest of the day and her twit spilled over to Tally by day's end. "You know," Tally said in a burst of insight, "we're acting like a pair of chickens with their heads cut off. We're yakking about what clothes you should take to Seattle, whether to travel by bus or train, how much money to take with you, where can you stay in Seattle, and we don't even know how long Dave will be in the states."

"So true. I've got to stop racing my mind until I hear again from him. Oh, hurry up my love and phone. The uncertainty is killing me."

"While you're pacing about like an animal cooped up in a cage, I'm going to calm my nerves and write Cory." Tally propped up his picture, smiled back at him, and lost herself in matters of her own heart.

April 4, 1944

My Darling,

Big confession. I'm longing for you tonight. While at work, my mind was everywhere but where it should be. Tom, my supervisor, gave me quizzical stares all evening, but so be it, tomorrow will be Saturday and I resolve to do better.

Why am I in such a state? Well, it began on awakening and finding your letter on my pillow. It starts the day with the signal that all is beautiful, God is in his heaven, and I love you.

I then looked out the window and watched the fog for at least a half hour. This is the first time I've seen it so heavy and low. The effect is fascinating, rather reminding me of Colorado before the snows. What's keeping it so low? Ah, the mysteries of nature!

Yes, I'm curled up in my favorite chair with you, my favorite man of the fleet, right in the foreground of my thoughts and foremost in my dreams. Sure and isn't the picture familiar, Mr. Z! I love you, Cory, for always and forever.

The day turned into a frenzy when Dave called Cindy from Seattle. She had seen him about six weeks ago when he was transferred to the West Coast from Washington D.C. after finishing training. They spent a short time together in San Francisco before he shipped out. She was resigned not to see him for a couple of years, so when he called today, she nearly flipped. I did my best to calm her down, but was a poor influence, ending up about as excited as she. She's in a flutter figuring out how to get up there. It wouldn't surprise me too much if they bounded for the marriage bureau. I sure hope she'll return here after his ship pulls out because, geeminy, I'd sure miss her. She brings so much laughter to the ranch.

Your poem in today's letter was precious, Cory. How you make the ocean come alive! What deep feelings the sea can bring out in you! Your talents are never ending. What are you doing fighting a war?

Now exactly what did you have in mind asking if I could survive in living quarters with space for just the bare essentials? Cory, darling, I love you. If you're testing the limits of my love, I pass with flying colors. I wouldn't quibble if there were no furniture at all if I could snuggle up on the floor next to you. So put that, sir, in your meerschaum and smoke it!

When I'm with you, details mean absolutely nothing. In case the simple point has slipped your complex mind, the lady is quite crazy in love.

Listen carefully, darling, and if you hear a rumble over the waves, it sure could be this heart o'mine because it's pounding so loudly. It knows that Sunday will be here soon and how special that day has become. It just expects to see you and simply can't understand what would not make it so. Ah, someday we shall have many Sundays, just the two of us, and then shall look back and laugh at this war which kept us apart, but gave us so much in allowing us to know and love each other. Good night, my darling. You are what makes my dreams so sweet.

Loving you always,

Mopsy

☆ ☆ ☆

Gil Harvey, boat commander, a brute of a man, over six-feet-three and in still the shape he was as an All-American football player, was sipping coffee in the wardroom with Cory. "Before we get to the business at hand, Gash, I want to congratulate you on your fine action last week. You saved a kid's life. I saw it from the bridge. I was impressed."

"Thanks, Gil, but it wasn't that big a deal."

"I think differently. It was quick thinking and it took guts. Has merit for a citation."

"Wrong on both counts. It was instinct not guts. And if I had used my brain, I'd have ordered the coxswain to do the diving and I'd have taken the wheel. . . . Fact is, it was stupid to have had Baker out of the well. So scratch the thought of any citation."

Gil laughed. "Zigler, you're a corker! I know guys who would scream for the Purple Heart if they got blisters on their butts while sitting in a foxhole."

"Medals are for heroes. Like for the guy willing to take a bellyful of lead to drag a marine off a reef at Tawara."

Gil touched his Silver Star. "Mainly flesh wounds. But, God, that was one helluva landing. A snafu from start to finish. Not enough prebombardment, no clearance of underwater hazards, gross miscalculations of the tides, and ridiculous bottlenecks on the coral reefs. The Japs did make one thing clear. They're on these damn islands to fight. Retreat is not in their book. But we're off the subject. I asked you here to tell you the Brass is working on something innovative."

"I sense trouble already."

"They think the night invasion might sharply reduce casualties. So they've selected us as the guinea pigs to test the idea. We're to land a battalion of marines in full battle gear on a simulated beach next week at the stroke of midnight."

"You keep saying *we*."

Gil cleared his throat. "Two waves will hit a beach marked off by blinking red lights on the southern tip of the coast. I've selected you to take in the first wave, and Scorch the second, following you in." He handed Cory a folder. "The complete plans and instructions are here. We'll pick up the marines at Oceanside, recruits from Camp Pendleton, and then drop anchor some dozen miles off shore."

"We have nine other officers in the boat division. What's wrong with drawing straws?"

"I'll ignore that."

"This calls for learning an entirely new set of signals."

"On target. Lights instead of flags. But you'll have a full week with crews at night to get the hang of it."

"I suppose the moon will be starting its new phase so we'll be groping about in pitch blackness."

"If the point of it all is to take the enemy by surprise, we sure as hell don't want a moon spotlighting the approach."

"The scene's getting all too clear: bows bumping sterns, signal lanterns falling into the drink, engines stalling on sandbars, boats drifting out to sea."

"Still worth a try, Gash. Any more questions?"

"Does Scorch know anything about this?"

"You tell him. The three of us will have a session after you guys familiarize yourself with the plan. So get started."

Cory headed back to the stateroom and tossed the folder on Scorch's lap. "Guess what, ol' buddy, we're now into night invasions." He reviewed his conversation with Harvey.

"God Almighty," Scorch reacted. "I sure hope the Coast Guard's in on this. All we need is to run into a hail of fire thinking our great shores are being invaded."

Cory laughed. "The Brass probably figures even if the worst happens, it would be no catastrophe. Our loss, considering where we are on the totem pole, would hardly alter the course of the war. But what hits my funny bone is the notion of a surprise attack. Here comes a flotilla of small boats flashing lights all over the area. Does the enemy think they're seeing lightning bugs! Sell me the London bridge! But ours in not to reason why. . . . Start reading, sea dog, while I take a peak at the sunset."

"And dream of a chick with jade-tinted orbs. . . . Wooeee!"

Cory sat on the upper deck, gazed at the dying sun, and with his lap for a writing desk, let his mind drift.

Dearest Mopsy,

The beauty of a sunset at sea is eclipsed only by the image of a colleen I once saw lighting up the ballroom of the Coronado. What's that dazzling lass been doing today? Tennis? Swimming? Dining at the Skyroom? Shopping at the Plaza? Dancing at the Square? Kicking up sand at the beach? As for me, it's living on a diet of boating, drilling, and standing watch as the navy seems intent on trying to make a sailor out of me.

San Diego keeps looking better to me when I view it from the distance of a ship. Guess I've never told you of my famous intro to the old mission town. It was no world beater. I was waiting on a street corner for a bus, tending to my own affairs, still somewhat self-conscious of my shiny bars, when this lissome lass with a bubble-shaped bum sashayed along, stopped, and stooped to scan the bottom row of a newsstand. A weather-beaten old salt, several hitches on his sleeve, bumbled by, instantly sized up the situation, tweaked the bubble and wheeled around the corner. By the time the lass untangled herself from the rack and bounced to her feet, fire spewing out of both eyes, naturally only one body was in sight. With the sinking feeling that words would only worsen my case, I spread my palms upward in a direct appeal to a higher court. After spitting out words to the effect that just because a gold bar rests on my shoulder I shouldn't think for a lousy minute that I could get away with that, she uncorked a haymaker, which I, frozen in my tracks, took flush on the jaw. Still dysfunctional, I thanked her and hopped on the bus, which mercifully had pulled up. All in all, I was ready to give the whole frigging town back to the Franciscans!

I must close, sweetheart, as a stack of material awaits my immediate perusal. Nothing earthshaking but fifty lashes at the yardarm if I dillydally. And that would make it painful to squeeze you, which, you see, is the last thing I would want happen. So beware! Squeezing you is a top priority when it's "land ahoy!" In the meantime give all at the ranch a squeeze for me, but you, Mopsy, be most discriminating whom you squeeze on those wild and woolly San Diego dance floors. I love you,

Cory

P.S. Tommorow's Easter. Happy Bunny Day! It's ho hum for us, but I can just see you in the Easter parade high-stepping in your bodacious new bonnet.

☆  ☆  ☆

It was a beautiful Easter morning. Gaiety reigned at the ranch, dampened by one thing. Debbie was nowhere to be seen. Her bed had not been occupied. The musketeers had made a pact to always keep one another informed with a note on the refridge door should one stray from the routine. There was no note and no Debbie. Cindy was less concerned. "I'm sure she's with a friend for Easter and forgot to mention it. Our schedules have been out of whack. Let's give it another day before we get alarmed."

"I'm still going to slip in a prayer at church," Tally said.

The girls dolled up in their Easter finery. Each laughed at the other when they put on their freshly purchased bonnets and struck out for the First United. Bird imitations were the fad for the season, and Tally sported a feathered little blackbird on the side of her bonnet and Cindy, a bluebird on hers. "At least we're in fashion," Cindy said.

The services were beautiful with the altar overflowing with flowers. The choir sang with open lungs the psalms of joy. Then came the solemn roll call of those killed in action. Tally felt faint. The list kept getting longer and longer each time.

Susan's parents invited Cindy and Tally for Easter dinner at their home. Tally accepted but Cindy declined on the possibility that Dave might call. She did agree to go with Tally that evening to the Square to dance to Jimmy Dorsey if no new developments were forthcoming.

After visiting Ted and dropping in on Charlie, but not staying long because she found him still in a highly agitated state, Tally took the streetcar to Susan's home in the outskirts. It was a sumptuous meal that had a stuffed but delighted Tally returning to the ranch. With no call from Dave, she and Cindy took off that evening for the Square to kick their heels to the band of Jimmy Dorsey.

With it such an active day, Tally wrote her letter to Cory in stages, beginning in the morning when home from church.

April 6, 1944

Cory Dearest,

Good morning, m'darling. Happy third anniversary. And happy Easter to you! Tis a most beautiful day, almost like summer. Spring's got a stranglehold on me, making me love you more than ever, making it nigh impossible for my pen to cooperate with my heart.

Cindy and I just returned from church. The service was lovely, being Easter and all. I got to show off my new bonnet, a crazy one, darling, with a little black bird perched on the side. Cindy showed off an equally silly one. We looked at each other and laughed. Ted was sure my eyes had failed me on catching his first glimpse of it.

Cindy's wound up like a top. She'll stay this way until she firms up her plans for Seattle. I'll miss her, of course, but her happiness is up there. But guess what? Know what I miss most? Mind if I scream it? YOU!

Susan's folks invited me over to join them for Easter dinner. Sweet of them to do so.

Debbie's not home and I can't imagine where she is, since she wasn't in last night either. We pin notes for each other so we can get in touch should the occasion arise, but this time there was no note, no Debbie, no nothing. I'm more than a bit concerned. . . . Later.

The meal at Susan's was delicious. I returned home stuffed.

Now things are quiet and peaceful and I'm watching the sun, a beautiful orange ball, go down. I'm wondering if you're seeing the same sun. A light fog is giving it its spectacular color. It looks so majestic on the horizon.

I'm going to the Square in a little while to hear Jimmy Dorsey. How about coming along, darling? Wonderful dance music. I shall be dancing with others, but no matter who he is, you'll be closest to me, deep in my heart. Cindy is going too. I hope it will divert her mind. . . . Still later.

I'm writing this letter in relays. We've just returned from the dance, and still no Debbie. My concern is increasing.

Dorsey was delightful. I had much fun, danced till I was weary, but all the time wishing you were my partner. I'm ready for the sack, as you guys put it, with a contented smile because I'll be meeting you in my dreams. Love always,

Mopsy

Cindy was still wide awake when Tally hit the pillow. With a twinkle in her eye, Tally asked her if Frank Sinatra had made her forget Dave.

"He is a cutie pie," Cindy admitted. "Can see why the bobby soxers swoon over him. But he's too skinny for me."

"But he does have a sexy croon," Tally countered. "Jimmy Dorsey's ratings took a jump when he joined the band. He's great with the Mills Brothers."

"Speaking of popularity," Cindy said, tossing the ball back to Tally's court, "how you do draw the guys! That marine captain was all over me trying to get your phone number. I finally had to tell him your husband was a marine colonel. Guess I better write Cory about this."

Tally laughed. "Didn't see you turning into the shy wallflower. . . . Tis a bit flattering when we have the ratio in our favor. But I do love to dance, and Cory's not the jealous type. He insists I have fun whenever I get the chance. . . . Well, lights out for me. Let's hope we hear tomorrow from Seattle."

They awoke the next day to discover with much relief that Debbie had arrived back sometime during the night.

"We should hang her by her thumbs," Cindy declared.

"At the very least," Tally replied. "I'm going to call her and see how she wriggles out of this one." She returned a few minutes later. "You were right, Cindy. Friends had invited her on the spur of the moment to spend the Easter weekend with them in La Jolla, and in her haste to depart, she plumb forgot to cue us in. Was most apologetic so I said we'd forgive her on the promise it'll never happen again. So one crisis is solved but another one is not. What have you decided to do?"

"Nothing for the time being. I figure Dave is waiting to hear something definite. He knows I'm on pins and needles so he'll call the moment he gets some closure."

"Makes good sense to me. The trick is being patient, bonny lass, if that's at all possible."

The day went by, the chores of washing and ironing filling the time, but still no word from Dave. "Tomorrow, we'll hear," Cindy said resolutely. "Tomorrow," Tally echoed. With that brief conversation ending, she set her mind on writing Cory.

April 8, 1944

My darling,

Tuesday—and I love you, just as I do everyday. So much, Cory, I find myself repeating it over and over, like a broken record, as if in so doing, I can convince myself it's not a dream and I'll not awaken to find my heart wildly astray.

I have a happy premonition this will be the week to bring us together. I may be optimistic because there's no firm evidence for it, but no firm evidence against it, either. The longing inside of me wants it to be true and I refuse to explore the feeling further for fear of jinxing the odds.

Thank you, darling, for your letter today. You sure know how to turn a fair maiden's head, sure know how to spoil her rotten, and sure know how to turn a phrase. I adore them! May I quote one: "Love is fullest when happiness is its food." How do you come up with such beautiful thoughts? I feel exactly the same way but never find the words to say it the way you do. I promise to feast on happiness.

Do not fret that I'm cutting short my pleasures. I'm not restricting myself. My happiness, darling, revolves on you and knowing that you love me. My days are crowded, my evenings full, and my worries manageable because you are with me both in mind and spirit. Each passing day, each letter, each dream finds me feeling ever closer to you, knowing you more, loving you deeper.

Cindy is chasing the ants tonight. They come in swarms to pay their social calls. Just when we think we've located their source, a new family springs up elsewhere. They are the most resourceful creatures. I'll try not to seal one in your letter.

Cindy's expecting to hear from Dave tomorrow. She better or the poor kid will be a nervous wreck. Her mind is so set on Seattle that it would be a calamity if the navy pulls the plug. I'm guessing the ship's in for repairs and all will work out.

Thank the good Lord the mystery with Debbie is solved. She spent the weekend with friends, the invitation so sudden and unexpected that she forgot to relay the message. She's full of apologies, but I could have spanked her! For a peace offering, she brought a new buddy for Homer. Homer is our china pig which proudly sits on the kitchen table. So far, no name has come forward for the new addition, who is quite cute.

Well, sweetheart, the arms of Morpheus beckon and before the ants decide to get too friendly, I best say good night and scurry to the safety of the bedroom. My dreams will be with you, of you, and for you. I know I'll see you soon. I'm counting the hours. Loving you,

Mopsy

It was a cold day for the beach but Tally and Cindy showed up because Mike Lashley, a fellow worker, asked a few friends to join him on the wake of his termination notice. Mike and his wife, Beth, were an older couple, in their midthirties, but very popular with the younger set. The news of their plight deeply saddened Tally and Cindy, which they were quick to express on arriving at the beach. In a consoling effort, Cindy said she heard yesterday that four in her unit also got the pink slip.

Mike took it well in stride. "I think this is but the tip of the iceberg," he said. "Most of us who got jobs in war plants after Pearl Harbor did so on Pentagon money, so when the military contracts dry up, so do the jobs. It's going on all over the country." He laughed. "Rosie the Riveter got so efficent that supply outpaced demand. Beth and I knew this would happen when we left New Jersey, but we didn't believe it would happen this fast. However, it's been a great ride. Speaking of rides, why don't you two sea urchins brave the elements and ride the air mattress in with the breakers?"

"I'm game," Tally cried. "Me too," sang out Cindy. And so for the next couple of hours, they shivered and giggled as they bobbed up and down crashing with the surf on the beach. Before leaving to get ready for work, they asked Mike of his plans.

"Beth has a teaching certificate, and thank God there's a teacher shortage. She's leaving Friday to go home and teach in the local high school. I'm staying a few more days to wrap things up here. I'm throwing a farewell beach party for Beth tomorrow at four o'clock and you all are invited—beer and cokes and games. Don't look downcast. I've checked with your bosses and Convair is compassionate over the firings. Promised to let our close friends off work to attend the party."

"Whoopee," Cindy shouted. "We'll be there."

Tally was one tired camper when day was done and she had yet to write Cory. The letter, she suspected, would be short.

April 9, 1944

My darling,
    Jeepers, it was a bit damp and chilly this morning. I lit the fireplace and that warmed me up. Also warming me up is the thought that your ship's getting mighty close.

We went out to the beach in the afternoon and couldn't resist riding Mike's air mattress in with the breakers, so in we went and nearly froze. Mike, as you wouldn't know, is a fellow worker who was terminated so he'll be heading east with his wife who will go back to teaching. They're an older couple who are awfully nice and full of fun. They always have a crowd of young people around and join right in with the activities. We'll all hate to see them go, but that's life in San Diego these days. With some of our military contracts not renewed, we can expect increasing terminations. There were four out of Cindy's group today. Hmmmm. I wonder what the next six months will bring. The pace of life in wartime stuns the mind. A year ago I never expected to find myself in California, but how glad I am that I came, that I stayed, that I chanced to meet you, darling.

I would love to ramble on but I know I must get up early for a downtown trip. Good night, dear, and when I become engulfed in dreams, you will be with me again. Forever yours with love,

Mopsy

The next two days were an emotional yo-yo for Tally. The first day began at the noon hour with a letter from Cory that had her leaping with joy. She read the key paragraph to her still sleep-groggy roommate: "Our orders are to return to Coronado base; your orders are to cancel all prior engagements for the 48 hours of this weekend. Details will follow. Have it from impeccable sources that sea legs can adjust to terra firma."

Tally whipped into her clothes and rushed to the hospital to tell Ted the good news. Then she stopped to check on Charlie and found his bed empty. She ran down the ward nurse for an explanation and found that he had been transferred to the neuropsychiatric ward. The nurse said disconsolately: "We lost all communication with him. He sank into a deep depression. I'm afraid he's a serious mental case."

Tally was distraught. "I liked Charlie. I just don't understand why he wasn't adequately prepared. The loss of the use of his legs came as a total shock to him. It devastated him."

The nurse put a hand on Tally's shoulder. "He's not an isolated case. But before you condemn the staff, ask these questions: How many surgeries do they do in a given day? How many surgeons do we have? How much time do they have to spend with a given patient? How much sleep do they average?" The nurse walked away without waiting for a response. It's true, Tally thought, war makes no allowances for human limitations.


The beach party brought out mixed emotions. Mike had invited all the layoffs so much hugging and teary-eyed goodbyes were intermingled with the camaraderie of volley ball, swimming, and beer guzzling on blankets. The word *goodbye* always triggered a deep-rooted chill in Tally, which she had traced back to the early breakup of her family. The day itself was sublime, capped off with a gorgeous sunset, the beauty of which brought to Tally's mind images of Cory, warming the fibers of her heart.

The Inner Circle collected for chitchatting at the ranch after the party. Debbie proudly displayed the red ribbon Lash had won for taking second place at the prestigious Convair Horse Show earlier in the day. She also excitedly announced the possibility of going to Missouri to see her boyfriend, Jack, should his short army furlough come through.

Tally remained concerned about Cindy. She had finally received a second phone call from Dave but was mysteriously silent regarding its content. Tally did not probe. She knew Cindy would ultimately divulge, but until she did, she would respect her privacy. The reticence made Tally think Cindy was weighing complex alternatives which were leaving her up in the air on a course of action.

The next day she suggested to Cindy they unwind and catch the early afternoon matinee of the movie *Greenwich Village*, a light musical starring Don Ameche and Vivian Blaine. Cindy liked the idea. While downtown, Tally purchased two tickets for the Sunday night performance of *Porgy and Bess,* certain Cory would enjoy it.

After work, in the comfort of their living area, Cindy finally broke her silence. "The deed is done," she sighed. "I've notified my boss I'm going to Seattle. Earlier this morning, before you were awake, I got a train ticket, called my folks to telegraph some money, and phoned Dave to get me a hotel reservation. It won't be easy, but I'm sure he'll wrangle one out. He still doesn't know how long the ship will be in dock, but has been told there'll be no leaves. So, I might arrive to watch his ship sail, or I might see him long enough to arm-drag him to the courthouse." Cindy laughed. "But I simply can't stay here and do nothing but bite my nails."

Tally hugged her. "However long you're gone," she said, "I promise we won't auction off your bed. Oh, Cindy, you know I'll miss you something terribly."

"I'll miss you just as much. But, I'll be back."

I'm not so sure, Tally thought, with no job to return to.

Tally talked to herself as she picked up her pen. Bonny lass, with all of this crazy excitement going on, you've been two days into the writing of this letter to your darling. Finish it tonight, choppy as it is, or you're not deserving of the name of Natalia Ann Dugan!

April 15, 1944

Cory Darling,

Joy, Joy, Joy! We'll be together before this letter reaches you, but I want to write anyway, if nothing more than to shout my joy that I will be in your arms this weekend. Oh! How I've missed you and how I look forward to seeing you!

Somehow, today has seemed short and it didn't have a thing to do with the time of my waking up. Perish the thought! Avis, a girlfriend, called about 1:30 PM to arouse me, which gave me just enough time to visit Ted at the hospital before going on to a beach party at four o'clock. Mike threw the party because his wife is leaving Friday. Sure wish you could have been with us; it was a fun outing. We stayed until nearly eight. The sunset was so romantic over the water.

So, here we all are at home tonight: Cindy, Debbie, Avis, and I. This was my first good talk with Debbie since she went on days. Lash took second place in the Convair show today, so she now has a red ribbon to add to her collection. She's thinking seriously of visiting her beau, Jack, in Missouri.

Avis is leaving so I'll say good night to you for now, darling, only it won't exactly be good night for you, will it? I should say happy watch, dear.

Later.

Good morning darling. I've been debating whether I should mail this since your address is changing. I may as well add a few lines while I'm chasing the thought around.

While downtown we saw "Greenwich Village" at the California. Enjoyed it. Cindy has been rather quiet since last hearing from Dave. Something definitely is weighing on her mind. In fact, I'd say she's been engaging in some pretty deep thinking.

Geeminy, darling, I'm agog. Just two days to go. I measure time in terms of how soon I'll see you. Mr. Barker, the driver of our car pool, asked about you and I told him. He reminds me of the nursery rhyme about the old woman in a shoe because he takes the time to listen and is interested in everybody's troubles.

I guess I've been lucky all the way around. I'm not sure how long the work situation will remain stable. I'm hoping this general state of confusion will soon clear up. The one thing I do know for sure is that I love you, darling, with every breath that's in me.

Later.

Cindy has finally opened up. She's decided to go to Seattle and see Dave in spite of complications too numerous to mention. In a flurry of actions taken today, she gave notice at work, called her folks, got tickets, and phoned Dave to give him her schedule. She seemed greatly relieved to make the decision. We hugged, cried, and promised to keep in touch. I couldn't ask for a better roomie and I feel she'll come back eventually.

I received a letter from my older sis telling me I am now an aunt. Looks like I've got a head start on you, darling.

Oh, incidentally, I was able to get our tickets for "Porgy and Bess" on Sunday evening—okay? Also our pictures turned out poorly; can barely make out what most of them are about, but shall save a couple for you, anyway. I must help Cindy pack and see her off in the morning. I'm excited for her but more excited over seeing you in a matter of hours.

I'll put this in the mail for you, darling. You may or nay not get it but my thoughts are with you, regardless. All my love, Cory, forever.

Mopsy

# *Together*

Tally fidgetted in her chair at work. I'm going to ask him, she kept repeating over and over to herself. After all, nothing ventured, nothing gained. The worst he can say is no.

Buck, sitting directly behind her, tapped her on the shoulder. "Why don't you ask Pops for Saturday night off?"

"I can't believe it! You're reading my mind again."

"Just call me Sherlock Holmes. Tally, you've been telling me for two days he's returning to the base this weekend to await ship assignment. Why else would you be in such a twit?"

"Okay, mind reader, how do you propose I win Pops over?"

"Well, you could throw a grand mal seizure. Better yet, you could blink those lovely turquoise eyes and tell him your long-lost grandmother has been found, and you promised to take her to the zoo."

"Buck Wells, if you weren't so big, I'd give you a boot where you've got the most padding. But at least you are agreeing that I should ask."

"He's alone in his office right now. Go, strike while the iron is hot."

Tally collected herself, stood up, walked to the office door, and softly knocked. She calmly laid out the facts, then asked for the favor, willing to make up the time either on a holiday or in overtime. Pops was surprisingly responsive. "I admire your forthrightness, Tally. Most workers would just report in sick." He thoughtfully rubbed his chin. "You've got my blessing. I wouldn't want to go down in history as the scrooge who stood in the way of true love at the time America was facing her greatest crisis since the Civil War." She hugged him.

While Tally, on her coffee break, was relaying the good tidings to Cory on the phone and setting up their weekend plans,

Buck slipped into Pops's office to commend his handling of Tally's request. "There won't be a heartbeat of work lost," he said, "the rest of us will pick up the slack."

Pops grinned. "I was counting on that."

Tally saw the springy strides in the distance through the living-room window, knowing Cory would be approaching from the bay. She didn't wait. She dashed through the door and sprinted toward him. Cory stopped, braced in his tracks, and met her charge with open arms. They bearhugged until they could barely breathe. Then they kissed until their lips hurt, in the full light of day, unblushingly, indifferent to the world about them, never wanting to let go.

Cory took a deep breath. "You smell like freshly mowed hay."

Tally pinched him on the nose. "Well, I never knew you were a farmhand."

"The career was brief, just several summers growing up, but the sweet scent of alfalfa left its mark. Smelling the lobes of your ears brings it all back." He lifted her like a feather and carried her into the house. "The sea legs just passed a major land test," he quipped. She yanked a clump of his hair.

"Put me down, Sinbad, and I'll treat my favorite sea rover to his favorite cocktail."

Tally returned with a tray balancing a martini, a decanter of wine, and several wine glasses. "Since I've told you about the Inner Circle, and all of them are here except Cindy who's off to Seattle, I thought you might like to meet them." She called out and in sauntered a sunburned trio of tennis players fresh from the courts and still in their playing togs.

Cory stood up. "Don't introduce us. While you pour, Tally, let me play the guessing game of who is who. Susan I recognize from the dance. I couldn't have pulled off the kidnapping caper without her and Cindy's help." She returned his smile. He then looked at Debbie. "Now here's a woman who seems loaded with horse sense. You must be Debbie." She laughed. "I salute," he said, "your derring-do. I've always kept a healthy distance from the equines, respecting the advice of my wise-owl grandfather who said never get on the back of a creature that has a mind of its own." The girls tittered. He smiled at Avis. "This is a person who strikes me as having impeccable tastes, which means her heart must belong to the navy. You have to be Avis." More giggles.

"Cheers for batting a thousand," Susan said, raising high her glass.

"Give the credit to Tally. She furnished the discriminating cues. Yet I don't know . . ."

Avis took the bait. "Don't know what?"

"How really democratic this group is. The excess of pulchritude makes me suspicious of elitism."

Susan laughed. "Just goes to show what a few days at sea can do to the eyesight."

"When modesty inherits the earth," was Cory's quick riposte, "I'm sure the headquarters will be here."

And so the light bantering and easy repartee went on until Cory suggested to Tally they best get cracking if they wish to do all that's on the slate. They bounded out, hand in hand.

"I can tell the girls adore you," Tally said. Then with a twinkle in her eye, she added: "And, begorra, with that blarney of yours, I'm thinking about getting m'self a ball and chain."

They took in the sights of Old Town until the hunger bug nipped them. They found a quiet eatery for a candlelight dinner. During dessert Cory confessed that in a moment of weakness he had agreed for them to drop by and briefly join his vagabond mates at their favorite watering hole, Paul's Passion Pit. "Transparent," he said with a warm smile, "is their motive. They seek to check you out, the doubting Thomases."

Tally's laugh rang out. "I would say the checking should go both ways now that the cat's out of the bag and I'm wise to where their night prowls lead."

The bistro was not the den of iniquity that the name implied. It offered the usual come-on features of muted lights, checkered tablecloths, and scantily clad waitresses. But, its biggest attraction was a live combo. By the time Cory and Tally arrived, the group had combined several tables and had the party rolling. After the grinding days at sea, the boys were ready to unwind. But they hadn't lost the manners of their upbringing as they bounded to their feet to greet the latecomers.

Cory grinned. "Tally, I'll cut to the chase and give only their sea tags as their civilian identity went out with the zoot suit. Clockwise we have Hammock Harry, Fearless Fosdick, Broacher Bill, Hutch the Mole, Madman Mulligan, Gooseneck George, and my woeful sidekick, Scorch." Each introduced his perky date.

Tally noted that Cory was called Gash, yet another name to be added to the list. She reflected on how boyish the lean-and-fit group looked to be saddled with the responsibilities soon to fall on their shoulders. She made a special effort to befriend Scorch on the premise that he would have the best after-school tales on her favorite sailor.

Joy swept through Tally to go once again to the dance floor with Cory, to nestle once again in his arms, to be guided once again by his firm hand that made following so natural. Well into the dance she teased him, calling him a seafarer with a thousand names and wondered how Gash made the list. He mumbled that it was just one of those freakish things. "I brushed against a boat propeller one day and got several nicks and scratches. Some wag saw a few splotches of blood on my sleeves and called me Gash, a moniker that's since stayed." Tally had a hunch there was much more to the story but would have to tease it out of his buddy.

On dancing with Scorch, she found him lively, lots of fun, and quick-witted. She could see at once how the strong friendship developed between him and Cory. She got Scorch to fill in some of the details.

"We met and hit it off in midshipman school," he said. "Cory had the edge over most of us with his solid background in math and physics. He finished in the top five percent of our class, which gave him a choice of duty. But the dolt chose to go with the majority of us into the Amphibs. Most lunkheads would have jumped at the chance of duty on a battlewagon or carrier, but not him. He responded where the need was greatest, which I blame on his Boy Scout complex, a character flaw which makes you want to both hug and boot him. Now, while Gash aced the exams, he was no bookworm. Anything but that. He's a natural athlete and will party at the drop of a hat, often one of the last to leave. The guy has talents to burn. At a Christmas service he soloed in "Holy Night" and had more than one black sheep taking a second look at the Nativity scene."

"How did he get the nickname of Gash?"

"There was a boating accident. One of the boathands fell off the LCVP, hit his noggin on the hull of the ship, and went out cold. Cory dove into the drink as the guy was being sucked toward the boat screw and nabbed him as he was about to meet the blade. He came up with minor gashes but well bloodied on the arms. Although the cuts cleared up in a week, the tag stuck."

"I suspected there was a little more to it than what he tried to pass off. Tell me, has Cory ever failed at anything? Has he ever really goofed?"

Scorch chuckled. "He's not the Second Coming, if that's what you're hinting. Before you think of canonizing him, ask about life in Mexico. And I wouldn't go so far as to say he's squeaky clean. Inquire if he's heard lately from the mermaid." Try as she might, Tally was not able to draw more out of him.

When back to dancing with Cory, Tally asked how Scorch got his nickname. "When the combo heats up," he replied, "you'll get a clue." He asked her if she liked to boogie-woogie, and when she said she was not adverse to the idea, he handed her to Scorch the moment the band cut loose, and wished her luck.

What jitterbugging! The navy hepcat had moves that would

envy a Ray Bolger! Tally got into the spirit of it. In perfect rhythm, he put her through contortions she never knew humanly possible. People around them stopped, clapped to the beat, and gave them room to fly. When it was over and she staggered breathlessly back to the table, a laughing Cory led the table applause.

"The saints as m' witness," Tally gasped, "the man could melt the wax right off the floor!"

For the last waltz the band played the tune that was high on the Hit Parade: "Always." Tally rested her head on Cory's shoulder, and he sang the chorus in a voice loud enough only for her ears.

> I'll be loving you always
> With a love that's true always . . .
> Not for just an hour
> Not for just a day
> Not for just a year
> But always

He pressured her hand. Nothing was said or needed to be said. It was their song. She looked into his blue eyes and felt toasty all over.

They left the party, headed for the bay, and poked along the shoreline, arms around waists, a full moon lighting the way. They chatted and joked as only crazy young love can do. They'd stop, kiss, and then he'd accuse her a wench, a vixen, a brazen jezebel for behaving so shamelessly before the innocent eyes of heaven, making the good saints blush. She'd break away from him and dash up the beach until his longer strides overcame her, and she'd grab a clump of his hair and call him Dracula, de Sade, or what other deranged monster that would come to mind. Then they'd kiss again and solemnly swear never to make public the awful truth about the other. They reached home at a late hour and, with the living room at their disposal, they snuggled up on the sofa and talked and smooched and smooched and talked until it was time for another wild dash to the pier.

Cory logged in and out of the base and returned at noon to the ranch looking remarkably fresh considering the winks he had. He was in casual grays, a dress uniform over an arm for the opera that night. They took off to the barn to see Debbie's champion horse and then hiked a trail until they found a secluded spot to lunch on apples and cheese and a bottle of wine that Tally had stuffed into a small picnic basket.

After sating their appetite and stretching out on the blanket that had served as their tablecloth, Tally, with a twinkle in her eye, adopted a quizzical air. "Darling, just how was life south of the border? And, tell me, what's it like rubbing toes with a mermaid?" She coyly rubbed her peace dove.

Cory gave a puzzled look, then broke into a grin and blasted Scorch for dirty pool. Then he suddenly lunged and pinned Tally's arms to the blanket.

"The punishment for illegal access to top-secret information in wartime, my seductive Mata Hari, is the five-man firing squad. Your only hope for clemency is to renounce all your false idols and declare me your one and only Lord and Master."

"What gall," she sputtered, "to accuse one of dirty pool and then attack without warning an unarmed, defenseless woman! The dastardly trick violates every rule of fair play."

"All's fair in love and war," he countered.

She strained against his superior strength and, then, resigned to the futility, mumbled the humbling words. Whereupon, she was rewarded with a tender kiss and a drawn-out monologue on the virtues of humility.

Tally held her tongue until she was free. Then she pounced astride him, settled a knee on each arm, and informed his lordship freedom would be granted only after he promised to end his shilly-shallyings and properly address the issues.

After feigning helplessness and bemoaning the demise of the whalebone corset, the bondage garment that kept women civilized, he capitulated but with the conditional reminder that forced confessions are inadmissible in court. Calling him the world's worst actor, she kissed him, hopped off his chest, and refilled their wine glasses.

Propped against a tree, his stomach a pillow for Tally's head, Cory asked which of the stories would the infamous Mata Hari insist on hearing first.

Tally humorously assumed a posture of fitful indecision. She paused, lifted her head, sipped a little wine, lowered her head back on his lap, and then after pausing again, softly spoke. "The story of the mermaid, my love."

He stroked her tresses and after a large gulp of fermented grape, asked for the spirit of Bacchus to give him the strength.

Twas a Sunday afternoon at the Coronado. Esther Williams was top billing. Scorch and I missed her act at the pool but arrived later for the dance underway in the ballroom. We were barely seated when Scorch nudged me, pointing to this table with a dazzling centerpiece screened off by a cordon of balding Neanderthals.

"Know who she is?" Scorch asked.

"Not the slightest."

"That's Esther Williams, you idiot."

Scorch, an autograph buff, boasting the Hancock of many a gem of show biz, would savor hers as the crown jewel. So I asked if he'd like to polka with the mermaid before bowing and scraping with pen and pad. His returning volley was that clods of my ilk kept bodyguards of their ilk in overtime pay. I had pegged the loathsome leviathans as PR, boring the lady out of her gourd. To settle the issue, I said I'd be willing to test the waters, and if they were not overly chilly he could wade in, but not on equal time since there was the possibility the hulks could be bouncers. With, of course, nothing to lose, Scorch shook hands on the deal.

On the way to her table, I mapped the strategy. There'd be no goggle-eyed stares, drivel, or kissing of the ring. Just the appropriate courtesy given to any fair maiden in pretty ballroom shoes. Making the customary bow as the band struck up, I asked for the pleasure. Somewhat startled, she looked at me, at her entourage, back at me, then gave thumbs up. She was Hollywood to the nines in her Christian Dior gown, Liz Arden make-up, and Coco Chanel scent. Now to hold an air of nonchalance while dancing cheek-to-cheek with a live goddess can cause a short in the brain circuit. It can also collapse a few synapses in a goddess, causing something like "You don't know me, do you?" to pop out. This had me babbling incoherently about two total strangers winding up with a paddle and neither with a canoe. Blushing fetchingly, she introduced herself. I gave the name of Henry Ford the Third. She gasped that I didn't believe her, which forced me to say it was my pedigree that seemed most contentious. As she struggled with that piece of pointless palaver, I offered to swap a car for a swimsuit. That did it! Unsure if the glint in her eye was telegraphing a laugh or a stamp on the foot, I ended the charades, came clean, and made the plea of how she could make Scorch the happiest gob in the fleet. The super good sport went with the pitch and smacked a home run. She finished out the dance with Scorch and penned for his his everlasting joy: "To Scorch, a fantastic dancer. All my love, Esther Williams." Scorch picked up the tabs for the rest of the week.

When she stopped laughing, Tally told Cory if she had been that lovely woman, she would have petitioned the Pope to have him exorcised. "I think I'm ready," she said, "to hear about life south of the border."

Cory drained his wine glass. "Mexico, next stop, so help me God!"

The High Command, always willing to try out new ideas in amphib warfare, saw possibilities in the night invasion. It did have its elements of charm. Strike, surprise, and rout the enemy in sleep. What could be more demoralizing than being routed out in long johns! Of course, such a sneaky attack would take time-consuming preparations, but the top brass seldom gave serious thought to such details if they affected only those of lower ranks. Our unit was selected for the experiment and I was tapped to lead in the assaults. The orders read: "Attack simulated enemy beach on southern tip of California. H-hour, midnight. Debark a regiment of marines and return immediately to parent ship. Execute with maximum speed."

It was an abominable night. We dropped anchor ten miles at sea in a savage storm with heavy fog. We scrambled down the nets to man boats bobbing in massive groundswells. Why more bones didn't snap or splinter was a miracle in itself. Finally, all boats were loaded and departed for the rendezvous area. We slowly circled, bows bumping sterns in total blackness. Finally, the attack signal was given. I broke my wave out of the pack and headed shoreward. The beach party during the day had set up a pair of red-blinking lights for markers to guide us in. My simple task, aided by the navy's most powerful binoculars, was to spot the lights and land the troops between them. The blowing rains, however, kept splashing the lens, making the glasses useless. It came down to the naked eye searching in zero visibility for the beach markers.

Scorch, in charge of the second wave, tailgated us, using our sound for direction. On approaching the fogged-in shoreline, I ordered the coxswain to ease the throttle to avoid running aground. The loss of power caused us to drift southward with the current. Suddenly, out of the soup rose two weakly blinking red lights. I gave the signal for full throttle; we roared in. It was a superb landing considering conditions. None of the crafts broached. The marines, bayonets fixed, stormed ashore in full battle gear. I somehow regrouped the boats and swung seaward with the relieved feeling of a perilous mission well done.

It took almost to dawn to find our fog-shrouded ship. I climbed aboard soaked, chilled, aching, but glad to be alive. I was immediately piped to the bridge to face an apoplectic skipper restricting himself to words of the bilges to inform me I invaded Mexico, a fiasco that would require a formal apology from the State Department. The blinking lights guiding me in came from the red-light district of Tijuana!

Tally went weak laughing. "I'm sorry, Cory, but I can't control myself. The image of battle-whooping marines with pointed bayonets charging the bordellos of Mexico has me in hysterics."

After her convulsions subsided, Cory said she could choose how they spend the remaining time before the opera.

A sparkle entered her eye. "After we drop off the blanket and basket, let's take the ferry to Coronado and visit the rock with the heartbeat, the one we scaled the night of the dance."

Tally dashed the final yards to the boulder, Cory right behind her. They climbed to the top of it, sat with their legs dangling over the edge, and gazed out at the open sea. Cory lowered an ear. "Its heartbeat is stronger, my love. This tells me you have been true to your pledge. You have not doubted its spiritual life."

"The beat of its heart is so beautiful because it beats in rhythm with the sea. I agree, darling. We must have first come from the sea. How else can we explain the tranquility that comes in listening to her sounds. Just the sitting on this rock magically vanishes my cares and woes. Even makes less frightening all the rumors on job terminations."

He rested her head on his chest. "Rumors are rampant in wartime, Mopsy. Don't let them get under your skin. The scare of layoffs is a throwback to depression days. Truth is, a war, for all of its ugliness, is a stimulant for economic growth. A war such as this one will be followed with an era of prosperity. Your pretty little head will spin at all the luxury about to descend on it."

She tilted her head upward and kissed the point of his nose. "Oh, Cory, you do see roses in the rain, and I so much want to do so too."

As she shifted to sitting position and pulled her feet up on the top ledge, he hooked an arm under her knees and straightened her tanned legs across his lap. "What extraordinary underpinnings!" he exclaimed. "So symmetrical."

"Oh!"

"Look. The arches of the feet match, the ankles match, the calves match, the knees match."

"Really."

"As we continue the anatomical ascent, the ratio of the thigh bones to the hip bones match the ratio of the bosom to the girth."

"Amazing! Now what are you saying, Cory?"

"I'm saying in a roundabout way that I love the beautiful, and you, Mopsy, are beautiful."

She flung her arms round his neck. "I always want to be beautiful for you, darling. Even after the hair is gray."

He caressed her auburn locks and held her in a tender embrace. "We best leave the rock. We don't want it to explode in our happiness."

As they were returning to the ranch to change attire for the *Porgy and Bess* opera, Tally spoke of her friends Mike and Beth Lashley. "I'd like to grow old in the way they do. They're middle age but very young at heart. With their zest for the fun-loving life having never diminished, they fitted right in with all of us young bloods."

"Only those with amnesia of the heart need fear the tyranny of time."

"Darling, how well you put into words the feelings I so bumble to express."

Cory changed into his dress blues and Tally into a black décolleté evening gown and spike heels for the night's entertainment. He surveyed her transformation. "An exotic Mata Hari," he exclaimed. "An outfit that could extract top secrets from MacArthur himself."

"A femme fatale, am I?"

"I just pray we don't meet any drunken sailors. I'm a bit rusty on my kung fu."

Tally laughed. "I could change to sackcloth and huarches, but then I'd insist you wear a toga and straw sandals."

After the opera they had a midnight snack and returned to the house with the living area again to themselves. They snugged up on the sofa. Tally kicked off her heels.

She sighed. "Oh, Cory, how long do you think this horrible war's going to last?"

He placed her stockinged foot on his lap and caressed it. "Just a matter of time now. The Battle of the Coral Sea ended their aggression. The Battle of Midway changed the balance of sea power. Victory in the Gilberts cracked their outer defense. Slowly the noose is tightening on Hirohito. When he's about to choke, he'll squeal: 'Boys, I'll make a deal. If you don't bomb my garden, I'll give you a peace dove for Christmas.'"

"Home for Christmas! I love your optimism, darling. And why not? Yes, peace by Christmas. That shall be my dream."

"Now that we've settled the war issue, Mopsy, let's get to more important matters. Us." He shifted position to have her lie next to him on the sofa. "We have just nine days before I head to San Francisco and a week of those are lost in work schedules."

"I know, I know. And I know very shortly you'll be making another mad dash to the ferry." She twined her legs on his and wrapped her arms on his head. Their bodies pressed together in a tight embrace. "Oh, Cory, I love you so. Every ounce of me loves you and always will." She smothered him with kisses and then pushed a finger between his lips. "And I want you to know I am not a Mata Hari. Nor a femme fatale." Her lovely laughter rang out. "I am a black widow, which means I shall ensnare you in my web, drug you with my aphrodisiac, and then devour you. What do you think of that?"

He nibbled on her ear lobe. "Rather you be a black widow than a scorpion."

"Oh!"

"The black widow kills in love. The scorpion just loves to kill.

Better that my tombstone reads here lies Sinbad murdered in passion than murdered in cold blood."

"Since when have you been an expert on the scorpion?"

"Since my wise-owl grandfather told me the story of the scorpion and the frog. This scorpion met this frog on the bank of a river and since scorpions can't swim, he asked the frog if he could ride on his back across the river. 'If I did that,' the frog replied, 'you would sting me and I would die.' 'But if I killed you,' the scorpion replied, 'we'd both drown.' So the frog let him sit on his back, and when they reached the middle of the river, the scorpion stung him. 'Now we'll both die,' the frog croaked. 'Why did you do that?' 'Because,' the scorpion sighed, 'I'm a scorpion.'"

"Aha," Tally exclaimed, "since we can't escape what we are, I shall love you to death, my prince froggy." She pressed her face on Cory's and smooched until he barely had running time to catch the ferry.

Tally's pounding heart made restful sleep impossible. She tossed and turned in wild dreams. She began the new day with thoughts of only Cory, drawn to his picture like iron filings to a magnet. With her feelings bursting for expression, she had to write before doing anything else.

April 29, 1944

Gash Darling,

Good morning, dearest! It's a good morning after all, for I find that life does somehow go on, even as I thought surely the world must end when you left last night. It didn't end, darling, for, as per your prescription, a few hours sleep brings a fresh light and in that light I have only to say that I love you, and then ask what is to happen to two people so terribly much in love? Again, I can only say, I have never, never before felt anything like this, and never, never thought it was possible to feel like this. There is a tenderness in your love found only in dreams. It dissolves reality and makes me feel immortal, never to grow old under its protective shield. Oh, how I want our love to be pure and right. As surely as I say this, just as surely, we could easily have fallen over the brink last night. People do, I know, and it's so easy to rationalize and live only for the moment with so much war and death hanging over us.

But, I plead, Cory, I want our love to be right, to be beautiful, to be something we can be proud of, not dwindled by shame or guilt, but something to hold and cherish through the frightening months ahead when we haven't each other's arms for protection. That shall be our strength because beyond that we have only words and letters to hold the bond, words and letters which can say and mean such a multitude of things. We've already glimmered the ache of separation and how it festers the agitated mind.

What can be done? I don't know. Each time I see you, it becomes harder to whisper goodbye. Goodbye, such a dreadful word, isn't it, darling? Rather, I would say good night for it carries the promise of a good morning. The answer may be in time itself. Looking ahead it's like trying to grasp eternity; looking behind it zips past like the night express. By most people's standards we have known each other only six weeks. But in my heart each second is a minute and each minute an hour, so in the heart where things really matter, I have really known you for ten years. So, we are not cheated!

Oh, darling, I love you so much it's like hanging the washing in the rain, it never gets dry. We have our love, yet we have it not, but let's not drift into the shadows. We can laugh, hope, and bear up today because of what might be tomorrow. The war brings out many moral irregularities but may our better nature prevail to guide our passions. Let us keep our love pure, darling, for a higher power to bless. May God forgive me if I love you too much. You have my heart. Forever yours,

Mopsy

Phone calls filled up the week. It came to both of them that Scorch and Susan would make a good pairing. So they planned a double date for Sunday.

It turned out to be an evening of laughs. Scorch, not short on talent himself, was a funny impersonator of celebrities. He had Tally and Susan in stitches with his mimicry of Groucho Marx and W. C. Fields. Then he and Cory teamed up in a minstrel slapstick, a Mr. Interlocutor and Mr. Bones routine, which had the girls holding their sides.

"You guys came out of vaudeville," a laughing Susan insisted.

Scorch saw Susan home. Alone in the living area at the ranch, Cory plunked on the sofa while Tally fixed coffee. When she returned, she curled up at his feet and rested her head on his knee while they sipped.

Cory ran a hand through her sheeny locks. "You guessed right, Mopsy. Scorch and Susan hit it off great. Too bad they can't have more time together. *C'est la guerre!*"

"And just one more day for us. Remember, you promised to meet me at the plant after work and take me home for one more big hug before going north."

"I'll be there, m' darling, with bells on." He massaged her neck and shoulders and inhaled deeply. "Ummm. You sure smell good."

"I know. Like freshly mowed hay."

"Don't downplay the sex appeal of alfalfa. Why do you suppose the expression *make hay while the sun shines* got so popular?" Tally twisted over and punched him lightly in the stomach.

There was a long silence. Cory saw her mood change and asked why the dour face. "I'm pouting," Tally said, "because of the darn navy. Because it's going to take you away from me, send you up the coast, then down the coast, and then . . . I just don't wish to continue with the thought."

Cory kissed her on the cheek and said, "Think only of the free hours we'll have together painting the ol' town red at the end of the shakedown cruise. And should red not be your favorite color, why we'll paint it whatever color you choose."

"Wouldn't surprise me one bit if the navy rescinded orders the moment the ship entered the bay and ordered it back to sea, leaving me stranded high and dry on the dock."

Cory lightly pinched her cheek and chided, "Ye of so little faith."

There was another long period of silence. "A penny for your thoughts," Tally said.

He scratched her back and spoke softly. "I was just thinking that at this very moment somewhere in Japan a soldier boy is kissing his sweetheart goodbye, telling her not to worry, but knowing in his heart she has every right to. He knows that the skies are full of American planes, the waters are patrolled by American ships, and the battlefields are crammed with American tanks. He knows that modern wars are no longer won by soldiers but by technology, and that he is fighting the most powerful industrial nation on earth. He knows only too well his chances of coming home are slim to none. We're lucky to be Americans."

"You sure are good at lightening my mood. Getting me to think about the plight of the poor Japanese girl takes me away from wallowing in my misery."

Cory drew Tally up on the sofa, pressed her body next to his, heartbeat against heartbeat, and said the words, the three little words, that make love tender. Their lips melded. Time faded out in the bliss of oneness and then returned with jolting reality as he shot out of her arms to beeline to the waterfront to jump on the last ferry just as the last of the stern lines were being cast off.

Tally went to sleep pondering more on Cory's thoughts on war. His attitude was so different from most servicemen. He truly did not harbor hate or resentment toward the enemy, propaganda notwithstanding. He saw both sides being victims of a system outside of their making, and but for the accident of birth, the uniforms could well have been switched. How difficult it must be, she thought, to humanize the enemy and carry out the mandates of war.

A frustrated Cory phoned Tally soon after she reached work the next day. He had to break the news that he could not see her as planned later that night. The boat officers drew straws as who would be in charge of the enlisted personnel heading to San Francisco. He drew the short one and so had to be at the depot early in the evening to head north with the crew. Tally vented her disappointment, understanding, of course, how the fates of war play out. She relayed bushels of love and a request for an abundance of letters. Her emotions quieted down at day's end, and she wrote to let him know she would survive in spite of the navy.

May 5, 1944

My Darling,

Jeepers, how I looked forward to seeing you tonight, and the navy ruined everything. I didn't do too well on the phone. But at least I can write a few lines and tell the most open secret of all—I love you, Ensign Zigler. A spot is reserved in this heart-o-mine for you that neither man nor beast can maneuver out of position. So there!

Even though we couldn't be together, just hearing your voice and knowing you are thinking of me means so much. Perhaps to a fellow it doesn't mean as much as to a gal.

There were a number of absentees at work tonight so some of us put in a few extra hours. They played music for us and it was enjoyable. If they'd do it all the time, it might eliminate a good deal of unnecessary talking and visiting. Our group, however, has to be careful because we work directly opposite the chief engineer's office. I do enjoy my little chats with Buck. You would like him, too, Cory. He's quite the philosopher and can always find a quote at the appropriate moment. He and Mr. Barker make a madhouse pair.

Debbie is home tonight and in bed early. Susan, who is staying with us a few days until she goes on day shift next week, is out at her folk's home.

I was reading the "Digest" and ran across an article which reminded me of what you once wryly said. May I quote you? "It takes two to make a marriage: a single daughter and a scheming mother." Sure glad you have a mind of your own, darling, otherwise, you might not have had a chance.

Susan came in so I'll say good night, my fair prince. Bon voyage, cheri! With all my heart come back soon. I love you, darling. All yours,

Mopsy

# Shakedown Cruise

"I don't envy you, buddy," Scorch said as Cory was packing his belongings at the base barracks. "These guys are going to see this train ride as their last hurrah stateside. Once on the Hudson, they know it's no return till it's over, over there."

"Don't rub it in, mate. I'm fully aware of what it means. It'll be a ride for the ages."

"At least you'll have troop inspection before boarding."

"A lot of good that'll do. Some of these salts, old enough to have sired you and me, have forgotten more tricks than we've ever learned. No matter how tight the inspection, it's a dollar to a doughnut booze in quantity will find its way aboard."

"So, maestro, what tune are you going to play?"

"I've a song and dance, Scorch, but I'm keeping it under hat. If it plays well, I'll let you in on it, but if it doesn't, you'll know because my address will be Leavenworth and my diet will be bread and water. Will tell you this much. I spent the best part of the afternoon over at personnel checking the files on the crew and let me say this, we've got our share of talent."

The San Diego depot that night was a human circus. Wives, sweethearts, mothers, and shrieking tots milled about in last-minute hugs and kisses. Cory let the farewells linger on until he got frantic signals from the conductor. He ordered Chief Petty Officer Murphy to line up the men for final troop inspection. Murphy efficiently carried out the order, brought the men to attention, and reported to Cory with a snappy salute that the company was all present and accounted for.

Cory and the Chief then moved rapidly down the lines to check for any signs of irregularity. The most they came up with was homebaked cookies, fresh fruit, hunks of salami, dice, and girlie magazines. Cory then addressed the bell bottoms:

"Men, I have now fulfilled navy regulations. Inspection has been completed. As the Chief reads off you name, file orderly on board and take a seat. I intend to go immediately to my compartment, lock the door, and hit the sack. When we arrive at dawn in San Francisco, I shall expect to find the train shipshape. The following men shall comprise the cleanup detail: Lasky, Horne, Pollak, Tidell, and Johnson. They will be responsible to see that the seats, aisles, and heads are clean and in working order. Chief Murphy, take over."

There was a roar of approval as Murphy, stationed by the platform, began bellowing out the names and the men filed aboard. When the last one entered, Murphy turned to Cory. "Curious, sir, why you selected that particular group for the cleanup detail. You have a couple of real hotheads in the mix."

Cory smiled. "I checked records earlier in the day, and they are our ex-carpenters and ex-plumbers."

Cory stayed faithful to his word. He entered his compartment, locked the door, and picked up a book, having no illusions of getting sleep. The decibels slowly increased with the consumption of the liquor, which, following prediction, had mysteriously appeared on board in oversupply. Tempted as he was to shelve the plan when the noise level reached bedlam, he knew that once he compromised, all bets would be off. So he held to course. At two A.M. a loud pounding was on his door. He cracked it open to see a hopping mad conductor with veins getting larger and redder as he spoke.

"In my twenty years on the circuit, I've never seen a rowdier bunch. I'm going to send a full report to the commandant of the Naval District, and you, sir, are going to have your ass in a sling."

Cory assumed a humbling, placating posture. "You've got every right, sir, to toss the lot of us in the brig, but before you write and submit your report, I ask one small favor. Come to my compartment at the crack of dawn and join me in an inspection of the damage." He gained the needed time.

At precisely 6:00 A.M., a sweating ensign and a stiff-necked train conductor proceeded to make rounds. The conductor's eyes bulged in disbelief and Cory heaved a deep sigh. The train was spic and span. Seats and heads were in good working order, aisles cleaned, and trash gathered and stored in appropriate containers. The conductor lifted his eyes and said in awe, "It's a miracle."

"No, just the navy," Cory replied with a straight face.

☆ ☆ ☆

"Still nothing from Cory," Tally fussed. "I got a brief note on his arrival to S.F. saying the trip went fine, has a good story to tell about it, and the ship will leave its slip in a week. He dubbed their crowded living quarters Goat Castle. And that's it! They've been at sea a full day now."

Susan, staying at the ranch during Cindy's absence, sought to appease her. "Really no big surprise," she said. "The boys have to get settled into ship routine and then when they have a little free time, take in the sights of the city. He'll be in touch soon. Cory doesn't impress me as one of those out-of-sight, out-of-mind sailors."

"How does he impress you, by the way, now that you know him better?"

"I still say, darling, if you ever decide to toss him to the dogs, let this bitch know first." She laughed. "Not that it would probably do much good."

"Susan, if you aren't the sly one. When it comes to oomph, you put Ann Sheridan, the original Oomph Girl, to shame. I bet you get more marriage proposals than the bureau at City Hall. I saw those heads spin at the pool today."

"You have a bad case of cross-eyes, Tally, if you saw them spinning my way. But on marriages, I'm of the opinion one has to be dumb, drunk, or masochistic to take the plunge in wartime."

Tally laughed. "Those were my sentiments until I met Cory.

Now I'm not sure what I'd do if he dangled an offer. But I'll never be tested because he's as adamant as you. He told me one night four things can happen and three are not good: He stays happy and she doesn't; she stays happy and he doesn't; they both stay unhappy; they both stay happy."

"Unusual to find a male both handsome and intelligent."

"I've been stubbornly refusing to write until I hear from him, but you've got me looking at it differently. Twas selfish of me to expect that when he gets a breather to have him lock himself up and write instead of taking in a little fun in the city."

Tally picked up her pen and Susan picked up a book.

May 12, 1944

My Darling,

Hi, m'love! How's everything after one day at sea? What I wouldn't give to be a stowaway! Hmmmm. What time did you heave anchor? Is my navy lingo improving?

Susan and I hit the sack fairly early last night—early for us, although well past midnight. Of course, we couldn't possibly sleep at that hour, so we gabbed into the wee hours, with men the main topic. She insists I let her know the moment we break up. Hmmmm. I think I better watch you two. Well, anyway, we unrooted ourselves from our respective beds around ten o'clock and tripped off to the grocery. If you could have seen how loaded down we were with sacks, you would have thought we were shopping for a harvest crew.

After squaring things up about the house, we went over to the park for a few games of tennis. Neither of us will make it to Wimbledon, but we're fairly evenly matched. It was a mite warm so we decided to follow up with swimming. We suited and casually strolled to the pool. A guard, looking WWI vintage, appeared and formally announced: "Young ladies, as of the first of the month, the U.S. navy has taken over this section and you are trespassing on government property." Needless to say, it wasn't sunburn that had us turning pink, as glancing about we suddenly became aware of a battalion of sailors gawking as though we were Esther Williams' double. We properly excused ourselves and glided out of there as inconspicuously as possible, getting a good laugh later on over it. That concluded our adventures before going to work. And now as the day ends, darling, in case you're wondering, you are here with me in my heart, in my dreams, and one hundred kisses to you for the fantastic day we had together. Loving you ever,

Mopsy

"I'm excited for two good reasons," Tally gushed, sipping coffee with Susan after their late-morning breakfast. "I got a letter from Cindy and she said she'll be back in ten days. I had misunderstood. I thought she resigned, but she actually had wormed out a leave. I had serious doubts she'd return without a job, so a big weight is lifted off my mind as I would miss her terribly."

"Not only that," Susan added, "but I ran into Debbie as I was clocking in yesterday and she said Cindy is on the day list, so it's no more swing shift for her. I also heard that I'll soon be transferred to days. Things are moving at a dizzying pace. . . . Well, what's the second excitement?"

Tally's infectious laugh rang out. "Surprised you haven't guessed. This afternoon you and I will have our first art class with Mr. Gilbert. It was you who persuaded him to take us on. I've always wanted to learn to paint. I only hope my talent comes close to matching my desire."

"Don't sell yourself short. I've seen some of your dabblings and they're not bad at all. But we are fortunate to study with him. He's one of the finest painters in the area."

"Wouldn't it be wonderful," Tally exclaimed, "to have at least one enviable skill."

The afternoon went not exactly the way she had pictured it. Mr. Gilbert took his small class out to the park. "Art is nothing more," he lectured, "than converting imagery into visual expression. It is inner perception externalized. Perception is unique. No two people see an object exactly the same way. We paint what we perceive. I can give you techniques to improve the projection but I cannot give you techniques to improve the processes giving rise to the imagery. That is God-given. The great artists differ from good artists in that they are able to see the essence of things. They catch glimpses of truths." He paused. "Now today we paint what all of us see everyday, yet each of us see differently, a tree."

He then spent his time going from student to student critiquing what he saw. When he came to Tally, he took a long look. "A most unusual perception of a tree, Miss Dugan. I suggest you forget about the limbs, the branches, the leaves and concentrate just on the trunk. Draw nothing but trunks."

"Trunks, sir?"

"Trunks, Miss Dugan."

Later that night in the peace and comfort of their living area, the radio on low, Tally in preparation to write Cory and Susan buried in a book, Tally suddenly broke the silence.

"Susan, just one question. How much of the tree did you draw?"

"Why, the entire tree: trunk, limbs, branches, leaves. Why do you ask?"

"No special reason." Tally turned to her correspondence.

May 13, 1944

My darling,

Just time ere I jump into bed to drop you a line. You will be with me soon, pleasantly disturbing my dreams. I wonder where your ship is mooring tonight.

It was another beautiful day. I spent the afternoon in the park with an art class, sketching tree trunks, tree trunks, tree trunks. I shall probably see you sitting on one in my sleep. I had never realized all that goes into painting a simple little tree. I started out on leaves, but Mr. Gilbert (you don't pronounce the "t") suggested the focus be on trunks.

The uphill slant to my writing is to be blamed on the magazine I'm using for a base. It has a lump in the center.

I heard from Cindy today and she should be back in ten days. I hope she can for I'm eager to see her.

Say hello to Scorch. I can see why you're so high on him. He's a great guy—and can he jitterbug! All of your buddies that I met seem top flight. I get the feeling all of you get along famously together. Wonderful that you are all assigned to the same ship.

I talked to Ted this afternoon and he's going to check with his doctor about a leave. I'll probably dash to the hospital tomorrow afternoon. Whoops! There's the phone. Who could be calling at this hour!

It was Avis. She called to cancel out riding in the morning. Which reminds me, I should get some sleep. Good night, my darling. I'll drop another line tomorrow. Loving you ever,

Mopsy

Tally relayed the good news on her brother Ted to Susan the following night. "The doctors," she said, "are so encouraged with his progress that they're giving him over a month's leave before the next scheduled surgery. He will get to go home to Denver and try to patch up his marriage. I have serious doubts it can be saved."

"He's such a nice guy," Susan said, "to have such tough luck happening to him. Doesn't seem fair."

"You don't know the half of it. It's material for a soap opera, but I don't want to burden you with it."

"Please do. I've heard bits and snatches, of course, but not the whole story. We've adopted Ted, you know."

Tally walked over and hugged Susan as tears misted her eyes. "It's not very pretty and I'll try not to ramble. After my parents divorced, we kids were placed with my mother, the usual arrangement, but she had become bitter and cynical. Life was not too pleasant, much bickering took place, and in most of the squabbles, Ted, who was a grade ahead of me, and I found ourselves on the outs with the others. Consequently, we became very close and somewhat seclusive. We confided in each other and shared our dreams and ambitions.

"As long as I can remember, Ted was set on becoming a civil engineer, doting on designs like of bridges and tunnels. He won a top scholarship to college, an exciting day because financial aid was his only hope of continuing his education. Then Jenny roared into the scene like the night express. They were crazy about each other, constantly on the go, together all the time, little sleep in a whirlwind romance. She wanted to get married, not wait, which put him in a bind. It would end his chances to be an engineer. In this sense, Jenny was selfish. She was the only child of a well-to-do banker and was accustomed to have things go her way. Patience was not one of her virtues. Her father, who'd do anything for her happiness, offered Ted a job in the bank. He was as fit to be a banker as I was to be a baker. Then came the stunning news that Jenny was pregnant. Well, that ended all speculation. Ted returned his scholarship to the university and following high-school graduation, in a big, expensive wedding, footed by papa banker, the two exchanged the vows. Ted became a teller in the bank.

"It was a terribly rough first year. Ted disliked his job and Jenny was not ready for motherhood. She resented what her pregnancy was doing to her young beautiful body. She increased her drinking. In her seventh month, a bit tipsy, she tripped on a top stair and tumbled to the mid-landing. She only suffered minor bruises but lost the baby. Ted was disconsolate. He had wanted the baby so much. I think he saw it as the exchange for his scholarship. Less than a month later, Pearl Harbor made the news. Ted, gung-ho patriotic, resigned from the bank and enlisted in the marines. He went to Parris Island for training and from there went with the First Division to Guadalcanal. He was not only badly wounded but, like many, picked up malaria and jungle rot. The hazards of the tropics were as feared as the enemy. Dysentery was common in the foul, smelly swamps. Jenny drove out to San Diego to see him. She was shocked at what she saw and he was appalled that she should see it. The relationship was further strained. Bitter arguments took place, divorce was brought up, and Jenny returned to Denver to decide what to do. In spite of it all, I think they still love each other, but the odds of the marriage working have to be slim."

The story deeply affected Susan. "What can I say?" she said. "The thought of these boys crawling in the steamy jungle fighting snakes, insects, poisonous mosquitoes just turns the stomach. On top of that, Ted has to cope with severe wounds, long rehabilitation, and a collapsing marriage. All of this happening to one so young makes it mind-boggling. And being as close as you two are, this has to be terribly hard on you."

"His physical progress has been so encouraging. I'm hardly aware anymore of his artificial eye, and the docs claim they can reconstruct his jaw. It's his mental state that's now most distressing. Too much of the time he's flat and broody. The spontaneity that was once his charm is gone. Cory with his contagious optimism has kept my spirits from dipping too low. Thinking of him gives me the urge to dash off a letter."

"You do that," Susan said, "and I'll polish off this novel." Tally flipped a mental switch, which she was getting good at, and began writing.

May 15, 1944

Gash, My Darling,

You've been gone only ten days now, so why should I be missing you so? Love makes such a mockery of time. Makes it seem forever since I last looked into those devilish blue eyes.

The world must be full of people like us who watch the hours pass into days and the days into weeks for those special moments to be together, and then repeat the process all over again. The sweetest minutes of all are those precious ones we can spend together. Yes, I do feel we've been fortunate and should be thankful for the time we've been together, be it only a fraction of a lifetime. Can you believe that Friday is another monthversary?

Exactly two months ago we met and danced and you sang under the stars what is now my favorite Irish ballad. I'll miss you twice as much come that day.

This has been an unusually busy week for some reason. Susan and I went to art class on Tuesday and discovered that Mr. Gilbert's birthday is Thursday. We stayed up to bake him a cake, one phase of the culinary arts neither of us stars in. The second cake turned out passibly edible in a modest way, but the first effort was a sorry, dilapidated specimen, the sight of which might put you in hysterics. But Mr. Gilbert was so touched to think that we had thought of him that it was worth the mess.

How easy it would be for me to drift asleep while I'm sitting here with you on my mind and the radio playing ever so softly so as not to disturb us. This has become the best part of the day for me—when I come home, relax, and be with you for a few minutes.

Avis called this morning to say she and her landlady were going to Tijuana and asked me to go along. (I know it's no longer your favorite vacation spot!) We did have a fun time, darling, and explored practically everything. It's not a very large place, quite colorful, with so many curio shops one hardly knows where to start. We stayed mainly on the main drag and sampled hardware, cosmetics, clothing, jewelry, etc. The city was easy to enter, but on leaving, one would think we were saboteurs, the way we had to sign our lives away. We did order a nice steak dinner at the Foreign Club. Only disappointment was your absence.

Ted got a leave of 38 days, which made him quite happy. He will go to Denver. I was hoping to tag along but since he's leaving so soon, I'm afraid I'll have to take a rain check. He's going Monday if he can catch transportation.

Not a word more from Cindy, but she must be on the road back. Her work leave is up Monday—I was wrong; she hadn't terminated. She'll be surprised to find she's been transferred to days. I'll be a little orphan working the swing shift.

Our group threw a party after work last night and it was not a howling success. A few clods got roaring drunk and things got wild and boisterous. Several of us slipped away a bit early. I guess there will always be those who have to hit the bottle heavily to get the courage to rise above convention. Well, this hasn't anything to do with us, darling, so it's not worth the time of day. Rather, it just makes me love you more for the person you are.

Write as often as you can, darling. I thrive on your beautiful letters. In the meantime, I'll keep on loving you with all my heart.

Mopsy

Another Sunday dawned, the day of the week that had become special to Tally. It was, of course, the only day the Inner Circle was free from work and could have a full day of fun together, be it riding, swimming, tennis, moviegoing, dancing— ending up usually being a string of activities. Now that their schedules separated them during the week, the day also became one of catching up.

As Tally became more aware of what little time remained before Cory would be gone and into the thick of things, her anxieties correspondingly mounted, and she turned more often to attending Sunday morning services.

And, of course, with Sunday the day of their first meeting, it took on a special romantic hue, which Tally enhanced with creating weekly anniversaries and private reminiscences.

On this particular Sunday, there was the added poignancy of Ted's first prolonged hospital leave, starting the next day, and the angst of still no word from Cory, on whom she had so relied for emotional sustenance.

Ted arrived at the ranch late in the morning to bid goodbye to the Inner Circle as his train was to leave the following day. They all hugged him, Debbie assuring him the mountain air would add color to his cheeks. Then Susan and Debbie went riding. Avis and Tally deferred, preferring to see the movie Dragon Seed, based on the novel by Pearl Buck. "I've read the book," Tally said, "and I'm eager to see how they made it into a movie."

After the movie, Avis and Tally stopped at a coffee shop before continuing on to the house.

"You seem a little subdued today," Avis observed.

"Ted's leaving and no letter from Cory has put me a bit in the blues. Has Mark had spells like this?"

Avis laughed. "Every time the big lug pulls into port. Sailors are all alike. When at sea, they write faithfully; in port they resurrect the double standard: You write, they play. At first I sulked, then I decided what's good for the gander is good for the goose. If he can play around a little, I can play around a little."

"I have no heart for that. Guess I'm a one man's woman. But it must be reciprocated. The moment Cory should stop loving me would be the moment the relationship ends. I'd never crawl, beg, or claw. That would be losing dignity."

"Doubt seriously that'll ever happen. "The way I saw Cory look at you on the afternoon I met him, I said to myself, I sure wish Mark would look at me that way." Tally smiled and squeezed Avis's hand.

Susan had the big surprise of the day. After dinner and all were lazying about in the living area, she jumped to her feet and droned with theatrical resonance: "Ladies, I have an announcement to make to all who are so unfortunate as not to be natives of this fair city. Tonight at the stroke of midnight under a full moon the grunions make their annual ride on the tide onto the sandy beaches of the Island of Coronado. It is a sight to rejuvenate the most jaded of eyes."

"Grunions?" Tally asked.

"Small whitish fish. They come this time of year under a full moon and a high tide to spawn. The females ride in on the tide at the bewitching hour, deposit their eggs in the sand for the males to fertilize, and then in about two weeks the tide washes the eggs out to sea and they hatch at once. It is a ritual beautiful to behold."

"We must see it," Debbie enthused.

And so at midnight an excited crew of Debbie, Avis, Susan, and Tally stole to the Coronado beach and thrilled to the fascinating reproductive rites of the grunions. Tally could hardly wait to return home and pass on the experience in her letter to Cory.

May 18, 1944

My Darling,

Tell me, why this intense longing for you on Sundays? Could it be I first felt your arms around me on a Sunday? That day will always stay special. While no St. Pat's Day is ordinary, I had no premonition of this one, of the turn it would take, or of the time it would last—way into the wee hours of the morning. Memories of that night will never grow dim: the dance, the serenade, the walk under the stars, the ride on the ferry, the wind blowing hair in my eyes, and the good night kiss, so gentle and yet so warming to every fiber of my body. Oh, how unsettled and confused were my feelings as I waited for the next Sunday, which seemed ever so slow in coming. You muddled up my thoughts about myself, my relationship with men, my outlook on life. My respect for reason told me all this could not be happening. But it did, Cory, and the love which caused it all goes as deep as the heart can be tapped. Compre? I hope you do, darling, because then you can explain it all to me.

Today has been rather quiet for a nice change. Ted popped in about 11:00 AM and we read and listened to the radio. Avis came over for dinner and we hopped downtown to see "Dragon Seed."

The real excitement happened tonight. The moon was full so we sneaked over to Coronado beach at midnight to watch the grunions run. They are a small fish which come in at full moon and high tide at this time of year to spawn. It's a beautiful sight to watch them make their nests by half-burying themselves in the sand. When you look on them as a whole, the sand seems almost white and the grunions appear to be standing upright, dancing.

Will close till next time. Love you, darling, just bunches and bunches.

Mopsy

☆ ☆ ☆

An amused Scorch eyed Cory plopping on his bunk after his watch with a couple of letters. "God, it was nerve-racking," Cory said, "having the old man breathing on the back of your neck and firing questions on how to handle emergencies while you're trying to carry out the orders of the day and keeping an eye on the helmsman that he stays steady on course."

"What's going on, anyway, between you and the captain?" Scorch asked.

"Whatcha mean?"

"I mean, what gives that keeps him giving you the short end of the stick?"

"Guess I don't follow you."

"Gash, you're pulling my leg or you're the most naive dude in the fleet. To begin with, did you catch the squint he gave you when Gil introduced the boat division to him?"

"Lord, Scorch, the guy's nearing fifty. Vision starts going downhill at that age." Cory then grinned. "Besides, he probably wanted a closer gander because I reminded him of his favorite nephew."

"The eternal optimist. That explains, of course, why you were the only one who got double watch while we were docked."

"The luck of the draw. Somebody had to get it, and I was the unlucky one."

"The same luck that tagged you Officer of the Deck while the rest of us denizens of Goat Castle got the lighter duty of assistant OD's?"

"Just goes to prove what a good judge of character he is."

"Okay, wiseacre, figure this one out. He makes you, who doesn't know beans about guns, gunnery officer of a forty millimeter, and those of us who grew up with firearms, gunnery officers of the twenty millimeters. And if you're still whistling in the dark, why would he assign you summary court-martial officer and not Gooseneck, who's had two years of Law School?"

"Okay, mate, now that you've spent the day gathering data to make a paranoid case, what's your conclusion?"

"I see only one explanation. He's run into you somewhere before. And not under the best of circumstances. Maybe he was caught in that barroom brawl when we were celebrating the end of midshipman school. God knows, the whole place got into it before it was over, and he may have been on the innocent end of one of your wild haymakers."

"Not a chance. You know me, Scorch. Once bottles and chairs enter a fray, I'm on my belly crawling out of the place. Okay, I'll come straight with you. I can't deny the skipper has a vendetta going, why is beyond me, yet I like the old buzzard. Maybe it's because he's a mustang and doesn't have the phony Annapolis polish. By coming up through the ranks, he knows his navy from A to Z. While I'm sure his heart was set on commanding at least a light cruiser, I can't think of a better person to have around when the chips are down. Well, we'll see how it all plays out. . . . Now, if you'll excuse me, old pal, I hit the jackpot in today's mail. Two letters from Mopsy."

Cory propped himself up in his bunk, ripped open the envelopes, and read them in sequence.

May 24, 1944

Gash Darling,

This is my first letter to you since Sunday. I've been waiting, thinking surely I'd be hearing from you. Now I feel something must have happened to prevent your writing, or, perhaps, even getting mail. Has some unforseen circumstance occurred? I fervently hope it's nothing drastic.

I realize, confined as you are to a ship, there's not much news, but, nevertheless, I still want so much to hear from you. Aren't I a terrible mess leaning on you the way I do? It seems absolutely ages since I've last seen you and yet I know it has only been three weeks. The days drag interminably when I think of the darn war keeping us apart. I must immerse myself in work.

Monday last, I met Ted downtown for lunch and saw him off on a train, heading home. I'd love to have hopped aboard with him, and yet I wouldn't, not wanting to risk missing even one minute with you. As I look at it, I can, should the need arise, go home at any time, but I can't see you at any time. And let me add one more thing, darling. As well as you know me, it's no surprise, but I still need to say it. As long as you want me, I'll be waiting, but should you, for whatever reason, ever feel differently, I have only to ask that you tell me. I am not afraid, for I know in my heart I love you. It's not something I have to bring up and ask myself or tell myself, it's constantly present. There is room in my heart only for you. That is why I realize now that I never truly loved Rex, my high school sweetheart, or Martin, who came along a couple of years later. Doubts always lingered and, therefore, I could never commit. What you have given me, darling, is priceless—the awareness that I am normal, that I can be free of doubt, that I can commit. Often in the end things turn out for the best, despite the agonies and struggles on the way. You know, Cory, it never ceases to amaze me whenever I look back to realize how short a time I've known you and yet how long a time you seem to have been in my heart.

Cindy came home Tuesday and is back on the job. She and Debbie are working days, so I've seen little of them this week. Susan is staying on with us for a week to adjust to the day shift before returning home. Here is our confusing schedule: Debbie and Cindy work from 7:00 AM to 4:00; Susan from 8:00 AM to 5:00; and I, of course, from 4:00 PM to 1:00 AM.

Later.

Hmmmm. Sure and tis a beautiful day. We girls went downtown for lunch so I'm only dropping in to say hello before dashing to work. I received a letter from Dad today wanting me to come home. If I did, I know he'd want me to stay. I couldn't, darling, because Denver now seems so disconnected. Even though we both have some second thoughts about San Diego, it's still a part of you as long as you're part of the navy.

I better get this in the mail for you. Please write when you can. I love you. Ever yours,

Mopsy

My Darling,

Hello, my heart. And what I would give to say hello in person! You took such a big part of me with you that I feel fragmented. I fear it will be this way until this awful war is over and you return. You've kinda grown on me, planting yourself deep here in my heart. Your heart really, for I've given you mine. Do you miss yours, darling? See what I mean. I'm all in a flutter and, begorra, it's all your fault!

The world may think me crazy, but as long as you can put up with me, that's all that counts. My hope, darling, is that somewhere in the space which separates us, our thoughts will meet and mingle in the oneness known only to those deeply in love.

Sunday has been a rather peaceful day. Susan and I played a few sets of tennis early this morning and later went to church at the Cathedral. It was my very first time in a Catholic church and I can honestly say it was beautiful.

Susan moved out to her home so Cindy and I are sharing the same room again. Of course, we have tons of things to hash over regarding her trip and matters in general. She had a wonderful time, hated to leave, but after finally relaxing, realized how worn out she is. Great to have her back even though our only time together is on Sundays. The good news is that Dave's ship is temporarily in anchor in Long Beach. He came down for several hours. Crazy, lovable kids! I told them they were eligible to join our club, which, after all, is fairly exclusive. By the way, both she and Debbie send their warmest regards.

Avis has been staying with me this week since her landlady is out of town and she's not keen on being alone. Last night, however, we stayed at her apartment and it was fun having the house entirely to ourselves, making all the commotion we desired. We sewed some during the day and lunched downtown on the lobster we had sworn we'd tackle before exiting San Diego.

I received a letter from Barbara, a dear talented pianist and close friend in high school, who is on a concert tour and planning to go to England. Jeepers! That's a long way! Hope she can find her way back! Also received a letter from Ted saying he made it home without mishap. It will do him so much good to traipse the old familiar haunts. I'm not sure how he's really dealing with his divorce. We were extremely close before he married, are still so, but have patterned our lives more independently the past several years. Dad insists I'm the stray sheep of the family, and I agree in that my interests vary sharply from the other members. I must write a short note telling him I won't be coming home right away.

And how is the gang of wave commanders liking their new quarters? You guys are crazy. Can't help but laugh at the name you've dubbed it. Goat Castle, really! Cory, you come up with the best zingers.

Tomorrow's another lesson in art. We've now advanced to vases. Gotta be something more stimulating to paint. The class is down to three. Mr. Gilbert can be a martinet, but he does know his stuff.

I suppose, my navy hero, I should be hitting the sack, so good night, dear. I know you'll be with me soon disturbing my slumbers. And, of course, I love it! I fear I should have a nightmare if you don't show up some night. Take care of the guy I love. Loving you ever,

Mopsy


As Cory finished reading the letters and dropped them in his special cigar box labeled Mopsy, a grinning Scorch wisecracked, "I suppose the ravishing colleen is still wearing rose-colored glasses when writing to her Prince Charming."

"At this moment, the ravishing colleen is poorly concealing a layer of miff at Prince Charming's procrastination in correspondence. The situation calls for immediate corrective action involving subtle subterfuge."

"Just what has Houdini in mind?"

"A plan is forming. I had intended on giving her a photo in my whites to cap off our last night in port, knowing how visually oriented she is. The picture, taken in San Francisco, turned out better than average, so I'm sure she'll be happy with it. I'm thinking of mailing it to her now and predate the attached note before these letters to give her the impression I sent the photo before knowing of her pouty state of mind. This might placate her. Was also thinking I might phrase the attached note in scientific jargon as science seems to impress her. Something like: The world is a variable, but my love is a constant. How does it sound?"

"More Machiavellian than Newtonian."

"The plan's jelling. A few days after the photo arrives, I'll write to express the arduousness of shiplife, trusting it'll ooze more compassion than contempt. What do you think?"

"I think I should write her and advise her to read Jekyll and Hyde, underlining Hyde!"

About a week later Cory entered Goat Castle waving a letter at Scorch. "This should tell us if the crisis has passed or if I'm still in the doghouse." He stretched out on the bed, hurriedly opened the envelope, and silently read.

June 1, 1944

My Darling,

What a heavenly, wonderful surprise to find your note when I arrived home this morning! I nearly gave up, you know! And your picture, Cory, in your dazzling whites. I'm already in love with it. So *sweet* of you to have had it made and sent to me. It doesn't matter now which side of the bed I awaken, because you are there either way. Don't get conceited, but you are a handsome Adonis! And you caused a minor riot today. The girls caught a glimpse of your new picture. You are in bad trouble. They're all in love with you. Think you can take it? Not much! At least they now know I haven't completely left reality. My lingering regret is the distance between us.

Our worlds, indeed, have been quite different. I was never truly close to my mother, her failed marriage embittered her, although Dad tells me that beneath her bitterness are some endearing traits. Once, when I was very small, I recall her saying, "Someday when you marry, Natalia, be sure it's with someone you can be proud. That was my big mistake." You pass on that one, Ensign Cory. I can't be prouder of you.

Ideas that materialize into guideposts often disperse of themselves when put to the test. For instance, to single out a person to fall in love with is much too rational. Falling in love must be spontaneous. You know it's right because the anima inside of you is drawn to the anima inside of him, like the moth to the flame. You flame, you!

Ted had unfortunate experiences in his marriage. Why is it that people must suffer through their own rather than others' experiences? Why can't they learn through the pain of others?

I wish I could fully express, Cory, how much you fill my heart, how much I crave to see you, how much I desire to be in your arms and hear the words over and over "I love you." But you must know. You have to know.

Life has been running fairly smoothly at the ranch. Went to art class yesterday and later saw a show. Had breakfast with Cindy and Debbie. Dave popped in Friday evening but had to catch the 2:00 AM bus back. Debbie keeps Lash in training, a full-time job. One of her girlfriends from the East is coming next month and will stay with us. I haven't seen Susan since she went home, although I've talked with her on the phone.

By the way, I'm glad you're not seeing me tonight! I'm red as a fresh-boiled lobster, the result of spending all of Memorial Day on the beach. But the water was wonderful . . .

Sunday.

June is here again, summer is upon us, and the world is beautiful.

This has been a wild day, which I lamentably confess is not too unusual for Sunday. People flowed in and out like it was open house. Several of Debbie's friends were over and they all went to Coronado this evening. It's good to see Debbie go out for a change. She's like a different person. With Jack so distant, she has concentrated exclusively on her horse. She can be so witty and when dressed up, quite the stunning woman.

Dave also popped in and he and Cindy have been in their own private heaven. I'm betting they'll be tying the knot ere long. He's a top-flight fellow, Cory. I wish you could meet him. He expects to sail out any day, but you know the navy.

Avis stayed overnight and we went to church at St. Patrick's this morning. We managed to get the gang together and went riding this afternoon. Then it's downtown for dinner and the movie "Kismet" at the Fox theater to give Cindy and Dave the house to themselves.

And what are you doing on this lovely Sunday, darling? Did you know I've decided to have twin boys someday with dark curly hair and blue eyes and raise them to be exactly like their father—double trouble!

We're set to leave for dinner so I'll say an early good night, my love.

I love you forever,

Mopsy

"Well?" Scorch inquired.

A relieved smile crossed Cory's face. "Can't ask for more. The photo brought out hearts and flowers. A letter now to belabor the rat race dominating our life since boarding ship should get me fully back into her good graces."

A week went by before Tally's reply arrived. Cory wasted no time reading it.

June 7, 1944

My Darling,

How glad I was to hear from you! By the time this missive reaches you, I can't imagine the state of mind it'll find you. Not hearing from you threw me into confusion and uncertainty as to what to do, so I waited for a cue. Your letter this morning lamenting the long hours of night maneuvers on top of daytime exercises clarified everything. I should have had enough faith to know you would write when you can. Forgive me, darling. We women are funny, as you have undoubtedly discovered in your young but wise years. I guess I'm a little like you in keeping things too much within myself, not intentionally nor con-sciously. I only know this because others have brought it to my attention. I'm sometimes guilty of forming my own answers before consulting the source containing them.

I might mention that I, too, have mixed reactions about San Diego. I like it because it gave me you, and dislike it for what it symbolizes—America at war. All in all, it does keep my life full, and I shall probably look back some day in amazement at how much it patterned my life.

Taint fair that a gal should miss a guy so much! What's she to do when every fiber within her says "it's Cory?" A whole month you've been gone; one whole month in which each day seems a month. There's such a difference in having a person so near and can't see him from simply knowing he is far away. And the difference is pure torture. For two cents I'd blast the whole navy with a few choice words! And all because I miss you so much, darling. Is it odd to miss a person you've hardly had time to grow accustomed to? No, is my answer, if you love him. I love you, Cory, and that explains it all. Love requires no logic.

Where was I in the homefront saga in my last letter? I'm a total blank. I hope I won't bore you with repetition. We had a model in art class this week. He better have a sense of humor, otherwise he might feel hurt at what he inspired on my canvas. Art is such fun but I haven't devoted the time I should to it. At least Mr. Gilbert ranks me high in imagination!

We've been on a tight work schedule this past week. Our department does its own lofting, which has us working on metal. You get accustomed to it, but for the first couple of nights you go home dizzy from drawing finely narrow lines with white paint glaring back in your eyes. But, there's a feeling of accomplishment when it's over. The termination scare, by the way, is simmering down. I'm fairly sure our department will have plenty of projects for some time.

Today was Mr. Marley's birthday, the chief engineer of the night crew. He's well-liked and we call him "Pops." We pitched together and got him a nice present to uplift his morale. There has been so much sickness in his home. When the whistle blew at midnight, everybody burst out with "happy birthday, Pops." He was genuinely touched.

I've had early morning visitors all week, which has cut into my quota of sleep. And now with the painting of the house in the offing, there'll be no sleep after 8:00 AM until that ordeal is over.

Haven't seen much of Cindy and Debbie this week, but will have brunch with them on Sunday. Dave is gone. I'll see Susan at a party at the Coronado tomorrow. My darling, I shall continue later. . . .

Sunday.

Cindy and Debbie were out late last night so we all slept in. A beach party tonight was a solid success. We scoured for wood to build a small fire for cooking. By eight o'clock we were famished and everything tasted good, even the sand. One of the fellows played the accordion and we sang. Then we waded along the edge of the ocean toward the hotel. When we reached the rocks, I could faintly see you there and wanted to run up and hold you tight. Then a big wave whipped in to soak me and wash away the image. We went home soon after because Susan had to get up in the wee hours.

Incidentally, darling, I'm not ignoring your question about the picture. The kodachrome which we were going to have finished was underexposed. No clear prints possible. As for the others, I will take care of them soon. That's a promise. . . . Good night, my darling, my dreams shall be of you.

Mopsy

"No need to say a word," Scorch said. "The Cheshire-cat grin says it all. The love life of one Ensign Zigler is back on track. She has obviously forgiven or forgotten your pathetic, procrastinating ways."

"Your compassion overwhelms me."

☆ ☆ ☆

"At last we have some relaxing time together," Tally said, as she and Cindy slowly sipped on sherry before dinner. "Now that you've caught up on your sleep and lost that horrible zombie look, it's high time I get a full and honest account of your wicked life in Seattle."

Cindy, in her usual bubbly fashion, described her trip north, of staying with the wife of a fraternity brother of Dave's, whose husband had been shipped to Attu, Alaska, and of her fun nights on the town with Dave that never ended till dawn whenever he got liberty from the ship. Since the ship's repairs were minor, it was a day-to-day uncertainty, with the stay longer than their most optimistic estimates. The added bonus was the few more days the ship lingered at Long Beach, allowing Dave to dash back and forth to San Diego.

"One thing that came out of the crazy experience," Cindy gushed, "is that I hadn't really realized how much in love I am with Dave. He's just pure gold."

"I picked up on that in the brief times he came bouncing in from Long Beach. I like his eyes. They have a warm, kind look."

"If anything should happen to him in this awful war, I would surely die."

"I feel the same way about Cory. Which brings up a question that's flitted through my mind. Do you think men have the same capacity for love as women?"

Cindy thought for a moment. "Probably not. For one thing they're less emotional; and they're not as romantic."

"Don't know if I agree entirely on that. Cory is very romantic. But the woman might have a greater capacity for love because of her child-bearing role. I guess it's debatable. But I've worried more than once on how well Cory's passion will hold up over a long separation. His love flamed so intensely in the few hours we had together. Can it burn out as quickly?"

"Cory adores you. No matter how long the war goes on, the flame will never die."

Debbie, who was preparing the meal, announced that dinner was being served. As they rose to their feet, Cindy gave Tally a hug. "Maureen O'Hara, banish thy fears. Zorro will never abandon thee." *The Mark of Zorro* starring Tyrone Power was currently playing. They laughed their way to the dining table.

It was a week of anticipation for Tally. The *Hudson* was winding down its shakedown cruise, dropping anchor at Long Beach with plans to reach San Diego in the middle of the next week. By Friday Tally could barely contain herself. She began writing a letter that night to update Cory on her activities, finishing it finally on Sunday and posting it so he'd have all the latest news to digest before their exciting time together.

June 15, 1944

Gash Darling,

Here's to another day which is gone. They do pass quickly when the work piles up. Such has been the case for the past two weeks.

Tis good to be busy to the extent of not having enough time to think too long about things, but not so busy as to be unable to drop a line to a special guy and let him know I'm thinking of him.

If I think too long, I get feisty over the forces keeping us apart. Life just seems so empty without you and so wonderfully fulfilling with you. My only consolation comes in looking forward to seeing you. And how much I do look forward to it, darling. The thought of seeing you—jeepers!—what it doesn't do!

There's been a pitter-patter of rain today, the kind of day to curl up in a chair with a good book.

Cindy was leaving work as I was going in so we managed an hello-and-goodbye routine. I'm told I'll soon be going on days but on such matters our plant is as unpredictable as the navy. Debbie is planning to go to Missouri in a month to see Jack.

I went to a luncheon today at one of the girls' home. She had several over with thoughts of a little tennis, but the weather nixed that.

Ted will be back soon so that ends the possibility of a trip home. Guess I was a little homesick when he left, but I'm over it. If he gets a discharge, he'll head back, so I may get a second chance. Also, an old school chum from Denver is driving back in another month. Cindy and I are giving some thought to going with him. Avis is terminating next month and has asked me to go home with her to San Jose, about 50 miles from San

Francisco. She makes it sound interesting, but Dad is probably right in suspecting a certain restlessness in my mood, and so I'd be just as well off staying put.

Things have been uncommonly orderly these past few days. Yesterday, I went to art class, but the rain discouraged creativity and we mainly coffeed and chatted. Mr. Gilbert was telling of his experiences in Burma and the stories behind some of his paintings. A most versatile man, but definitely of an artistic temperament. I can almost feel his mood when walking into the room. He was recently commissioned to do a sketch of "Romona's Home."

If you'll pardon me, darling, I'm a bit on the drowsy side so will continue later.

Saturday.

Well, I just had a good night's sleep after leaving you last night, and here I am about to say good night again. How do you like that! Always saying good night in the morning and good morning in the afternoon.

Cindy partied tonight, I begged off, and she just slipped in, bubbling to talk about it. You can bet we'll sleep late tomorrow. So happy it's Sunday. We just raided the ice box and found some good fried chicken. Aren't you sorry you're not here! Ooops! You might be on rations so I won't go on.

Avis, her boyfriend Mark, and I played a couple hours of tennis before going to work. A nice warm sun beat down on us. The arms of Morpheus are starting to look good. I feel a dream in the making and I'll see you in it, darling. Loving you.

Sunday.

I *will* finish this protracted missive today, darling, and post it for you. We were up at eleven to make it a rather short day. Debbie has taken off for the stables and the gray overcast makes it a perfect day to loaf at home. Wish you could too. When's the navy going to let up? You guys have been on a slave schedule for a long, long time.

Cindy said she got a letter from Dave "over there" and he's getting the same treatment. She's buckling in for a long wait. As usual she gives you a big hello. She's one of your staunchest supporters (along with Susan), starting back at the St. Pat's dance.

Avis just called and we will take in "Mr. Skeffington" at a theater in North Park. We'll have dinner at the Embassy.

Jeepers, I'm sitting here kind of shivering—in June. Would you believe it? I definitely need you here to warm me up. Thinking of you fills me up inside like a toy balloon.

As I've often told you, you're not truly away because you left your heart with me. I love you.

Mopsy

After posting the letter that Sunday night and then returning to the ranch, Tally was startled to get a phone call from Cory at Long Beach. All of his previous calls came during her coffee break at work. He said he snuck away to the phone booth on the dock to tell her how much he loved her, missed her, and looked forward to having her in his arms in a couple of days. He told her to get her paint brush out because the old mission town needed a coat. Then he subtly injected that the ship's stay in San Diego might be less than what was planned.

Tally's sensor instantly shot up. "Why would you say that?"

"Just a hunch. They've scratched the original cargo orders here at Long Beach and are loading a bunch of new stuff. This suggests other changes may be in the wind. The gist, darling, is stay flexible and don't put all your marbles in one basket."

A twinge of anxiety swept through Tally. The phone call ended with Cory promising to notify her as soon as possible should there be any modifications in orders.

The following night, Monday, Cory called Tally during her coffee break at work. His news was devastating. The *Hudson* had received sailing orders for the next morning. There would be no mooring in San Diego. No time together. All libertes have been canceled. This would be the last phone call.

Tally went speechless, her mind a blank. Cory filled in the interval reminding her it was quality not quantity that makes a relationship strong. Theirs was bonny first class. He then spoke the words of their song: "Loving you always, not for just a day, not for just a year, but always." She was able to muster up a "me too" before the time had run out.

Buck saw a red-eyed Tally return to her desk after the break. "The world is coming to an end?" he asked.

"You've read my mind again. . . . Cory was due here tomorrow and his ship is heading out instead. I was deprived of seeing him the night before he went to San Francisco because he was put in charge of the crew, and now I'm deprived of seeing him before he goes overseas because the navy revised the ship's orders. It isn't fair, Buck." She choked up.

He put a sympathetic hand on her shoulder. "War is unfair, Princess, but it's also impersonal, which means its madness is random. No one is picked on or selected out. What happens to whom is the whimsy of the dice. But bear in mind, your disappointment can't be any greater than his. He has to be miserable, too. Don't let yourself mope in self-pity, turn your thoughts on ways to cheer him up."

"Oh, Buck, you are so right. And, you know, that's exactly what Cory did. What little time we had on the phone, he used it to buck me up." She let out a short peal of laughter. "No pun intended, Buck."

He grinned. "Princess, as long as you can laugh, I don't have to worry about you."

With both Debbie and Cindy on the day shift, Tally had the living area to herself on returning home from work. She turned the radio on low. The Charlie Spivak Orchestra was playing "You Belong to My Heart" and tears welled up again in Tally's eyes. She wiped them dry, picked up her pen, and began writing.

My Darling,

Forgive my weakness, but I'm too distraught to control my feelings in the anguish of knowing that your ship will leave in a few hours for that part of the world which is the last place I want you to be. How I prayed that I could have cozied up at least one more time in your loving arms and feel your heart beating against mine before having to face a winter of loneliness. How strong and reassuring was your voice and how hard I tried to reciprocate. I make a poor soldier. At least I didn't break down on the phone. I know you have tried to prepare me for this possibility and I know how crushingly disappointing the outcome is for you, too. We deserved at least one final hour together. To have been so close and yet so far is a torture that should be suffered only by the condemned. In calmer moments, I guess I may see that even a full evening together would only temporarily ease the pangs of a starving heart.

Forgive my bursts of immaturity. I'm sure others face similar ordeals with less blessings, but I have a long way to go to be the stable, steady person I need to be. I must remind myself you are with me in my dreams and I must not, as you so well put it, let my thoughts diminish the joy of the wonderful hours we have spent together. They have been truly beautiful, Cory, from the very first moment I felt the tingle inside and knew instantly all that mattered most was you. I am thankful, my love. I guess human greed ever asks for more.

How little I know how long and lonely it might be, but like a taste of the bitter, your sweet outlook makes it bittersweet. I know time will pass as I plunge into a busy schedule, but I know it can never move fast enough to bring you back to me.

With your help, darling, I feel I am growing a little in maturity. I now realize life cannot be measured in months and years, but by how it's spent. Each passing day will bring me one day closer to what is in our hearts. The thought alleviates but doesn't stay my restlessness. Yes, I am restless, my dearest, as are probably countless others like us who are waiting for that special day when we can look squarely at the world and know the price and

THE RED-RIBBONED LETTERS

meaning of peace as no other generation can. And then what? It doesn't matter—only that you come back safely. You must, my darling. I cannot bear to think otherwise. To that end my prayers shall follow you. Oh, my love, how I pour out my heart and soul to you, like I never have to anyone before or will to anyone after. You have my love forever,

Mopsy

# *Stoneface*

Captain Martin of the Surgery Unit took Tally to one side while she was on volunteer duty. "I have a patient, Corporal Randall Scott, nineteen, whom I'm rather concerned about. We've done all we can with surgery, but he's now into major depression with psychotic episodes. Until there's space available in the neuropsychiatric ward, we can only hope to ease his symptoms. I'm sure there's much guilt at the root of his pathology, but it stays repressed. Here is where you can be of help."

"I'm afraid, Dr. Martin, you've tapped the wrong person."

"That's where you're wrong, Tally. I've observed you. Patients respond to your genuine warmth. If we can get Randy to open up, it should lighten his depression and give valuable information to the psychiatrists when he's transferred."

"I'll try. Give me a tip on how to begin."

"Your first goal is to establish rapport. Once he trusts you, he's more likely to talk. But I have to give you the same warnings that I've given the staff. Under no circumstances make physical contact with him. The mere touch of his hand can induce a psychotic rage. And never mention any aspect of the war. That will likely send him into deep withdrawal."

"What had happened to him?"

"A mortar shell tore up his stomach at Tarawa. He was found on the beach unconscious and nearly dead from loss of blood. He must have taken a hit wading in from the coral reefs. It was a miracle he made it ashore, and certainly a miracle that he survived the surgeries. The kid has an incredible constitution. But we're now into no man's land. Good luck."

Tally went to the nurses' station and glanced at the corporal's chart. A wave of sadness gripped her. Most of his stomach and parts of other internal organs had been removed.

The head nurse advised to begin easy and not press.

Tally opened the door to Randy's room with trepidation, taking a deep breath before moving up to his bed. Expecting to encounter a wild, feral look, she was taken aback to see big brown eyes peering softly up at her. She relaxed. "Hi, my name is Tally. I'm told yours is Randy."

His eyes flicked with little expression.

"Everything's going to be okay. I'm not a doctor or a nurse. I don't stick people with a needle. I'm just a volunteer. I talk to patients and try to get them things they need." She smiled at him. "The first thing I notice about meeting people is their eyes. Randy, you have beautiful brown eyes."

He still showed no tendency to respond.

Don't press, Tally reminded herself. "I can tell you're not in the mood to talk, so I'll leave you alone. But I promise you one thing, Mr. Brown Eyes, I'll come back to see you the beginning of the week."

Tally left the room and returned to the nurses' desk. "He didn't say a word, but I'm sure he understood every word I said." The head nurse smiled and said he only gets psychotic when upset.

"A question," Tally asked. "Is Captain Martin a good surgeon?"

"One of the best. Why do you ask?"

"He doesn't talk like a surgeon."

Tally went on to work. She found that the project she was working on just needed finishing touches, which she was able to do in several hours. Being Saturday night, Pops was reluctant to start her on a new project, so he had her doing mostly piddling things. She still had time left over and got the sudden impulse to surprise Cory with a brief letter on company stationery. She felt a little guilty stealing company time, but not that guilty.

My Darling,

Of course you won't know by the letterhead that I might be writing you at work. This has been one useless day as far as work productivity goes. I finished my lay-out early and the boss doesn't like to give us a new job on Saturday night, so I'm doing little incidentals and clean-ups, trying my best to look busy.

We ate in the cafeteria tonight where a group of us had a reserved table. Reserved because we happened to get there first. The lunch hour is divided into two shifts—ours at 8:00 and production at 8:30. We always seek to return before 8:30 to avoid the deluge of humanity coming and going. In hurrying, one tends to ignore the painted words on the step: "safety first, watch your step."

At nine o'clock every night but Saturday, we have a half hour of recorded music. How nice it would be to have music while you work all the time.

I'm mailing this crazy, short letter only to let you know my thoughts are with you at all hours. All yours, darling,

Mopsy

Randy was very much on Tally's mind when she sat down the following night for her Sunday letter to Cory. Then it dawned on her why. It was young marines like him that Cory would soon be landing on the beaches. A shiver went through her as her fingers tightened on her pen. She would never write Cory about him.

June 22, 1944

My Darling,

Tis a Sunday, which, I suspect you know, is my favorite day. The reason you also may know. Tis sprinkling outside, contrary to all the brochures on sunny California. The locals, of course, never use the term rain. Only high fog. But, whatever, I do enjoy it. Do you like to walk in the rain, darling, or has all of the beach landings in the sea spray taken the romance out of it? At the moment there's a big puddle across the street by the park, and it's been amusing watching the cars as they're about to hit it swerve sharply to miss it.

Debbie and Cindy were up when I came home from work so we girl-chatted and slept in late. I can report no great changes in our lives this past week (imagine that). Debbie is still running in circles because Jack himself is not sure of what lies directly ahead for him in the army (imagine that!).

We've been told with some assurance that we'll be transferred to days within the next two months. The rumor is a ten-hour day, five days a week. I wouldn't be a bit unhappy having weekends free, but this is only talk, which I've learned to take with a grain of salt.

Avis, Cindy, Debbie, Susan, and I are dining together this evening and taking in a show. Tis good to have an evening with just us girls, because it's getting harder and harder for us to swing it, and I have the uneasy feeling the Inner Circle will be soon breaking up.

The day has been rather quiet so far. We've had some good music on the radio—you've reawakened, maestro, my love of the classics—and everybody's writing.

How about you, darling? How's it going? The papers give us somber reflection. I fear your hours are long and tense. The big offensive is exploding in the Pacific and it leaves me with such a helpless feeling. All I can do is put in more time with the wounded at the hospital. Some look so young and put up such a brave front, yet I know many will never live a normal life again. I read to them, hold their hand, let them talk, and then go home and pray for your safety. Who would have dreamed my life would have taken this heavy turn even two short years ago!

Tomorrow is Cindy's birthday so Avis and I are cooking up a little surprise for her. The evenings are rather lonely for her as Debbie has Lash in training and needs to ride him every night.

Oh, that I could kiss you good night, darling, rather than relay it on paper. I love you always,

Mopsy

Tally saw Randy on a regular basis. She came to predict his mood through the expression in his eyes. The vacuous look was depression; the intense look, rage or the start of psychotic withdrawal; the soft look, inner peace. Talking to him in a calm and reassuring tone of voice would often reduce the intensity and get the soft look to return.

At first his rages frightened her, but less so as she came to understand she was not part of the scenario. The drama was created by the demons in his delusions. The insight enabled her to weather his storms and help restore his equilibrium. But when he withdrew into the fetal position, nothing she did or said could lessen his rigidity. He was out of contact with reality. She would then quietly leave the room.

The wall he formed to protect himself seemed impenetrable. Even when those big brown eyes turned soft and attentive, the best she could elicit were mundane, impersonal comments. Tally would smile and patiently say, "Randy, you can talk to me on any subject you want, anytime you want. I'll listen and I'll care, no matter what." She could sense her words being processed and perhaps some trust being slowly built up.

One day he surprised her. A crack appeared in his wall.

"Tally," he said, "you asked me once where I was from."

"Yes, but you never answered." She saw his eyes soften.

He measured his words. "I grew up on a farm in Indiana. The nearest town was Richmond, some twenty miles away. It was a special event going there, the farthest we'd ever get from home. When Pearl Harbor was attacked, I joined the marines over my mother's wishes. I lied about my age, wasn't yet eighteen, but when our country was attacked, I figured it was my duty to defend her. I can handle a gun as good as the next one. My younger brothers could help Dad with the farm." His voice suddenly cracked. This has been the most he's said since entering the hospital. His eyes began to drift.

Tally had the urge to hold his hand and tell him he was safe with her, but she recalled the admonition not to touch. She controlled the impulse. "Tell me more about the farm," she said.

The softness returned to his eyes. "I loved the sweet smell of the clover in the fields, the odor of the livestock in the barn, the smell of hickory logs burning in the stone fireplace with the snow falling outside. I enjoyed the picnics in the family woods and the socials at the little white church, on whose burial grounds rest my grandparents and great aunts and uncles, part of the pioneering stock of eastern Indiana. Wild honeysuckle grows there to sweeten their bones."

Tally saw his eyes harden, his body shake, and she knew he was back into the world of demons. She felt he had said enough; she stole softly out of the room and reported the conversation to the staff. They were excited. This was the first dent in an armor that had withstood the assaults of even sodium pentothal, the truth serum. Captain Martin seized Tally's hand. "You've established a link of trust," he enthused. "We could be near a breakthrough."

Several days passed before Tally saw Randy again. The head nurse reported good gains. "His rages are less violent and are less frequent," she said.

Tally gave Randy a big smile. "The doctors and nurses say you're doing much better. Goes to show how much it helps to talk. Telling me about your farm in Indiana has been the best medicine thus far for your spirits. What would you like to talk about today?"

Tally saw tears well up in his big brown eyes, something she had not seen before. Again, her urge for physical contact was strong, to share through touch his sadness, his struggles, their friendship; but, yet again, she suppressed the instinct. Instead, she whispered, "It's all right to talk and I'll listen to every word."

Randy's eyes clouded and looked distant, and when she thought she was about to lose him, he spoke, the words coming out weakly, haltingly, with great effort. "My buddy Hank and I made it through the Solomons, not too many in our company did, and we were part of the reserves in case things went badly in Tarawa. They did. Red Beach II on Betio Island took a beating on the first day and we were rushed into action the next day. Hank and I were in the same assault boat. It grounded on the coral reef, the draw of the LCVP was too deep. We were more than five hundred yards from shore. The ramp opened, we piled out, the gunfire began. Hank was hit, sank into a hole in the reef, cried out. I wanted to go to him but orders were to move fast." Randy began to sob. "I should have disobeyed, gone to him, but I didn't. I left him to rot in the bowels of the reef. I scrambled over the reefs and ploughed toward shore, shells exploding, men screaming, the water getting redder. Then I suddenly felt a piercing pain in the guts and it moved upward. Blood in my throat choked off my scream. I saw a huge bottomless cavern before me. I wanted to slide into it. I fought off the desire. I slogged on and then I felt sand. I made it. Then nausea hit me. I lay against a pile of rotting bodies in the hot sun. The odor filled every pore of my body, made me puke, then everything went black."

Randy's eyes became fiercely intense and his body shook uncontrollably. Tally tried to calm him but he was beyond hearing words of comfort. He began thrashing. She rushed for a nurse, and he was injected with a large dose of morphine, which put him into a deep sleep.

Tally, lightheaded, weeping internally, reported the breakthrough to the staff, who reacted ecstatically. "Just what the psychiatrists will need to help work through his guilt," Captain Martin said.

The next day being Sunday, Tally and Cindy went to church. On the return Tally told Randy's story to Cindy. "Most heartrending," she added, "to think this could be happening in the twentieth century."

"The individual case is much more powerful than abstract statistics," Cindy said. She forced a smile. "Guess we need a mood transfusion from Cory."

"Even Cory has his bad moments," Tally replied. "He wrote in his last letter—the one so long in coming—about an event in San Francisco that had a profound affect on him. On their last night in port, he had dinner with his coxswain, Rob Roy, who introduced him to his wife, Jeanie Mae, and their one-year-old baby. He said Jeanie Mae and baby came all the way from Georgia to celebrate her eighteenth birthday and watch the christening of the ship. In his usual quaint way, Cory described her as a porcelain doll that would break into a million pieces if dropped. He was appalled that she was this young to have a baby and have to care for it alone during the long months ahead. Then as he rose to leave, she clutched his arm and whispered to him to take care of Rob Roy because, to use her exact words, 'he is all that we have.' The pure simplicity left Cory, the man so adept with words, able only to gently squeeze her hand."

Tally declined going to the dance that afternoon with Cindy, Avis, and Susan at the Coronado, choosing instead to go to the hospital to check on Randy and then home to hear some relaxing music before writing what she had come to consider her Sunday evening hour with Cory.

She was relieved to hear that Randy had a good day, calming her fears that he might have had a bad mental relapse following the disclosure of his nightmare at Tarawa. The head nurse did report a minor incident of a broken water glass at supper which Randy, very apologetic, helped clean off his tray.

Tally popped into Randy's room to say hello and to promise him a long visit on the morrow. She had never seen his eyes look softer. He nodded, replied he had a letter to write, and waved goodbye.

Still drained from the emotions of the weekend, Tally was content to be left quietly alone in the house. She curled up in her favorite chair and listened to Mozart, letting her thoughts dwell on her favorite sailor. Oh, Cory, she said to herself, I'm understanding more and more your love of the masters. Time neither weakens the joy of their works nor takes away their freshness. As Mr. Gilbert would say, genius gets to the essence, which is truth, which can never be boring. She drifted off into musical fantasies until set to write.

June 29, 1944

My Darling,

You know my thoughts are with you as I sit to write, but you can never know how much. Tis quiet at this hour. Cindy and Debbie have found the sandman, and I, the night owl, have a Mozart symphony to keep me company. How sad to think that one who gave such beautiful music to the world died so young. I find it hard to see a design in a world where people of genius die young, the good and brave get shot up in war, and the derelicts live on forever. There's so much I don't understand, darling.

I went riding this afternoon at the Elroy stables. Hutch, my horse, was quite stubborn, balking all the way up the trail, but coming back became full of life, knowing he was heading home. I could barely contain him. I'm dearly paying the price now!

I talked with Ted. Going home did him so much good. The wonderful news is that he and his wife are trying to work things out. I'm keeping my fingers crossed. They've had such a trying, wretched two years. He's due for another operation tomorrow, and Jenny may come here if recuperation time is lengthy.

I haven't seen much of my roomies today. Cindy went with Avis and Susan to the dance in Coronado and Debbie's been riding as usual. They all dragged in and found the pillow pronto.

Oh, where might you be tonight, Cory? I'm almost afraid to think about it. When, oh when, will the ship's compass swing and point east? Your letters keep me from despair. I read and reread them until they're locked into the heart, so much do they mean to me. If people knew, they'd probably think I'm loco. But, begorra, let them.

Buck is taking a long vacation starting tomorrow, so he'll miss our Fourth of July party. Hey, how about that! Shall we make a date to light the sky with Roman candles? As long as we're celebrating, we might as well make a full day of it and take in the sights of San Diego. But where to begin? Better yet, let's not fight the crowds, but cuddle up at home with the old masters. I heard Delius the other night—morning. Beautiful, haunting music.

Tell me about Goat Castle. Is it still one for all and all for one as the saying goes? I shudder to think of the long, hard hours of work. All of you must be fit for the Olympics. Just the cream of the navy. Now, you know, of course, how I'd love to trade places with one of your buddies—well, for at least a day. On further thought, I'm not sure I'd be up to ramming one of those boats through a high surf. Guess I'd better stay where I am.

Good night, my darlin'—I love you. Yours ever,

Mopsy

Tally arrived earlier than usual at the hospital the next afternoon to have what she hoped to be a long, fruitful conversation with Randy. She had lost all fear of his flights from reality because the rages no longer threatened her. She felt the staff had exaggerated his potential to be dangerous. She had never seen any of his violent behaviors focused. Those big brown eyes evoked more compassion than anxiety when they drifted, and she was beginning to feel an affection, too strong to be comfortable, which she knew would make objectivity more difficult. She wondered if Ted's long monthly leave had made her vulnerable for a substitute. Such were the thoughts running through her mind as she entered the ward.

She picked up on the pall at the nurses' station. "What's the matter?" she asked. She saw the eyes of the head nurse shift toward Randy's room. "No," Tally cried out, sensing horror without being told. She dashed into the room without waiting for the answer. The room was empty and the bed was made up in clean sheets.

The nurse came to the door. She spoke quietly. "Randy committed suicide last night."

Tally screamed. She partially recomposed. "How?"

"He hid a sliver of broken glass from his supper tray. After the sleeping pill and night check, he slashed his wrist at the angle so as to not botch the attempt. The sheets were soaked in blood this morning, his lips curved in a peaceful smile."

Tally's tear-filled eyes stared into space. "Why would he do this to me?"

The nurse handed her a short note. "His one and only message was this note to you."

Tally dabbed the tears from her eyes to see to read.

> Tally, I'm writing you because in smelling my awful stench, you can understand what I must do. The smell of rotting flesh is in my blood and will stay as long as blood runs in my veins. I now have the strength to do what I must do to take my place in the churchyard without stinking up the other graves. Goodbye, thank you.

"Oh God!" Tally sobbed. "Why, oh why, didn't he stay on the farm!" She refused the sedative Captain Martin had left for her.

She later learned that the official report simply stated that "Corporal Randall Wilson Scott of the United States Marine Corps, recipient of the Purple Heart, died of wounds suffered at Tarawa."

Sentimental over holidays, the day before the Fourth of July found Tally in a nostalgic, reminicent mood. She took a stroll in the morning in the park and visited the zoo, her mind rehashing the things she and Cory did on that wonderful Sunday afternoon. With the bittersweet consciousness of Cory so close and alive in her thoughts but so far away in reality, she would keep him close over the holiday with a protracted letter covering the period, beginning before she went to work that very afternoon. It never ceased to amaze her how the mere activity of writing would strengthen the illusion of shortening the miles between them.

Hello Darling,

Hey, begorra, the Fourth is slipping up on us and it looks like we won't be able to keep our date. Mr. Barker also broke his date, for you see, he invited several of us for dinner, then began tearing down the partition between his kitchen and dining room, but hasn't been able to finish the job in time.

Jeepers, what a great day to have been with you. The thought just fills this heart-o-mine to the brim. When I relive the good moments we've had together, tally them up, the score is fantastic, making me realize how very lucky I am. And now all I ask of the good Lord is to see that no harm comes to the jewel that I've found.

The sky has been interesting to watch today. Light fluffy clouds keep hanging unusually low, making the sun reluctant to peek through. I'll see how long the pattern holds as several of us will be eating at an outside cafe before going to work.

I've seen little of Cindy and Debbie this week, but hopefully we'll be on the same shift before too long. They're tearing the office down in the engineering room to make room for the second shift on days.

Well, darling, I wish I could linger longer, but I must be getting into the "swing" (shift, that is). . . .

Later.

A new day and so far, uneventful. Debbie's at a horse show and Cindy's going out with some friends of her father for dinner. Avis is coming over for dinner and we're going to a formal dance at the Women's Club tonight. Susan, whom I haven't seen for some time, will be there. Whenever I dance these days, I close my eyes and imagine you are my partner.

A gang of us will be going to Tijuana tomorrow. A bull fight's on but I doubt if we'll take it in. The main idea is getting together once more. . . .

Still later.

Well, my darling, I'm remiss in finishing and posting this. Here tis Tuesday morning already. Avis and Debbie bounded in about the same time Sunday to take me away from you, and I'm now just getting back. The dance, by the way, was enjoyable and Avis stayed overnight with us. Seemed we had barely dented the pillow before the driver arrived for the Tijuana trip. We had loads of fun, but after work my weary bones collapsed into bed. "Stay busy," you keep telling me!

Our work schedule is light. It seems to go in cycles. We have days that we dawdle and days that we can barely catch our breath. Feast or famine.

Saw little of Cindy over the weekend. She did say Dave was going through a bout not unlike yours: long hours, exhausting duty. I know all of you are in the thick of things and I could worry sick if I let my mind dwell on it.

Must dash to the grocery before art class. I think this will be our last class for a spell. Mr. Gilbert will be taking a vacation.

I'll say "au revoir" for now, darling. I eagerly await your next letter. I love you bunches and bunches, always and forever.

Mopsy

☆ ☆ ☆

Big Gil Harvey called a meeting of the Boat Division officers the day after the ship left Long Beach. "Guys," he said in his usual casual manner, "I'm sure you've figured out why the shakedown cruise was cut short. I can now make it official. We're on our way to Hawaii to pick up marine reserves and rush them to the Marianas. Operation Forager has hit some snags. In every damn island we've invaded, we've underestimated our opponent. Saipan is no exception. Plans were to take this piddling island, two miles at its narrowest width, five miles at its broadest point, and fourteen miles in length in a week. We'll be lucky to take it in a month, and the casualties are accumulating. So instead of playing a backup role as originally scheduled, we're getting shoved into the middle of things. I'll keep you updated as plans keep changing. As of now, consider Hawaii the last mail delivery. No letters will be sent or received once we leave for the battle zone. That is all. Gash, hang around for a minute."

When they were alone, Gil came to the point. "I understand

you volunteered for the graveyard watch." He smiled. "What brought that on?"

"Simple logic. The navy operates on the caste system. As the bottom man on the totem pole, lowest in rank, last in seniority, it was a *fait accompli* I'd be assigned the watch, so why not make points by volunteering for it."

"Smart cookie."

Smarter than you think, Cory said to himself. The real reason, which he was not about to reveal, went much deeper. This would be the only watch that the skipper wouldn't be breathing down the OD's neck, the only four hours of the night that he slept. Adding to that appeal was the fact that Cory had just found out from a reliable source that the captain's vendetta was based on the incredible coincidence that he, Cory, of all people, could pass as the twin brother of the culprit who had eloped with the captain's only daughter. Discretion being the better part of valor, Cory set about to keep a low profile, and the graveyard watch was a major step to that end.

"I also understand," Gil continued, "that you and Hawk have teamed up as bridge partners and are cleaning the clocks of your opponents."

"Hawk is a genius. He has a photographic memory. The guy can reconstruct entire hands. He is teaching me his fantastic system of bidding. But, for your general information, we're putting our ill-gotten winnings to a worthy cause. The loot goes into Hawk's safe, and when the war is over and the ship docks in San Francisco, we're going to throw a celebration party to last to the last nickel. Every man on board gets invited."

"Play those cards!"

"Gil, to change the subject, I gather you've picked up some casualty figures on Saipan. Was the landing as bad as the one at Tawara?"

Gil's body stiffened. There was a long pause. "Depends on how you measure it. At least there were no reef problems."

"Can't help but notice that just the slightest mention of Tawara tightens you up like a drum. Still living with it, aren't you?"

"Always will."

"I've heard it sometimes helps to talk."

"Like I just said, Gash, play them cards."

"Sure, Gil."

Cory returned to Goat Castle and found Scorch already stretched out on his bunk. "What'd you think of the meeting?" Cory asked.

"About what I feared. We're gettting into this mess, old buddy, sooner than I thought. Wasn't at all happy with Gil's comment that the brass continues to underestimate the Nips. Our intelligence reports stink. It looks like we're in for the long haul. I had hopes that once we got within bombing range of Tokyo, the warlords might toss in the towel. Now it appears it'll only stiffen their backbone. I'm predicting they'll stick in to the bitter end. What do you think?"

"The key is Hirohito. Being god to the people, they'll do whatever he tells them to do. So as the God of the Rising Sun, he'll determine when it'll set. But he's about as easy to read as the sphinx. . . . Meanwhile, I'm going to write Mopsy and tell her the crazy story of why the old man has it in for me."

"So you've finally figured it out."

"Hawk clued me in. It turns out that I'm the damn look-alike of the SOB who ran off with his precious daughter."

"I can't believe it!"

"Nor I. Life in the navy, old sea dog, has its crosses to bear." Cory sat at his desk and pulled out his writing material.

June 21, 1944

Dearest Mopsy,
    With the *Hudson* purring along at the high speed of 16 knots and all quiet on the upper decks, there seems no better time to

introduce you to our intrepid leader, Captain Jonathan "Jack" Pettigrew, known behind closed hatches as Old Stoneface.

The man is a throwback to the days when ships were made of wood and men of steel. He's perpetual motion twenty hours a day, energized by a dark premonition he's the only competent sailor aboard, a foreboding not founded entirely on arrogance. His is a Horatio Alger story, a swabbie who through sweats and smarts gained top billet in a three-decker oceangoing vessel.

Then papers on his new officers arrived, a steady inflow of "90-day-wonders," overachievers who accomplished in three months what took four years of hard grind at Annapolis. Stoneface was stunned. He couldn't believe the Pentagon would stoop this low. How could they do this to a devout patriot who sacrificed thirty of his best years to Old Glory! His one and only hope, he gravely understood, to escape certain shipwreck, was to oversee every move of every officer aboard. In the mass munching of tums this required, he overlooked his luck of the draw. The batch of greenhorns assigned to his command, impressions notwithstanding, happened to be a group of fast learners.

Small world that it is, a 90-day-wonder had eloped with his only daughter, ruining what aspirations he had for her. It also solidified his suspicions on that strange breed of officers. Making the world smaller yet, I happen to be the spit and image of the ne'er-do-well, which suddenly clears up all the extra duties dumped on me since arriving aboard. Yet, as the saying goes, every cloud has a silver lining. Seeking to keep a low profile, I volunteered for the graveyard watch, zero hour to zero four in navy lingo, knowing that those were the only hours Stoneface slept. I rediscovered the joy that comes with no hot breath on the back of the neck and the peace that comes when most of human life has drifted off into slumberland. To preserve my good fortune, I have to periodically send out strong distress signals to ensure that my all-heart mates don't have a relapse and offer to swap watches.

While in a storytelling mode, my angel, I must tell you the strange thing that happened today. The chaplain, risking his reputation, spent time with me on deck. As we gazed seaward I noticed a tiny blob on a whitecap. I had never seen anything quite like it. "What could it be?" I asked.

The man of the cloth adjusted his binoculars. "Why it's a human soul," he declared. When he saw my raised eyebrow, he puffed out his lower lip and informed me that the spotting of lost souls took up the first year of study in Divinity School. He then assumed the burden of broadening my spiritual education.

"Souls," he lectured, "are like snowflakes. No two exactly the same. They all share, however, the common trait of reserve. Once they discover they're under observation, they vanish. Thus, we must keep our voices low."

I asked if he would do a psychological portrait on this one. His eyes brightened as he was now in his element. He whispered: "This is no ordinary spirit. Notice the buoyancy. Means it's full of vitality. Now detect the delicacy. Means it could only belong to the fairer sex. Look how free it is of blemishes. Means it has the purest of hearts. See its soft edges. Means it has a romantic disposition. Finally, observe its grace of movement in the way it bobs. Means it's full of spontaneity."

His analysis abruptly ended as the apparition suddenly disappeared. He gasped. "O heavenly father, what sensitivity! Softly as we spoke, how could it have sensed our presence? Alas, we shall never know its source or the purpose of its mission."

Here I had the edge on the chaplain. Not only was I certain of its owner, but I had a good idea of what she was up to. You had plotted a spy trip to m'heart, and had it been successful, you would have stolen this little rhyme tucked in one of the chambers.

Love you, Mopsy, forever and a day,
Love you in each and every way.
And should the flame of life go out,
The love will live, be not in doubt.


The graveyard watch is about at hand. So tis time to say au revoir, pax, and sweet dreams.

Many XXXX's, darling.

Cory

Tally was in heels and hose, continuing the custom of the Inner Circle when out on their special luncheon, but this time she was alone, seated at a table in the Skyroom. She glanced about and she caught the eye of Robert Graham, who was also sitting alone at a window table, nursing a cocktail. He smiled, stood, and approached her table.

"Expecting company?" he asked.

"A lone wolf," she replied. "My girlfriends have deserted me for the day shift."

"Well, I, too, was stood up and so am lunching alone. Would you care to join me?"

She smiled. "How can one resist a window table! I'd be delighted."

Robert ordered a margarita for her and a second manhattan for himself. "And what occasion are we celebrating?" he asked.

"None really. Now and then I get the urge to dress up and partake the good life. Of course, to justify the dent in the budget, I have to cook up a rationalization. Today, for example, I'm making a big production over the good news that the swing shift, which is my shift, is returning to the standard forty-hour week. This means I'll have both my Saturdays and Sundays off."

Robert grinned. "I'll drink to that. I'm hearing that factories, in general, are getting their inventories back to normal so we can expect more easing up."

Tally found Robert an easy conversationalist. Although on the reserve side, his wry observations on the human rat race as viewed from atop San Diego's tallest building kept her in laughter.

During dessert, he suddenly changed the topic.

"Tally," he said, "I've just come up with an idea. My boss has been needling me for some time to get more involved in PR activities, not exactly my cup of tea. He wants me to represent the company in more social events, more specifically the cocktail and dinner parties engaging the big cheeses of companies who are potential clients. In other words, he wants me to get more into the social network. This would call for a female companion, a woman with the social graces to freely mingle. You would be a natural. Would the role have any appeal to you, particularly now that your Saturday nights are open and most of these events would take place on the weekends?"

Tally was taken slightly aback. "So flattering of you to think of me, Robert, and I certainly would enjoy the opportunity to wear some of my pretty cocktail dresses that are collecting dust in the closet but I'm afraid I'll have to decline. You see, I'm involved in a relationship with a man in the navy who at present is overseas."

His eyes brightened. "That would make the arrangement even more perfect. There would be no hidden agenda. Since I have no intentions of entering a serious relationship while the war is on, and since you are already in one and have that need satisfied, we'd both be motivated not to let personal feelings interfere."

Flashing through Tally's mind was Cory's repeated insistence that she keep an active social calendar in his absence. The chance to attend some of the finest balls and parties of the season with no strings attached would clearly fall within the boundaries he had in mind. She looked at Robert and smiled. "This does cast a different light. I accept the offer, Robert, on one condition. If at any time for any reason either one of us wishes to terminate the agreement, the other shall readily grant it with no questions asked or hard feelings caused."

"Fair enough." Robert raised his goblet of brandy he had ordered with the desert. "To good times only. No arm twists, no temper tantrums, no poisonous letters if either wishes to back out."

Tally laughed. "To good times only." They clicked glasses.

At the ranch on the following Saturday night, her first Saturday not at work, Tally informed Cindy of her pact. Cindy gave it thumbs up, saying it would surely meet Cory's approval. "I think you're quite safe with Robert. He doesn't come across as a wolf in sheep's clothing. And I envy all the swank parties you'll be attending." Then she tossed out a bomb of her own. She confided that she was giving thought to quitting her job ahead of the pink slip and moving back home. She had told her parents that she and Dave will get married at the first chance, and they have put the pressure on her to come home and get a local job, if she insists on working, because once their little girl gets married, it will end the kind of family life they had long shared.

"I can understand their feeling," Tally said. "And I can understand your feeling of having, perhaps, one final long visit to the nest. You have a beautiful home and a beautiful family, but I want you to know that you also have a very special place in my heart. I'll miss you terribly."

Cindy threw her arms around Tally. "You're the biggest reason for making the decision hard. We've had so much fun together. But no matter how far apart we may get, we'll always keep in touch. Let that be our pact. I love you, Tally."

☆ ☆ ☆

The battle of Saipan raged on. The *Hudson* poured in the reserves for the Twenty-fifth Marine Regiment, which had suffered severe losses in the early days of the invasion. The landings took place with light opposition as the bulk of the Japanese defenders had retreated to defense positions back in the woodsy terrain. The task of the boat divison, round-the-clock duty, was mainly salvage and the evacuation of the wounded. The number of landing boats that had been destroyed was awesome, clogging the beach for days, making difficult the moving in of supplies and equipment. At night the silence would be broken with banzai charges. "I swear," Cory said to Scorch, "I heard some yell Babe Ruth before they charged to their death."

The casualties kept mounting. "On the final count, it'll be between fifteen and twenty thousand," Gil predicted. "And we'll have killed at least twenty-five thousand Nips in the blood bath."

It stunned Cory. "Gil, you're talking of a total between forty and fifty thousand dead and wounded on an island not fifteen miles long and a stone's throw wide. We had two thousand midshipmen in our class. When we had dress parade, four abreast, we covered five football fields. Extrapolate and it becomes unthinkable! All I know right now is that I've smelled the stench of death for ten days and it's an odor I'll not forget."

A moment later a pale, shaken Scorch joined the group. "I can't believe it," he stammered. "We were up at the northern rim loading some wounded when my coxswain pointed upward. We watched in horror, helpless to do anything, as hundreds of women and children, followed by ragged soldiers, leaped off the high cliff to their death. They obviously believed the propaganda that death is preferred to surrender and torture at the hands of the Americans."

"Don't waste your tears," Madman Mulligan piped up. "Can you think of one damn thing we've got in common with the bastards?"

Cory, aware that Madman lost a brother in New Guinea, suppressed his initial reaction. He simmered down and said, "At last report, Madman, we both have gestation periods of nine months." He turned to Scorch. "Have you noticed that the Japs have no hospital ships. Makes their policy altogether too clear. Keep shooting until you're out of bullets or haven't the strength to pull the trigger. Then fall on your sword or jump over a cliff. God! War is ugly!"

Gil Harvey called another special meeting of the boat division officers.

"I hate these meetings," Scorch whispered to Cory as they entered the room. "Gil only calls them when he's got bad news to pass on."

"Misery loves company," Cory replied.

"Guys," Gil began, "first, congratulations on your baptism of fire. You've worked long hours, tough duty, and carried out your jobs well. Even the captain lauded your efficiency. Saipan has finally been secured. The cost was great but we now have a landing field to bomb the hell out of Japan. This should quicken the pace of the war. Any questions?"

Cory spoke up with tongue in cheek. "Gil, the skipper made clear when we boarded ship that we were on duty seven days a week and twenty-four hours a day. Any chance of forming a union?" The group laughed.

Gil smiled. "We live in a free country, son, but I should remind you that mutiny in wartime is on the list of offenses that allows hanging on the yardarm." More laughter. "Which brings me to the main reason for this meeting."

"So who are we hanging?" Scorch blurted out. The group cracked up.

Gil had enough. "The next wiseacre gets crow's-nest duty for the rest of the night." The group quieted down. "The next target is Tinian, a small island about twenty square miles some three miles south of Saipan."

"Why are we bothering with that rinky-dink?" the Mole asked.

"Harassment. It has four airstrips. When the Fifth Fleet departs, they can fly sorties over Saipan. They can also sneak boats in and play guerrilla. The garrison has about ten thousand troops. So the brass says take it."

"After Saipan it should be like taking candy from a baby," said Hammock Harry.

"Wrong," replied Gil. "There's limited access to the island: two small beaches in the north and two larger ones in the south. The landing could be fiercely contested. The difficulty with White Beach I and II in the north is that they are narrow, making the movement of large equipment hazardous, and they are protected by steep cliffs, making a heyday for snipers."

"So," Hammock Harry said, "we hit the south beaches."

"Wrong again. The brass figures that Colonel Ogata, heading the defenses, has reasoned likewise and has shifted his troops to the south. So we engage in a bit of chicanery. We go through the motions of a landing in the south: battlewagons blasting away with their sixteen-inch guns, carrier planes bombing and strafing the beaches, transports anchoring to unload troops, while the Twenty-fifth Marine Regiment, the real invasion forces, are sneaking across the three miles to the White Beaches. If the ploy works, many lives are saved."

"So," Cory said smiling, "we're part of the decoy. We sail to the south and fake a cargo of troops."

"Wrong," Gil replied. "With our familiarity with the Twenty-fifth, we get the honor of boating them in."

"Suppose," Cory said, "Ogata decides to leave a regiment in the cliff?"

"Then it will be a massacre."

☆ ☆ ☆

In the shade of a coconut palm on the atoll of Enewetok in the Marshalls, Cory and Scorch stretched out their frames enjoying warm beer and reading letters accumulated during the blackout period of the past invasion. The island junket was the navy's way of dissolving stress of combat and regenerating spirits for the next campaign.

Cory raised his bottle of beer. "To Ogata, who went for the decoy and saved our hide for another day."

"To Ogata," Scorch reiterated, "wherever his soul might now be roaming." He gulped some beer and made a face. "If necessity is the mother of invention, how come the tropics didn't invent the refridge? This stuff tastes like you know what."

"We're lucky," Cory said, ignoring Scorch's complaint. "We could have been lambs led to the slaughter. The boys at Guam, they say, ran into a buzz saw. Our boat division is still fully intact.

. . . Scorch, what I dread most about this ugly business is not the fear of death but the loss of parts. I'd hate going through life a paraplegic or in need of a seeing eye dog."

"Perish the thought. By the way, have you heard about the *Colorado*? The word is that she took some heavy hits."

"Tally's roommate had her fiancé aboard. I hope he made it. Guess I'll find out soon enough from Tally. Well, enough of this prattle. I still have several more of her letters to read, and I'm eager to get at them." Cory cracked open a fresh bottle of beer and removed the letters from his shirt pocket.

Scorch sighed. "You've got yourself one sweetheart there. She's not only a knockout, but a true-blue correspondent. She keeps the letters coming. You're a lucky guy, Gash."

"Amen!" He arranged the letters chronologically and then drifted away from the world of khakis and ant hills.

July 14, 1944

My Darling,
  The weeks are creeping past us. It will soon be four months since we met—four, short, unforgettable months. A whole third of a year! (See how good my math is coming.)
  The sun and clouds are alternating this morning, neither wishing to appear dominant. When a little girl in summertime, I'd lie on my back and stare with fascination at the clouds. I still love to watch cloud formations.
  I went to the hospital to see Ted. They have a specialist now attending him. He's making progress but it's a slow process. He'll be confined for some time. When he's discharged, he's hoping to go to school. The good word is that the divorce has been cancelled and his wife is planning to visit next month. I'm still keeping my fingers crossed for them as they have some big adjustments to face.
  I baked some small cakes yesterday and have been wrapping them in brandy-saturated cloths. So, darling, if you catch a strong whiff of liqueur on opening this letter, don't you dare accuse me of being off on a toot!

Saw Cindy checking out from work yesterday as I was checking in. A brief smile and nod was all that was exchanged as stepping out of line is highly frowned upon. Avis has been limping all week, having stubbed her toe against a table and bent her toenail back. It's downright sore, but her excitement on going home in a couple of weeks has kept her spirits up. Debbie's sister and husband are coming up this weekend. The family's home is in Berkeley. She still hasn't heard from Jack regarding his transfer. There will be two very disappointed people if they can't get together.

Cory, I love you so much I could stand on the roof and shout it to the heavens. Love and kisses, darling. Yours ever,

Mopsy

July 17, 1944

My Darling,

Hi! Good morning. Our fourth monthversary and I love you, love you, love you! I got up rather late, having gabbed at length on returning from work last night. Cindy told me she was leaving, Cory, for good this time, and it came as a jolt. Her plans are to rest at home a couple of months and then get a job. Jeepers, one thinks about these things happening, but when reality strikes it's all so different. We've been together nearly a year and have grown very close. It'll be a wrench to see her go, although I can hardly blame her. She has a beautiful home to go to. But with all we've shared, she'll be taking a part of me with her.

Ted, too, will be leaving when his discharge finally comes through. I know he needs to. Avis, of course, will be leaving in a couple of weeks, and Debbie and Jack will be exchanging vows as soon as the army lets them. With you millions of miles away, darling, there's little reason for my staying in San Diego. Yet, I'm reluctant to leave because I still connect it with you. Odd how seemingly unimportant places and insignificant things can come to mean so much. And don't you dare call me a sentimental slob! Denver has lost its charm because I feel so detached. True, I'd like to see dad, but I'd have to keep very busy to stay.

Please forgive me, Cory, this letter is beginning to sound gloomy. It was not my intention to be glum, especially on Sunday.

We've been poking about today. Cindy, Debbie, and I are having dinner at home. One of Dave's fraternity brothers is in town and he and a friend are taking Cindy and me to the Square tonight. A dance or two should brighten things up, but nothing could do it better than you, darling, right here in my arms. Loving you always,

Mopsy

July 21, 1944

My Darling,

Bursting with joy best described my feeling on seeing the familiar handwriting on the envelope that greeted me at the head of the stairs. I held your letter tight for a long moment as though it might suddenly vanish or turn out to be a mirage.

Then I could not stem the tears as cruel reality crashed into mind carrying the fact that thousands of miles are between us and the training days are long over. Real guns are pointing at you on every beach you now land. These are the days I've dreaded and tried in so many ways to block out. I now understand the urgency of those quick sailing orders which deprived us of one more night together under the stars. They had invasion plans written all over them, but you would never tell me a word—and still don't—ere it would upset my pretty (airy) head.

Oh, how I chide fate for not giving us more time together, not even one more hour. Such a small request. Just think! One more date would have rounded out our times allowed together to an even half-dozen. Know what we would have done! Begorra, we would have taken a blanket to a secluded piece of shoreline with the nearest human a mile away. We would press our bodies together under God's brightest stars, speak not a word, and let our hearts beat as one. I would smother you with kisses and caress every ounce of your adorable body.

You have your Irish gall to imply impairment in my judgment! Were I to do it over again, hindsight and all, it would still be you, and it would still be you no matter how many separations we'd have to live through. And with each new one, I would be just as cowardly and full of self-pity as with the last one. Don't you dare ever think of taking from me the privilege of worrying over you. Everybody worries about somebody these days, and I've chosen my somebody to be you. Oh, darling, I do love you so, I'm terribly proud of you, and you must return safe and sound.

Cindy terminated yesterday, got her belongings together, and I saw her off. We hugged long. A lump formed in my throat. I knew it would be a long while before hearing the ring of her laugh again. When she left before, I felt she'd be back soon. Not now. Very few of the original group are still left. Debbie has a friend, Laura, who is coming to live with us on Saturday, so there will still be three of us here. We'll be playing musical chairs. I'm taking Debbie's room and she and Laura are taking the one that was occupied by Cindy and me.

This weekend is au revoir to Avis and Dave's friend. He's on his way to New Jersey for advanced training. Seems to me I should be getting quite adept at these goodbyes. The word is still one of the ugliest in the language, and one that the two of us shall never use.

Had my first exposure to a pipe today. We girls lost a bet on the races against the fellows in our group, so as a penalty, we had to bring a pipe to work and smoke it. Caused quite a riot! Me thinks I won't become addicted. I'll save the pipe for your return. Poor Buck had to excuse himself and leave the room rather than see his fair flower defile herself. Oh, me!

Darling, I put a picture in the mail for you. I don't know when you'll get it, but I hope soon. It was the only print made, because, being the most satisfying portrait I ever sat for, I wanted you to have the only copy. I hope it will help soften the pain in the long days ahead. I love you, Cory, every particle of you, from curly hair to pinkie to tiny toe. All yours,

Mopsy

Cory slowly pocketed the letters, his countenance reflecting a somber mood. Scorch tossed him a beer and cracked open one for himself. "Hey, brooding mate, don't tell me all's not well on the homefront."

"Tally's beautiful as ever. Her letters got me thinking that life for a working girl in a port town during a war is no bed of roses."

"What got you on that track?"

"The dizzy pace of life going on there. Jobs are temporary, can terminate without warning, friends get suddenly married and leave the area, lovers overseas go into no man's land where life and death is touch-and-go, and then families come on strong putting pressure to return home."

"You've forgotten the dances, beach parties, four-star restaurants, theater. I'd still swap places."

"There's no haven in this cockeyed world. Take the ranch. In the four short months I've known Tally, the Inner Circle's about made full circle. They'll soon be back to square one with a new cast. The only one really holding the fort is Susan, and that's because her home's there and she's in no panic to get hitched. Incidentally, you two seemed to hit it off quite well."

Scorch laughed. "Almost too well. A couple more dates with her might have put a major crimp into my life plans. The chick has plenty of pizzazz."

On their return to the ship, the mail boat had made its second run and there was a thin, do-not-bend envelope for Cory. He opened it as the denizens were gathering in Goat Castle, and he set a framed portrait of Tally on his desk. With Cory's fondness of long hair, she had let it flow off her bared shoulders and come to rest on the lace trim of her decollete dress, which was all the photographer provocatively allowed to be seen in the photo. "Since you heathens have never been close to the likes of an angel," Cory quipped, "take a quick peek." They crowded about.

"Some chick!" Scorch exclaimed. "The doll's fabulously photogenic."

"She'd do mighty well on a screen test," Madman opined.

"The epitome of pulchritude," Gooseneck aired.

"What I'd like to know," the Mole asked, "is why would a glamour puss like that want to hook up with a sea bum like you?"

"All right, chumps," Cory said, grinning, "you've had your look. Pull back before you get singed from a halo. Angels don't cotton well to infidels. . . . Besides, if I don't shoot off a fast reply, I'm in deep doo."

"Give the lad space," Scorch said sarcastically, "he wants to think. The last time he worked his brain this hard he had a petit mal attack." They drifted off.

After a long daydreaming gaze at the centerpiece on his desk, Cory picked up his pen.

July 28, 1944

Dearest Mopsy,

My old friend the leprechaun has made his appearance. Guess what! He handed me a photo of a beautiful angel.

"She thought your bare desk needed a decoration," he said.

"How did you ever get aboard the ship?" I asked him bewildered. "We're miles from nowhere in the world's largest ocean."

He looked at me with the disdain of one who had to put up with an idiotic question. "I'm disappointed, m'lad, in the size of your brain waves. If an angel is capable of dancing on the head of a pin, why does it surprise you that a leprechaun is capable of walking on water?" Suddenly, he vanished.

I am now staring at the most absolutely divinely angelic portrait ever to set my eyes upon. When my wits recover, I shall compose a poem to commemorate the event.

In the meantime many XXXXXX's, darling.

Cory

# The Pearl Necklace

Cory followed Hawk into his stateroom. "Another seventy-five bucks to the cause," Cory beamed. "Those marine captains were a soft touch."

"Indeed," Hawk replied. "But had you played a couple of hands a bit smarter, we'd have been over a hundred."

"Jeez, Hawk. Here I thought I was reaching the top of the game."

"You're getting there, Gash. You've got natural card sense, which is why I selected you for a partner. And you've caught on fast to my bidding system, which gives us a head start before a card is played. It's just that you've got some bad habits to overcome from the days of college bridge."

"And I was considered a whiz in college."

"That's what makes the habits hard to break. Poor opponents let one get away with bad plays. Plays that would be fatal against good opposition."

"How about an example."

"College kids finesse when unnecessary. Good players finesse as the last resort. They connive to get their opponents to finesse. A bird in hand is always worth two in the bush." Hawk then laid out several hands that cost them because Cory was too quick to finesse when other better alternatives prevailed. "Comprehendere?"

"Clear as a Swiss bell," Cory replied.

"That's another one of your good points, Cory. You don't get defensive, wasting your energy justifying mistakes."

"I keep reminding myself of your comment in the beginning not to take criticism personally. If I did, you said, I'd be a cooked goose with all the unlearning I have to do. Now that I'm beginning to see the difference between a good and poor bridge player, I'm curious as to what you see separates the great from the good."

"Good question. Both the good and great player are fully cognizant of the rules and the probabilities. So I'd say, the main difference is psychological. A great player, like Jacoby, has the uncanny knack of anticipating his opponents. He quickly picks up on their strengths and weaknesses, their indicators of stress, when they get conservative and when they take risks. Also the great player has the card sense to know when to violate the rules. Every rule, however fundamental, should at times be violated. The trick is to know when."

"I can see why you're a top beachmaster. It's a bridge game to you."

Hawk laughed. "I like the metaphor."

"Speaking of beaches, since I know you have a pipeline to the brass, what's next on the docket?"

"Keep this under hat, but all signs point to the Philippines. Troop movements are focusing on an October invasion. MacArthur can get the egg off his face by retaking the islands. It's general knowledge he goofed in losing them." Hawk chuckled. "Since we'll be working with the army, we should get some cracks at them on the bridge table. From all I've seen, they should be pushovers. But remember, Gash, always console poor players on their bad run of cards and assure them that luck will fall their way the next time."

"Hawk, you're a fox!"

When not under preparation to enter a war zone, Cory found life aboard ship routine with occasional variation. The graveyard watch was mostly monitoring course and speed, leaving time to gaze at the ocean with wonderment at its energy and enormity. After relief of the watch he would get in a few winks before general quarters for the sunrise alert at the battle stations. Following breakfast he carried out the routine inspections of an assistant deck officer; and, as the recorder of the summary court martial, he prepared the proper papers for BUPERS in Washington, D.C. Then he got in a few winks before lunch, the censoring of mail after lunch, and with the time left before the evening meal, reading, writing, and personal chores. After general quarters for the sunset alert, it was usually bridge or workouts until time to read the log notes before going on watch. He became so adept at catching snatches of sleep, he would do it standing against the 40 mm gun, since the dawn and dusk alerts never prompted enemy action.

Having no expertise with weaponry, Cory made a deal with his gunnery chief, who knew guns inside out and outside in. "Chief," he said, "putting me in charge of this forty millimeter points up the absurdity of the navy caste system. From this moment on, it's your charge, and I'll defend to the death every decision you make." The chief grinned and shook hands.

Of all the extraneous duties, the one Cory found least boring was censoring letters, required throughout the fleet to keep damaging information from falling into enemy hands. Dull days at sea inspire the imaginations of sailors, giving rise to colorful fabrications in letters home. This one lazy August afternoon, some of the stories passing through Cory's hands struck him so amusing that he had to write Tally about it.

August 10, 1944

To the Sweetest of the Sweet,
One thing the movies downplay and the novels ignore, Mopsy, is the boredom of war. But it's true. Much of our precious youth is frittered away in the dull routine of shiplife. Even the ocean, outside the typhoon season, can get lazy and lethargic. One escape from the monotony comes in censoring the mail. As you know, all out-going letters are censored to quiet the paranoia of the top brass, who fear if a mailboat falls into enemy hands, our great war strategy will be compromised. Point #1: No mail boat to date has fallen into enemy hands. Point #2: If one did, it would most likely shorten the war. The confusion

would send the enemy into full retreat. The imagination of a bored sailor at sea has no parallel. Here are typical lines from a gob to his gal on a totally uneventful day like today:

"Sugarplum, I'm still having the shakes. We've been under attack since dawn, one dive-bomber after another zooming down, sights on our ship. Our big guns have been spewing hot lead without break. All's quiet now, but had one of those babies that nicked our crow's nest been inches lower in its fiery plunge into the sea, I'd be writing this from Davey Jones's locker. But the Lord was on our side. Keep the prayers going, luv, because all signs point to more of the same tomorrow."

Anyone interested in reconstructing the war from the letters of sailors have the stuff for a blockbuster novel.

From what you write, nothing is ever dull at the ranch. Now that Cindy intends to plunge into the sea of matrimony with, of all things, a navy man, don't you think the only decent thing for you to do, with your knowledge of that branch of the service, is to advise her to see a brain specialist? I'm starting to think that Susan is the sanest in your circle. Notice how she avoids foreign entanglements. The prudent lass seems not about to plunge into any sea until the waters have been fully charted. Who, besides the all-wise gods can possibly predict the direction of the currents when this crazy tide rolls back to sea!

However, the important thing to remember in this nutty year of 1944 is that I love you, Mopsy, and would climb Mount Everest for a sweet kiss from your sweet lips. Shelley said it all in these words:

The mountains kiss high heaven.
The moonbeams kiss the sea.
What are all these kisses worth,
If thou kiss not me?

Loving you even though we're on opposite sides of the Date Line. (Weak pun)
XXXX's,

Cory

P.S. Ye gods! The noise is suddenly deafening. Shells are tearing up the forecastle, raking our decks, blasting holes in our hull. Tojo knows if he sinks the pride of the fleet his dimming star will glow in Tokyo. Eureka! The guns are silent, the enemy has vamoosed, our vessel still floats. Tojo's great gamble failed. He no longer rules the Pacific. The turning point of the war happened this August day of '44. Save this PS, Mopsy. Future historians will kiss your big toe for it.

☆ ☆ ☆

The events of July 1944 weakened the core of Tally's support system. It began with Avis and Cindy resigning from work, in advance of termination notices, and returning home. As it was, Tally was the only one of the Inner Circle still on the swing shift. Job cutbacks had other good friends leaving the area. Then the rash of new arrivals at the hospital were grim reminders of action accelerating in the Pacific. News of the shelling of the *Coronado*, although Dave was reported safe, increased her fears of the dangers confronting Cory.

The upside of Ted's continued progress in rehabilitation was tempered with the downside that his discharge and departure would be soon an issue to face. His many surgeries had brought them even closer together, and she would dearly miss him even though she knew how important it was for him to return to Denver and try to put together the pieces of his marriage. She also knew his going home would increase family pressure for her return, although she no longer felt connected to Colorado.

Adding to her stresses was the cessation of art classes since Mr. Gilbert had dropped the day class, continuing only with the night class, which conflicted with Tally's work schedule. She had found art therapeutic.

Debbie had a long-standing friend, Laura, from her hometown who she thought would be a good replacement for Cindy. "You will like her," she told Tally. "She is cheerful, easygoing, a neat but not obsessive housekeeper, and bunches of fun." She laughed. "Besides all that, she loves horses. Her husband, overseas, is an officer in the navy."

Tally perked up. "Sounds good. Grab her if you can."

And so, Laura Branson, tall like Debbie, sweet like Debbie, delightful like Debbie, moved in at the ranch. Laura and Debbie took the bedroom shared by Tally and Cindy, and Tally took Debbie's old room.

As Tally sat down to write her late-hour letter to Cory, she was sensing more than ever her dependency on him, seeing him the one anchor of stability among the myriad of changes constantly affecting her life.

July 23, 1944

Gash Darling,

Again, 3:00 AM! Tis a crazy hour to be up, is it not? Wonder what hour it might be at your sea hideaway? You've been a pest today, persistently with me, persistently refusing to go, and I loving it.

While each passing day brings me a day closer to your arms, each passing day also makes me miss you more. Oh, how many more days are there to go? I dare not think on it. Must every generation go through this? We will make it.

For the moment not much is happening outside the usual routine in our limited little world. Avis and I are doing some sewing, trying to finish her suit before she goes home. Always things to be done at the last minute.

I visited Ted in the hospital this afternoon. His long ordeal has brought us ever closer together. He's encouraging me to go home for at least a vacation. I'll go, I guess, but not right away. Seems that the plant is getting a funny hold on me. I feel something exciting is in the air and I want to be there when it happens. All very vague. The design of a plane, for example, that will break the speed of sound. It will happen some day, you know.

I caught the "Special" to work this afternoon and it broke

down just as we started over the royal gorge. The poor little conductor got so hysterical that he had everybody in laughter. Several men helped him get it started. Then we really took off on a wild ride as he was trying to make up for lost time.

The night shift still controls my life, and the "ranch" has taken on a new look with a face-lifting paint job and two new housemates. Laura is very much like I pictured her. She's tall, very friendly, and judging from her collection of ribbons and cups, an expert horsewoman. Her husband's a lieutenant in the navy and is overseas on a cruiser. I don't know too much about the other girl as she came with Laura, unpacked, and then disappeared.

I stopped by to see Mr. Gilbert. He has dissolved the day class, which leaves me on the out because my working hours conflict with his night class.

It's terribly still tonight. The only noise is the scratching of this pen. I know there's danger all around you, so please be careful, my darling. Nothing must happen to you because I love you so.

I best close now, plumb out of energy, but full of love for that guy out there.

Mopsy

The coming aboard of Laura at the ranch filled a void for Tally. She once again had a daytime companion at home. Laura was in no particular rush to gain employment as the money coming in from her husband, Chad, amply met her current expenses, including her part of the rent.

Tally found Debbie's assessment of Laura on the mark. She adapted to the loose lifestyle, had a good sense of humor, and was happy to do her share. Tally took a quick liking to her. "You've been here but a week and already fit like an old shoe," she said.

Laura laughed. "I'm beginning to feel like an old shoe."

The war also played its dirty tricks on Laura. Her honeymoon was barely over when the attack came on Pearl Harbor, changing dramatically the newlyweds' plans. Chad joined the naval reserves to avoid the draft. He then bounced about the country to different training centers until he was finally attached to a cruiser as a line officer. He saw action at Midway and in the Central Pacific campaigns. Tally saw in Laura, like in Cindy, a bonding through the common anxiety of a loved one caught up in the turmoil of the Pacific. It helped to lighten her spirits as she began her weekend letter to Cory.

July 27, 1944

My Darling,

Hi! Dropping a line to let you know you're at the top of my most wanted list.

Jeepers, it's going to be easy to "hit the sack" tonight because it's been a hectic day, but with lots of fun and frolic. Being Friday night, folks were more in a jovial mood. Six of our group are starting vacations and three are terminating. It's getting to the stage where everytime you look up or turn around, some one is saying goodbye or good luck or have a nice trip.

Laura and I had a session of house cleaning before I went to work. You should see the kitchen—positively shining and we're so proud of ourselves. Now don't you dare ask when it was last cleaned!

The new girl, Ann, will be with us only a short time. She's a friend of Laura's and is visiting her husband who's in the marines.

Cory darling, I'll be with you tomorrow. For the moment, goodnight and sweet dreams. My mind has ground to a halt with just one thought remaining in it—I love you.

Later.

Good morning! Isn't it wonderful what a few hours of sleep will do! Tis beautiful today, Cory. The sun is out in all of its glory. Debbie and Laura are out riding and I've just stirred from bed. Susan is coming over this afternoon. Since this is Avis' last day, we'll have to cook up something in the way of celebration.

Back to us. I know I'm only one of many who would like

things different, but I realize, Cory, it's just as frustrating for you. In saner moments, which I sometimes have, I know I have little to really complain about and should be thankful for what I have. Darling, without you, my thoughts would be barren. You are my joy and life. God keep you safe wherever you may be. I love you.

Mopsy

Tally went through her well-stocked closet. She picked out a form-fitting powder-blue cotton dress and matching satin slippers. She pinned up her hair in a high bouffant and meticulously applied her makeup. She attached pearl earrings, a silver bracelet, and her silver peace-dove broach. All of this was in preparation for her first social engagement with Robert Graham, who was escorting her to a black-tie dinner party at the mansion of a wealthy industrialist. Tally pranced into the living area for a last-minute inspection from Debbie and Laura. "How do I look?"

"The belle of the ball," Debbie said.

"Not a strand of hair out of place," Laura added.

"But guess who's on pins and needles," Tally replied. "Robert told me I'll probably see more diamonds on display than in a jeweler's showcase."

"The rich are just people too," Laura said. "None walk on water."

Tally answered Robert's knock on the door to find him holding an orchid corsage. She admired his formal attire. "Very debonair," she said. She ushered him in, introduced him to the girls, and pinned on the orchid. "It's beautiful," she gushed. "And it matches my dress."

"Beauty becomes beauty," he said. After a brief cordial exchange with the girls, he and Tally took their leave.

The sumptuous dinner party was the extravaganza of Albert and Angela Swain. "They manufacture flying boats, sea-rescue planes," Robert said. "Our company is seeking to be a supplier for them. Angela Swain reputedly can be most persuasive in the decisions of her husband."

Tally took an immediate liking to her hostess. Angela in her prime must have been an arresting beauty, she surmised, because she still has the captivating features of dark eyes, high cheek bones, and a finely chiseled chin.

"Dugan, you say your name is," Angela repeated. "Not Dugan of the Dugan Plumbing Company, perhaps?"

"No ma'am. Dugan of the Dugan Construction Company."

"Don't believe I'm familiar with it."

A twinkle appeared in Tally's eye. "Not surprising, Mrs. Swain. The company is in Denver and while the name is old, the company is small. A one-man operation." They both laughed.

Tally felt the liking was mutual when Mrs. Swain insisted before the evening was over that she be called Angela, and then as Tally was leaving, Angela warmly pressed her hand and expressed the hope that they would see each other again soon.

Robert beamed while driving her home. "You hit it off super with Angela Swain. She told me your refreshing candor reminded her a lot of herself in her younger days." He then added, "I hope the evening was not too stuffy."

Tally smiled. "Why, with white-coated waiters, imported wine, dinner on Wedgewood pottery, and dessert under a flame, how could it possibly be stuffy? While diamonds the size of marbles lit up the room, no one sported a lovelier corsage. Thank you, Robert."

At home, Tally undressed, put on her p.j.'s, and still stimulated, began a letter to Cory. She decided not to mention the fabulous feast, not from a sense of inappropriateness, but from the fear it might put salt on the wounds of one perhaps freshly bitten by ants while eating canned Spam and washing it down with warm beer, having been marooned on a primitive island.

Dearest Gash,

Whee! At last we've been notified in writing that we go on days next month. I've been in this morass of uncertainty long enough, and it's such a relief to know what's up.

How are you, my darling? I can only hope in the best of fettle. I know you'll write when you can, and I look forward to each day with the thought that this might be the one. Your letters are a pure treasure. They are my strength in these abnormal times. Your love shines through them in so many different ways: in the simple but beautiful way you see a sunset at sea, white caps in a storm, the ocean in moonlight. Only the eyes of one in love can capture beauty the way you do. Perhaps someday I can do it painting.

I'm sure my letters have a boring ring of repetition because I report on a life with much more routine than variation. But this is how it is, darling. You insist I enjoy myself and I do manage a fairly active social life, but I confess it doesn't have the pizazz of yore. A critical ingredient is lacking. I'm becoming increasingly more content with quiet evenings and good music. Begorra! Am I growing old before my time?

Sunday.

Susan, Avis, and I saw "Arsenic and Old Lace" and afterwards we sat on Avis' trunks to get them closed. We saw her off on the early morning train and there was a slight rise of dew in our eyes. Susan went straight on to work but I got in forty more winks.

Monday.

We had an interesting day at the blood bank. We got a dedication card which was attached to the bottle, so, of course, I dedicated mine to you. They asked me to pose for a picture, which, I guess, will appear in the local paper. After coffee and donuts I went to work. With people still on vacation and the walls torn down, the workplace was mildly in chaos.

I heard from Cindy today and she's happy at home.

Well, darling, I guess my letter writing at 3:00 AM is about a thing of the past, which I bet is a relief to you. Maybe I'll make more sense from now on. I did enjoy working swing, but I'm looking forward to a more normal routine.

Good night, Cory darling, you have my love. Forever yours,

Mopsy

The next weekend began with a special joy for Tally. She had just received in writing that she would be transferred in two weeks to the day shift. The happy news warranted a little self-indulgence. She intended on sleeping in Saturday morning, but her dreams were interrupted much earlier with a gentle shake. She popped open an eye to see a smiling Laura bending over her.

"I know," Laura said, "you planned to snooze till noon, but I thought you might wish to alter plans on learning that the postman brought you three letters from you-know-who."

Tally bolted upright in bed. "Three letters! Begorra!"

Laura laughed, dropped the letters on the bed, and moved toward the door. "I also got a couple from Chad. Appears the boys used the same post office."

"They're safe," Tally exulted. "They're out of the war zone, because their letters are free to go." She propped herself against a pillow, opened all three letters, arranged them according to their dates, and read them in proper sequence. The first letter acknowledged the arrival of her picture, as only Cory could romanticize it; the second letter included a poem, a beautiful poem that made her heart flutter in knowing how much the photo must have meant to him, and the third letter had the poet-philosopher expounding on the mystery of love. Tally read and reread the letters before joining Debbie and Laura for morning coffee.

All of them were in a glowing state as Debbie, too, had received a letter from Jack.

"All goes well with Chad," Laura reported. "His chief complaint is lack of sleep the past month. How about Cory?"

"His letters are always so upbeat I'm never sure what his

concerns are," Tally replied. "He makes fun of situations that would depress most. That's one of the things so endearing about him. Also his unique way of seeing things. The philosopher came out of him in one letter in which he got into analyzing the duality of love."

"What's his theory?" Debbie asked.

"Better yet, read what he says," Laura requested.

Adequately persuaded, Tally slipped off to her room to retrieve the letter.

"I'll read the sentence leading up to it," Tally said. "For your info, Laura, Cory nicknamed me Mopsy, going back to our first meeting when the wind kept blowing my hair in my face."

What a perfect night it was to be on watch, Mopsy. With moonbeams dancing on gentle whitecaps, an engine purring on all cylinders, and a helmsman holding steady to course, the thoughts of Sinbad the Sailor turned to the mystery of love. Ah, and what a mystifying paradox it is! The one emotion of which most is said but least is known.

What a double-edged sword! Love has the power to zap or revive, depress or exalt, enslave or free, pare or enrich. Why is this so? Can it be rationally explained or is it merely more grist for the poet's mill?

I suggest the key to the paradox is not to be found in the mystic writings of the Muses but in the simple wording of elementary physics. I refer to the minor section on spinning objects. It posits two opposing forces act on a spinning object. One force, centripetal, draws the object toward its center; the other force, centrifugal, thrusts it away. So what's this got to do with love? Since we all agree that love spins the head, we're back to spinning objects. The centripetal force, pulling inward, constricts love and makes it egocentric. The centrifugal force, thrusting outward, expands love and makes it altruistic. Hitler exemplifies centripetal love at its worst. Francis of Assisi is a good example of centrifugal love at its best.

Thus, love can be ennobling or degrading, depending on the balance of the pull. Mopsy, we must strive to keep our love more centrifugal ere we be drawn into the vortex of the very evils we're risking our lives to destroy.

Debbie was the first to break the silence in the room. "Cory would be good at debate. He lines up his ducks."

"I agree," Laura said. "Once he got me thinking the sword was double-edged, all that followed made sense."

"Hasn't he struck a truth?" Tally asked. "Don't all of us struggle between selfish and selfless love. Don't all of us, on the one hand, get the urge to withdraw and self-protect, and on the other hand, get the urge to help others? Only centrifugal love can transcend the self."

Debbie smiled. "With so few St. Francises of Assisi around, I'd say the urge to self-serve does most of the pulling. Too much centripetal love may be the cause of most of the mess we're in."

Tally's day was topped off with a grand feeling of relief as she settled down to write to Cory. While his letters were always a great source of joy, those today were especially special in confirming that the *Hudson* had come through its first big test unscathed.

August 7, 1944

Darling,

A bonanza day! Imagine! Three letters from you—each one priceless. The censor himself must have been agog. Guess what? I've cancelled all extraneous activities to spend the day just with you. You are so upbeat! I love you.

You are so reassuring, Cory, that all is right and all will work out for us. I want that with all my heart, more than anything else. Darnit, I get so blasted sentimental just thinking of you, darling, and so bumbling trying to express myself. I know of no one who can put words on paper to move the heart the way you do. Sometimes I would like to share them in a world filled with so much sorrow, but I know they were meant for my heart alone and it would be a betrayal of love to do so. When you come home, darling, I warn you, I shall follow you like a trained puppy, afraid to let you out of sight, lest the ocean should swallow you again.

I'm not afraid of what we may have to face after the war. Nothing can compare to the anguish of being apart, which tears at every fiber in my being. My father once told me that love was largely a matter of proximity—you come to love those whom circumstances let you share a great deal of things. There may be a grain of truth in it, but where would that leave us, darling? It's not our fault we can't be together. All I can say for sure is that I've fallen head over heels, never had before, but now that I have, I wouldn't want anything to stand between us which we can't share.

Susan's folks invited me for dinner last Sunday. They certainly have a lovely home. I think what I missed most in first coming to San Diego was the lack of a real homey atmosphere. During my last year in Denver, I developed a very close friend. She had no brothers or sisters so she and her folks sorta adopted me for about five days of the week. I stayed at their grand home, only leaving the paradise to help Ted in his rehabilitation here. That opened a new world. I met someone who means more to me than any other living soul. After due deliberation, I've come to the weighty decision that he's not for sale, for rent, for loan out, or giveaway!

Cindy wrote today. She's planning a week in Chicago with her father. It's business for him but fun for her. Debbie and Jack will marry as soon as the army will give him a few days off. They hope to marry either here or at his home in Los Angeles, probably the latter. Looks like they won't have much time together before he goes overseas, although there's an outside chance he may go to Officers' Candidate School.

Well, darling, not too long I'll be getting up at predawn to reach work at 7:00 AM. I enjoyed swing except for the time you were here. Why didn't I drop work and follow you to San Francisco? Such wild ideas can only come out of my head because I love you, I miss you, I hate being apart from you. Love and kisses,

Mopsy

Several days later Tally steeled herself for a poignant scene when Ted announced there'd be a short ceremony to honor him and two others with the Purple Heart. A small group of close family members gathered in the conference room at the hospital to hear a colonel in the U.S. Marine Corps praise these young men for their heroics in the Solomons, fighting against odds in a steaming jungle fraught with malaria-bearing mosquitos, venomous snakes, and tropic diseases to halt Japanese imperialism.

Tally's eyes misted watching the boys stand stiffy erect in their starched uniforms, one with a leg missing, a second with an arm missing, and the third, her brother, with an eye missing, showing faces belying their ages, getting the badge of honor pinned on their breast. The thought obsessed her of those many names that were read in the church pulpit, boys who received the honor posthumously.

After the ceremony, Tally brought Ted to the ranch where Debbie and Laura had a decanter of wine to give toasts to the honored hero. Ted was grateful but his spirits were subdued. The lightness of the girls could not shake his mood. He finally excused himself, called a cab, and said he thought it best he return to the hospital. Before leaving, he quietly removed his decoration and handed it to Tally. "For all that you've put up with, you deserve this as much as I. Further, I'd just as soon not see it again. It reminds me of things I'd rather forget."

Tally hugged him. "I'll keep it on one condition. It will always be yours. Whenever you want it, for whatever reason, you'll get it back."

When Ted left, Tally turned to her roommates. "I'm sorry you didn't know Ted before the war. He was so handsome, so alive, so much fun. Maybe time will bring about full cycle." After a long pause she said, "I think I'll go to my room and write Cory. Thinking of him always cheers me up."

My Darling,

Sure, and you're a bit more than wonderful! Another letter this morning. That alone makes this a great day.

I went to the hospital this afternoon. Hadn't seen Ted in almost a week. He's up for another operation, depending on the doctor's schedule. The surgeries are now cosmetic.

Debbie will be in limbo for the next several days. Jack's at a camp between Los Angeles and San Francisco. He calls every night but things remain indefinite. Doesn't know if he'll get a furlough or be sent directly overseas—sounds suspiciously familiar. Laura and I are caught up in the drama. Debbie, of course, is Miss Poise, but you know she's churning inside.

Yesterday was a typical day. As I passed through town on my way to work, people were lined up at the shoe stores, frantic that their coupons might be canceled like their food stamps were last week. Seems a bit silly to me, as if their very lives were at stake if the coupons aren't spent—my humble opinion.

The vacationers are dribbling back to work, except Buck, the king of mischief, so things are still relatively quiet.

Know what? The move is finally underway and it's days for me starting Monday for sure. Whee! It's hard to believe. Geeminy, it'll be a hard pull getting me out of bed Monday morning. And I'm not expecting much sympathy from your quarters. We've been evacuated from our little teepee and we'll begin life in our new one, straight across the room. Advantage: We'll no longer be sitting directly across the boss' office.

It was a scream watching the movers. They had the navy to help. Our tables were screwed to the floor, but that did not slow down their removal. They just yanked them up and when they lost a leg or two, they let the maintenance crew take over.

I walked down to the shop during the rest period and saw the mock-up of our newest plane. Jeepers, one feels quite insignificant when getting to the place of actual assemblage. One doesn't realize how huge they really are. But, it feels a mite good to be part of the process contributing to the final product. In the middle of work, we sometimes wonder what it's all about.

In visiting Ted, I shed a tear at the little ceremony that took place in which he was awarded the Purple Heart. He gave it to me saying he'd much rather forget. I could understand with all that he's gone through, and told him I'd keep it until he feels differently. I hope and pray, darling, that you will never receive one.

Cory, your letters are so precious I sometimes wonder how I deserve you. I love you so, so much. And what I wouldn't give for just one tiny glimpse of you. But, my terrible greed would have me stealing all of you, locking you up, and throwing away the key.

I'll return your kiss before saying good night, honey. Bon soir and sweet dreams. Yours forever,

Mopsy

Tally and Laura were back at the ranch sipping coffee after having put Debbie on the bus early Sunday morning to marry Jack, who was waiting orders at the army camp near San Francisco.

"These farewells," Tally said, "really tug at the heartstrings. First Cindy, then Avis, and now Debbie."

"At least Debbie's coming back. May take several weeks, but she'll be back."

"Oh, these crazy times! Most of us, I'm sure, would never have accepted anything less than a church wedding with flower girls, gowned bridesmaids, a champagne reception, and a Niagara Falls honeymoon. Now we'll settle for a courthouse, a reception at the nearest pub, and a honeymoon in a bivouac!"

Laura laughed. "There's no stopping love. Join the madness, Tally."

"Cory's keeping me sane. Which brings to mind something I've been wanting to say. I'm more than delighted that you've come to the ranch. You've made a wonderful addition."

"It had to have been fated. If my friend Ann hadn't had a horse trailer, and if her husband hadn't come to San Diego to be shipped out, I surely would not have accepted your and Debbie's offer because I could never leave my horse behind."

"It worked out well for everybody."

Laura smiled. "Guess I better get to the stables. I've got two horses to care for until Debbie's back."

It was a rare Sunday at the ranch, not the usual madcap activity. It allowed Tally to do personal chores and get organized for her first day on the day shift. The Sunday was also the fifth-month anniversary of her courtship with Cory. As the sun was setting, she curled up in her chair, the radio playing, writing material before her, and drifted off into romantic thought.

August 15, 1944

Darling,

Tis Sunday, I'm home, salutare to our fifth monthversary. I love you. It's been quiet, not the usual pell mell one can expect at the ranch on break day. Right now the sun is setting and I've never seen it more spectacular. The sky is a brilliant purple, which in reflecting from the houses makes them purplish too. Everything is so still that I can hear the crickets all the way over in the park. All of this is saying my heart aches to be near you.

Things have been hopping up to now. Laura and I saw Debbie off this morning in another moving scene. She and Jack have decided to get married in spite of the roller-coaster conditions. Tomorrow night she should be Mrs. Jack Hollins. Laura's down at the barn but should be returning soon.

The sunset is gone and the shadows of dusk are spreading. I've had a good week, but I think I'll like days once the body gets adjusted. We'll still have a car pool in the morning which will be a big help. My workdesk leaves a little to be desired. Our old group has been scattered and I'll be seated between two madmen, meaning I'll have to hustle to keep up. It will be terribly crowded. Mr. Barker kidded us Friday night, saying he should call a meeting instructing us how to act on days so we won't disgrace him. He's really a grand person and we all like him.

Darling, Laura just popped in and we're going to have late dinner, so I'll close in order to help with preparations. I hope I dream of you tonight—it would make such a nice memory to go to work on. My love always,

Mopsy

Tally bounded in late Monday afternoon full of energy. She caught Laura returning from the stables and insisted they celebrate her success with a glass of wine. "I've survived the first day on the day shift," she boasted. "I got up on time, got my mind clicking on the job without a hitch, and stayed awake all day. It was fun renewing some past acquaintances. Let's make it a double celebration. Name a success you had today."

Laura laughed. "All I've accomplished is surviving a rigorous workout for two spirited horses. Cheers!"

As the night wore on, Tally discovered the big adjustment was yet to be made. She was wide-eyed at bedtime. She hoped writing Cory might beckon on dreamland.

August 16, 1944

Gash Darling,

Aren't you proud of me! I've survived. This is Monday night and, to be truthful, the first day on the regular shift wasn't all that bad. I got up on time, clocked in on time, but the real test has yet to be passed—getting sleepy on time. It's past 11:00 PM and I'm sitting here wide-eyed looking at your handsome picture. It's wonderful to see your smile, so warm and just a teeny bit shy; but, begorra, you aren't shy—the way you carried on with Esther Williams!

Loving you, Cory, m'thinks is causing a swelling of the heart. Should it burst, I'll hold you responsible. But if you come home right away, I'll drop all charges.

It does seem strange working days. It's a much more subdued atmosphere. Also, there are more men than women on the day shift; just the opposite at night. It was like homecoming running into so many of my former night-time friends. The down note is the 12-cent-an-hour pay cut. My prodigal life is over.

I received a letter from my sister saying her husband may be swinging through San Diego. He's a trucker but most of his business has been east. Maybe I can weasel out a ride to Denver.

We were hoping for a call from Debbie to fill us in on the day, but she's probably too wound up to remember.

Laura is going to school for a short time to brush up on her typing and shorthand, so we both will be early risers. I suppose, darling, I should give the sandman a chance. Good night, sweetheart, I love you forever. I continue to pray for peace.

Mopsy

The week flew by. Debbie did finally call to confirm she was a married woman and will be returning sooner than expected because the honeymoon was cut short with Jack's sudden orders for overseas duty.

"The army is as bad as the navy," Tally said. "The thought of sudden orders gives me the dreaded feeling of another invasion in the air."

Laura was silent for a moment. "Army means MacArthur. Lordy! Does this mean the Philippines? I recall the general did vow to return."

"So senseless," Tally conjectured. "The Philippines are farther from Tokyo than Saipan. But, then, who am I to question the military mind? I just hope Cory doesn't get involved."

Saturday was Tally's second major venture with Robert. She was edgy as the social affair was a penthouse cocktail party, a new experience. Laura teased her as she flitted about nervously rechecking her final appearance. "You better be careful hobnobbing with the upper crust. It might start rubbing off on you, and before you know it, that morning-fresh look of innocence will be gone and replaced by that jaded jet-set look."

Tally laughed. "Not a ghost of a chance. True, the rich are fascinating but so are the inhabitants of the zoo; yet I'd never want to be one of them."

Robert arrived, again the bearer of an orchid corsage. "You are so thoughtful," Tally said pinning on the flower. Then with a deep breath and the wave of a hand, she uttered, "To the penthouse let us go."

Tally's eyes dazzled in wonderment the moment she entered the spacious living area with its priceless Victorian furniture, lush oriental rugs, and huge glass panels with their spectacular view of the bay. Flowers and exotic hors d'oeuvres flavored the room and a mahogany bar ostensibly displayed every conceivable variety of alcoholic beverages. Tally chose Portuguese sherry. The women were ravishing in their haute-couture gowns and jeweled accessories, and the men dapper in their prewar Hong Kong made-to-order silk suits. Tally animatedly entered into the flow of the conversations, gaining smiles of acceptance and winks of approval from Robert.

On escorting Tally to his car on leaving the party, Robert heaped on more praise. "Once again," he said, "you were great, fitting in beautifully with the strangers about you. It's remarkable how quickly people warm up to you. I got the distinct feeling that our hosts, Madalene and Harvey Thompson, would adopt you in a hairsbreadth moment as a daughter. My boss will do a double flip hearing that."

Tally smiled. "Our arrangement does seem to be working well, doesn't it, Robert? The pleasures for me have been nothing short of wonderful. Like the hors d'oeuvres we had today were fabulous. I never ate canapes with more delicious toppings. At the same time, you seem satisfied with how I'm fitting into my role. Any suggestions for improvement?"

"Absolutely none. Keep being your natural self."

As they were approaching the ranch, Tally let out a deep sigh. "Goodness, I do feel I've had a bit too much to drink."

"Stomach upset? Shall we stop for an antacid?"

"Stomach is fine. Can't believe I overdid it. I only had a couple glasses of sherry."

"What makes you think you did? There's no slur to your speech, and there wasn't a trace of weaving while you were walking to the car."

"I have an internal regulator which kicks in when I exceed my limits. I tend to get narcoleptic." She laughed. "I'll never abuse alcohol because I'll fall asleep first."

"Hang on," Robert said. "In a couple of minutes you'll be safely home, and then in another couple of minutes you'll be safely between the sheets. But while you're still with the living, let me reiterate that I, too, am most pleased with our pact. I think Cory is a lucky guy."

Tally had a long sleep and by the next night was fully recovered and in fine fettle to send off her night message to Cory. Yes, darling, she thought as she picked up her pen, we shall make our love centrifugal. But you will have to help me.

August 22, 1944

My Darling,

If you were here, you'd find me once again curled up in my favorite chair, writing to my favorite sailor, listening to soft music, and chatting with Laura at intervals. The music makes me lonesome for you, but I love it all the same. Jeepers! Know what's now playing? "My Prayer Is To Linger With You." What could be more appropriate!

We have a patient in the house. A friend of Laura's had his tonsils out and he was moaning and feeling so abused that Laura jokingly offered to take care of him. Lo and behold, he took her up on it! Now she's stuck with holding to her end of the bargain.

Debbie and Jack have called to confirm they had tied the knot. The honeymoon is shorter than they hoped for. He has only several days before being shipped out. Debbie will be on her way back ere long.

Susan and I went to see Mr. Gilbert the other night. We were fascinated with his paintings of Bermuda, listened to baroque on his phonograph, and were regaled with his world adventures. I'm looking forward to taking up art again.

Strangely, I don't mind getting up early as I thought I would. Days go much faster than nights. And there's something very nice about being home in the evenings.

Honey, I was all set to write you Saturday night, but I collapsed. I was sitting and the next thing I knew, Laura was shaking me. I staggered to bed and slept 15 hours, sound. Ted moseyed in at 10:30 AM to breakfast with me. I really felt refreshed, took a long hike, and dressed up for dinner at Susan's. Was out there till ten o'clock.

Cory, darling, I'm forever thinking about you in the far-off Pacific, wondering what you're doing, telling myself over and over that you're safe, worrying if the navy is treating you right, and asking again and again oh when, oh when will this be over. I miss you so much. There's nothing like a letter from you to lift my morale, not to mention the happiness it brings me. I make no secret of it. I love you. No matter how many ways my pen tries to express it, it always boils down to those three simple words.

If my writing's difficult to decipher, blame my neighbors. Whatever they're rolling about is shaking the entire house—oh, me!

I'll say good night, darling, but I shall always be with you. Loving you forever and a day,

Mopsy

As the last Saturday arrived in the month of August, Tally and Susan returned to the ranch after a couple of sets of tennis to find Laura holding a small package. "This came for you, Tally," she said. "It's from overseas so I'd judge it's very important."

An excited Tally ripped the wrapping off a thin white cardboard box, opened it, and gasped. She removed and held toward the light from the window for the others to clearly see, who also gasped, a necklace of natural pearls.

Squeals of gushing surprise came from the girls.

Tally was too taken aback to speak. As her eyes slowly returned to normal size, she read aloud the attached note: "An optical illusion, Mopsy. The pearls look strung but there's no strings attached."

"Typical Cory wit," Susan said. "You must get to meet him, Laura. He's something else!"

"He's so precious," Tally interjected. "I'm so lucky. I think I might cry." As the mist formed in her eyes, she dug into her pocket for a hankerchief.

For the rest of the day, Tally was outside of the earth's orbit. She would fondle the pearls, put them down, go for a short walk, return and pick up the necklace, and fondle the pearls again. Susan smiled, finally gave up, and went home. Laura took off to visit friends, leaving Tally to spend the evening with her precious necklace, listening to music, and forming a response to Cory.

August 26, 1944

My Darling,

I'm totally breathless! I adore the pearls. You shouldn't have done it. Natural pearls cost an admiral's salary! But now that I have them, I wouldn't part with them for anything, not for all the diamonds in Africa! I am wearing them while I'm writing. Darling, you are most conservative in your values. Only a thousand kisses a pearl? I wouldn't think of anything less than a million.

Oh, how I hope we can make up for all the time we've missed, and that we'll never grow too old to take our love for granted. I couldn't stop loving you, Cory, even if I lived past one hundred. Just think of all the happy years we have ahead of us! I'm all butterflies inside again. Oh, my darling, is it humanly possible that others love as deeply as we? All is so right!

I think you would especially like what you see of me at this moment. After work yesterday I indulged in a complex bouffant coiffure, and I dare say there must be a touch of femme fatale in it, judging by the whistles strolling home (from sailors—if you haven't guessed).

The moon looks suspended in mid-air and the stars, so thick and bright, shine like diamonds in a sky cut into cross-sections by the arching searchlights. Beautiful sights always make me think of you.

It's unusually quiet. Laura is out and the neighbors are not making any racket. The quietness has me pining for you. Thanks again, darling, for the beautiful pearls. I'll think of you always when I wear them, my precious amulet of protection. Nothing now can ever go wrong. Forever yours,

Mopsy

# The Amazing Hawk

"Wonder what Hawk has in mind?" Scorch asked Cory as they reached the beachmaster's stateroom.

"I've got a good idea," Cory replied.

They knocked, entered on command, and closed the door after them. Hawk was waiting with Scotch drinks on his table. He passed them out.

"Just as I thought," Cory said grinning.

"Cheers," Hawk said, "to the promotions of two ensigns." They clicked glasses.

"A question," Scorch said with a puzzled look. "How did you smuggle the liquor aboard?"

"Gash never let you in?"

"I took you at your word," Gash said, "that it was not to be general knowledge."

"I'm impressed. The fact that you kept it even from your closest buddy tells me you are a man to be trusted. Well, I'll let you in on the secret, too, Scorch, assuming you can also be trusted with showing the proper discretion."

"Nothing goes beyond this room, sir."

Hawk took a long sip. "I suppose I should first lay the foundation. When I graduated from Wharton Business School back in the Roaring Twenties, I headed straight to Wall Street. Times were booming and I discovered scores of suddenly rich people chomping at the bit to buy stocks but not knowing beans about the market. So I opened the first investment-counseling agency. Others quickly followed. The timing couldn't have been better. One could throw a dart at the financial page and whatever was hit was a sure winner. No brains needed. Now for the denouement." Hawk took a long sip of Scotch for the dramatic effect. "Walking to my office one day in September of '29, I had the

'Road to Damascus' experience. In a blinding insight I saw the bubble bursting on the Exchange. So I quietly advised my clients, the only agent to my knowledge to do so, to sell. When the market collapsed, I was dubbed the Wizard of Wall Street, which was no better moment to sell out. Being a man of modest needs, I retired entirely from the workforce, bought a seafaring yacht, and vacationed a major part of the year on the beautiful isles in the South Pacific. By the time the war with Japan exploded on the scene, very few living souls had more familiarity with the lands beyond the hula skirts. I was a cooked goose. When the navy tracked me down, my only recourse was to bargain. One of my successes was full immunity from stateroom inspection." Hawk smiled. "Hence, my closet stays well stocked with no possibility of confiscation. This knowledge is shared with very few, and I might add with careful selection."

"You've definitely earned the loot," Scorch said. "Gil heaps kudos on your action at Tarawa where he said you two worked the same beach."

Hawk sighed. "Gil was one of many who ran into very rough sledding there. I had hoped the navy had learned something from that ill-managed campaign but so far I haven't seen it. We made a lot of the same mistakes in the Marianas."

"Gil still doesn't talk about Tarawa," Cory said. "It must have been hell."

"It was the damn reefs. I was suspicious that the draw of the boats might be too deep and suggested a dummy raid to precede the invasion, but once the military is on a mindset, it's like trying to change the direction of a mud slide! We've also got to increase the prelanding bombardment. Three days is not enough. It doesn't knock out the beach guns. It still shocks me that our dead and wounded at Tarawa, an island no larger than Central Park, exceeded three thousand. Christ!"

Cory quietly finished his drink. "I wouldn't take your job, Hawk, for all the booze in Kentucky. Wave commanders are called the 'expendables' but beachmasters in my book are the suicide brigade. My hat's off to the bunch of you. I don't know how you do it. If I were commander-in-chief, I'd pin the Congressional Medal on you guys after directing traffic for just one day on a hot beach."

"Get the hell out of here, the two of you," Hawk barked. "If I spend any more time with you, I might get the big head."

As they entered Goat Castle, Scorch said to Cory, "Thanks for the Scotch-for-Scorch drink, old buddy."

Cory laughed. "You're thanking the wrong person."

"No. The toast was really for you, being Hawk's bridge partner. As your best buddy, I rode along on your coattail, which is okay with me. Say, that was some story Hawk told us."

"Like I've said before, the guy's a genius. Brilliant in everything he does."

"Sure glad he's aboard our ship."

"Not so sure about that."

"Whatta you mean?"

"The navy's figured out how competent he is, too. You can bet they'll have him in on the toughest invasions."

"Hadn't thought about that. Oh, by the way, Gash, there's a question I've been meaning to ask you. I can understand, of course, how a man with my impeccable record got promoted, but who's the guy in BUPERS that can get a man promoted who almost started a war with Mexico?" He ducked out of the room before Cory had a chance to respond.

Cory glanced at his watch and saw that he had time before the evening meal to write to Tally. With Hawk still much on his mind, he decided to make him the subject of the letter.

August 28, 1944

Dearest Mopsy,

I've told you about our skipper, his rags to riches climb on the navy ladder, and the ungodly coincidence that I'm the spit and image of the scoundrel who ran off with his Sunday daughter. Now I would like to introduce you to Commander Hawkins, best known as Hawk; who, in my estimation, is the most intriguing and brilliant officer aboard the *Hudson.*

A genius of the first water, he finished college in the early 1920s with a degree in finance, went to Wall Street, set up the first investment-counseling service, and was the rare bird who got his clients to sell before the market crash of '29. Still not out of his twenties, the guru of Wall Street sold his agency for top dollar, retired, and bought an oceangoing yacht. From then on he divided his time between the Seven Seas and an apartment on Park Avenue where he perfected his bridge skills to become a top tournament player.

His familiarity with the Pacific Islands—nobody more so— put him in demand when the war with Japan broke out. He agreed to the title of beachmaster in turn for several concessions, the main one being that the closet in his stateroom stays sacrosanct, free of inspection. He has it well stocked with the best of brand liquors, which he prefers to label medicinal restoratives, which he generously shares at judicious moments with a select few. I happen to be among the privileged because he chose me, pickings being as slim as they are aboard ship, for his bridge partner. He has reorganized my entire thinking about the game. To control greed from staining the picture, all of our winnings are put in his safe for a ship's victory party at the end of the war.

Now in case you might be wondering how he bargained so well with the navy, including a full commander's ranking, you have to understand the role of the beachmaster in the amphibious scheme of things. He goes in with the first waves and is in complete charge of the beach until it's secured. He coordinates the entire shore operation: organizes the evacuation of the wounded, the routing of supplies, the removal of bottlenecks, the deployment of reinforcements, and the defenses against possible counterattack. His decisions affect many lives, and they are often made under the stress of heavy enemy fire. Hawk's skills in these matters are, by themselves, in my opinion, worthy of the highest medal. But military decorations are generally given for wrong reasons and often to the wrong people. I'll expand on that viewpoint in another letter.

Outside of our skipper, Hawk is the only true sailor aboard

the ship. He can match Stoneface sea story for sea story. Hence, he's the only one invited topside for dinner. Hawk, by the way, was the one who alerted me to the horror that I was the double of the felon who whisked off the captain's daughter. Despite all of Hawk's efforts to defend my character, the skipper has stuck with his own criteria for spotting rascals. As Hawk quotes him: "For one thing," pacing lumberingly back and forth, "you can bet the farm they're light on their feet."

Darling, the dinner hour beckons. It's a flagrant breach of naval etiquette to pop in late at the table without an ironclad excuse, so I best close this pronto, adjust the tie, button the sleeves, and hit the wardroom at the striking of the hour. A barrelful of kisses.

Gash

☆  ☆  ☆

"Incredible," Laura exclaimed when Tally informed her that Ted was lined up for yet another surgery. "How many times has he been under the knife?"

"I've lost track. But all of the recent ones have been cosmetic. They've removed all the shrapnel they can from his chest. What they've done to repair his face has been remarkable. If you had seen him when I first came here, you would hardly recognize him."

"Debbie told me it was a modern miracle how they've reconstructed his face."

"The plastic surgeon still thinks he can make his jaws a bit more symmetrical. Imagine hearing talk like that!"

"What will he do after discharge?"

"His latest idea is to return to work at the bank as the first step in patching up his marriage. This also bothers me. I know how much he hates inside work. I'm afraid it'll start the tensions up between them again. I suggested he go to school and develop some outside skill, like surveying. But he seems fearful of venturing into something new. So unlike his former self."

Tears welled up in Tally's eyes. "How his ego has shrunk. . . . Best I get on with my Sunday letter to Cory."

"And I think I'll practice on my typing, now that the house is spruced up for Debbie's return."

It was an unusually damp and cool night as Tally, donning her pearls, turned her thoughts to the man who knew they would be her favorite.

August 31, 1944

Dear Darling,

Tis a wet Sunday evening, raining most of the day. And a tiny mite chilly for this time of year. Perfect for cuddling. Why aren't you here? Give me the number of your CO.

Laura and I are home tonight, having worked like beavers tidying up the place. It's gratifying to have a clean house even if it does take a day like this to prompt us. She's practicing typing while I'm penning. She starts a job Monday as secretary to an insurance firm in the Bank of America Building.

Debbie wrote that she should be back tomorrow. She confesses she likes her husband, being queen of the understatement. Funny how you don't miss people until they're gone. Now, I think I've just made my understatement of the year.

Remarkable how fast the weekends go and then how slow the rest of the week passes. One of the ironies of life. If the whole week would go fast, your return would be that much sooner. Sometimes I awake with a chill because in my dream, time moved at a snail's pace. Uncanny! As hard as it is to express my feelings, how easy they betray me just at the mention of your name. Must be because I not only love you, darling, but because there's no one like you this side of heaven. Oh, would I know where you are tonight, if only to know you're out of harm's way. Should anything happen to you, I don't believe I could breathe.

Linda, a girl at work, and I moseyed out on the field yesterday to watch the planes land and take off. They never cease to fascinate me. Every time I see one I have a yearning to be up there. Didn't know I have an Amelia Earhart complex, did you? Maybe after the war I'll do something about it. How would you like to be buzzed from above? Hmmm. After work we got a wedding present for one of the girls in the group, and while downtown we dined and saw "Hollywood Canteen." Twas perfect for the mood we were in.

Susan and I had an inspiring evening on Friday. We had dinner and then heard the Don Cossack choir at the auditorium. They were absolutely magnificent.

It's enjoyable having free evenings again. No rushing about to get to work on time after a special event, and no urgency to go to bed right after work.

Ted called today to say hello. He's going up before the survey board tomorrow, can you believe, for yet another operation. He said to give you his regards.

We're having company next week. Friends of Laura's. An ensign and his wife will be staying a few days. Debbie will be back so we'll have a full house. Incidentally, our patient fully recovered and left several days ago.

The searchlights are on again. It's a big show as dozens of them are scattered about, making an impressive sight.

I cherish my pearls, Cory. I wear them just about everywhere. I adore the guy who was so thoughtful. I'm a very lucky girl, darling. Really, you should meet him sometime—truly a prince. Love and kisses,

Mopsy

Mondays, usually anticlimatic after the Sunday jamborees, did not follow the pattern this time. First of all, there was the excitement of Debbie's return from her truncated honeymoon. Tally stopped on her way home from work to buy an expensive bottle of wine for the occasion.

"I know," she said, "you'd much rather be in the company of the groom at this hour, but maybe some sips of vintage Madeira will help soften the disappointment." Debbie hugged her.

Over the wine, Debbie regaled them of the high drama of the breakneck pace required to get the license, find a preacher and a chapel, and the fast bribing to get a bridal suite. Then after all that came the heartbreaking shipping-out orders.

"With hindsight would you have done it differently?" Laura asked.

"No," Debbie replied emphatically. "I wouldn't have changed a thing."

Laura had cooked a special dinner, and the girls chatted well into the evening with a million things to catch up on.

The second highlight of the day for Tally was a letter from Cory. "I know it sounds silly," she said after waving its arrival, but the first thought that comes to my mind on seeing his handwriting is that he's still safe. I'm so grateful that I always want to write him as soon as possible."

She excused herself, collected her writing material, and began what seemed her zillionth letter to him.

September 1, 1944

Gash Darling,

How it warmed the heart to hear from you today! Surprised? All your letters affect me this way, fading everything, except our private little world, into oblivion.

In your gentle fashion, you raise some points which I need to address and not be too illogical. My darling, a third of a year has slipped by since our lips touched, rather quickly but not nearly as quickly as the six weeks you were in the area. How I wish we could have had more hours together, to know each other more intimately. I know how you feel about marriage. Something not to be entered into lightly, a total commitment, full involvement. While you say it best, I feel much the same way. To me it's the most important event of life. It would be for keeps. Having seen directly what wrecked marriages can do to families, I want more than ever to see my children grow up in their own loving home and be given the love and security which are their rights by birth. Darling, I could never marry anyone if I could not give myself fully to him, without doubts, without compromises, regardless of the circumstances. The true meaning of love is the one gift, and the greatest gift, you have given me. Once we talked briefly of war marriages and we both agreed, as I remember your words, their attractions do little for their longevity. Actually, we know little of the other because we took so little time to talk of anything but our feelings of the moment. I know we are not bound to each other; we have made no pledges, and are free to do as we wish with our lives. But inwardly, my freedom is in jeopardy because my heart beats in its own Morse code—I love you, I love you, I love you! The same message over and over in constant rhythm.

I've never really desired marriage before, but I had never felt towards anyone as I do towards you. I guess it's possible in the abstract for people to have more than one great love. However, I'm clear about my feelings for you, darling. I know for certain in the heart that I love you and could not share you with anyone else. If you should suddenly appear in the flesh tomorrow, my love for you would overshadow all else. You have all that I could ever want: intelligence, humor, compassion, a beautiful soul. I love your philosophy of life; not to mention, begorra, you're as handsome as the Irish has ever made them!

What I'm trying to say, dearest, and probably doing it poorly, is that while I know you love me, I want you in no way to feel that it carries with it any obligation. We have made no promises. I love you. That is my dowry. I want to give only happiness.

I believe in being loyal to one's ideals, be they popular or unpopular. And I believe our debt to nature is to try to restore the beauty we've taken from her, no matter how small. Sometimes the smallest things are the most beautiful.

So, here I go rambling on unable to keep from baring my soul to you. I hope, darling, you do get the gist of what I'm fumbling to say. Guess it all adds up to this: I love you, Cory, and as long as you want me, I'll be awaiting. Good night, sweetheart. I enclose all my love.

Mopsy

☆ ☆ ☆

In late September of '44, the *Hudson* dropped anchor at Pearl Harbor, and Gil Harvey was having a brief meeting with the officers of the Boat Division in the wardroom.

"Guys," he began in his characteristic way, "here's the dope. We'll be here only a couple of days to load up the holds and then set sail for the Solomons, stopping first at the Marshalls. We'll pick up troops and lead in the assaults on the Philippines. The specifics will come later. Any questions?"

Scorch spoke up. "Why the Philippines? We've got air bases in the Marianas, and they're a helluva lot closer to Japan than the Philippines."

"I'll refer that question to MacArthur." There was a ripple of laughter. "If no more questions, we adjourn, with the reminder that the last mail boat leaves the ship tomorrow."

Scorch walked out of the meeting with Cory. "Name me one advantage, buddy pal, of retaking the Philippines."

"It will lock up the naval blockade of Japan."

"Always the man with a positive. And how many body bags will it take?"

"War is ugly, Scorch."

There were sudden shouts on the main deck. "Can only mean one thing," Cory exclaimed. "The first mail boat's back."

Mail boat it was, and it was loaded. Scorch saw a big smile on Cory's face after mail call. "I see it from ear to ear," he joked, "that the chick's still falling for your line."

"If you'll pardon the pun, ancient mariner, it's a red-letter day. Three of them, no less, from the most gorgeous doll on the Coast. Now if you'll just give up the ghost for an hour, I'll shift my thoughts to a higher plane."

"Who am I to impede your struggle to conquer lust! If you see it's a losing battle, join me at the Betty Grable flick."

Cory looked long and lovingly at Tally's photo and then dreamily opened and read her letters.

September 8, 1944

Dear Darlin' Gash,

Devil that thee be! What happened when I opened your letter this morning but find you bragging on meeting a lady on an exotic island. Had me sharpening m'feline claws until you finally let slip it was a mock invasion, the lady was 90, toothless, and the island's only surviving inhabitant, standing her ground against 500 charging marines. What exactly do you mean that she brought me to mind!!! In spite of all the flattery, I still love you all the way from here to wherever that exotic island is.

While on the subject of putdowns, what's the idea of typing a letter and typing better than I! Stop giving me an inferiority complex. By the way, I recited your funny ditty to Laura and we both had a good laugh. She can't wait to meet you.

Yesterday was Sunday. Ted called at 7:30 AM, knowing I love the sunrise. This one was truly magnificent and it set the tone for the day. It displayed the full spectrum of colors. He joined me for breakfast and we took a nice long hike. He's finally beginning to cast a glow of health. I can't begin to count the number of operations he's been through.

We have a new driver. Mr. Hines found us a sweet little lady of 60, living only a block from us, to replace him as he's now a passenger in a different pool. We had our first ride this morning and she's loads of fun.

I seem to be caring less about going out these days. Must say though, the town is a haven for single girls, with guys available on every corner. But, for me, I impose a measure of comparison and—surprise, surprise—you always come out on top, darling. The evening starts out with a promise of fun and frolic, but as it progresses, you suddenly bubble up and all bets are off. You are so darn sweet, Cory. The day when the high tide drifts you ashore will be my happiest one.

Debbie and Laura are out riding. While writing, I have on the Firestone Symphony Hour. A full moon is out and the sky is clear. I'm counting the stars in anticipation of the kisses one day I'll collect. Cory, darling, I couldn't love you any more than I do. All yours,

Mopsy

Dear Darling,

I'm writing during the latter part of the lunch hour. The stationery rather gives away the setting. A threatened downpour broods outside. Most of us brought our lunch and are huddled inside, safe and dry. Tis a Friday, which is always welcome, for tomorrow begins the weekend.

We're all in a cheerful mood today in spite of the gloomy weather. The rain does seem to freshen things up, giving us more motivation for pushing the pencil. Usually we walk out on the field after lunching, but not today.

I can't think of anything to raise my spirits more than spending a few minutes with you. Linda is reading, which reminds me, I started "The Robe" about two weeks ago and am now on page 25. Woe is me, how my reading is getting neglected! Maybe I should try a different book.

Buck's making a file of some kind while keeping us amused with his philosophical lamenting. Enclosed is a little book he wrote. The lunchers are coming back. A fellow in the rear is bowing a violin and I love it. And in case you haven't got the word, I love you, too. Darn, there's the whistle; much rather remain in the fog with you. . . .

Later.

Just arrived home from work. Still drizzling and a fog is settling in. The kind of night to be with you, snuggling in your arms. Hmmmm.

Tis the night for art class. I'm learning much from it. We're examining the different ways artists express the same object, and we continue to focus on the human figure.

I think it's wonderful you're playing with the thought of writing a book. With your way with words, you'll never lose the reader. But how can you find the time for it now? I'm sure you'll think of a way.

And speaking of thinking, I was thinking what a terrible drain it must be on your family to have their only son so far from home. Please give me a report on them. I'd sure love to meet them, especially your mother and your big sister, Kathleen. Laura should be here any minute and so I'll stop and help

Debbie with the dinner. The two of them will be riding tonight. Laura has a new saddle to break in. She's been trying it on for size on the bannister.

The smell of food is overcoming me. Would you like to join the table? No mutton, I promise! I love you always,

Mopsy

September 15, 1944

My Darling,

A good morning to you! 'Tis another beautiful Sunday. The sun's come out to glisten the fallen raindrops. I called Ted and he's coming over for breakfast. Laura and Debbie are out riding again. They're on a three-hour jaunt to have breakfast with friends in the valley. Ted has to report back early, so I'll meet a girlfriend, Sally, for church and lunch.

Susan and I took in a movie last night. Too much war violence in it so we skipped the end. I don't want to think about you in that mode. The thought edges in anyway, too often, without having to watch movies on it. Susan picked up my anxiety and insisted we leave.

Later.

Little news to report, just to let you know my thoughts, darling, are of you. We've finished dinner and Laura and Debbie are worn out from bouncing in the saddle all day. Laura has her saddle on the floor and is trying to mobilize the energy to clean it.

Debbie and I have decided, in a flush of patriotism, to toast to "our men." To you, Cory, and the special person that you are. À votre santé! . . .

Much later.

What do you know! Monday's passed, Tuesday's not far behind, and know what else? 'Twas exactly six months ago today, m'darling, that we met—a whole half year ago that a love-tipped arrow found its mark from the bow of Cupid. Seems infinitely longer than that. Seems I've known you always. Was it you who kept appearing in my little-girl dreams after reading about the knights of the Round Table? I have said the war brought us together. At times I feel we would have met without a war. Fate is more powerful than clashing armies. The forces of destiny prevail no matter what. Do I sound like a sorceress?

Do you mind if I miss you just bunches, darling? Sometimes I can't help myself when I start thinking of how sweet and dear you are. Oh, just to see you once again! To be near you, to be in your arms, to be held tight, is worth an heirship.

Here I go, letting my heart run away with my pen. It's so easy to do, especially on one's sixth monthversary. My heart cries out, I love my darling ever so much. Please take care of him.

Just a colleen who's crazy about a mick with a touch of the kraut!

Mopsy

Cory replaced the letters in their envelopes, stored them in his special cigar box, and immediately started a letter to get it off in advnce of their next stop at Eniwetok in the Marshalls.

September 24, 1944

Dearest Mopsy,

Six months have elapsed since the prettiest colleen to ever set foot in San Diego scaled the Coronado dunes with none other than the notorious pirate Timothy "Black Beard" O'Reilly. The time sometimes seemed to him only six days; sometimes six years, so warped becomes the perception after endless hours on the high seas. However, the beautiful portrait on his desk ends speculation that it might have all been a hallucination brought on by too many sprays of salt water over his LCVP. Now, my Irish lass, should his ship ever take a cigar, I mean a torpedo, he shall bring the portrait with him in his lifeboat for solace. I trust you are gaining awareness of your indispensable role, even though the beguiling twinkle in thy eye might cause approaching sea-rescue ships to collide.

The denizens of Goat Castle keep flashing high-fives to you

on passing your picture in spite of my efforts at enlightenment that an angel would break a wing if she tried to stoop that low to recriprocate! Enough said of my cretin cronies!

I think I once mentioned my lack of enthusiasm over medals. This may seem rank heresy in a culture loving heroes. But, the simple truth is all that glitters is not gold. Let me give you two examples.

One day I happened to notice a highly decorated sergeant in my boat. I took him aside during a break and told him how lucky we were to have a man with his record in our company. He smiled weakly and said, in all truth, it's not all that it seems. He went on to describe his heroism. His platoon had scaled a hilltop with orders to hold it at all costs. They dug in. He soon realized they'd been cut off so retreat was no longer even an option. Through his binoculars he saw the build-up of Jap infantry and artillery. He did a life-review but most of his thoughts settled on a blonde waving farewell at St. Pedro Bay. He wished he'd spent his time a bit better with her. Suddenly, all hell broke loose, shells exploding everywhere. Then, all was silent. The dust of battle slowly cleared and as he peered cautiously out over his foxhole, he saw the hillside littered with dead Nips, cannons pulling back. He slowly pieced it together. The Japs had crossed signals. The infantry charged and then the artillery opened up. When the general arrived on the scene, he saw the slaughter on the hill, Old Glory flying on the crest, and a platoon of marines calmly enjoying a smoke. Sarge saw little to be gained in reporting all the facts, but figured a medal dangling on his chest might make an impression on a certain blonde in southern California.

By the same token, I had in the same boat a corporal busted to a private. I was finally able to draw out his story. It happened in the jungles of Bougainville. He had wondered off from his scouting party, got lost, and believing he was headed toward friendly lines, stumbled instead into an enemy detachment. Displaying quick wits, he burrowed under a fallen tree trunk, but to his horror, the unit decided to bivouac there for the night. His log became their sitting bench for the evening meal. He could easily reach up a hand and pat butts. Somehow, they had purloined a case of navy beans and mixed it liberally with their standard portion of rice. Unaccustomed to American cuisine, they spent the night breaking wind, yet he lay motionless until they broke camp at dawn. He eventually found his unit but got busted for absence without leave. Now, Mopsy, just how many in the entire U.S. armed forces do you think capable of holding their silence through a night of ants, mosquitoes, and exploding beans? The moral of the story, plain to see, is that the truly heroic acts most often go unrewarded in our system of values. Like I said, all that's gold doesn't glitter!

I best bring this letter to a close, darling, so that it can catch the next mail boat. Though it may be a little while before you hear from me, as sometimes we get a little busy training troops, it goes without saying that you're always in my thoughts.

Many XXX's to a colleen who's tops on my kiss list.

Cory

That evening the news spread like wildfire throughout the boat division. Hutch, the Mole, was doing handsprings on the quarterdeck. He had received sudden orders to report at once to the amphibious base in Coronado. He was soon deluged with phone numbers and addresses from men of all stripes and rank.

"Lucky stiff," muttered Hammock Harry, "how do you rate?"

The Mole puffed up. "Shows that there are some brains after all in the bureaucracy. Obviously, they have noticed my talents and are eager for me to be an instructor at the base." He pulled out a little red book he had purchased at ship's service. "Anybody you want me to contact?"

"My grandmother," Harry cracked.

"What do you make of it?" Scorch asked Cory on the side.

"Looks like we've all underestimated the Mole."

"Or that he knows somebody in higher circles that he's kept under hat."

Hutch's euphoria went unabated until the following morning. Scorch bumped into Cory supervising the loading of cargo at his hold amidship. "Have you heard what happened?"

Cory shook his head negatively.

"The Mole's orders were rescinded. Turns out he was the wrong Hutchins. And he had already packed."

"What state's he in?"

"Ready to kill. If you value your health or longevity, don't get within a ten-foot pole of him."

Cory chuckled. "This goes to prove what I've been saying all along. The Japanese propaganda boys have missed the boat. They have sultry-voiced Tokyo Rose on the air night after night bashing the fidelity of the American female, telling the GI that his sweetheart's in the arms of a 4-F while he's rotting in the jungle or upchucking on a rolling ship. Now, what red-blooded American male is going to buy that story, believe that his true love would pull a low trick like that! Maybe the other guy's gal might, but not his. Thus, Rose always brings on a good laugh. Now if she really wanted to start an epidemic of bodies overboard, all she would have to do is say: Guys, spread out the map of the Pacific. Stick a thumbtack where you are now, one on where you were six months ago, and one on Tokyo. Then prorate the number of years it'll take to reach Tokyo. Sad to say, when the war's over, Rose will likely hang on the gallows instead of getting a ticker-tape parade for bolstering American morale in the Pacific."

☆ ☆ ☆

It became Tally's wont to share with Debbie, Laura, and Susan the parts of Cory's letters not touching on the romance. She was closely secretive of the parts on intimacy, especially his love poems, which always charmed her vanity. The girls much enjoyed his vignettes on his fellow officers and his discursive reflections, like on love and the awarding of medals. "He has a way," Tally said, "of whatever topic he brings up of tickling my funny bone. I never get a letter that doesn't give me at least one good laugh. The Lord knows we can stand more of that."

"I noticed," Debbie said, "he never talks much about the war, even when censorship permits."

"War is ugly to him," Tally replied, "and ugliness has no place in his world. And, then, he seems to have imposed a mandate not to let my worry index jump off the chart."

"So," Susan grinned, "you and I go see a war movie."

"I doubt if either of us thought it would be so graphic. And I owe you bunches for insisting we leave before we got to the worst part."

"Regarding medals," Laura injected, "Chad feels as Cory does about them. I think medals mean more to those who've never been in combat."

"My brother Ted goes along with that. As you know, he gave his Purple Heart to me."

"It's the old story," Debbie said, "we crave for heroes and the need seems greatest in wartime. Every movie now has its hero who wins against all odds. We leave the theater purged."

"Well," Tally said smiling, "it's time for me to write to my hero. Cory's letters are always so interesting, even though he's confined to shipboard life, and mine, with the whole city of San Diego to draw on, are dull as dishwater."

"Guess what," Susan said, "I bet Cory reads every line with the gusto of a little boy eating ice cream."

"Amen!" Laura agreed. "I bet that holds for all the guys."

Tally laughed. "Susan sure has a knack for buoying up the ego." Tally picked up her writing material as the confab broke up and sank into her favorite chair.

September 29, 1944

My Darling,
    What a welcome relief Friday night is! Merely knowing that I might sleep in late if I wish is manna. I was set to spend a quiet, leisurely evening at home and what happens? Susan came by and we impulsively decided to go swimming at an inside pool.

Turned out to be refreshing and I'm glad we went. Susan is spending the night with us and we all had a nice gabfest on returning home. I now have some quiet moments to be with you.

It's a clear, starlit night, which always stimulates the thought of what you might be doing somewhere near the other side of the globe. By the way, darling, the snap you enclosed in your last letter fits perfectly in my billfold. Sure, and it shall remain there! Thank you so much. And how'd you guess I had just the right space for it! A sixth sense, no doubt.

We had an evaluation party at the art class. It's the annual exhibit and some of the oil paintings were outstanding. They made my charcoal, my pride and joy, look a mite forlorn beside them.

Last Wednesday I went riding with Laura and Debbie and being a bit out of practice, I pleaded to deaf ears the next day for a standing job. I was learning to post and caught on fairly quickly.

Oh, me, it came to me that whenever you are out of touch with the mails, my letters are likely to pile up. Thinking of the mental strain correctly reordering them will put on your faculties, I've decided to lessen the burden and number the envelopes in sequence. Seems I began this once before, but something happened after I passed digit one.

Tomorrow promises to be a busy day. Ted's coming in the morning and the rest of the crowd later. We'll probably play tennis or something equally foolish. But, what won't be foolish is that I'll be thinking of you, darling, with my every breath. I love you always.

Mopsy

Susan and Tally had planned a full agenda for Saturday: tennis in the morning, lunch downtown, a matinee in the afternoon, and dancing at the Square in the evening. Gusty winds nixed the tennis match.

The resourceful Susan suggested an alternative. "With a nice wind in our face, what a great day for riding! What say we get a gang together, go to the Hazelwood stables, and afterwards sit around a campfire, eat, drink, and sing the old songs?"

"Wonderful idea. Who'll be in charge of the picnic?"

"We'll ask the guys to come up with the food and we'll bring the drinks. If worse comes to worse, I'll finagle some hot dogs and marshmallows out of my folks."

It was a fun afternoon. Ten outdoorsy souls piled into two cars, reached the stables in midafternoon, and rode high-spirited stallions on trails until nearly dark. They then found a campsite on the outskirts of town, built a fire, and heated ribs and drumsticks that the guys furnished. The girls brought beer, and they all ended the active evening making sweet harmony.

"Oh, if only Cory were here," Tally whispered to Susan. "His beautiful tenor is exactly what we need."

It was a weary but happy Tally who returned to the ranch sometime after ten. She still had enough zest to write Cory of the day's fun.

September 30, 1944

Dear Darling,

Nope! I didn't do it! I didn't sleep late after all. Up, mind you, at eight o'clock, begorra, and do I ever feel I've cheated myself! Do you like to sleep late, darling? I'll bet you're one of those early risers, getting that active, fertile mind off and running. When I woke at the usual time, 5:00 AM, I sighed gently, closed my eyes, and stirred only when the sun struck the window. Only then did I jump out of bed.

Been a joyful day. A bit too windy for tennis, we packed a picnic lunch and went riding at the Hazelwood stables, two miles out of the city. It was midafternoon starting, but we got in a nice ride, returned about dusk, built a small campfire, ate, and burst our lungs singing. When the vocals wore down, we listened to music on a portable one of the fellows brought along. Oh, darling, how I wish I could have shared the shadows of night with you. It was such a grand feeling out in the country with the crickets and coyotes. Yes, they were howling far off. How your beautiful voice would have added to the festivities. Hmmm.

It's still early Saturday evening for most people, a little past ten o'clock, but to me it signals what I most welcome, time to float into the arms of Morpheus and dream of you, sweetheart.

Your Mopsy

A week passed. Laura, giving a quick and approving inspection of Tally who was dolled up ready for a ritzy evening, smiled as she said, "From drumsticks to quail under glass. Some difference between two Saturdays!"

A twinkle appeared in Tally's eye. "Diversity, my love, is the spice of life. Robert tells me that when Boeing puts on a bash, it's as big as their planes. They're the hosts tonight for an eight-course orgy, ranging from caviar to crepes. They've sent a couple of VIPs from Seattle to present slides afterward on their B-29 bomber. And there'll be, of course, an open bar the width of the banquet hall to usher in the activities."

"Robert is certainly giving you quite a sample of upscale living. The floor show is about all that's left, and that'll probably come next. What does Cory think of your dissipation?"

"I haven't mentioned the pact to him but I'm sure he would approve. He's made it clear that I shouldn't in any way put any restraints on my social activities. I've not written about the conspicuous-consumption orgies because it wouldn't seem right to flaunt a menu of fillet of tenderloin with Bordeaux before one on a diet of canned Spam and powdered milk. While the high life has its fascination, the truth is, Laura, if I had to make a long-term choice, it would be beer and drumsticks."

It was a large and noisy affair, filling the huge ballroom of San Diego's largest hotel. The smoking and drinking crowd soon created a haze so thick that eyes burned during the slides presentation. The moment it was over, Robert touched Tally's elbow. "Let's get out of here. I've had about all I can take."

"I'm ready," Tally responded.

Robert suggested as soon as they hit fresh air that they stop at a coffee shop since the night was still in its prime. Tally was all for it. They found one to their liking and took a back table where it was quiet and not crowded. When their order came, Robert induced Tally to go into more detail about Cory.

She animatedly told him of their meeting at the St. Pat's dance at the Coronado, of ducking out with him at intermission—a definite no-no for hostesses—and of their magical stroll along the beach into the wee hours of the morning. Although they've actually had very little time together before he went overseas, they write regularly and her heart has never beat quite the same.

"Love at first sight?" he asked.

"Head over heels," she replied. "But, enough of me. Let's talk about you. What are your plans after the war?"

"I'm getting out of big industry. I don't like the politics and I don't like the toadying to big cheeses. But as long as one is in the game, it only makes sense to play by the rules. So, I've decided to get out of the game. I will say that you have helped make playing the game much more palatable, and for that I'm most grateful."

"I've had fun, Robert, and your skills as an escort have put me at ease. But, like you, this kind of life is not my cup of tea. I have no desire of ending up a jaded dowager with a bloated liver. But, back to your plan. What do you think you will do?"

"Get into real estate. I see great opportunities. The secret of San Diego is a secret no more. Umpteen servicemen have been exposed to its ideal climate and will be pouring in to make it their home after the war. I'm predicting a population explosion. The housing industry will boom."

"You sound excited."

"I've already started taking courses. I'm doing it, of course, on the q.t. I should get my license in six months. I have enough of a nestegg for a nice office and for the expenses of getting started. I should be on the ground floor with the growing metropolis of San Diego. And, to boot, be my own boss."

"I think it's wonderful your life is so well organized."

"What are Cory's plans after the war?"

"He's still got some schooling left. Then, he's talking about grad school. The life of a college professor has appeal to him. Making money seems to be low on his priorities. But, of course, everything is still vague. Right now he's caught up too much in the war to focus on what comes next."

"Of course. And I admire the part he's playing. At times I feel I'm a slacker, having the good life while others of my age are pouring out the sweat in the trenches."

"Nonsense, Robert. It takes people in all kinds of settings to win a war. While people like you and me are out of the range of bullets, we're still making important contributions."

"Yours is a good attitude, Tally. Well, I suspect I've delayed you long enough. I'm sure you have loads to do, including correspondence, and I wouldn't want to hold you up."

"You are always thoughtful, Robert."

The usual soporific effect of cocktails hit Tally on arriving home and she went straight to bed. She had a big riding day scheduled on the morrow, and it would be Sunday night before she could finish the letter she had started on Friday.

October 5, 1944

Dear Darling,

The week is about over and it moved quickly, running on the same monotony of routine—working, sleeping, eating—all in all consuming the 24 hours I'm told we have in a day. Sometimes I have to stop and count them, thinking a few might have dropped by the roadside.

Susan and I are alone. We went shopping after work and just

traipsed in. We had a brief downpour without a moment's notice. Jolly fun! At first we tried keeping out of it, but it seemed to follow us into every doorway we found. When it started gushing up through the ends of our toeless shoes, we gave in and waded through. You should see us now trying to nurse our pretty, rationed shoes back into shape.

We were planning on going riding Sunday, but the wetness makes it doubtful. Laura and Debbie are out to dinner, but I'm satisfied to stay put. Of course, if you were here, I'd be ready to kick up my heels. As is, I'll settle for music on the radio.

The other night we went to the auditorium to see Paul Draper, a tap-dance artist, and the accompanist who played the harmonica. They drew a full house. They were top-flight.

A new road opened, cutting across town to Pacific Highway. It's great. We went over it for the first time today and reached home at 4:20 PM, a big time saver. We all made a wish (old wives' tale) driving over the new payment—sometime I may tell you what mine was.

Dad has been pushing for a visit. I'm due a vacation and with you so far away, it's worth mulling over. But, traveling is no cup of tea these days.

Oh, wonderful Friday night! Tomorrow we can sleep late. I'm going to bed with a book, "Magnificent Obsession," and then, darling, I'll dream of you all night long and hope your obsessions are magnificent, too. I love you. . . .

Sunday.

It turned out a fine day after all. When Debbie and I awoke this morning, the sun was shining across the foot of the bed, a welcome sight. Then, I glanced up on the dresser and smiled back at you, and the day was off to a wonderful start. This magic spell you have woven over me, darling, energizes me and pops me right out of bed.

We did go riding; the sun had dried all the wet spots. Ted came over at eleven o'clock, the rest of the gang at one. We rode till dusk. This time we took a different trail and discovered an old deserted house just waiting to be explored. The stairs collapsed under Paul, Susan's date. He fell half-way through and then got fully stuck. To top it off, he had the worst horse of the lot, which kept stumbling. But Paul had a good sense of humor and took it all in stride. Earlier, we had collected a little fire-wood for a cookout on our return. We were now famished. Twas a beautiful night, Cory. Our kind of night. The moon was out full. Hmmmmm. Oh, darling, our time shall come. We stayed until the embers died out and the batteries in the radio gave out. Meanwhile, the stables had closed and we couldn't call a cab. Guess what! We hiked four miles to the streetcar line. We cut through a hill, thinking it would shorten the distance. It extended it.

I'm bone weary and tomorrow starts another week of work. Our driver has taken the week off to move, so Debbie and I are taking the trolley in the morning. Wish us luck! Be good, dar-ling, my thoughts are with you always, and my love forever.

Mopsy

# *A Shellback Is Born*

Tally and Ted were having Sunday morning coffee. "I suppose I should give serious thought to a visit home," Tally said. "Dad's been pestering me, and I know he's not in good health."

"He'd love to see you. And maybe you could twist his arm to see a doc. He puffs like a steam engine after climbing a few steps. But when I suggested he get a checkup, he balked like a stubborn old mule."

"We're not a close family. I don't feel a real part of it. After a couple of days home, I know I'll be chomping at the bit. Now that Aunt Bess and Uncle Roy, who are the only ones I deeply care about, have moved to Wichita, I'd likely spend most of my time at my girlfriend Lois's home. Still, filial obligation gnaws at me to go."

"No question, we have a dysfunctional family. Yet, on the bottom line, we do love each other, so it's puzzling as to exactly what went wrong."

"The love is centripetal."

"Run that through again."

Tally laughed. "Guess I've never mentioned Cory's letter on the paradox of love, referring to its power to create or destroy. Since the head spins when one's in love, he borrows from the physics of spinning objects to unravel the paradox."

"Sounds interesting."

"According to physics, there are two opposing forces that act on a spinning object. One force, called centripetal, acts to draw the object toward its center. The other force, called centrifugal, acts to thrust the object away from its center. The stronger force prevails."

"With you, so far."

"So, centripetal love draws people toward themselves, making them selfish, self-centered, self-serving. On the other hand, centrifugal love thrusts people away from themselves, making them other-oriented, altruistic-minded, touting the common good. The stronger of the two forces determines the character of the love, whether it's outward or inward channeled."

"A clever analogy."

"The more I've thought about it, the more I see a fundamental truth in it. Applying it to our family, it's clear that self-interest dominates. Each one out for oneself. No one inclined to enter the world of others or care for their needs. That's centripetal love."

"Maybe that's what went wrong between Jenny and me. We're centripetal. I want things my way; she wants them her way."

The phone suddenly rang. Tally returned in a few minutes, a smile on her face. "You won't believe this! Talk about mind reading! That was Pat, our brother-in-law. He's in town unloading his truck, will be heading back to Denver in a couple of days and wondered if anyone would like a lift. I told him there's a good possiblity and to check back before leaving."

"Fate has decreed it."

"This seems to be as good a time as any. Pops was just saying the other day that we're between contracts and work will be slow for a while. With little to do, I'll be a wreck trying to keep my mind off of Cory getting ready for another invasion, this time the Philippines."

"Now, how would you know that? Censorship is very tight on these matters."

"I'm becoming an expert reading between the lines. I also think I'm developing a sixth sense about Cory. The word I believe is telepathic."

"All right, my crystal-ball sister," Ted said with a touch of sarcasm, "get honest and tell me just how you arrived at the notion he's heading for the Philippines."

"In his last letter, he said life is busy aboard ship. It's dull and boring unless it's preparation for an invasion. He also said they'll be training troops. He didn't say marines. So it must be army. That means MacArthur and the Philippines."

Ted threw up his hands. "I give up." He rose to his feet. "I'm going back to the hospital. Let me know what you finally decide."

Tally dropped by the hospital to give Ted the latest scoop on Tuesday. "Saw Pops yesterday and he was most cooperative. He said this was the perfect time to take leave because work is caught up and will be for some time. He immediately started the paperwork and completed it today. I can take up to a month if I wish. So, big brother, since Pat's picking me up on the dot of eight in the morning, I best be on my way to pack a couple of suitcases." She gave Ted a big hug. "I'll pass on your best regards and give you a full report on my return, which will probably be in a couple of weeks." Tally bounded off.

☆ ☆ ☆

Cory strided into Goat Castle where the gang was loitering before dinner. "Well, guys," he said, "I just talked to the navigator. October eighth is the day."

"The inscrutable oracle speaks," Scorch cracked. "Just what is supposed to happen on the eighth. An eclipse?"

"The shellback certificate, my dimwitted polliwog."

"So that's the fateful day we cross the equator," Gooseneck piped up. "May Providence keep the rites civilized. All we need are a few broken heads!"

"Never know about these things," Scorch said. "All it takes is for a hairbrained smartass to ruffle the feathers of a crusty old shellback to let the tiger out of his cage."

"The smart thing to do," Cory said, "is to take a business-as-usual attitude for the day and let the chips fall as they may." He then added, "But who expects the smart thing to happen with this wild bunch!"

By the time the boatswain piped general quarters on the morn of the eighth and everyone was settled at his battle station, the word had been passed from bow to stern. Fisheyes, chief electrician, a crusty old shellback, had been attacked in his sleep, bound, blindfolded, and stripped of his wax-tipped handlebar mustache with several swift swipes of a razor. All aboard ship were fully aware that the mustache was Fisheyes's cherished symbol of masculinity.

"I can't believe even a cretin would do this—rile up an electrician," Cory gasped. "This means all-out war."

A more accurate prophesy has never been made. No ship that floated the high seas, barring piracy or mutiny, had a scarier day than the *Hudson* on that special trip into the South Pacific. The strongest of the initiates could barely crawl to his bunk when the curtain of night fell. Sickbay overflowed. Cory was motivated by a special incentive to endure. He knew awaiting his survival would be Hawk's restorative. After getting amply replenished, he stacked his bunk with borrowed cushions and wrote Tally of the day's massacre.

October 8, 1944

Dearest Mopsy,

This was the day I shed my polliwog skin for a shellback hide. Here is the story, if I can muster the strength.

In time, sailors in Balboa's ocean are certain to cross zero latitude, better known to landlubbers as the equator, that invisible line separating the hemispheres. The physical insults that transform polliwogs into shellbacks can have side effects not unlike the aftermath of a torpedo hit.

Hearts raced when the order came for us to join a task force assembling in the South Pacific. As we approached the moment of truth, a predawn incident occurred that forever unbalanced the scales of sanity. Several polliwogs sneaked to the bunk of Shellback Fisheyes, a chief electrician whose concept of masculinity never progressed beyond a meticulously groomed, wax-tipped handlebar mustache. Slipping a pillow case over his head with a cutout for the mouth, they pinned down his arms, and with an adept use of the razor, left not a trace of his coveted symbol of virility. The tone was set. In deference to your dainty sensibilities, I shall be circumspect in describing the carnage that followed.

The booming PA system announced that the uniform of the day for polliwogs was athletic briefs and sweat socks. Jock straps were advised but optional. We assembled at the barbershop to have our heads and eyebrows shaved. After a tar shampoo, a hair piece of goose feathers was set in place. No goose ever looked so ridiculous! The call for polliwogs on deck came at high noon. The sun blazed directly down (confirming zero latitude) as we went through *warming-up* exercises, such as running in place for 15 minutes, 50 pushups, and 100 sit-ups. Then, on hands and knees we began scrubbing down the hot steel deck with thin-bristled toothbrushes. Fisheyes, who had spent the morning perfecting a phallic symbol that shoots beams of high voltage and low amperage (maximum shock with minimum burn), stood behind us jabbing away most indiscriminately. If you can picture hopping jack rabbits in goose wigs pushing a quarter-inch-wide brush back and forth on scorching steel, you've captured the quiddity. To soothe parched throats, kippers on salty soda crackers were rammed between baked lips.

Saved for very last was the ever popular gauntlet run. Drawing on our last ounce of reserve, we crawled on hands and knees through the spread legs of shillalah-wielding shellbacks to kiss the greasy fat belly of King Neptune to receive the treasured Certificate of the Deep. Those beyond responding to Fisheyes's stimulant were carted off to sickbay. The rest of us, somehow still showing flickering signs of life, made it back to our quarters under our own steam and let a salty shower on wounds revive us. If the enemy had opened fire, I know of one ship that would've gone under without a return volley. And where was Stoneface during all of the fun? He was on the bridge, deadpan throughout, vicariously revenging the S.O.B. who stole daughter fair.

But, my princess, all is well that ends well. The enemy has not attacked, the injuries all appear superficial—not one of the

200 bones X-rayed was broken—and reliable ol' Hawk came through with his patented restorative. And now I shall lay me head on me pillow and let sleep conquer all. Love you,

Cory

Within a week the walking wounded had healed, the task force had formed, and the invasion plans had been outlined. Cory was in Hawk's stateroom following an evening of bridge. Hawk was unusually complimentary. "Your game's getting solid as a rock, Gash. The only goof tonight was the hand in which you opened with a spade. Had it been a heart, we'd have set them. So, I would say you are no longer an apprentice but qualify as a full-fledged journeyman. I'd be happy to introduce you to tournament bridge after the war."

"Kind words, Hawk, but, as you know, I've still got more schooling to finish up when this mess is over. That is, if it's ever over!"

"Don't be impatient. We're getting there. After the Philippines it's just a couple of more islands before the big one."

"Are you expecting a tough landing in the Philippines?"

"Hardly. With over seven thousand islands, there's way too much waterfront to protect. Manila will be the tough one. Here's another piece of consoling news. The general's planning to set ashore at Leyte. I doubt if they'd let him step on a hornet's nest. So this one, Gash, should be a piece of cake. Still, put away extra victuals because it'll be a long day. Plans call for landing sixty thousand troops on the first day alone."

"Three divisions. Fantastic. Well, getting near watch time. Stash away the loot, Hawk."

The invasion off the east coast of Leyte on October 20 went off as scheduled. Major elements of the Sixth Army hit the beach with light resistance. Hammock Harry was not so lucky. His boat took a howitzer shell on lowering the ramp. He died instantly, the first loss in the boat division.

Great fanfare took place early in the afternoon. About four hours after the first waves landed, the general strided ashore with his entourage. Before a passel of photographers, he delivered a terse statement of arrival. The message was flashed from shore to ship: "I have returned."

It was twenty-four-hour duty for the boat division, rushing in troops and supplies and keeping lanes cleared for heavy equipment. The initial goals were met. Some sixty thousand troops landed the first day. The beachhead was rapidly secured and Hawk's work was over. He returned to the ship wearing a big smile. "Like I said," he commented to Cory, "it was a piece of cake. With early control of the sea and sky, we met only token resistance. However, I heard we lost a man."

"Hammock Harry. He must have had a premonition. Asked me the other night to write his mother should the bells toll. This will be tough. He was their only child, you know."

"Better get used to it. Don't mean to sound callous, but from now on there'll be no pieces of cake. The last push will be a donnybrook. But, our work's done here. As soon as we dump our ammo and load up with the wounded, we move on out."

But what should have been routine wasn't. Three days later the *Hudson* was still in Leyte Gulf stuck with its ammo. Operations on the beach were more fouled-up than organized. It was clear that Hawk was no longer running the show.

Then the war horizon suddenly darkened. Reports of an approaching Japanese fleet put all ships on the alert. A navy show-down battle was taking shape off Leyte. The Japs were in a make-or-break mood. They threw the works—battleships, carriers, cruises, destroyers, subs—into the fray, and for three days the biggest battle in the annals of naval warfare raged, the *Hudson* a spectator on the periphery, witness mostly to dogfights between

Zeros and Hellcats, which, nevertheless, kept the men at their battle stations round the clock. It was a crushing defeat for the Japanese, the end of their navy, including the sinking of their "indestructible" dreadnought *Musashi*. The tonnage loss, heavy on both sides, was ten to one in our favor. The ammunition still remained aboard the *Hudson*.

The lack of sleep was beginning to affect all hands, but the boat division, with ship duties as well as amphib duties, felt it most. Scorch spoke the feelings of the group. "Let's dump the damn ammo in the drink and get the hell out of here. Another night without sleep and we'll all be having bats in the belfry."

Cory mustered up a grin. "Some dudes never catch on that the barrel of a gun makes a good leaning post for a catnap. I've got the feeling Stoneface won't be hanging around here much longer. Wouldn't say he's the most patient skipper in the fleet. He'll deposit the ammo one way or another."

Then as tensions began to relax, a new menace clouded the picture. The Japs sprung the kamikaze, the suicide plane. The sky suddenly swarmed with all types of obsolete aircraft loaded with explosives and with just enough fuel to reach the target area. They came in low under radar detection, down through cloud protection, and in a straight line. There was no pattern. Damage was severe. A sister ship to the *Hudson* sank in eighteen minutes. Bone-weary gunners again manned their guns round the clock, so groggy that they fired at everything in the sky. Many American planes were shot down. Chaos reigned.

The skipper had seen enough. He sent Lockhart, the communications officer, ashore with instructions not to come back until the army took the ammo. Ironically, an order for it came soon after he left the ship. And turning the irony to tragedy, a 'kaze hit the shore installation, killing Lockhart as he was stepping inside the makeshift facility.

"Now what?" Scorch said to Cory on hearing the news. "The ammo's gone, we're leaving in the morning, and no com officer."

"No time for a replacement," Cory said. "The skipper will have to appoint someone temporarily until we reach port, and the whole crew's dead tired."

"Who could he posibly choose?" A diabolical grin appeared on Scorch's face as he looked Cory squarely in the eye.

Cory flushed. "No, not on your life! Stoneface wouldn't do that. Taking anyone from the boat division would be pure sadism. Especially me who doesn't know beans about communications. Hell, I've never even been in the shack. All I know is the Morse Code which we learned in midshipman school. No, Stoneface would be plumb out of his mind to even consider selecting me."

"Of course. He's much too savvy to do a dumb thing like that. But, then, didn't he appoint you recorder for the summary court-martial board and a gunnery officer on a forty millimeter?"

The PA system suddenly blared. "Mr. Zigler, please report at once to the bridge. Mr. Zigler, please report to the bridge."

Cory looked at Scorch. "No!"

Scorch looked at Cory. "It can't be."

A half-hour later Cory returned, his face ashen. Three words escaped his lips. "He did it."

Scorch's grin reached from ear to ear. "You're the new com officer?"

"Stoneface was adamant. He refuted every argument for incompetence, asking what's new on his ship. I told him I'd never been in the shack. He said I will now. I stressed I never coded a message in my life, and he asked if I had passed sixth-grade reading. Finally, I told him I hadn't slept in a week, and he replied, 'who has?' I tell you, Scorch, this is a nightmare. I've got the manual, the size of the Bible, to read and digest before morning. The captain assured me my relief will be the first item of business the moment we hit port. All that can save us from calamity is fair weather and a sleeping enemy."

"I think I'll sleep in my life jacket." Scorch was still grinning.

☆ ☆ ☆

To Tally's amazement, her visit home lasted a month. Part of the time was spent in Wichita to see her Aunt Bess and Uncle Roy, and a good part of the time was spent in Denver at the home of her good friend Lois. The remaining time was spent with her family. Her first act on returning to the ranch in San Diego was to drop off her suitcases and head directly to the hospital to give her brother a full rundown on her trip.

"Now that it's over," she said in conclusion to Ted, "I admit I'm glad I went. It was good seeing old friends. The only letdown, which was no surprise, is that the family hasn't changed. All going their own way. No closeness. I did have a warm feeling toward Dad, finally getting to know him after all these years. And you are right, Ted, he's in bad health, but in denial. He claims it's just overwork and now that he has a nest egg, he'll ease up and regain his strength. When I suggested that he see a doc, he snapped he'd rather see an undertaker because he can't do any harm."

Tally then left, telling Ted she had yet to begin unpacking. At the ranch Debbie and Laura greeted her with big hugs. Seeing her tired look, they suggested she wait till the morrow to tell them the highlights of her trip. They didn't get any argument from her.

After taking her suitcases to her room, the first thing to catch Tally's eye was a letter on her pillow. Recognizing the handwriting, she jumped with joy in the awareness that another invasion was over and Cory was safe. She read the letter slowly, devouring every line as it had been so long since she last heard from him. Tired though she was, the poem he enclosed was like a shot of adrenalin and stimulated her to dash off a reply before the sandman took over.

November 6, 1944

Gash Darling,
   Begorra, it seems ages since I last wrote and I guess it has been. My paltry excuse is that I've been home the past month. A

month that went so swiftly that now that I'm back, I hardly realize I was gone at all.

Darling, how happy I was to be greeted by your letter on return, which tells me another crisis over there is over. And you composed a beautiful poem for me. It's absolutely precious, one of your finest, and I shall keep it always in my heart.

I didn't have my mail forwarded since I hadn't planned on being in Denver more than two weeks. I was toying with the thought of going on vacation ever since hearing of my dad's declining health. Well, my brother-in-law phoned from Los Angeles and invited me to ride back with him. On the spur of the moment, I decided to go, and in a truck of all things. Twas a new experience for me and although the trip was slow, it was not as bad as I feared. We stopped the first night in Las Vegas, a wide-open town. During the better part of the next day, we challenged the mountains of Utah, reaching Salt Lake City at night. We ran into snow, which made me feel nostalgic. The first I've seen since leaving Colorado. We struggled two days in freezing rain before entering Denver. From there I took a train to Wichita to visit my favorite aunt and uncle. It was so good to see them, Cory, that I had a hard time getting away. I returned to Denver the following week and was on a frenetic pace, like having wings flitting from place to place. I stayed mostly at my good friend Lois' home. Dad is staying in a hotel. He hadn't been feeling sparky so I convinced him to take a couple days off and see a doctor. He nixed my suggestion of spending some time with me in California. I saw quite a bit of my younger sister since she's not working. We didn't really fuss the whole time I was home, a record. Also saw my younger brother, who's about to sprout wings, and my older married sister. That's the family, darling. I wish we were close, like one big happy family, but we're not. We all pretty much lead our own separate lives—each one quite different. Ted and I are the only really close ones. I hope my children will grow up knowing the true meaning of a home. Oh, but they shall. I guess there is virtue in learning to accept things as they are. In fact, I have so much more to be thankful for than most people, and most of the time I'm aware of that. At any rate, I do know I'm glad to have had a vacation and am equally glad to be back here in the confines of good ole San Diego.

Darling, I'm in a particularly devilish mood tonight. Come, my prince, and let me practice my satanic spells on you. ABRACADABRA. You are now in my power. I will appear each night in your dreams and give instructions you'll be helpless to resist. So beware!

In case my handwriting appears unnatural, fear not, I haven't had a stroke. I'm trying to write this letter on my lap on the bed and both my pen and thoughts are bouncing all over the place.

I do miss you so much, darling. Now, if you take the next ship home, I'll be on the dock, begorra, smelling like a wagonload of alfalfa. Meanwhile, I'm going to read the poem again and then fall asleep loving you with all my heart. Yours forever.

Mopsy

"Well," Tally said laughingly as Robert escorted her into the Coronado Hotel for a cocktail party, "what have I missed in the month I was gone?"

"Very little. Being election time, it was mostly boring political shindigs. Like today, it's a victory party for the Democrats." Robert grinned. "My company supports both parties so we can't lose."

"Roosevelt wins big again. Let's see. He succeeded Lincoln, didn't he? My father was very secretive about his voting. I remember as a little girl asking him if he voted for Roosevelt or Hoover. With a wry smile he said he voted for the man with two o's in his name. Is FDR beatable?"

"The person who might be as popular would be the man with the squashed hat and corncob pipe. MacArthur's profile is splashed all over the papers these days."

"Cory was in that invasion. And here we are in the Coronado, the hotel where we first met. I think I shall have a martini, his favorite cocktail, in celebration."

"Two dry martinis," Robert ordered. He clicked glasses. "To a man after my own tastes."

"Skoal," Tally said with a twinkle in her eye.

Robert watched her take a healthy sip. "Easy on the olive." He smiled. "We don't want you dancing a jig on the table."

"I promise I won't embarrass you. I get sleeply before I get drunk. Remember!"

While Tally was later able to walk in a straight line to the car, she was too sleepy to write Cory that night. As it turned out, it was Friday at work before she started her letter, justifying the use of company time on that it was not only a slow day but that it was the eighth monthversary of the magic meeting.

She debated if she should bring up the pact with Robert, but again nixed the idea in fear it might be flaunting a feast before one reduced to a Spartan diet. Never mention cake when there's a shortage of bread. The letter took a couple of days to finish.

November 17, 1944

Dearest Darling,

Writing at work and why not! It's our eighth monthversary, two-thirds of a whole year. How much I miss you, Cory.

Concentration is affected by the noise and confusion of the workers above us who are scraping black-out paint from the overhead windows, the official recognition that the threat of a Japanese invasion is over. Hooray! What joy to be working in genuine daylight again. It's a lovely day outside, the kind of day which always gets me wandering about the globe with you.

We're taking the streetcar to work this week because our driver is on the rest of her vacation. The people on the trolley are unusually friendly and cheerful. In the few days Debbie and I have been aboard, they recognize and speak to us. Getting into the Thanksgiving spirit, I guess.

Gosh, my mind's been flitting on many things lately. Even thinking about school after the war—providing I can make myself settle down. I wish it would have been possible long ago, but perhaps I still can. What do you think, darling? I'm also wondering if I should go back to Denver and be with dad since he continues to be under the weather. My ideas keep jumping from one thing to another, and not lighting too long on any one.

The excitement of my vacation has finally worn off and life is back to normal and running smoothly again. I've rejoined the mass of workers. Susan went with me to art class last night and afterwards we coffeed and chit-chatted. She would like me to move down to the club where's she's staying, but I'm still much undecided as to what I want to do.

By the way, shellback, have you fully recovered from the initiation? Sounded like a day to remember. Your description of the events couldn't keep me with a straight face. I know it was brutal, but I'm sorry, you have a way of tickling my funny bone.

There goes the first whistle so I must stop for the moment. My thoughts are especially with you on this very special day. . . .

Sunday.

What a perfect time to be with you! Tis my favorite day and I have the house all to myself. Laura and Debbie are at the horse show in Green Valley, having taken off quite early, before I relieved myself from my "boudoir." I had planned on seeing Ted, but he had to report to his doctor, which cancelled that.

Went to church after he called, prayed for your safety, and am now squandering the remainder of the day cleaning and mending, which has fallen behind schedule—and ironing.

I just reread your last letter on the hazing. You know you have my full sympathy, but your storytelling of it is a riot. Darling, it's wonderful to know your sense of humor hasn't weakened over these horrible months. We've been cheated of a big hunk of time, but if we can somehow survive what still lies ahead and get you back in one piece, we'll take the time to catch up for the lost months. I sometimes get frightened looking ahead at a world changing so fast and moving in such strange directions. I look to you to keep me in balance because I don't believe I came into the world "guaranteed" to be a wholly rational being. The waiting for the world to straighten itself out becomes more tolerable when there's someone in particular worth waiting for. I count every day that you are gone, darling.

A fall chill is in the air so I lit the fireplace and am curled up in front of it. The soothing piano music of Satie is playing on the radio. I close my eyes and imagine what a thrill it would be to open them and look into your blue eyes and run my hands through your curly hair. Oh, dear heart, I love you so much. All my love always.

Mopsy

☆ ☆ ☆

Scorch and Cory were having a warm beer after a pick-up game on the makeshift diamond in Ulithi in the Carolines, an island spared of war as it was evacuated a month before our first troops arrived. "We haven't got a bad ballclub," Scorch commented.

"Pitching's the name of the game," Cory replied, "and we've got a good one in Gil. He throws the heat over ninety miles an hour. I asked him if he thought about pro ball after the war, and he said he'll be too old for that."

"To change the subject, I assume you're planning to inform Tally of your brilliant performance as a com officer. It might do wonders to correct her distorted perception of your value to the navy, especially, if you let it be known we'd now be at the bottom of the sea scraping barnacles off the ship if the flag had waited for your SOS before sending a destroyer to us."

Cory grinned. "I'd rather tell her there's a mouse in her petticoat! Man, if she heard that a sub had its periscope on our ship, she'd be a year on the shrink's couch. And, wise guy, considering what percentage of my brain was still alive after all that sleep loss, I'd rate my performance superior just in finding the coding machine. . . . Say! The mail boat should have returned and I'm betting on some letters from Tally. Let's head back."

Indeed, three letters awaited Cory on getting aboard ship. One roused a tinge of nostalgia as it was written on Thanksgiving Day, the holiday he always remembered for his mother's exuberance, who, as an avid reader of early American history, would cap the day reminding the family of the reasons why they should be thankful to be Americans. Cory plopped on his bunk and entered his beautiful world of Tally's letters.

November 20, 1944

My Darling,

A terrific wind is blowing. You should hear our windows rattle. Sounds as though they may shatter into pieces at any moment. Some cardboard boxes we piled out back have long since sailed up the street. Hmmmm. Wish you would blow in.

I have art class tonight and am eager to go in spite of the weather. I'm into my first pastel and I'm fired up. Susan is planning to go with me. Class ends next month and I want to get in as much work as possible. Mr. Gilbert gave us a lecture on Chinese art last night. I'd like to study it when I have more time to devote to the fine arts.

Debbie's down at the barn having a jumping lesson and Laura has yet to return from work. Her horse, Star, took a third and fourth in the horse show Sunday and Lash took a second. We were laughing this morning realizing the only time we seem to see each other is during our pajama parade, which we stage every morning and night.

I finished "Magnificent Obsessions" today. Quite an accomplishment for me, much as I enjoy reading. Seems I started it sometime in September. Cory, darling, could I send you anything to read or, for that matter, anything at all? You know, my Lord and Master, your wish is my command. If there is *anything* you would like, let me know, huh!

Jeepers, I'd do anything to be with you. Can't you see me scrubbing the deck! Toting the pail!

One of the girls in our group invited us to the christening of her four new Siamese kittens. They are preciously tiny.

Incidentally, by the way, in passing, and in closing, I love you, I love your poems, I love every beautiful bone in your body, and, sure, I love resigning myself to the spell you weave over me. Forever and ever, darling,

Mopsy

Hello Darling,

Thanksgiving has slipped up on us. How about a turkey date? Can't be, I know, but I hope, darling, the navy has at least a plateful of goodies awaiting you wherever you are.

A couple of dinner invitations fell through for a variety of complicated reasons, so a group of us made reservations downtown for munching turkey. The girls are taking in a show tonight but I declined. I selfishly decided to curl up in front of the fire, relax, catch some good music, and dream of the one I love. A Beethoven concerto is fitting beautifully into my mood.

Darling, I do have so much to be thankful for. I've made good friends in San Diego; I enjoy my work; Ted is going to survive his wounds; but most of all, you have come into my life. I've read about love, heard people talk about love, had some flirtations, even experienced a couple of serious affairs, but nothing remotely compares to the passions you stir. Not many women know the true depth of love because very few men can tap the heart so deeply. That I have met one of such gentility makes me eternally thankful. I bare my soul to you, as I've declared so many times, in ways I could never possibly do to anyone else. Oh, happy Thanksgiving, my dear darling, wherever you may be, and God keep you safe in the dreadfully scary months ahead. You'll flood my dreams tonight.

As our song goes, I'll be loving you always with a love that's true always. Not for just an hour, not for just a day, not for just a year, but always.

Mopsy

November 25, 1944

Gash Darling,

Tis Sunday again and the sun shines. The air is a bit brisk, but I enjoy it. Took a little walk with Ted and I told him about your initiation. He passed on some of the devilish things that happened to him on crossing the equator. Dear darling, I suspect the bruises were painful.

Susan and I visited Mr. Gilbert the other night. He's doing a huge mural for the "Y" and has a year's work ahead of him. I'm glad for him because he's so talented. Susan's coming over for tennis. Do you like the sport, darling? We enjoy the game.

Want you to know I walked clear home from town the other night after visiting Mr. Gilbert. The evening was so lovely; you were the only missing part. I got to wondering why and what this crazy world is all about and guess I'll never really know. But, still I always try to do what I feel in my heart is right. Excuse me, there's some commotion outside. . . .

Later.

What do you know! It was Susan and the gang. After thinking I'd kept it to myself, I may as well have shouted it to the whole world. Today I'm 22. It was a big surprise and lots of fun. We played tennis for a while and then returned home for a feast. We ended up with that stuffed, holiday feeling. Laura and Debbie joined in and the evening passed in chatter and game playing. Oh, happy day! It's a warm feeling to know there are so many thoughtful friends about.

Tonight I'm a mite weary. It's ten o'clock and I'm ready to turn in. But, first, let me tell you about my wonderful yesterday. I heard from you, darling, not one letter but two. I wish I had the words to match the emotions within me. Would be easier to catch the words of the wind and the trees. You, Cory, of poetic heart, must have a glimmer of what is beyond my ability to express. I only understand that I love you terribly much. With all my heart, I'm yours for keeping.

Mopsy

After doting on Tally's warm, loving letters, Cory carefully stored them in his cigar box, which was getting close to full so regular has been her correspondence. He wished he could claim the same consistency, but long periods of sleep deprivation simply diminishes efficiency. Would she understand? How could she?

Even when conditions return to normal, the graveyard watch and the battle-station watches every morning and night keep the sleep patterns irregular, making impossible any buildup of energy reserve. He was still feeling the lag effects of the last invasion as he picked up his pen, determined in spite of his exhaustion, to dash off a letter. If Scorch was jokingly concerned that Tally had him, Cory, on a pedestal, he needn't worry further, he laughed to himself, once she receives this hodgepodge of thought.

December 10, 1944

Dearest Mopsy,

I'm dog-tired. Ratchet that up a notch. No dog's been this tired. Too little sleep over too long a time. If I can string words together to make a sentence and stop when the sentence is made, chalk it up a miracle. But knowing you, a run-on sentence is better than no sentence at all!

The days have blurred. Hard to tell one from another. Also memory's playing tricks. One moment it seems I was in college yesterday; the next moment it seems it was in another lifetime.

Ah yes, the college days! They bring to mind the goose. The goose, you know, has no past or future. Each day is a brand-new day. So it was in the rah-rah days. We lived for the day. Never thought about yesterday, couldn't care less about tomorrow. The goose, the happy-go-lucky goose, dear Mopsy, was our model, our idol, our hero.

The war has killed the goose. Take Goat Castle. Eavesdrop and you'll hear nothing but stories about the good ol' days or frets about what's coming next. Nothing on the present. Isn't that what old age is all about—reliving yesterday, ignoring today, fearing tomorrow. War makes one old before one's time.

But your letters, mavourneen, talk happily of the day. This makes you still a goose. Whoops! Scratch that. What I mean, like the goose, the day counts most. Most endearing.

War not only puts time out of joint but wipes out choice. Why do you suppose we wear ties to dinner in the Tropics? By choice? No way. Because John Paul Jones shivering in the frigid

Atlantic gave the order. Navy regulations control our lives. War runs on authority. Nothing democratic about it. "Yours is not to reason why, yours is but to do or die."

You'd think by now we could connect a craft to a davit in our sleep. All it takes is sliding an iron hook through an iron eye and—voila—up she goes. But in heavy seas it can be an adventure. Like the other day when the sea was spouting up gushers like Old Faithful. Gave my coxswain fits in his approach. The rolling ship had the hook swinging and the rocking boat had the eye bobbing. We staggered in the well like drunks trying to thread a needle. Two passes went for naught. As we circled for the third try, Simon Legree, bellowing unprintable obscenities from the bridge, told us to hoist the G-D boat. That did it! With a monkey leap at the swinging hook, I caught a whack on the steel helmet. Then, bouncing like a gymnast on a trampoline, I connected the hook to the eye in the split-second nature gave us. That might have saved us from getting tossed to the sharks! Now when general quarters is sounded and the scramble for helmets goes on in Goat Castle, I have no problem grabbing mine. It's the only one in the pile egg-shaped!

So life goes on aboard the mighty *Hudson*.

Our bridge earnings are piling up. Hawk and I skinned a couple of light colonels the other night, who swore they never saw such a bad run of cards. Incompetent players always blame the cards for their losses. Hawk and I, of course, fully agreed with their assessment and promised them another crack to get even. It's getting to be like taking candy from a baby.

I warned you, Mopsy, I'd be rambling and disconnected, and so I am. But having floundered onto a positive note, nay a winning note, tis best to end. I should, however, warn you, there's still enough life in the corpse to fling a barrelful of kisses to the night fairy with orders to dump them into the dreams of a colleen who shows the outer shell of an angel but is stuffed with the devil's own food. . . . Love and XXXX's,

Cory

P.S. Happy "double two" birthday, or is it two plus double tens!

"What are we celebrating?" Laura asked, breaking out in a broad smile.

"You're as bad as Buck. You're reading my mind. What gave me away?" Tally finished pouring three glasses of wine, their dinner aperitif, and handed Laura and Debbie theirs.

"When I saw you pouring from a pricy import, it had to be a celebration."

Tally's contagious laugh rang out. "Well, to keep you from dying of curiosity, we're celebrating Cory's birthday. Today's the first of December and December's his birth month. . . . I read that as long as you drink to celebrate and not to drown sorrows, you'll never have a drinking problem."

"I'll drink to that," Debbie piped up. "Which day did Cory first see the light of day?"

"I'm embarrassed to say, I don't know. But by toasting on the first of the month, we can't be late."

"I'll drink to that," Laura chirped.

"Really, it's so hard to get Cory to say much about himself. When I asked for his birthday, he wisecracked the same month as the Savior and made the boastful point his was first. That leaves us, if my math is right, twenty-four days to play with. You know, I never even knew he was promoted until I saw the j.g. on his return address. He can be so private!"

"Tish! Madly in love with a man who keeps his past hidden. Might he be on the FBI's most-wanted list?" Debbie teased.

"And then there's Robert," Laura chimed in. "Equally mysterious. Could that smile be concealing the snarl of a wolf?"

Tally took to the rise. "Robert's no wolf. The best animal metaphor I can think of is the teddy bear. Believe me, he's no lothario. He hasn't so much as extended a peck on the cheek, so faithful is he to our pact."

"Men are all alike," Laura said jestingly. "They may not show it but you can bet women are somewhere in the back of their minds. I wouldn't even trust Robert, the ultimate gentleman, to stay platonic after three martinis."

Tally laughed. "I swear, I think you two are getting as bad as Susan. She thinks all men have a one-track mind. But seeing how she's constantly having to fend them off, it's quite understandable. Oh, I agree that Robert has a one-track mind, all right, but it's solely on business. He's already making plans for the postwar world."

"The smell from the kitchen suggests dinner is ready," Debbie interrupted. "The wine, Tally, was delicious. You're fast becoming a connoisseur. That's one benefit we all get from your hobnobbing with the affluent set."

They polished off the rest of the bottle with dinner, and Tally, in a pleasant glow, decided to end the good day with a short letter to Cory.

December 1, 1944

My Darling,

How goes it with my favorite sailor? The week is over, started with a bang and ended the same way.

One night we tried our hand at candymaking, anticipating the Yuletide. Turned out surprisingly well. If I mailed a batch to you, it would arrive in a sorry state, so we'll give handouts to friends with small children. Another night was art class and I went to Susan's afterwards. She's thinking of moving back home, stimulated by the rumor that our jobs are once again on shaky turf. I'm supposed to be transferred soon, but don't know where. All I know is that it'll be different kind of work. Debbie's worried about her job, too. Some people are starting to show panic, but I don't feel that way. I'll look at my options before acting blindly.

Well, it's not my intention to bother you with all of this, darling. Let's return to Friday. I started the day taking a shower with my slippers on. By the time I awakened enough, they were a sorry sight. Cory, darling, whatever will you do with me? Big, big problem. Friday night I did the rites in the kitchen and bathroom and stole off to the bed sheets to let another week slip by.

The girls having finished chores are heading directly into dreamland. This is the part of the day I like because it's the time to join you. That is what my dreams are made of. Loving you always, darling. All yours,

Mopsy

During the next several days the rumors continued to fly that military contracts will be drying up and Convair will be forced into more layoffs. It was the main conversation piece at the water coolers. Susan, Debbie, and Tally felt particularly vulnerable because they were still dependent on soft money. Tally's insecurity was greatest because the prospects of no income had the more serious repercussions. It would call for some painful personal decisions. To keep her anxieties in check she adopted the policy of trying not to think beyond one day at a time. She also vowed not to involve Cory with her insecurities. Nevertheless, the uncertainties and their underlying anxieties were not entirely controlled in her next letter to him.

December 3, 1944

My Darling,

It's cold and drizzly outside and I'm warming up in front of the fireplace. My wish is to have you suddenly materialize and crush me so tight I can barely breathe. Oh, my darling, how long has it been since I've even heard your voice!

All is quiet in the house tonight. My roomies are out riding and I'm preparing for art class. I received a letter from you, precious as always, so all is right in the world.

We're still up in the air over our status at work. Susan expects to be terminated this week. We knew the temporary nature of our jobs on accepting them, but reason and emotion don't often go well together. It seems now that the inevitable is happening. I'm trying to take it as a strong signal that we've amassed all that's necessary to achieve victory, slow, oh ever so slow, as it may be in coming.

I'm proud of you, Cory, proud of what you're enduring, but most proud of the person that you are. Of course, I'm having to find out most of these things on my own. Dave wrote Cindy he saw your ship at Tinian where his ship, the Colorado, took heavy shelling. You, naturally, wrote absolutely nothing about it. I didn't even know you were promoted until I saw your return address. The war has to be a terrible strain on all of you, yet your letters are always so upbeat and humorous. You're so protective of me. The toll must be heavy, keeping so much within yourself, absorbing the violence that doesn't belong in your gentle world.

Little do we know what course our lives will take from day to day. It's the unknowing that makes life both exciting and scary. Who could have foreseen our meeting and powerful attraction? The scary part is our being apart. I sit down and have a serious talk with myself, ending up convinced everything will be all right. It will, darling, it will.

For now I must run off to class. My heart I leave with you. All my love always,

Mopsy

It was Saturday and Susan and Tally were lunching together downtown.

"Well, it's official," Susan blurted out, "I'm jobless starting Monday. A bunch of us are being laid off, including my younger sister."

"The rumors are proving right," Tally replied. "I've been hearing all week that pink slips are in the mill. Why do they always come at the holidays? Last time it was around the Fourth of July, and this time it's at the Christmas season. I guess that's one sure way of getting people home for the holidays! What are your plans, Susan?"

"First thing, I'll move out of the club and back to my parents. Then loaf awhile, probably through the first of the year, and then pound the streets for a job. My boss was most gracious. Promised a flattering reference letter."

Tally reached across the table and patted Susan's arm. "I'd say you have the situation well in hand."

"We've all seen it coming. As the war moves on toward its climax, more layoffs will come. Get ready, Tally."

"Pops has already indicated I'll be transferred to another division. I'm taking that as the first step toward severance. Don't know what I'll do then. I had originally planned to stay in San Diego only as long as I could be of help to Ted, but after meeting Cory, I'm not sure what I'll do."

Susan smiled. "I suspect Cory will be of help in making that decision. But you know, if the rent gets due and the pocketbook's empty, you're more than welcome to dump your suitcase in our house. Nothing would please me or my parents more."

"You're a dear friend, Susan. You have a beautiful family and I'll keep the kind offer in mind." She laughed. "Let's just hope my spendthrift habits won't come home to roost."

Susan turned serious. "One lesson I've learned from this war is not to put all of one's eggs in someone else's basket. Some day— I don't know when—I'm going to be my own boss and have my own business—I don't know what—and then I'll not be dependent on anyone for survival." Tally had never heard Susan's voice sound more resolute.

The girls put their troubled thoughts behind them and had a fun weekend together: seeing a movie in the afternoon, going to a concert in the evening, tennis and riding on Sunday and in the evening dancing to their heart's content at the Coronado. Monday found Tally holding to her good spirits as she received a letter from both Cory and Cindy. She squeezed in time to write Cory before taking off to a party Monday night.

December 9, 1944

Dear Darling,

Tis a gorgeous day. Debbie and I just arrived home from work. I'm heading for a party at a girlfriend's home just a few blocks away. So convenient I shall walk.

As the war progresses, I can't help worrying more about you, Cory. I pray to God that he will keep you safe. He shall, dear darling. He shall in spite of the shells and bombs and torn-up beaches. "When Cory comes back" begins all of my thoughts. When this is over, I would declare it our private holiday were it not millions of others would want to share the exuberance of that wonderful day too. Our grandchildren will never begin to comprehend what all this means unless they, too, get caught up in a monstrous war, which I pray to God will never happen.

As for setting up housekeeping for a future college professor, I'd be most happy to oblige, even if it meant selling apples on the corner to meet expenses. It would be worth every apple, because you are the most important and worthwhile person in my life. This would mean, I'd guess, much more schooling after the war. I want you to, darling. For a while I thought I'd like school, too, but the way things seem to be shaping up, we may all be needing a job. I've a feeling there will be massive lay-offs. Both Susan and her sister were terminated last Saturday. I'm hopeful when the time comes, I'll be able to get into something I like. But, don't worry about me, dearest.

I got a letter from Cindy today and she's working in the bank at home. She misses Dave so much.

Begorra, testing me again, eh! Of course I'd be willing to lounge in a sarong, a la Lamour, on a desert island munching crackers, provided, of course, you'd be coming in the next boat in a loincloth. So there! I love you and there's not much you can do about it. Forever-n-ever,

Mopsy

# Operation Smokeboat

Tally came bounding down the steps with a letter in her hand and a smile on her face to join the small group lounging in the living area. She turned toward Susan. "We got a response from Cory on the photo."

"What photo?" asked Debbie.

"Guess I never told you and Laura that over Thanksgiving this imp Susan plied me with wine and then got me to pose in swimsuit and heels and send the snap to Cory."

Susan interrupted. "As you all know, Betty Grable started the rage with her pinup to the boys overseas. So, why shouldn't Tally, with her figure, do the same with Cory? And you should have seen the photo! It was a knockout! The guy will love it. I'm betting it'll be his best Christmas present."

Tally blushed. "I still have mixed emotions about it. But, anyway, let me read Cory's response to it."

While the cheesecake, Mopsy, deeply tapped the primitive passions, I must say your tape measurements cannot begin to reflect your *true value*. It can only be properly expressed in immortal verse.

Speaking of figures
I gotta declare
You've got the numbers
To win anywhere

Yep, you have a figure
That's got me impressed
But I dig the shape of
Your bank account best.

When they stopped giggling, Susan immediately commented, "I always knew Cory was three-parts devil; now I'm beginning to wonder about the fourth part."

"Cory, of course, knows only too well the pitiful shape of my bank account," Tally said. "He's fully aware that my budgeting skill has me living from paycheck to paycheck. I will add that he got back into my good graces with his PS that said I've replaced Betty as his pinup girl."

"His humor tickles me," Laura said.

"Then you'll get a kick out of the last part of the letter in which he lampoons the admirals who came up with the smoke-boat as the answer to the kamikaze."

"Kamikaze?" asked a puzzled Debbie.

"The press barely mentions it, but the wounded coming into the hospital from the Philippines talk freely about it. It's a suicide plane in which the pilot deliberately flies his plane loaded with explosives into a ship. Can cause great damage. I guess the Pentagon isn't ready yet to alarm the public about it. Cory was careful not to be too specific to avoid the censor. Here's his tongue-in-cheek anecdote."

Of grave concern to us in the lower ranks has been the rapid proliferation of admirals. The crisis arises when the supply exceeds demand. What to do with the surplus? Of all the crazy things, many get siphoned into brain tanks. Now a thinking admiral, really an oxymoron, is a health hazard to all within his radius of influence. Those in doubt should hear about Operation Smokeboat.

The curtain opens during an island invasion. The enemy brings out of hiding a dreadful weapon, the kamikaze, or suicide plane. A brain tank, given the task of finding a solution, came up with the smokeboat, conceived on the brilliant notion that for the kazes to be effective the targets must be visible. Fog-generating smokeboats have the power to make targets invisible; alas, they also make everything else invisible. (More on that point in a moment.)

Since all attack transports move in convoy escorted by destroyers to protect them against submarines, they become sitting ducks for kazes. Thus, it follows they would be the first to test the admirals' scheme. As Stoneface scanned his roster for a smokeboat officer, what name do you suppose caught his eye? When the alarm sounded on this ink-black night, the coward crawled slowly out a skinny boom and down a swaying Jacob's ladder into a smokeboat manned by a sleep-deprived mutinous-looking crew. As we began laying smoke, along with boats from other ships, a fog was created so impenetrable that I couldn't see the coxswain who was inches from me, who couldn't see the compass which was inches from him. The boatman couldn't see the six-foot boathook in his hand. Three blind mice! When the all-clear signal came through, we hadn't the foggiest, pardon the pun, idea where we were. We idled the motor to save fuel, and after a long night sweating out visions of drifting into lanes of destroyers or out into the open sea in a tiny boat with but three days of provisions, daybreak mercifully broke. Through the diluted haze, we somehow found our ship, our nerves frazzled.

I proposed selling the plan cheap to the Japs, which the brain tank rejected, convinced that the human eye with adequate practice can adapt to zero visibility. The project was not abandoned until the neuropsychiatric cases surpassed losses from kaze hits. So, angel, in your evening vespers ask for a moratorium on high-level promotions. Those of us in the bottom echelon will suffer fewer nightmares.

"Well," Susan laughed, "it appears Cory has finally caught up on his sleep. His wit is back."

Tally found the Christmas season of 1944 replete with social activities. There were parties galore, both at the ranch and on Robert's calendar, dances throughout the town, and special events at the hospital. The house was decorated top to bottom with holly and the other symbols of Yuletide. The exciting news was the unexpected arrival of Chad, who was on a holiday leave, which sent Laura into rhapsody. Also arriving were several of Laura's hometown girlfriends trying to connect with itinerant husbands, which turned the ranch into a hubbub of confusion. Despite all the commotion, Tally never lost sight of December 17 and wrote Cory to tell him of it.

December 17, 1944

Dearest Gash,

Today is Sunday, our ninth monthversary, darling, and a beautiful sky greets the occasion. I sorta overslept this morning. It's noon and Ted and I just finished brunch.

We have excitement at the ranch. Laura's husband, Chad, flew in yesterday from overseas. She's bubbling all over. Also, four of her girlfriends with husbands in the navy hereabouts swarmed in. With everybody trying to get in touch with everybody and everybody trying to get together at one place, the situation is hilariously confusing. But faces are beaming. Wonderful that they will have the holidays together. The perfect ending would be your parachuting from the sky and landing on our front lawn. Can you manage it, darling?

Later on today we are going to see the rodeo at Mission Valley. A good sunny day for it.

I won a $25 bond at work Friday. It's a drawing each month at the plant for those with a perfect attendance. How, now, could that possibly happen to me? Mr. Dina declared he had a cut coming for all the times he reminded me to clock out. I also won the check pool which we have every Friday. The number on our checks corresponds to a poker hand and the best one wins. And if it's more good news you want, I've been given the word that I have a good chance of keeping my job if I want it.

Yes, so many nice things have happened to me lately. Dad wrote and said he's feeling better. And Ted radiates more health each time I see him.

Had an interesting time last night, Cory. Remember my telling you of my little friend Linda getting mixed up with two beaus in the navy? Well, the first one pulled into dock last week. He must have got wind of something because he up and married her in Los Angeles. They returned to San Diego and a group of us went out to their place for cocktails. My, oh my!

What does the crystal ball predict over the next months? Wouldn't we all like to know! Just as long as I know you're safe, darling, I shouldn't ask for more. The dream of being in your arms keeps me going. Guess this green-eyed colleen must be hopelessly, impossibly in love. All yours, sweetheart.

Mopsy

☆ ☆ ☆

The *Hudson* steamed into Hawaii and dropped anchor for the holidays in the wake of one of its wildest adventures since being commissioned. The adage when it rains it pours never had a more literal meaning. Following the flurry of kamikaze activity at the Philippines and the sub scare in the open seas, came a typhoon while the ship was at anchor, loaded with troops, about to depart for Hawaii. For three days the storm flexed its muscles in a concerted effort to sink all ships afloat, but the *Hudson* weathered every sling fired her way. Although steel bent on her deck in the violence, she still kept her nose above water.

"Never been so damn scared in my life," Scorch muttered. "Thought sure the tub would capsize. I froze at the thought of what I'd do. I figured if a 'kaze hit us, I could swim to something floating; but, Jesus, in a typhoon the groundswells would slam you silly. Did you see how they picked up and flipflopped small craft in the air?"

"Did I see it!" Cory exclaimed. "I had the deck during the peak of it, remember? I saw the beach littered with torn-up boats. I still don't know how we avoided all the vessels crashing about us. But, I'll say one thing. My hat's off to the guys who designed these babies. More than once I was confessing my sins and seeking absolution, convinced we were heading for the deep when the ship would correct its list. But, old sea dog, we survived and finally made it to Pearl. Things happen in threes, so I'm told, and we've had our quota of spine-tinglers, so maybe we'll have a calm and quiet holiday."

"Let's trust the navy's not so barbaric as to make war on Christmas Day. But, then, strike when the enemy least suspects is the motto of the navy."

"Which reminds me, Scorch, of an idea that I'd like to run through with you. We're all in need of a pick-me-up. And I don't mean one of Hawk's restoratives. I've been thinking we might work up a skit to bring a few laughs on Christmas Eve."

"I'm listening."

"I'm leaning toward a takeoff on the navy bigwigs running the show."

"Count me in. Put your evil mind to work. But make it short so we won't have too many lines to get down."

"Only time for one act. However, first things first."

"I know. A letter to a chick in San Diego to update her on the heroics of her hero."

"You're getting telepathic, Scorch. "But, I'm forgoing the heroics for the tale of the coward before the storm." He picked up his pen.

December 17, 1944

Dearest Mopsy,

"Alone, alone, all, all alone. Alone on a wide, wide sea," if I may quote the words of Coleridge in his *Rime of the Ancient Mariner.* Such described the feeling I had on riding out a rip-snorter in the Pacific. Here's the story.

Our convoy was all set to sail from a lagoon off a supply base in the South Pacific (exact longitude and latitude would incense the censor) when we got word of an approaching typhoon. Our pulses quickened. Departure time was indefinitely delayed. All hands rushed to batten down the hatches, secure all movable objects, and toss all loose personal items into foot lockers. The galley crew worked feverishly boxing up pots, pans, glassware, mugs, whatever. It would be cold cuts and chips until the all-clear message sounded.

I glanced up and saw blackness swallow the last piece of open sky. The heavens retaliated with a cloudburst. Giant waves, howling, crashed over the main deck, bending steel in their path. The ship screamed back as she strained at her seams. I began wondering is she was going to split in two? The storm reached its peak, I swear, the moment I took the watch.

What chaos! With a line around my waist and two seamen achoring the ends, I stepped onto the bridge to check the wind velocity. I yelled at once to be hauled in as I was suspended in midair. The needle had swung to its max.

How strong a wind was that? With anchor down and engines ahead full speed, our 16,000-ton ship dragged backwards! The force of the onrushing waves sweeping across the deck peeled paint. Time and again the ship rolled on its side seeming about to capsize only to miraculously right itself. Ships banged together, smaller craft broke in half, boats in the bay got pitched high and dry on the beach. I had never seen nature more rambunctious, and I was never so glad to get relieved of a watch.

I tied myself to my bunk and tried to sleep, but the constant crashing of dishes in the nearby wardroom made it impossible. The boxes kept slamming into the bulkheads as they slid from one end of the room to the other.

After about 48 hours of ceaseless pounding, the worst was over. As the storm gradually lightened, a semblance of order began to appear. The good ship had proved her seaworthiness. She maintained her poise throughout the entire ordeal. I pray she's seen her last typhoon. I'm also happy to say that the innards of Sinbad the Sailor, too, remained essentially intact throughout the trial. At least no glaring evidence to the contrary. When calm seas finally returned, anchors were lifted and the convoy got underway.

Slowly but surely I'm finding out that we have some good athletes aboard. We get together when time permits and play a little volleyball when one of the holds is cleared of cargo. The game gets interesting in a choppy sea. We've also formed a baseball team and when we're between campaigns mellowing out on some recreational island, we challenge other ships' teams. Banged-up fingers beats sitting on anthills guzzling warm beer. Of course, having my druthers, I'd much rather be mellowing out on the pine dance floor at Paul's Passion Pit with a leggy, auburn-haired colleen. Any idea who she is? A clue: She leaves a trail of perfume as sweet as a field of fresh-cut fescue!

Or, I might follow Omar Khayyam's recipe for the good life: "A book of verse, a jug of wine, a loaf of bread, and thou beside me." So, Mopsy, off to the countryside we shall go.

Guess what! I have a job offer when back in civvies. A shipmate's dad owns the garbage rights in San Francisco Bay. He collects garbage from ships in anchor, and for an outrageous price he dumps it in the ocean beyond the restriction zone. He charges about a nickel less than what it costs a ship to crank up its engines and make a round trip. He intends to pass the lucrative scam over to his son after the war, who asked if I'd be interested in making a quick buck. The lure notwithstanding, I found myself somewhat disenchanted at the thought of spending the rest of my employable days in the enterprise of garbage collection—no aspersions intended on the sanitation trade. But, knowing me, I fear it would be oil mixing with water. However, nice to know you're wanted!!

UnAmerican as it appears, my passion for learning seems to override my passion for money. From what I've seen of campus life, professors make enough to buy the necessities but very few of the luxuries. No big cars, big homes, big yachts. (Perhaps a questionable return after the starvation years of degree collections.) However, the tranquil life of books makes it seem a fair swap. But, then, who knows what life will be like in postwar academia!

Well, at least we can accurately predict some aspects of postwar life. You can remind the depression-smitten girls at the ranch, Mopsy, when the spirits are down, of the good life awaiting them once the country's done with rationing. Imagine loading the icebox with steaks, the closet with shoes, the car with new tires and a full tank of gas! And should they fear about jobs when guns and tanks are out of fashion, have them think about the baby carriage business. With 12 million vets returning, the industry should have back orders for years. So, sleep in peace, my love, a great day is coming. XXXXXX's

Cory

☆ ☆ ☆

Tally spent the Saturday afternoon before Christmas as a candy striper in the hospital. It was wrenching to pass holiday cheer to boys with little to cheer about. The violence of war made the celebration of the birth of Prince of Peace seem hypocritical to her. As she was moping the feverish brow of a young marine without hands, he suddenly asked her if she had a "fella." She smiled and said she has a fella who lands marines like him on the islands. "Oh, one of the expendables," he replied. The moment he saw the pale look on her face he knew he had committed a faux pas. "I'm sorry, I was only kidding. A sick joke." She patted his cheek. "No harm." In the heart she had come to accept that the truth hurts no matter how hard the brain numbs it.

Before leaving the hospital, Tally, as usual, stopped by to visit Ted. She was especially eager this time as she knew he had a meeting earlier with his doctors. "How went the powwow with the medics?" she asked breezily as she popped into his room.

"The good news is that the plastic man is basically finished with me. Says that since he now has me looking like Cary Grant, he doesn't want to mess it up. The bad news is that the ward doc tells me I'm going to have to live with the piece of shrapnel near the heart. It's too close to the aorta to remove. If the piece moves I'm a goner; if it stays put, no sweat. I have to abstain from vigorous exercises and heavy lifting."

"Sounds like it could be worse."

"Sounds like I'm a bank teller for the rest of my life."

"When will they discharge you?"

"As soon as all the infections clear."

Tally left the hospital with a heavy heart. She knew that Ted was the outdoorsy type. With his marriage on shaky grounds and now his vocational choices limited, his adjustment problems still remain major.

When she arrived home, a magnum of champagne conspicuously adorned a table. "What's this?" she gasped.

Debbie had a big smile on her face. "Robert dropped this by. He said he and several friends will be spending the holidays at a hunting lodge and he wished us to pop the bottle to welcome in the new year. He insisted, however, we not uncork it until New Year's Day."

Tally at once brightened up. "How thoughtful." Then she suddenly laughed. "Do you remember, it was exactly last New Year's that I first met Robert?"

"How could we all forget! You arrived home as sparkling as the champagne. Delightful as was your performance, we'll try to see you won't have as big a hangover this time."

With the sun putting on its final encore on this the shortest day of the year, Tally sat by a west window with writing pad on lap and turned her mind to thoughts on the South Pacific.

December 22, 1944

Gash Darling,

What a glorious feeling! The sun is bursting through the window and the wind is whistling through the trees. The lady next door, right on schedule, is taking her dog for a walk. I could set my watch on their appearance. Her bulldog, knowing his path, bounds gleefully forward, indicating all is right with the world.

Cory, you'd like Laura's husband. Chad is easy-going, lanky, with a nice, friendly grin. He, too, is on a transport. You may have passed ships. His is the *Morton*. At the moment the two of them are at Long Beach, soaking up what little time they have together, while his ship's undergoing minor repairs. Debbie and I are running the ranch alone. She's now at the stables, having Laura's as well as her horse to care for.

Susan's moved back home but hasn't begun looking for a new job. I was at her place last night for an engagement party in honor of her sister, Lois. In the enclosed snapshots, she's sitting in front on the steps. Wouldn't you say we make a snazzy trio? But where you are, darling, anything in skirts probably looks fantastic. The other Lois is my girlfriend in Denver who is graduating from music school and going to New York next summer. The picture with her was taken during my last vacation.

Looking ahead, what a wonderful summer it would be if the war suddenly ended and you were back. What a tantalizing thought! If you can't make it in person, you'll always be here in mind and spirit. Cory, I miss you beyond the words to convey. It's tolerable only in knowing what we have to look forward to. In low moments I remind myself it was the war that brought us together, so I must control my fury towards it. I must see the good with the bad. I feel I've grown some (don't despair) in the sacrifices demanded. When I look honestly at myself, I was certainly a pretty frivolous thing at one time. The party girl was I. Life was one big dance. Then came Pearl Harbor, life changed, especially when a special guy in navy blue showed up. You know the rest.

After a little ironing—two weeks' worth—I'm going to retire to my dreams with you, sweetheart. I love you very much.

Mopsy

The parties accelerated. The confusions multiplied. Tally never saw so many strangers come and go at the ranch, some briefly introduced themselves with drink in hand and then disappeared forever. Underlying the frenetic festivities was a sense of urgency, not entirely unfounded. For many it was a last reunion with sweethearts, an all too brief prelude before a long dark period of separation. How long, no one knew, or even wished to contemplate.

Of all the people passing through, Tally had found Chad the most interesting. He had become the executive officer of a transport and carried an air of quiet confidence about him. He told

Tally she should be proud of Cory because the wave commanders were the blood and guts of the Amphibious Corps. "On the bottom line," he said, "if they don't do their job and get the assaults ashore, the best laid plans go for naught."

He was somber about the war in the Pacific. "While victory is no longer in doubt, the final cost will be a shock to people. Attrition is the only hope the Japs have for an honorable peace, and they'll waste lives to do it."

Tally felt a pang in her heart. "They are a fanatical lot, aren't they?"

"In a profoundly mystical way. They believe they are a destined nation. It began in the Middle Ages when the powerful Mongols approached their shores with a massive armada which was devastated in a typhoon. The Japs claim it was a divine wind. Now their hopes ride on the kamikaze, which literally means divine wind. From what I hear, they have more volunteers than aircraft."

"The suicide plane must be a devastating weapon."

"Such courage and sacrifice on our side would warrant the Congressional Medal. The price of peace, I fear, will be dear."

While many carols were sung, presents opened, and eggnogs consumed, it did not seem like Christmas to Tally. For one thing, there was no snow outside or roaring fire inside, the essentials of a Colorado Christmas. But most important, there was no Cory. The sight of other lovers with moments together only intensified the void. She consoled herself in the thought that the vast majority of lovers in the world were also separated and were probably sadly reflecting on how many more holidays must be endured before it's over.

She upbraided herself for her mood, which Cory, she suspected, would label self-pity, an example of centripetal love. She must conquer it. She walked to the zoo and laughed at the funny expressions of the animals. They're laughing at me, she thought, and well they should for my lack of gratitude for all the good things that have happened to me the past year. She reminded herself of the improvement in Ted's health, the addition of so many good friends, the good fortune of finding an interesting job, the joy of taking art lessons, and, finally, the meeting of the man who gave new meaning to love. Tally returned to the ranch with a new resolve, and closed out the holidays with two letters to Cory.

Christmas, 1944

Darling,

Begorra, what a day this has been! Started off with a roar when I awoke this morning to find the girls full speed into holiday celebration. Nothing like spiked punch on an empty stomach! Mistletoe was strung all over the place and crazy people, many of whom were new to me, were strung out everywhere. It was wild but no one completely out of their senses. Darling, have you ever been in a crowd and yet felt alone? It's a strange sensation. Here you are, swamped by people, laughing, imbibing, living it up, while you, too, uproarious with them but really apart from them. It's a kind of crazy world of make-believe. Well, it's Xmas, but doesn't seem like Xmas. No family, no big dinner, no tree, and raining instead of snowing. I know it's much worse for you, Cory, so I shouldn't complain.

I was planning to spend the day with Ted, but he's stuck at the hospital. We'll have New Year's Day together. I wanted to call dad tonight but wasn't able to get a line through. I also dialed the South Pacific but, darn, you didn't answer your phone.

We're not short on gifts. Xmas wrappings are piled in the center of the room, don't know what from whom, so sorting-out time comes later on. I don't know what's on your schedule, but I do hope it will be a day with at least some fond memories.

Somehow, this doesn't sound like me. Xmas has always been a rather sacred—perhaps semtimental is the better word—day. And I've loved the day. Hmmm. Debbie is writing a letter, too. I wonder if hers is as scattered as mine. I'm getting so I can't even think anymore, darling. Guess I better leave my heart in this letter and jump into bed. Yours to keep with all my love,

Mopsy

Gash Darling,

Another grand day and another day of longing for you. I think of you each morning as I look out on the bay going to work. Usually there are a couple of ships anchored there, which is all it takes to stir my fantasy, envisioning one of them yours. Lovely, wishful dreaming which lasts until the dong of reality has me in line punching the clock. By this time, I punch mechanically. Nevertheless, I'm thankful to be still one of the priveleged few.

The days move faster now that I'm in a new group and everything is different. I was glad of the chance to be transferred because it means I'll hold my job longer, even though it hangs on a string over my head.

Darling, here we are at the end of a roller-coaster year—can you imagine one more dramatic! How are you going to celebrate? On watch, I bet.

What a perfect time to share with you! But once again frustrated by pitiless fate. My New Year's wish is that no future lovers will ever have to face the trauma of indefinite separation.

Ted continues to make progress getting his marriage back on track. He and his wife are talking about spending some time in the mountains next year. The war about destroyed their marriage, although it was always shaky from the start. Someday, if you like, I'll tell you the full story. If we marry someday, God forbid there be a war to keep us apart and create breeding ground for misunderstanding! Ted has gone to Los Angeles on a three-day pass with a friend. So, tonight, I'll party with Susan and some of her friends.

The day is great for walking. Join me so we can talk. We have so much to talk about, so many dreams to explore. Yet, I know, the moment my hand feels the warmth of yours, normal discourse will fly with the wind and the heart will do all the talking and nothing else on this green earth will matter. I must stop wishing what cannot be and accept what will be. Perhaps that should be my New Year's resolution—stop wishing for the impossible. But, sure as I breathe, I'd break it the next day.

How are all the vagabonds? You know how impressed I was

with the ones I met. The creme de la creme, I'd say. So boyish, yet so gentlemanly, all with a touch of class. Still, I suppose, crowded living conditions with no relief can strain even the highest of nobility. I still laugh at what you call your living quarters—goat castle.

Yesterday could not be called a productive day at work. Too many started the end of the year celebrating a little early and didn't show. So the rest of us piddled.

My darling, when I see the new year in tonight, you'll be foremost in my mind. I'll send you a love message. Keep your antenna up high to receive it. Although we're starting out the new year apart, we can dream of ending it together. Happy New Year, darling. A very happy New Year. A very happy, happy New Year. I love you always. . . .

Later.

The party's over, crazy but fun. It ended at the Square with rice, confetti, silly hats, and whistles. It was a gay, hilarious crowd, almost like old times, but underneath an unspoken grimness. Everybody now has someone very close overseas. We all know deep in our hearts that this year will be a struggle; for many, a tragedy.

I've never seen San Diego so crowded at one time. The sidewalks were jammed. People used the streets to pass. Traffic was at a standstill. The streetcars inched along behind the milling crowds. We were numb with cold riding the ferry. On returning, we took in an early morning show, "San Diego I Love You." And so it was, my darling, the way we brought in the Year of the Lord 1945.

Cory, darling, we are starting this year together. You are in my heart always and I'll love you forever and ever. Forever is so short when in love. Too short to waste in bitterness, in pity, or in doubt. We'll be very happy and we'll always end whatever disagreements we have with laughter. Forgive me, my darling, for loving you so much. All yours,

Mopsy

# Christmas Eve

"Susan's here," Debbie yelled.

"Coming down," Tally yelled back.

Tally held an envelope in her hand as she bounded down the steps into the living area where Debbie, Laura, and Susan had gathered. "Now," she said, "this is the surprise," waving the envelope. "Cory sent me a skit he had written. He and Scorch put it on for the ship's officers on Christmas Eve, with several other members in the boat division playing minor roles. It's a spoof on the top-ranking admirals, which he titled 'A Star-Studded Cast.' I think it's a riot. I especially wanted Susan to hear it because she was with me the night those two nuts put on a low-comedy vaudeville act. She'll have no difficulty picturing them in action.

"I've been practicing on the inflections and have them down about as well as I can—no Sarah Berhardt! In the spoof Cory plays the dual role of narrator and Admiral Slitz. Scorch plays Seaman Third Class Gorky, his orderly."

Tally cleared her throat to gain everyone's full attention. She lowered her pitch to get her best sound quality for the reading. "And now, ladies, without further ado, let the curtain rise and the show begin."

A Star-Studded Cast

Act I

Narrator: Ladies and Gentlemen: Scratch that. Sea life breeds wishful thinking. Let me start afresh. *Gentlemen:* Two caveats. First, any resemblance between the characters in this play and persons in real life, as familiar as some may seem, is purely coincidental. Second, the play has not

been cleared by Naval Intelligence, nor is ever likely to
be. You are here at your own risk. . . . You may wish to
don life jackets.

To picture our Chain of Command, visualize a huge
pyramid with a cluster of gold bars at the base and a single five-star at the apex. This loner, Commander of
Fleets, COF, known as "The Hack" behind closed port-
holes, is so remote from the chain that all of his messages
are relayed through a camouflaged transmitter situated at
the intersection of the equator and the international
dateline. At this salient compass point, he divided the
Pacific into quadrants: Quadrant I, northeast; Quadrant
II, southeast; Quadrant III, southwest; Quadrant IV,
northwest. He put a four-star in command of each.
These admirals, Budd, Miller, Pabb, and Slitz, all of the
famous class of 1910, the year of Halley's comet, know
his name, but use only his in-house sobriquet of
"Sixpack." With his invisibility, his role fortunately is
minor in the skit. The leading principals are the highly
visible well-decorated four-star admirals, the real heroes
of the navy.

Act I spotlights Admiral Mortimer Slitz of Q-IV; the
setting, the Strategy Room on his flagship, the U.S.S.
*Rhode Island,* anchored off ugly Mug-Mug Island.
Present are the admiral and his orderly, Seaman Third
Class Ludwig Quintin Gorky.


Slitz: (puffed up) Just between us, Gorky, the more I think
    about it, the deeper it sticks in my craw.
Gorky: Exactly what, sir?
Slitz: (pacing the floor) The Rhode Island.
Gorky: You disapprove of battlewagons, sir?
Slitz: (annoyed) You miss the point as usual, Gorky. Hasn't it
    occurred to you my flag is flying on the *smallest state?*

Gorky: Never thought of it that way, sir.

Slitz: The salt on the wound is that Budd, bottom of the class, holds forth on the *Texas,* the *largest state,* at balmy Waikiki Beach.

Gorky: Smells like rotten fish, sir.

Slitz: Low-handed double-dealing, all right. But getting a grip on it is like trying to grab an eel. Gorky, looking at the whole enchilada from the perspective of the rank and file, does anything hit you—er—as a bit odd?

Gorky: Well, sir, now that you mention it, the names of the Quadrant leaders do catch the eye.

Slitz: Budd, Miller, Pabb, Slitz—names ringing solidly of heartland America. What are you driving at?

Gorky: Well, sir, they also have the ring of the suds. The premiums, of course, sir.

Slitz: (thoughtful) Suds, eh! Hmmmm. A curious piece of coincidence. Or is it? COF got his moniker because of his weakness for the hops. Hmmmmm.

Gorky: I wonder, sir, if the eel might be wiggling its way into a corner.

Slitz: (touching his medals) Valor at sea second fiddle to accidents of birth? Preposterous! (Eyes squinting) Even so, why am I the one to languish in the hellhole of the Pacific?

Gorky: I guess, sir, it comes down to winning a few and losing a few.

Slitz: There you go again, Gorky, cryptic. Come to the point.

Gorky: Well, sir, as we would say in the rank and file, Sixpack must have got blowed out on a bottle of Schlitz.

Slitz: (showing excitement) Something's starting to worm its way up through the ol' gray matter. Got it! A poker game. The four of us played a practical joke on the old man. While he was dealing (ho, ho), we dropped a dead

worm into his bottle of beer. When he poured it out into
his mug, he tossed his chips ten yards. . . . Lord
Almighty! I can see the label! . . . It *was* a Schlitz.

Gorky: Excuse me sir. The other admirals have been piped
aboard. Shall I show them in?

Slitz: (sigh) What must be done, must be done. Gorky, now
about the suds—just between us and the yardarm,
understand?

Gorky: Quite on the q.t., sir.

Slitz: And, Gorky, once the meeting gets underway, don't hesi-
tate to voice an opinion. I'm always open to the perspective of the rank and file.

(Enter Admirals Budd, Miller, and Pabb. Several minutes
elapse in warm handshakes, nervous heehaws, and hearty
backslapping.)

Slitz: Gentlemen, best we get on. The agenda, I fear, tilts
toward the heavy side. We have two items instead of the
normal load. Orderly Gorky will take notes. While our
wits are with us, I move we take on the most pressing
item, the menu for Thanksgiving dinner.

Gorky: Sir?

Slitz: (smiling) What is it, Gorky?

Gorky: Sir, considering it's Memorial Day, with the Fourth
and Labor Day yet ahead, the admirals might prefer to
handle first the item marked top secret and urgent.

Slitz: (after a long pause and hard stare) This isn't the time to
bring up personnel matters, Gorky, but your statement
compels me to point up the deficiency that keeps you
mired at seaman third class: degenerative myopia. The
sine qua non for promotion in the U.S. Navy is the
vision to see the forest beyond the trees.

Chorus of admirals: Hear, hear!

Gorky: Yes, sir.

Slitz: A myopic mind would give top priority to an urgent top-secret document, but remove the blinders, Gorky. What is more vital to a nation at war than the morale of its troops? And what could boost morale higher than a gastronomic delight on the day America gives thanks to a benevolent Providence for a bounteous harvest!

Chorus of admirals: Right on! Right on!

Slitz: Gentlemen, nice to gain your approval. Let it be so recorded. Now that we grasp the gravity of our task, may I invoke the immortal lines of John Paul Jones: "Damn the torpedoes, full speed ahead."

Gorky: Sir, I believe it was Faragut.

Slitz: (a bit annoyed) Faragut, Jones, Perry—all the same stripe. Gentlemen, success depends largely on our choice of the main entree. Think deeply.

Pabb: A great American dish is chicken and dumplings.

Budd: Almost as American as roast beef.

Miller: Gourmets would prefer leg of lamb.

Slitz: (beaming) Excellent recommendations. I would say the floor is ready for discussion.

Gorky: Sir?

Slitz: (showing contained annoyance) Yes, Gorky?

Gorky: The rank and file, sir, tend to be nostalgic on holidays. They would strongly favor the traditional table.

Slitz: There you go again, vague and abstract. Get concrete. What are you recommending?

Gorky: Turkey and dressing, sir.

Pabb: It forcibly strikes me that the turkey is more connected with Thanksgiving than the chicken.

Budd: I had a gnawing feeling that the steer wasn't kosher. Withdraw the beef.

Miller: (sigh) Scratch the sheep. Too Australian.

Slitz: A commendable input, Gorky. On rare occasions you

show brief flashes of promise. I can see, gentlemen, by your satisfied looks that further discussion is superfluous. The principal entree is turkey and dressing. Gorky, are you getting all this down?

Gorky: Yes, sir.

Slitz: Gentlemen, we're progressing ahead of schedule. Let us now put our collective genius to work on the more subtle entremets. I shall open the brainstorming with stir-fried turnips.

Miller: Buttered hearts of artichokes.

Pabb: Cheese-coated avocados.

Budd: Candied apricots.

Slitz: Any possible additions from the rank and file?

Gorky: Corn on the cob, mashed potatoes and gravy, baked beans, tossed salad, hot rolls, pumpkin pie, sir.

Slitz: (eyes glowing) Gentlemen, to quote a great living American, we've crossed the Rubicon. The die is cast. We've forged a culinary triumph. Gorky, rush this menu (to the aside—delete turnips, artichokes, apricots, and avocados) to every chef in the Pacific to be posted on the third Thursday of next November.

Gorky: Sir?

Slitz: (painfully annoyed) What now, Gorky?

Gorky: May I remind you, sir, of the proclamation of the commander-in-chief. He decreed Thanksgiving the fourth Thursday in November.

Slitz: Sticky details. The hobgoblin of creative minds. Very well, Gorky. Substitute fourth for third in the memo. (Sigh) Thanksgiving will never be the same that distant from Halloween.

Chorus of admirals: Hear, hear!

Slitz: Let us now concentrate the remainder of our creative resources on the final item.

Chorus of admirals: (sighing) What must be, must be.

Slitz: I've a memo here from Sixpack detailing the summer schedule of events. First, is the Island of Saipan, which, frankly, took most of the morning to find on the map. Since it happens to be in Q-IV, it comes down to being my dance. The Stars and Stripes must fly over it on the Fourth, so we can't dally. The formidable task is finding a rendezvous site. My old eagle eye noticed that Saipan is but a hop, skip, and jump from the great American fortress at Guam. Thus, I can think of a no better place to gather the flotilla.

Chorus of admirals: Right on! Hear, hear!

Gorky: Sir?

Slitz: (a withering glance) What now, Gorky?

Gorky: With permission, sir, I should advise that the island surrendered to the enemy two years ago.

Slitz: (gasping) A revolting turn of events! This calls for sacking Plan A. But, be not in despair, gentlemen. Always thinking ahead, I have backup Plan B, proposing we gather where a proud fleet, now only a hallowed memory, once anchored. Those in favor of Pearl say . . .

Chorus of admirals: (dabbing at the eyes) Aye, Aye.

Slitz (raising a fist) Gentlemen, we've just scaled a mountain. I can work out the incidentals: scheduling D-day and H-hour, allocating troops and supplies, coordinating air and sea forces. So keep your coding machines well oiled. Since I'm interpreting your silence as consent, I'm happy to state, gentlemen, we've concluded our taxing agenda and the meeting is now adjourned.

(The visiting admirals file out after more vigorous handshaking and backslapping, leaving only Slitz and Gorky in the Strategy Room.)

Slitz: Gorky, you know how I deplore details.

Gorky: Yes, sir. The hobgoblins of creative minds.

Slitz: Therefore, I leave all the logistics up to you. During your off-hours the next several days, pore over the intelligence reports, the aerial photographs, and, of course, the fine print in COF's instructions, and then draft the invasion plans. Specify the landing units, the assault divisions, the back-up reserves, the ship and plane escorts, and a full listing of critical supplies. No snafus. Remember, we'll be on Movietone News in theaters all over the United States. Any questions?

Gorky: Perfectly clear, sir.

Slitz: (clearing his throat) Gorky, back to the suds. I've figured out how I got marooned in Mug Mug, but what puzzles me is how Alphonso Budd got the plum of Waikiki. Er, would the rank and file have any thoughts on that one?

Gorky: Sir, we'd suspect there was more to that poker game than what met the eye.

Slitz: (eyes flashing) Don't be coy. Speak up.

Gorky: Sir, in the air force when there's a crash, the rule of thumb is to hop right back on a plane to avoid fear of flying.

Slitz: For chrissake, Gorky, stop skirting around the poop deck. Get to the point.

Gorky: Well, sir, what exactly did happen after Sixpack spotted the worm?

Slitz: Hmmmm. Good move. Let's see if I can put it together. We're doubled up trying to control our guts. Aha! That is, all but Alphonso. He's busting butt to the cooler and returning with a bottle of—I'll be an uncle's monkey, er, a monkey's uncle—the SOB returned with a bottle of *Bud.*

Gorky: Sir, you got the bastard eel by the testicles.

Slitz: (fist clenched) The scam's clear as crystal. Budd, the snake in the grass, planned the caper the moment that he spotted the worm. Well, have to admit, Gorky, as a sounding board, you've been of some help. Makes me tempted to reopen your files and refiddle with the promotion material.

Gorky: Thank you, sir.

Slitz: (scratching his chin) The sticky problem is to cover up the myopia.

Gorky: Yes, sir, that's the rub. The trees are too tall for the size of my forest.

Slitz: (staring off into space) What really cuts to the barnacles is that Alphonso, 75th in a class of 75, had the savvy to pull it off.

Gorky: Intelligence is a funny thing, sir.

(Curtain Falls)

When the girls stopped laughing, Tally said Cory wrote that the skit was so well received that he and Scorch have given thought to a sequel. She drew his letter from the envelope. This is what he said:

For a sequel, we're thinking of getting the brass together over a bottle of brandy to hatch up a plan to end the war early and become the biggest heroes of WWII. After enduring many false fits and starts, exacerbated by their increased consumption of brandy, they concoct the daring plot of sneaking Mae West, an undercover agent disguised as a Geisha girl, into Tokyo Bay in a gig to kidnap the emperor. The ransom would be the heads of the warlords on a silver platter. By the time the bottle is empty, they have covered all contingencies and have evolved an ingenious foolproof scheme. Then one of the admirals casually remarks that he will furnish the gig which will transport the busty blonde on her mission. This suddenly ends the camaraderie as all realize that the lent gig will undoubtedly become a national treasury, most likely enshrined in the Smithsonian, with all the glory going to its owner. None are about to grant that honor to one of the others. The skit ends in a free-for-all, with the tragic consequence that the brilliant plan is scuttled.

"Oh," Susan cried out, "I'm laughing already. I can just see Cory and Scorch making whoopee over that one. What a farce!"

"I so agree," Laura said. "Meanwhile, may I make a copy of this one. I've a feeling that Chad will love it."

"I'm sure Cory won't mind," Tally replied. "I intend on sending Cindy one."

When the chatting ended and the girls dispersed, Tally, still in a giggly frame of mind, picked up her pen to share her mood with Cory.

January 4, 1945

Dear Darling,

Yes, if I can stop laughing long enough, I do promise to get this posted for you tonight. Your skit, "A Star-Studded Cast" is a riot. What a sense of humor you have, darling. I've read it several times and I keep breaking out laughing each time. I hope you don't mind but I read it to Susan, Laura, and Debbie and they loved it. Laura wants to send a copy to Chad. Okay? They think you should skip grad school and go directly into the theater. Your dry wit and humor are just one of the things I adore about you, Cory.

The moon is out and the air is cool. I imagine where you are the air is warm night and day.

I finished the uninspiring task of emptying the trash. I paused on the back step to change the air in my lungs. A wave of nostalgia suddenly swept over me. Remember? It was here on the back porch that we said our first good night and had our first kiss. Crazy little things about that night flashed through my mind. Like that cute little waitress at the snack bar who had a little crush on you. She asked what you did and you told her you were a wave commander. Her eyes widened at that and with a straight face, you told her you trained female WAVES, and that you were training a select group on how to kill with a single blow of the hand in preparation for a secret mission in the Pacific. You were so convincing that I might have believed it had you not nudged me on the knee. And our first kiss, so natural, so gentle, so dreamy. If that didn't make me a goner, the few lines attached to the peace dove sure did. Remember:

But sure and twas Irish luck
To meet and fall for you
For tis the darlin' of my heart
Thee be and always will be too

Exactly my sentiments, darling.

Mopsy

# Mail Call

Over coffee after a cocktail party, when Robert asked Tally what brought her to San Diego, she felt sufficiently comfortable in their relationship to go into the details of Ted's struggles.

"Life hasn't been too kind to your brother," Robert sympathetically responded.

"The war not only hurt him physically but mentally. He's lost much confidence in himself and is emotionally down too much of the time. Right now he's on furlough to Denver hoping he and Jenny can revive their marriage."

Robert looked intently at Tally. "And the war hasn't been too kind on you, either."

"I don't wish to leave the impression it's been all bad. The war did give me a good job, new friends, and, most importantly, brought Cory into my life. But it's also kept us apart. In the ten months of our courtship, I can count on one hand the times we've actually been together." Tally took a long sip of coffee. "What I don't understand, Robert, is what makes civilized nations so ready to go to war, when war itself is so uncivilized."

"It does seem that advanced cultures jump to the beat of drums as quickly as the primitive tribes. I've come to believe greed is the common denominator. Nations, like people, keep craving for more than what they have. Once they build up their muscles, they get into empire building."

"Muscles?"

"Their military. Invariably, a strong military precedes aggression. Even a nation like ours that places a premium on human life is no exception. In flexing our muscles with Mexico, Spain, and, don't forget, Native Americans, we've expanded from thirteen states to forty-eight. Had the War of 1812 gone our way, we'd probably have Canada in our empire. And if France hadn't sold us the Louisiana Territory, I've no doubt we'd have taken it by force."

"So if Japan had not been greedy to build its empire, there would be no war today in the Pacific."

"Wilson may have been on the right track pushing for a League of Nations. We seem to need a higher power to control the ambitions of individual nations."

"All quite complicated, Robert. Best I go home. My feeble brain is muddled enough after several cocktails."

That night, curled up in her favorite chair, having downed enough caffeine to battle the soporific effects of alcohol, Tally blocked out all thoughts of war and concentrated on a Chopin étude on the radio to get in the right mood to write Cory.

January 8, 1945

Gash Darling,

Hi! I'm sitting at home soaking up the moon beams through the front window, the window through which I saw you a long time ago stride up from the ferry. All is peaceful. Chopin is playing on the radio.

Yesterday I received a wonderful letter from you. All of your letters are wonderful to me, darling, but this one was incredibly sweet. Ah, with what delicacy you do touch the cords of a girl's vanity! I love it. Bask in it. I'm flabbergasted at your accuracy on my measurements. Hmmmmm. Lt. Zigler, this suggests tons of practice. By the way, since you gave Betty Grable the bump (with a bank account slightly exceeding mine), I'll deign to be your pin-up girl. Yes, I still have that red-and-white dress I wore on our first date. Geeminy, how many guys would remember such a minor thing as that!

Just think! Last year at this time I was on the swing shift and Cindy was here. It's hard to realize how much can change within a year—and it's not over yet! I didn't think I'd be in San Diego this long—yet here I am. Who knows what surprises another year will bring!

Debbie's taking early repose, and Laura and Chad are still having fun in Long Beach. I received a letter from Ted and he had a ball on his furlough. He's on his way back for hopefully his last set of tests.

Seeing people so happy together makes me yearn even more to be with you, gabbing, laughing, just being us. What say we take a stroll? or stay home with good music? or dance at a cozy nightspot?—anything as long as we are together. You know, sometimes I get to day-dreaming like this at work, and some-times, like yesterday, I get caught. Buck ambled by, rapped on my table, and said, "Natalia, you have that special glint in your eye," and all I could do was stutter. (A brilliant riposte, wouldn't you say, darling.) With my fairyland vanished, I picked up my triangles and returned to nasty reality.

Geeminy, my arm's getting a crink in it. Guess I better shift positions. Ah! Feels better. I turned over.

We're going to picnic at the beach tomorrow, Sunday, weather permitting. Promises to be full of fun with a big crowd shaping up. Two of us are in charge of the food. I've counted red points in my sleep (red points, darling, relate to meat-ration points). It's going to be hot dogs for the main course. I've invited Susan—since you declined—to be my guest. She, by the way, started working at Ryans on Monday and has run into six familiar faces from her old department at Convair, so she feels right at home. . . .

Sunday

We had the group beach party. I'm now nursing sun and wind burns, but the picnic was a huge success. Can you believe, counting the young of families, 40 people in all!

I'm glad you enjoy tennis. Now I've been warned. I'm gonna have to step up the level of my game. You have an annoying trait, lieutenant. You become so good at whatever you do that you give your opposition an inferiority complex. . . . And yes, I would like to become a good bridge player. You can be my teacher but bear in mind if you steal all the tricks, I'm capable of tossing a fit! . . . Indeed, I've seen you cutting a fine figure in uniform, but in tweed pants, green coat, and red hat; well, that array of color calls for a suspension of judgment! And I'm not too sure a hat should cover up that black mane. Hmmmm.

Laura called from Long Beach and will be gone two more weeks. I'm so happy they can have this much time together.

Debbie's out for dinner so I'm going to turn in. Everything is so still. I can hear the animals over in the zoo like I do in the morning going to work. Good night, my love. Someday we'll forget the pain of this war and laugh at the funny side of it. Yes, someday, darling, we'll laugh a lot together. Nobody makes me laugh the way you can. Sweet dreams, God bless and keep you safe. Lovingly yours,

Mopsy

Several days later Susan caught Tally in a stare while they were sipping a coke after a late-afternoon tennis match. She piped up, "Why the ogle? Is my slip showing?"

Tally blushed. "Didn't mean to be so obvious. Was just musing on what an interesting case study you are."

"Ah, Dr. Freud, and what's the diagnosis?"

"After an extensive in-depth analysis, I arrive at no diagnosis. You're entirely too complex to label. The reason, of course, is that you are revoltingly opaque. You never talk about yourself."

"I unfurl the white flag," Susan said smiling. "What is it that you want me to talk about?"

"The person inside. On the outside, I see a smart, well-educated female who is a happy product of a loving family. And I see a chic, attractive bachelorette who is also brilliantly adept at dodging long-term attachments."

"A bit overdone but not without a kernel of truth. Tis true as marital bait I do seek to keep the hook away from the biting fish. I defend my teasing manner this way. The war is dramatically changing the status of woman. Because of male scarcity, it has opened job opportunities never before available to her. And she has risen to the occasion. So well that she'll be a bona fide competitor in the postwar job market. This will have its impact on sex roles and relationships. The traditional model of the submissive domestic happily serving the male breadwinner will become increasingly anachronistic."

"Is this good?"

"Who can say? It'll be dicey. All that seems certain is that marriages will not play out the same after the war as before the war. What worked for mom and dad will not work for you and me."

"Strikes me there'll be a crazy period. Both sexes floundering about trying to find their role."

"My conservative bones say commitment right now is high risk. To throw one's lot in with a brick from the old school is no guarantee he won't be crumbly clay in the new order."

"You sound a lot like Cory. He doesn't want to commit until after the war. Too many unknown currents, he says, to jump into the sea of matrimony."

Susan laughed. "Cory has a brain. But, never you worry, Tally. However treacherous the currents, he'll risk them swimming to you. How could he resist that Irish sparkle!"

"I'd feel better if you'd said that charming cosmopolitan air."

"Give the man credit. Beauty for him is more than skin deep. He knows a diamond in the rough when he sees one."

"You haven't read my letters. Hardly profound."

A smile creased Susan's face. "Where he's at, I doubt if that matters much."

That thought lingered with Tally as the day wore into evening. Indeed, she pondered, what is important to one "Alone on a wide wide sea?" a favorite line of Cory's. She remembered a letter in which he doted on the sailor's joy of mail call. She dug it out and reread the section:

> The moment the ship drops anchor, a boat is immediately dispatched to pick up mail and movies. Binoculars scan shoreward for the return, and cheers ring out when the mail sacks are spotted. Movies are the consolation prize if nothing arrives from home. Old corny Westerns are seen night after night simply because they're made in good ol' USA, the next best thing to

stepping foot on home soil. Even gifts like chocolate-chip cookies and homemade fudge which usually arrive as melted goo bring out smiles. Sometimes socks are crammed in the package, giving color to the goo. Cigarettes are a bit of a strain since they're cheap and plentiful at ship's service. On the list of needs they're about as in demand as woolens in the tropics. But, it's the thought that counts. Like the day Scorch received a silk stocking from an old flame with the attached note that its mate is anxiously awaiting a hand-delivered return.

More times than the navy cares to admit, it goofs and sends the mail to the wrong port. When this happens the closest thing to a mutiny takes place. The boat crew, returning emptyhanded, is the scapegoat, and roars of string 'em up on the yardarm ring out. But when the boat is loaded with sacks and the mail gets sorted, the ship quiets down almost as much as at the preinvasion devotionals, as men of all stripes drift off into sweet fantasy reading and re-reading the perfumed pages from home.

Sailors at sea are nostalgic, Tally told herself. A sachet scent may leave a more lasting impression than wise words. But, then, Cory was no ordinary sailor. She sighed inwardly. All that her letters really offered was what was in her heart: a love without guise; a love without boundary. What he read was all that she felt, nothing more, nothing less. Oh, she thought, if only they could have had more time together. Brooding such, she began another heartfelt letter to him.

January 17, 1945

My Darling,
Do you know this is our tenth monthversary? Can you believe St. Pat's Day is not that far away? After four days of rain, the sun is smiling again.

The work week is over. Two of the girls in the car pool were terminated yesterday so that leaves only three of us. The engineering department hardly seems the same with every other seat vacant. The project I'm working on is still in the experimental stage, so I'm on indefinitely.

Susan was over today for tennis. Laura called and will be back Friday. We're looking forward to seeing her. Seems like she's been gone forever.

Cory, my darling, what's the chance of getting you home soon? Oh, why do I ask? I don't know. Habit? An obsession? I know, of course, the chances are slim. The war still rages on. Yet, do not condemn me for asking, especially on this very special day.

Judy, a girl in our group, is leaving tomorrow. Her husband was a prisoner of war in Italy and is coming home. The poor thing, in all her rush, has six Siamese kittens to take along. She had planned on selling them, but they aren't old enough to separate from the mother, and the pet shop won't handle them. We took her out to dinner and a show last night for a final fling. We ate at the Chinese place on Eighth Street and asked for chopsticks. Such fun! We began seriously, but realizing our futility, broke out in laughter. We finished the meal in a record two hours.

I'm having a shower for Lois and Dick here at the house. They're marrying in two weeks.

I'm getting a good night's sleep for an event tomorrow I'm not relishing. I lost a bet to one of the fellows at work, stupid of me, so I must be his guest at the fight arena. I can think of a number of things I could enjoy more than cheering on gladiators, but honor demands no retreat. For the rest of this night, however, I shall relive the fun we've had together and dream up new frolics for the future. That's much more appealing.

Sunday

The stars are out tonight following a sunset that simply outdid itself. The horizon, starting off a brilliant red, graduated into a soft pink and then into a pastel blue. Moments of beauty bring me close to you, get my mind revolving like a broken record, repeating over and over, I want to be with you, I want to be with you, I want to be with you.

Ted has returned and is ready for discharge. Says dad is ill again and unable to work. My younger brother failed his physical because of bad eyes. He's classifed 2B and is crushed. He wanted to follow in his big brother's footsteps.

Laura arrived today with Chad. He expects sailing orders soon. I think I told you he's the executive officer on his ship. His prognosis for the next several months in the Pacific put a lump in my throat. He wasn't specific, only said that the intensity will go up a notch and things will get tougher before better. I quickly changed the subject.

Debbie entered her horse in the show today at Mission Valley.

Darling, the fights weren't so bad after all. I even found myself getting excited in the second round. I doubt if I'll become a rabid fan, but it was something different.

I've let my art work pretty much drop since the class ended. I must get back to it, but something always seems to pop up. Tonight, for instance, I have to shampoo my hair. So it goes. I'll say good night, my darling. I love you ever.

Mopsy

Later in the week, Ted and Tally were having dinner at the Skyroom. "Sis," he protested, "this is an awfully expensive restaurant to be taking me out to dinner."

"None, but the best, I say, for my favorite brother on his last night in San Diego. That's why I reserved a window table and have ordered the house special, steak au poivre."

"All good and well, but I'd feel lots better if we divided the tab."

"And I'd feel lots worse. It would mean I'd be obligated to see you off at the depot tomorrow. I hate depots. They remind me of funerals. Everybody comes to say goodbye. Goodbye is the ugliest word in the English language."

"At least let me buy the wine."

"If you don't stop this, I'll send you back to the hospital with a broken shin. I'm wearing high heels, you know. Now, cast your good eye below. The area you see is historic Old Town. Let that be the look you remember best of San Diego."

Ted clicked glasses. "Here's to the missionaries who made it all possible. How I wish I could have seen the town under different circumstances."

"I know. It's been a roller coaster for more than a year but the ride ended much better than either of us thought. I'll never forget the shock the first day I walked into your room. The change has been fantastic."

"I'm still no Cary Grant, but at least I've got rid of the Frankenstein mask. Jenny can now look at me without turning white as a ghost."

"Speaking of Jenny, would you have enlisted if she hadn't lost the baby?"

"Sis, when Pearl Harbor made the news, all I heard was the sound of the bugle." Ted paused to steady his voice. "I heard it playing Reveille, not Taps. It was neither Jenny nor the bank that was the key to my enlisting. It was all me."

Tally nodded. "I'm glad you feel that way. Resentment would be a big hurdle in getting your marriage back on track. I'm sure pulling for you two to work it out."

"Jenny's willing to give it a try. That's all I can ask. I know it's mostly up to me. You've been a great help, Tally, but it's time that I begin to pull my own oar. I just wish I could feel better about myself."

"The docs say it helps if one talks about his horrible experiences. Otherwise, the emotions stay bottled up and never lose their force. You've never talked about those terrible days in the jungle and especially that day you were wounded."

"Reliving them in nightmares is enough for now. To shift the subject, are you still madly in love with the wave commander?"

"Madly is the word, Ted. His letters are beautiful. I don't know how he does it with all the ugliness about him. He always writes upbeat. But I think I'd fall apart if he didn't. He's so protective of me. He never mentions invasions. He touches my funny bone with stories on his fellow officers and touches my heart with romantic fantasies and poems. I've decided he's three-parts leprechaun."

"Has he made a commitment?"

"Wants to wait until the war's behind us. We've had actually such little time together. When we're together it's ninety percent chemistry. We're more emoting than informing. Yet, he's given so much to me. It's hard to explain."

"Love is never easy to explain."

"Hey!" Tally said to lighten the air, "let's think about dessert. What about mousse? Their chocolate mousse is out of this world!"

Ted left for Denver the next morning, and Tally struggled for several days with the void. Always close, his trials and tribulations brought them even more so, which she had not so poignantly realized until his departure. Her funk had her chastising herself. Silly dame, begorra you are. You cried the first day you saw him and you cry the day he's gone, though he's a thousand percent improved. Tears should come only if he could never leave. Idiot!

The thought that her mood was not conducive for writing Cory helped shake her out of her mental lethargy. Then she found she had to overcome a sixth-sense forboding that an invasion was imminent before she could stir to write a light and airy letter.

February 1, 1945

My Darling,

Today was a typical routine day at work, but receiving a letter from you made everything shiny bright. I'm at home tonight, Debbie's riding, and Laura's still in San Francisco. She's on a day-to-day schedule, most likely coming back this week. Ted has been discharged and is home to stay. I'm so glad his long ordeal is over.

Susan and I played a little tennis yesterday. Neither of us were too sharp. I received a letter from Cindy and she still seems happy at home. I'm glad for her but sure miss her. Debbie rode in the horse show last Sunday at Balboa. It was a wet and rainy day. An old hen had been sitting on her tack box so somebody put pheasant eggs under her. They hatched Sunday, so besides two horses, Debbie has 16 baby chicks to look after. Her comment was if her family keeps increasing, she and Jack will have to add a wing to their proposed ranch house.

Jeepers, February is here and I'm beginning to whiff the scent of spring, which I love so much. There's a chance I'll be up in Los Angeles for a weekend soon. A high-school girlfriend, whom I haven't seen since, will be there for a week and asked me to come up. Right now, however, we're all wrapped up in Lois' wedding. Susan and I appear as excited as she. We're just having loads of fun.

And speaking of weddings, I've a lulu to report. Remember Avis? She wrote to say that she and Mark crossed the state line last Saturday, married in Las Vegas, and dashed back Sunday for him to pick up his ship setting sail for the high seas. It was done on impulse and her family is in shock. I hope them the best. Mark is a nice guy, but what a crazy way to start out life together.

Back to us. Darling, I miss you so much. How I would love to see you! How I would love to be in your arms, but I hardly dare let myself dream along these lines (except when I sleep and then the most wonderful things can happen). Yes, tis true. I love, love, love, love you always. Good night, my love. Your valentine,

Mopsy

☆ ☆ ☆

The bridge game was over and Cory was in Hawk's stateroom watching him stash away their night winnings. He said nothing, astonished though he was. Hawk, the brilliant bridge player, the razor-sharp mind, had made not one but two major blunders that significantly reduced their winnings. Hawk made no attempt at explanation, seemingly oblivious or uncaring of his subpar performance, either one hard for Cory to understand.

"Let us have a drink," Hawk simply said as he moved toward his booze closet. He mixed two strong highballs. "We're still in port, the skipper's ashore, so your watch tonight is not needful of vigilance. Savor well."

Cory studied Hawk's countenance. He had never seen him look this old, well beyond his fortyish years. Something had to be in his craw, but it was up to Hawk if he wanted to broach the subject. Cory respected his privacy. "Skoal," Cory said.

Hawk tapped glasses. Still out of character, he drained half his glass in one gulp. Then he opened up. "I was at a briefing today. It's set in concrete. Iwo Jima is next."

"Never heard of it."

"You will. It's in the Volcano Islands, midway between Saipan and Tokyo. Its location is its importance. Its airstrip would be handy for emergency landings of our B-29 sorties from the Marianas to Japan." Hawk took another large gulp of whiskey. "I visited the island several years ago. A miserable place. No vegetation, no animal life, mostly ash, barren caves, and canyons. Not fit for human habitation, the Japs colonized it years ago for sulphur mining. The grim part is that it has all the makings of an underground fortress. Its many caves can become interconnected, and an ugly five-hundred-foot mountain surveys its southern tip."

"How big is the island?"

"Small. Shaped like a pork chop, I'd say not much more than ten square miles. The brass thinks it can be taken in three days with two divisions and a third in reserve."

"What do you think?"

"It'll be a blood bath. It'll take all three divisions and God knows how long. Those caves are deep and won't be touched by the air strikes. The only beaches are on the southern rim of the island so you can forget about surprise landings. Gash, this will be the roughest campaign we've had in the Pacific. Since it has no natural supply of water, I wish we'd just blockade it."

Cory sipped the rest of his drink in silence and then exclaimed, "Hawk, this is insane. Over sixty thousand invaders and likely forty thousand defenders on an island half the size of San Diego Bay!"

"Strictly hand-to-hand combat with many no returns."

Cory returned to Goat Castle shaken, determined not to mention his conversation with Hawk to anyone. What good would it do? He plopped on his bunk, still some time before his watch.

Scorch gave him a hard look. "You look down, man. Tough night at the bridge table?"

"Naw. Into the woe-is-me syndrome. Here I am, confined in a monastery, figuring that Tally's out with dudes night after night having a ball at dances, picnics, parties, the fights, whatever. And I don't want to hear that since angels have wings, it would be cruel and unusual punishment to keep them caged."

"I do detect the green sprouts of jealousy. The hobo must be in love. Say, how'd you like to have the address of a mail-order house that sells chastity belts?"

"Jeeze! At least you're right on one thing, Scorch. The hobo's in love. And being the skeptic that you are, to back my words with action, I hereby bequeath to you my little black book. Every chick in it comes guaranteed to satisfy your perversion for revelry."

Scorch, shaking his head, took the book. "I'll be damned," was his oral summation as he slipped the book into his desk drawer and headed for the wardroom for a cup of coffee.

On February 17, the *Hudson,* loaded with marines of the Twenty-seventh Regiment of the Fifth Divison and the elite core of the Thirty-first C.B.'s, left Saipan in convoy to assault the beaches of Iwo Jima. When well at sea, Gil Harvey called together the boat division.

"Well, guys," he drawled, "this meeting is to dot the i's and cross the t's in the plans we've rehearsed for days and will implement on the nineteenth. Here are the specifics for the *Plan of the Day*. It starts at 0145 with the call for the cooks and bakers. Reveille for the troops is 0245 and their breakfast is 0300. Reveille for the boat crews is 0330 and breakfast is 0400. General quarters for dawn alert is 0500. Condition 1 ABLE is set for 0515. All hands will stand in to hoist out boats and debark troops. We arrive at the transport area at 0616. Sunrise is 0707 and H-hour is 0900.

"I don't have to tell you that this is the closest invasion yet to the Japanese homeland. Strong resistance to the landing is expected. You've studied the aerial photos until you're bored, but by now you should know that after the planes drop their napalm bombs and the ships fire their rounds of shells, there'll be no resemblance between the pictures and the terrain. The major consideration is to keep proper distance between the waves and between the designated beaches. Instances of these failures at Saipan caused crowded waves and crowded beaches, which unfortunately added to the casualties. I'll be in the control vessel should unforeseen problems develop. You have the code. Any questions?"

"How long are we likely to be there?" asked the Mole.

"The plan calls for two days. But keep a spare tube of toothpaste in the first-aid kit." Laughter. "We're adjourned."

"Can't ever accuse Gil of dragging out meetings," Scorch remarked to Cory on their return to Goat Castle. "What does Hawk have to say about the operation?"

"You know cool customer Hawk. He was more concerned over lining up two light colonels for bridge tonight." Why, Cory reminded himself, should I say more?

Cory stretched out on his bunk and tried to get his mind off what he knew lay ahead. He picked up and reread Tally's last letter, which just made the mail boat before their leaving Saipan.

My Darling,

Your letter tonight was wonderfully reassuring. I can't begin ever to tell you how much your letters mean and do for me, Cory. I wish I had your strength, your hold on reality. You live with danger, yet it is I who is quick to read between the lines, things which likely don't exist at all, and also clutch for things too preposterous to attain. Perhaps I'm overly severe on myself. Perhaps most sentimental girls, madly in love, frightened by a war that never seems to end, would be just as unstable. Who knows anything for sure nowadays!

I am hearing some wonderful music on the radio, a Brahm symphony, and all else is quiet ere this scratchy pen. Gosh, I've dropped it, bent its point, and yet it still writes. Debbie is at the stables and Laura accompanied Chad to San Francisco where he's now shipping out. They had their fourth anniversary Friday and our house is covered with roses, compliments of their folks. A florist shop we do have! The roses are truly gorgeous.

Being Sunday yesterday, Susan, Lois, and I spent the day at one of their friend's home on the edge of town. It's a big rambling house built on top of a hill overlooking the bay. The climb to it is a half-mile high. Everything about it is rustic and the moment you enter the grounds, you feel completely divorced from San Diego. It was one of the most peaceful days I have ever spent. Wouldn't it be wonderful to wake up each day amidst such wooded splendor! After dinner, we got into the fundamentals of bridge. I'm sure I'll enjoy the game once I really get the knack of it.

Lois is getting more excited as the day of her wedding approaches. I had fun after work picking out a new dress for the event.

Cory, darling, I like your broadminded view. You are right postponing serious talk until you return and the stresses of war are behind us. I only hope we won't have to wait too long. Not that *any* time would be too long, darling. I just sorta miss you terribly much and wish we could be lonely together. Good night, darling, I give you my love. Sweet dreams always. Yours forever.

Mopsy

# FEBRUARY–MARCH 1945

# *The Fateful Letter*

It was Saturday near noon in late February of 1945. Debbie and Laura were out of town participating in a weekend horse show, and Tally, still in her bathrobe and slippers, having enjoyed a late sleep and a leisure breakfast, checked the mailbox. Her heart jumped, as always, when she spotted a letter from Cory. She plopped into the chair by the window where the sunlight flooded the room and eagerly opened it.

The salutation caught her eye. Instead of Dearest One or Darling One, it was Dear One. A bit constrained, she thought, but she shrugged it off and went on to the opening lines.

> Don't be deceived, Mopsy, by the idle rumors that the war might soon be over. Nothing could be further from the truth. The chant "out and alive in fifty-five" has more merit than the "Golden Gate in forty-eight." An earthquake swallowing up Honshu might change the timetable, but I've noticed God's use of miracles these days are fewer in number and much smaller in scope.
>
> I know the foe only too well. He thinks on a different plane from us. He is on a mission driven by a fanaticism seen only in primitive religions. He would rather die for his emperor than live for his loved ones.
>
> The glory of his last act is measured by the numbers he can take with him. We dominate on land sea, and sky, yet he will defend to his very last breath every inch of his sacred soil. Surrendering is dishonorable. Death only is acceptable.

Tally felt a pang. Why would Cory begin in this vein? He with the glass half-full. He with the undeclared mandate to keep her spirits up and morale strong. She read on.

No cruelty cuts deeper than those idle rumors that each campaign will be our last. What fiendish delight can there be in dangling the carrot of false hopes? Orders will never be issued to jeopardize victory. As we get closer to Tokyo, the enemy will put up even more resistance. The High Command will be forced to stay with the battle-proven. Only the walking wounded will be sent stateside to train the recruits on the ins and outs of amphibious landings. Sure as the sun rises in the east, those of us who are still ambulating in Goat Castle will be ferrying the troops across the emperor's moat!

Tally's antenna was now up. Cory knew full well that the prospects of stateside orders made bearable the awful pain of separation. It kept alive the hope that Cory might be home for Christmas, the one gift she constantly prayed for, the only gift that really mattered. Why should risk be the lot of the few? Why shouldn't it be shared? Why must those with experience be condemned to face repeatedly the guns of war? How long can the odds be beaten? The props began to crumble under her; a mist formed in her eyes, a dull pain in her head. Then she rallied, took a deep breath, and told herself that when she turned the page she'd read: Mopsy, stop being so infernally serious. Have you forgotten I'm part leprechaun. This is a joke. I'm setting you up for April Fools' Day. Truth is, the Nips have had all of this bloody war they can stomach. Thery're ready to boot out the warlords and bring in the peaceniks. The emperor actually is a dove hiding in hawk's clothes. The reassuring words never appeared. There was no winking leprechaun. Instead, the gloom deepened. Cory next touched upon the godlessness of war.

We know that an all-powerful and compassionate Being would never let the best and the brightest become so much cannon fodder unless He was no longer on the watch. One can only assume that human folly has exceeded his threshold of patience. God knows I can fully understand that!

Tears began wetting Tally's cheeks. Cory was knocking out her every prop. What was the purpose? He had to have a reason. He knew the comfort she gained in putting her trust into the hands of a higher power for his safe return. He had to know how helpless she felt without leaning on a strength beyond hers. Would he have her desert Him?

The last paragraph was a brief reflection on love. He asked and seemed to answer his own questions.

> How deeply do we understand our tenderest emotion? Very little. The dazzle of it blinds us from seeing its true essence. Is the better measure how well we laugh together or how well we cry together? The sadness of love rests in its illusions.

A chill went through Tally's body. Cory knew their love flowered on fun and laughter which, in part, gave it its dazzle. Did that make it frivolous? Flawed? An illusion? Was he implying it was shallow? A dagger pierced her heart.

Tally was glad she was alone when she read the letter. She went up to her room, flung her body on the bed, and sobbed. She suddenly became all visceral. Her hands and feet turned cold and clammy, then numb. Her heart struggled to beat, rebelled against working. She could not form clear thoughts. Only hazy images flitted in and out of an aching consciousness.

Her body had absorbed the message her mind had decoded. Cory had lost his ardor. The fire had burned out. She picked up his picture, looked into his eyes, saw the passion shining through. Love was there. Nothing could be of more certainty. But now it was gone, dissolved, a casualty of war that is never recorded. Why else would he focus on the things that would puncture her dreams, dash her hopes, induce despair!

Tally was unable to stop the onrush of tears. Her body convulsed with the flow. The flood finally subsided. She drifted into a feverish sleep.

She awoke and it was nighttime. She craved fresh air, to go to Coronado Beach to draw on Cory's strength which she always found there, to keep herself from further disintegrating. She changed into her red and white dress, worn on their first date, put on a sweater to break the night chill and took the ferry.

Tally had the shoreline to herself as it was not a night for strollers. The swirling wind kept her hair in her face. She buttoned up her sweater. She strided the beach, venting fury to the sea and sky. The sobs of rage were not directed at Cory. She saw him like herself a victim. He had lost no nobility in her eyes. He was still untarnished truth and integrity. He had loved her and wanted her until the forces of a higher fate took him from her. Her rage was directed at a war callously indifferent to young love and to a God seemingly unwilling to do anything about it.

The brisk pace seemed to be helping. Clearer thoughts were beginning to sift through the inner chaos to suggest her brain was coming out of its partial paralysis. But they were disturbing thoughts. Thoughts raising the specter that fate may not be the entire story. For the first time, the possibility of a rival loomed up. How foolish, she chided herself, not to have entertained the idea before. Only the abnormal times could explain why it never crossed her mind. In the limited time they had together, she was intent on living each moment to the fullest, to think of nothing else. Life for her began anew when Cory entered her heart; events of the past faded away, became unimportant. She assumed that Cory was experiencing the same thing. What right had she to think so? So naive!

As the crisp night air began cooling down her feverish brain, the argument for a rival grew stronger. Why would there not be a special somebody before the war? As Scorch implied, Cory was a man of all seasons. A distressing scenario began taking form. She saw a woman of charming sophistication weaving her tantalizing web even as she and Cory were first meeting. This was not to suggest that his love for her was ever insincere or compromised.

No, she could not have been misled on that. She reflected on a letter in which he expressed the belief that it was possible to have more than one great love, which she took then as a point of theory, but now wondered if he might not have had himself in mind. His love for her rival would also have to be genuine. Tally could not imagine it any other way. It was not in Cory's nature to live with deception.

The triangle theory meshed with other facts. It went along with his insistence on no commitments, no long-range promises, no social restrictions. But, what could have caused the balance to tip in favor of her rival? Her heart sank. Of course! It had to be the letters. How drab must appear the everyday events of an ordinary working girl compared to the glamorous adventures of an educated world traveler. Misery now fully engulfed her. She couldn't cry any more. Her tear glands were empty. The hour had become very late. She retraced her steps, took the ferry home, and crawled between the sheets for several hours of fitful tossing before the dawn broke.

Tally had resolved to keep her pain to herself. If anyone should notice her washed-out look, she was prepared to blame it on a contagious bug. She nibbled on a little food, returned to bed, and dozed off till noon. She finally dressed and returned again Sunday afternoon to Coronado. This time she climbed the huge boulder overlooking the ocean that she and Cory usurped as their rock. It was mysteriously romantic because one could hear but not see the surf lapping at its base, emanating a steady heartbeat of its own. Her mind was now fresher and her emotions more subdued, although it would take very little to unleash more tears. She felt close to Cory as she gazed out toward the infinity of waves. She could feel his anguish radiating toward her. How ironic! She who wanted most to make him happy now saw herself blocking his way.

The crux of Cory's plan loomed ever so clear. In puncturing her dream balloon, he would open the gates to a reality she had not let take root. Her practical side would then come to the fore and have her see the folly of trying to nourish a romance through a war that seemed to be dragging on without end. Anything planted in barren soil ultimately dies on the vine. A strategem, centering on preserving pride and self-esteem, would be Cory's sensitive way of resolving conflict.

Oh, how he has misjudged the strength of my love, Tally sadly reflected. I would have endured a thousand wars and a million tortures! But he must never know that she had bareboned his plan. And he must never know the grief that it brought to her heart. She could not bear to let that happen. She could not forget what new dimensions he had brought into her life. She must make him believe his stratagem was working. But had she the cleverness to do it? She had grave doubts. Nevertheless, she saw no other course of action. And she strangely found by turning her mind on what she believed would lighten his pain, she had somewhat lessened her own.

Tally spent the afternoon mentally composing and discarding a dozen letters. None satisfied her. Her weary mind needed rest. It was time to start back, and she hoped a new day might inspire better results. She took a long lingering look at the white caps, and her eyes again brimmed with tears. She could not block out the agonizing question: Why, oh why, my precious love, must this be? If leaping to the jagged rocks below would somehow help, she had the courage, but even her tormented soul understood that would only make matters worse.

As Tally boarded the ferry to return to the city, she suddenly remembered that Robert had made a dinner date with her before he left on his last business trip. While this was a deviation from the past, it appeared spontaneous so she accepted, never doubting the propriety. Today was the day. Her first impulse was to call when she reached the ranch and cancel out, but then she reconsidered. Wallowing in self-pity would only raise curiosity in her housemates, now likely home from the horse show, whom she did not yet wish to involve. Further, she had come to respect Robert's judgment and trusted his confidentiality should the issue present itself.

Tally showed resilience. Draining as the day had been, she showered, dressed up, made over her face, and put forth a false buoyancy when Robert arrived. She chatted airily all the way to the restaurant, which was situated away from the noise of the city, isolated among tall palms overlooking the ocean.

Robert ordered cocktails, a dry martini for himself and a brandy Alexander for Tally. After they had several sips in silence, he gently asked, "What is wrong, Tally?"

"Whatever do you mean?"

He smiled. "May I make a suggestion? Never get yourself into a high-stake poker game because you could never pull off a bluff. Under stress you wiggle your toes. You wiggled them all the way to the restaurant."

She laughed and then atypically downed her cocktail without pause. "Please order me another one. I promise not to fall asleep, and it'll give me the dutch courage to open up."

Robert ordered refills and gave Tally all the time she needed to frame her thoughts. She slipped a handkerchief from her purse and dabbed her eyes. "Thank you, Robert, for putting up with me. I received a letter yesterday from Cory that still has me reeling in a state of shock. The gist of it is that he's had a change of heart. The passion that once flamed has died out, or perhaps I should say has been redirected."

"There is another woman?"

"What else would so cool his ardor?"

"But he actually hasn't admitted it?"

"That would not be Cory's style." She again dabbed her eyes. "Even in ending a relationship, he would be protective of the girl. The strategy underlying his letter, in a nutshell, was to stress the hopelessness of a romance born and bred in the crucible of a war that has no end in sight, relying on my practical side to then grasp the reality, suppress the sentimental aspects, and initiate steps toward withdrawal. My desire is to make him think I have come to see his point, and I should like your help in making it seem convincing."

"You want him to believe his ploy has worked?"

"If the relationship must end, I want him to believe it was done at my instigation. I don't want to stand in the way of his happiness."

"Tally, this is incredible. Most women staggering under a similar blow would fight hurt with hurt, but you are more concerned with his well-being. This rare quality, I must admit, is most admirable."

"It's not all that noble, Robert, when it becomes clear how much I really owe Cory. Through him I have come to better know myself, to realize my potential for love, and to be more tuned to the beautiful side of life. So if another woman can best give him happiness, I have no wish to be seen as a roadblock." Tears again welled up in her eyes.

Robert glanced away pretending not to see them. "Yes," he said, "I can see it's important how you phrase your response."

Tally forced a smile. "I already feel some relief because I can tell you understand where I am and where I wish to go."

Robert sipped on his drink for an extended silence. The waiter interrupted his thoughts, and Robert ordered for both of them. "You need to keep up your strength," he said. "A tenderloin steak accompanied with a vintage wine should met the doctor's approval." He then paused again to sort out his words. "I suggest in writing Cory you openly admit to certain troubled feelings which in all good conscience you could no longer leave unaddressed. Tell him of the existence of our relationship, the circumstances bringing it about, and the ground rules that guided it. Then tell him of the totally unexpected turn of events transpiring this one night when he crossed the lines, confessed his true feelings, and made a proposal of marriage. Tell him the startling development threw you into temporary shock, made worse by becoming suddenly aware of your difficulty in immediately rejecting the proposal."

Tally was touched. "That's a most gracious gesture on your part to allow yourself to become involved in my plight, but I fear Cory would instantly see through the gambit."

Robert's voice lowered to just above a whisper. "No gambit. It's the truth. I really don't know how or when it happened, but it did. All I can say with certainty is that when it happened, I was taken aback. Logic, which had controlled my life, abandoned me. The timing of it could not have been worse. I fell in love with a girl I had no right to love, and if I told her, it would mean it would be the last time I'd ever see her."

Tally's eyes were big as saucers. "Robert—"

He quickly waved a hand. "Please let me finish. I, who prided myself in having my life plans so neatly blueprinted, found my intellect and emotions at crossed purposes. My emotions refused to listen to the will of reason. They dominated my waking thoughts and ignored the hard facts of reality. I debated what to do and decided I could not continue to perpetuate a hypocrisy. The honorable thing was to be up front with my feelings and accept the bitter consequences. The colossal irony is that it was to be at this dinner that I was to let the truth out.

"Then when the conversation took the turn that it did, I saw at once that the confession could be put to your advantage in dealing with your current crisis."

Tally, still wide eyed, fumbled for words. "Robert, I had no idea! I had never allowed my personal feelings to go beyond the terms of our arrangement, and I assumed the same was going on with you. You were right. If I had sensed any amorous developments, I'd have withdrawn. As a one-man woman I would be adverse to even entertaining the idea. But under the present circumstances, I do see, as you've suggested, the possibilities of this knowledge helping me in framing a response to Cory. I know it's leaving you in a way dangling in the air, which is not at all fair to you, but I just haven't the wits to cope with our situation, too."

"Nor would I want you to even try. Your first obligation is to Cory. Sorting out where we are can wait."

"Robert, I can't oversay, how kind and thoughtful you are." Tally put down her fork. "I'm sorry, but my appetite just isn't up to all of this delicious food." They left the restaurant with a good portion still on her plate.

When Tally got back to the ranch, she was surprised but glad that Debbie and Laura had still not returned from out of town. She desired to be alone, to frame her letter without distraction. She did not even turn on the radio. She did have Cory's picture at her side.

In contemplating how to form it, she decided the letter would be, as truth would imply, brief, straightforward, no frills, and to the point. She would tell Cory of her pact with Robert, the startling disclosure, and her ambivalence. The ambivalence would be his window to close out the relationship according to the strategy he had set in motion. She picked up her pen with heavy heart.

February 24, 1945

Gash Dear,

I feel so strongly the need to write you; I want to write you, I must for my own peace of mind. I won't try to conjure up a multitude of excuses for the pickle I'm in because I want to be up front and let you know the facts as clear and honest as I can. By now you're probably guessing there's another person and my difficulty is in conveying a changed heart. That would be terribly misleading, Cory. That would belie the struggle going on within me, the struggle to straighten out my mind, to straighten out my thoughts and feelings, which are all mixed up. There is another person, that is true, and I have to address that.

The person in question is one whom I've known since I first came out here. Why things should get complicated now, I don't know. He knew of you when the friendship began and he understood friendship was all that I wanted. He never attempted to alter the relationship, and left me comfortably certain nothing would ever change. I guess it was the fact of being together so much of the time that we slowly grew on one another. Then he left on a trip and I wouldn't admit unto myself that I missed him. On his return, in an astonishing and dramatic turnabout, he asked me to marry him.

My feelings are most confused toward him, Cory. I'm very fond of him, but can't sort out the muddle beyond that. He's occupationally deferred from the military and is six years older than I.

Although I don't feel up to a decision at this moment, I know, in fairness to all, I must do so reasonably soon, hurting at the thought that no one leaves unhurt. It was just something that I hadn't foreseen.

Perhaps you did see it, Cory, which was why you wanted no promises. As usual, you were wise. No matter what takes place, I'll never forget the fun we had together, the sweetness you brought to my life. How I wish you were here to talk to. If in admitting my confusion, I have pained you, may God forgive me, but I could never hold anything back from you.

Please write soon. I want so much to hear from you, and in the meantime, I hope I shall be able to straighten things out in my mind.

Loving you,

Mopsy

Tears welled up in Tally's eyes as she sealed the envelope.

During coffee break the next day at work, Tally phoned Robert to tell him the letter had been written and posted. She expressed the wish to stay busy in the interval awaiting Cory's response. She thought it best not to inform the Inner Circle of the happenings until after she heard from Cory. Robert was

Johnny on the spot, saying he was flexible and would happily adjust his schedule according to her needs, again assuring her of absolute confidentiality.

Tally also desired limited social activity as it would be exhausting to maintain a front of gaiety and lightness. Robert understood and, after a moment's pause, said he had the perfect remedy. He went on to tell her that he and a friend jointly owned a sailboat and suggested that they go sailing in the late afternoons after work. It would be quiet and peaceful. She thought it a wonderful idea, but reminded him that being a mountain girl, she had never sailed or been tested for sea legs.

And so it was, Robert would come to the ranch after Tally came home from work, take her to the marina, and they would sail in the bay until sunset. They would then have a snack to finish out the day.

Tally found the outing wonderfully refreshing. "Sailing is so relaxing and so much fun," she bubbled. "I can see how one could get addicted to it."

One afternoon on an unusually beautiful day on the water, her mind becalmed, Tally turned inquisitively to Robert. "In the months we've known each other, I've babbled about the traumas in my life—my broken home, Ted's tragedy, job insecurity, crises with Cory, the woes of the Inner Circle—but I've never given you the time to talk about yours. So, tell me about the trials and tribulations of one Robert Graham."

He laughed. "Low drama compared to yours. I was born and fed here in San Diego, pretty much with a silver spoon, got a degree in finance at UCLA, and worked in sales ever since. My father made a bundle in the stock market in the twenties and lost it in the depression with the help of several bad investments. How bad they were, I never realized until after he and mother died in a car wreck and I was the executor of the estate. He had not only lost his savings but also bequeathed a heavy debt. Although I was not legally obligated, I was determined to pay every cent he owed.

After the good life he provided me, the least I could do was to see that his good name would not end up sullied. Complicating matters was that I had a kid brother born mongoloid who had to be placed in a private retardation center. It broke my mother's heart to have him taken from the home but he needed special custodial care. I thus had to contend with the expenses of his upkeep. He died a couple of years later, not too surprising as people with Down syndrome have a short lifespan.

"The positive side of all this was that it forced me to put my shoulder to the wheel and learn the meaning of hard work. The slate was cleared by the time of Pearl Harbor. The war then opened up financial opportunities, allowing me to build a nestegg and begin to enjoy the lifestyle I was born into. And, by the way, I have completed the requirements for the real estate license, so I can start my new career whenever I wish, most likely after the war."

"What impresses me most, Robert, was your resolve to clear your father's debt and let him rest in peace with his reputation unsullied. Most sons in your situation would have taken the easy route of bankruptcy. What you did reflects integrity, and to me that is a cardinal virtue."

The more Tally learned about Robert, the more she liked.

When the letter from Cory arrived, Tally, with heart beating fast, waited until Laura and Debbie left to tend to the horses before opening it. The tears began to form just on reading the opening sentence.

March 3, 1945

Dear Tally,

I'm responding quickly to your letter because I feel delay would only prolong the anguish.

Problems of the heart, I've always felt, are best resolved by the heart. From the tone of your letter, I venture that the conflict is more between your mind and heart than within your heart. The heart seems to have made its decision, reflected best in the candor of the letter, but the mind seems yet to accept it. Do not torment yourself this way. Honor has not been breached. I see no deceit, no manipulation. What is so sad is that we do not control the stars that control our destiny.

Is it painful? Yes. But the pain is bearable because the memories, so beautiful, are safely stored in the heart. Memories in the heart never fade. And they always stay fresh.

I shall probably never meet the thief who stole the gem I found in Coronado. It would plague me if I thought for a moment he lacked the sensitivity to value its quality, but if he were a philistine, I'm sure that little voice inside of you would have vehemently protested. Its silence indicates any such concern is unwarranted.

Love,
Cory

The tears flowed again down Tally's cheeks. Cory's reply closed out further speculations. The sensitively crafted letter, hallmarked with tenderness and acceptance, gave no evidence that the dialogue should continue, which could only mean, as she originally feared, that his ardor had been redirected.

She pulled out a handkerchief and dried her tears. She swallowed the little moisture still in her mouth to soothe the dry lump in her throat. As her mind's gyroscope paused in its spinning, she took stock. Cory was right. Delay would only serve to prolong the agony. The least anguish would have her focus solely on the unspoken agenda, the request to terminate the relationship. Yes, she shall comply and shall do so with dignity. She shall act swiftly and with a modicum of emotion. She summoned every ounce of her strength to pen what she knew would be her final letter to Cory.

Cory Dear,

You have been so kind and I want to write and thank you for your very sweet and sincere letter. It was so like you, always so tender and protective of a girl's heart. What you are makes me feel so privileged in knowing you. My opinion of you, Cory, has not altered nor will it ever. I still think you are wonderful. I hope your opinion of me will always be charitable.

I won't forget you, Cory. May your life be filled with happiness as deep as the ocean which separated us and with grief as light as its foam. God bless you and keep you always. Good night for now.

Mopsy

Tally, her composure under rigid control, called Robert to tell him her ties with Cory had formally ended. "Cory's letter came," she said. "He dealt with the ambivalence as his window to close out further dialogue, which confirmed the handwriting on the wall. So, to continue the role of the strayed lover, I wrote him a brief letter thanking him for accepting so graciously the unplanned turn of events." Tally then told Robert she would like a little time in solitude to get her emotions moving toward even keel. As usual, he understood, said for her to set her own pace, and call him the moment she felt comfortable.

The next day, Sunday, Tally once more took the ferry to Coronado in the afternoon and visited the "Rock." Her eyes gazed seaward as she stood on the top edge. Her mind was remarkably clear, her emotions well reined in. She talked aloud in a steady voice to the busy waves forming white caps on the seascape.

"Oh, Cory, you do know I love you. There will always be a special place in my heart for you as I hope there is in your heart for me. Our love, now secret between us, will always be healing, never destructive. This is because you have given me the meaning of mature love, love that flows outward, love that is centrifugal.

"Oh, Cory, I now understand when my little voice would cry out. It was telling me that my love was too immature, too possessive, too self-serving. If it stays quiet with Robert, it is telling me I am not on the rebound. I could not abide that. Love on the rebound is centripetal love."

Tally climbed off the rock. This time there were no tears to cloud her eyes. And for the first time she was beginning to feel inner peace. It was time to call Robert.

# The Unthinkable

On the following Sunday, a lovely springlike day, Tally, Susan, Laura, and Debbie enjoyed the afternoon on horseback in the countryside. They returned to the ranch rosy-cheeked from the airing and gathered in the living area to whet their tonsils with a glass of sherry before dinner.

This was the moment Tally had chosen to inform. She lifted her wine glass. "An announcement, fellow musketeers," she said in a raised voice. "Mark your calendars for an Easter wedding. Robert and I are getting married."

Dead silence filled the room. Tally smiled faintly at the room of bulging eyes. "Come alive, m'lasses. Begorra, I announced a wedding, not a wake."

Debbie was first to recover. "We noticed that Robert's been banging on the door of late more often than the Avon lady, but we had no inkling things had gone this far. Fill us in."

"Robert returned from a business trip several weeks ago, took me out to dinner, and out of the blue calmly made known that he was in love with me, had been for some days, and could no longer keep the secret even if it meant the end of our companionship. He then asked me to marry him. Needless to say, I was flabbergasted and speechless. He had always acted the perfect gentleman, never deviated the slightest way from the terms of our agreement, and never gave a clue of any change of feeling. I, in turn, never had a second thought on a romantic liaison between us. Robert, in his usual perceptive fashion, broke the awkwardness commenting that since his confession did not provoke instant outrage, I take the time to sort out the flood of feelings that are undoubtedly besieging my mind before responding. I thanked him."

A pin could have been heard dropping on the floor, so riveting was the attention in the room. Her toes wiggling, Tally took a sip of sherry before continuing. "When I slowly regained my wits, I was startled at my hesitation in not summarily rejecting the proposal. Instead, I was filled with ambivalence. I became suddenly aware of how much I had come to enjoy Robert's company and admire his many qualities."

"Propinquity is a factor in human relations," Susan thoughtfully said. "The war has clearly deprived you and Cory in that respect."

Laura broke in. "Another important difference is commitment. Robert seems to have provided it; Cory, I gather, has not."

Tally continued. "I delayed giving Robert an answer until yesterday. During my vacillations, he remained considerate and patient, never pressing me. On convincing myself that I could be the kind of wife he needed and wanted, and he could give the love and security I needed, I told him I'd be happy to marry him. I also told him if he wished to hold off the date until he had more evidence of my emotional stability, I could well understand. He gallantly replied that any delay would be to his disadvantage."

"And so," Susan said, "the boss gets two weeks' notice and a justice of the peace gets put on notice."

"In a pig's eye! Begorra, it's going to be a chapel wedding. I called Cindy and after her shock wore off she agreed to be matron of honor. Ted will give me away since my dad is too ill to come. Then I plan to corral the rest of the Inner Circle for bridesmaids. Getting everybody together in less than two weeks would be expecting too much."

Laura raised her glass. "Well, begorra, then here's to our ravishing bride." The glasses clicked and Tally blushed.

That night Tally had one more soul-wrenching task to perform. On making her commitment to Robert, she resolved she would do everything in her power to keep the shadow of Cory from popping up between them. She pledged never to make comparisons and sought not to even bring Cory's name up in conversation. She then made the hard decision to rid herself of the things that would encourage reminiscences. This meant photos and letters. She would keep his first and last letter and the fateful letter among her other correspondence as they lacked the intimacy of the others and contained no love poems. She could not bear to part with the peace dove and the pearl necklace, but vowed to store them and not wear them as long as Robert lived. She also would keep her copy of the skit. Resolutely, she then took his handsome pictures and the many beautiful letters down to the fireplace and set a match to them. Teary-eyed, she watched them slowly turn to ashes, the cremation of a beautiful dream.

The wedding, small but charming and full of dignity, went off with consummate grace. All of the Inner Circle—Cindy, Debbie, Avis, Susan, and Laura—attended. Ted came alone from Denver. Special selected friends, such as Buck and Pops and members of the car pool, made up the wedding guests. Cindy and Susan had the most difficult time. While they had no qualms that Robert would be a loving, caring, and a well-providing husband, they struggled with the concept of a substitute for Cory. Gash and Mopsy was a match they firmly believed was made in heaven. Tears dampened their cheeks when the vested cleric asked Tally, "Do you take this man . . ."

Robert had thoughtfully planned out the honeymoon. Aware of Tally's fondness of mountains and snow, he rented a snug cabin high in the Sierras where the winter's last snowfall still covered the ground. He had figured the isolation, too, would be a balm for Tally's emotions still tender and on the mend.

Tally picked up at once on Robert's thoughtfulness. The moment she entered the cozy cabin, she threw herself into his arms. "Oh, darling," she gushed, "you have been so wonderful, so patient, so understanding these past weeks with such a sorry, fickle, emotionally mess of a girl. But I promise I will become the best wife that ever graced your harem." She kissed him with passion and he held her long.

It was an idyllic week in the mountains. The scenery revitalized Tally. Resorting gleefully to the child of nature that never had left her, she would run and jump in the snow, make snowballs, and pepper a ducking Robert. She made artistic snowmen. Inside, she would lie in his arms on the leopard-skin hearth before the blazing logs, sip champagne, tweak his nose and ears, and smother him with kisses. "French champagne!" she'd exclaimed. "You're spoiling me rotten." Early on she asked, "Darling, just how many children do you want?"

He thought for a moment. "Four would be ideal and max. Two of each."

Her infectious laugh rang out. "In that case, begorra, we best get started. I don't want to be an old lady in shawl when the last one arrives."

A bubbly and fully refreshed Tally left her pastoral honeymoon cabin to begin domestic housekeeping in a modest apartment Robert had somehow found in the housing-shortage city. Tally loved it. It was the perfect beginning to a new life, and Robert, in his steady fashion, was forging an anchor of security that had always eluded her.

She was getting happily settled when a letter arrived that was forwarded from the ranch. Curiously, it came from Scorch. A feeling of apprehension gripped her. She was alone as Robert had left for work when she sat down on the sofa and opened it.

April 8, 1945

Dear Mopsy,
    No letter has ever been harder for me to write. But, I owe it to the best friend I ever had. Grip tightly the arm of your chair. This morning we buried Gash at sea. Full military honors. He died from wounds inflicted at Okinawa.

The sound emitting from Tally was much like the plaintive cry of an animal in the wilds that had been impaled with an arrow. For a moment her nervous system stopped functioning. The letter fluttered down on top of the coffee table. When she stirred and slowly regained awareness, she groped for the brandy decanter. She quickly downed a jigger to prevent another blackout. Had she read correctly? She picked up the letter and refocused. It was true. Cory was buried at sea. The burning thought that she had stopped praying for his safety seared her mind. Tears exploded in her eyes. Hysterical convulsions followed. When her vision finally cleared, she forced herself to read on.

> He did not suffer. He was in a coma throughout. I was thankful he was transferred to our ship where his closest friends could give him the final rites of his choice. It seemed most fitting for him to find lasting peace in the sea that both you and I know he so profoundly loved.
>
> There wasn't a dry eye on the deck. Gash affected us all. He did not have an enemy in the boat division. To me he was a brother. My heart goes out to you, Mopsy. No finer love have I seen between two people. How well I remember the night I first met you and watched the two of you on the dance floor. I could see then that this relationship was definitely more than a fling on the town.

How strange, it leaped out at her, that Scorch was writing as if the relationship was still ongoing. Probably psychological regression brought on by overwhelming grief. Or was it possible that Cory kept the rift all to himself? But what reason would he have in keeping his best friend in the dark? More likely Scorch knew but was just being discreet under the circumstances. He surely knew about the other woman. She returned to the letter.

> Cory's one big fear never materialized. In one of our seldom serious talks—he was always upbeat, as you know—he said it

was not death but half-death that he dreaded most. The notion of becoming a burden on others was intolerable. The guy was fiercely proud. Well, his wish was granted. Had he survived he would have been permanently brain damaged.

Other than overwhelmingly sad, I'm also pissed-angry. One thing we all learned early in the amphibs was that we don't volunteer for anything. Gash violated this basic principle. Before the Okinawa invasion, there was a call for volunteers for frogmen. These are the guys, the underwater demolition team, who go in first to clear the obstructions, so hazardous that only volunteers are considered. I couldn't believe it and told Gash he was crazy when he said he planned to sign up. He had too much going for him, not only a great future but one of the prettiest girls on the West Coast waiting for him. In fact, we just had our last mail call and as usual there was a letter from you. At least he had that moment of happiness before the end. When I asked him what made him think of doing this, he shrugged and said that he's one of the few that carries a rabbit's foot. I really think that damn Boy Scout complex got the best of him. It turned out to be our last conversation.

Oh, no! Tally reflected. Scorch *was* totally unaware of their split. He was present when Cory received my last letter, and yet Cory chose not to let him know that our affair was over. She continued to puzzle on. Why would Cory volunteer for an assignment of such danger, especially now that he was free of the one impediment to his greater love? Was it, as Scorch suggested, his Boy Scout complex? With her heart weighting down with pain and confusion, she weakly finished the last paragraphs.

He nearly made it. In their last sweep, a booby trap was touched off, killing several outright and wounding more, Gash the most severely.

I'm still numb over it. The landing itself was much easier than Iwo. The casualties didn't begin to mount until the marines poured into the hills beyond the beaches. We left the island taking a shipload of wounded to a base hospital.

What's ahead? I guess Japan itself, but, I confess, my heart's not into it. Goat Castle, already thinned, won't be the same.

If there's anything I can do, Mopsy, please let me know. Any gal with the moxie to have reined in a free-floating spirit the likes of Gash has my entire admiration.

Yours in grief.

Scorch

Tally poured herself another shot of brandy. It dimmed reality and strengthened denial. It can't be true, I don't believe it, her mind told her over and again. Not even the pitiless soul of war could commit such an unthinkable act. How could it choose a victim with such a beautiful orientation to life, one with so many gifts to bestow? There has to be a mistake. So often a body is wrongly identified. Scorch's letter tomorrow will say so. The tears flowed again. The illusion could not be maintained. Oh, God! Oh, God! I know it's true. Cory is gone.

Robert arrived home to find a red-eyed, strung-out bride curled on the sofa. He immediately knew something was wrong, very wrong. He quietly sat beside her and drew her into his arms.

"Oh, Robert, hold me tight, please hold me tight," Tally grievingly sobbed. He held her tight. All of her vital signs raced. Her bosom heaved. He needed to slow down the inner agitation.

"Before you utter a word," he said softly, "I'm going to fix us a drink—a brandy Alexander for you and a martini for me."

"Make it light, I've already had two shots of cognac."

He went light on the brandy and heavy on the gin. He rejoined her on the sofa. "Now, Tally, what's it all about?"

A couple of sips helped steady her composure. "A letter was forwarded to me today from Scorch, Cory's closest friend on ship, that said Cory was killed at Okinawa."

Robert gasped. "Shocking news!" He pressed her hand. "You have to be devastated."

She dabbed her cheeks with her handkerchief. "You must

understand, Robert, it is not the romantic aspect of my relationship with Cory that has me so devastated. I had come to terms
with those feelings before I could accept your proposal. My love
is as bound up with you as is Cory's with the other woman. You
must know I couldn't be happier since I've married you. My main
distress relates to the terrible loss and waste. Cory was blessed with
so many talents that will now never reach full bloom. A tragedy
which can never be measured and which, sadly, will all too soon
be forgotten. Wars do that. Wars destroy lives in such numbers
that any given one rapidly fades into a statistic."

"How was he killed?" Robert asked.

"That, itself, touches on Greek tragedy. According to Scorch,
Cory volunteered to be a froggie, a duty so perilous that only volunteers are taken. The froggies go in before the landings to clear
out the underwater hazards. A booby trap detonated to fatally
wound Cory. He died aboard ship apparently never knowing what
happened. Scorch said had he lived he would be a vegetable. I've
seen too many of those at the hospital."

"Yes," Robert mused, "there are things worse than death." He
rose and fixed himself another martini. "Moments like these," he
said, "raise my guilt over deferment. Guys like Ted and Cory go
the last mile getting peanuts for pay, while guys like me live fat
off the hog. Makes me want to enlist."

Tally stared in alarm. "Don't you dare think about it, Robert.
One more deeply loved one out in the battle zones would put me
in the asylum."

He put an arm around her shoulder. "Nothing to worry
about. It's too late now, anyway. The Japanese can't hold out much
longer with no planes, no ships, and all their paper cities going
up in flames." He finished his drink. "Why don't you dab your
cheeks with a little rouge and we'll hunt down a quiet cafe. You're
in no shape to be messing about in a kitchen."

Tally hugged him. "Robert Graham, have I ever told you that
you're one peach of a guy!"

It was another rough emotional time for Tally. She wrote each member of the Inner Circle of Cory's death, and they, shaken over the news, did little to facilitate her healing process in their distraught efforts to convey sympathy. Robert remained throughout the turbulent period the solid rock of support, handling her moods with tenderness and care. His favorite expression was, "Tally, things will be all right."

One late afternoon in mid-July Robert arrived home to find a frosty martini awaiting him on the coffee table. "And where is madam's cocktail," he inquired as Tally gaily joined him on the sofa.

"I've decided against one." She then agilely climbed astride his lap, kissed him, and twisted his ear lobe. "And I don't believe I'll have one for at least nine months."

Robert's eyes instantly lit up. "No!" he gleefully shouted.

"Yes!" she shouted back. "The doctor confirmed today. Now, shall the first one be a boy or a girl?"

"By all means, a boy, of course!"

"Then, a boy, begorra, it shall be."

Robert picked Tally up and danced with her round the room. "God," he said, "you're beautiful."

About a week later a box arrived for Tally forwarded from the ranch. It was from Bridget Zigler. M'Lord! Tally ejaculated to herself. A box from Cory's mother, the woman several months ago she would have given a king's ransom to meet, but now as she eyed the box, an uneasiness gripped her. With high curiosity as to its contents, she tore it open. Her eyes popped. There were all the letters she had written Cory, and on top of them was a letter, in excellent penmanship, written by his mother.

July 15, 1945

My Sweet Girl,
    Although we never formally met, you are no stranger because Cory had introduced you in his letters. In fact, it was after his

last letter that I became keenly aware of how very special you were to him. I intended on dropping you a hi-I-am-Cory's mother kind of note, but I dillydallied and by the time I got pen to paper, my world suddenly stopped. I haven't had the heart to pick up the pen until very recently.

Of his personal correspondence, Cory saved only your letters. What a source of comfort they must have been to him! It is my feeling that they were not meant for other eyes, so I am shipping them for you to handle as you see fit. The sheer quantity of them betrays the depth of your love. I can understand in part what you must be feeling because in the first World War, I had a similar relationship with Cory's father, who, too, was overseas. He did return safely, we married, and God blessed us with Cory and his sister, Kathleen. The war did not leave me entirely unscathed. My dearest brother, perhaps the most gifted member of the family, was devastated at Belleau Wood and returned home non compos mentis until his death some fifteen years later. I have asked of the dear Lord how much longer we women must suffer the pain of loved ones at war, and I get no answer. I dread the thought that the seeds of a third world war might have already been sown.

Cory wrote of some length about you in his very last letter, dated February 10, 1945. It occurred to me it might bring you some comfort in hearing his glowing report. I shall quote:

Mother dear, you ask: What does Natalia look like?

As an old movie buff, if you take the best of Mary Pickford, Lillian Gish, and Theda Bara, mix, stir, and pour, you have created a Tally. She lights up a room. Much of her charm is her obliviousness to her charms. I've met no lass more natural, spontaneous, incredibly herself. There's not one affected bone in all of her body. I love the softness of her hair, the way it blows in the wind. Mopsy, as I call her, fits her to a "T" (or should I say to a "Z"?).

Most notable hobbies: sports of all kinds, music, painting, star-gazing, walking in the rain. She dances like an angel and laughs with the wanton that would warm the cockles of the devil's own heart!

But, alas, no one is perfect. She's incorrigibly flawed, like someone else I know, with a prominent sentimental gene. She turns positively maudlin to the schmaltzy strains of "The Rose of Tralee."

If this blankety-blank war ever ends, I'll bring her home and let you see for yourself how truly well I've painted the canvas. Moreover, I'd say that a high possibility exists the two of you may get along famously.

And so it seems I have lost not only a handsome son but a beautiful daughter. But life must go on. It is to be lived. All things do pass. Cory's signature was his zest for life, and he would want the same for those whose lives he touched. You, my dear, have many good years ahead of you. Make the most of them. I, too, with much less time, shall strive to persevere. God bless you always.

Bridget Zigler

# *Scorch's Visit*

Tally forbiddingly saw the letter from Cory's mother as keeping the waters stirred that began with Scorch's letter. She, too, apparently was unaware of the broken relationship. Why would Cory not inform his own mother of the rift? And, then, on top of that, why would he wish his mother to believe that he would introduce the two of them after the war?

But even more disturbing was learning that the only personal letters Cory saved were the ones she had written to him. How could he not have saved the letters of her rival? A light bulb lit up. Of course! A woman with the obvious sensitivity of his mother would try to give as much solace as she could to all parties affected. She undoubtedly sent the same message to the other woman.

Even granted, the general tone of both letters had a chilling effect. It gave rise to Tally wondering if she had been on a false scent, had let her imagination run amok, had let her grotesquely twist the facts. Surely, she thought, I'm not that unstable. The fatality in Cory's letter was very real. There was no fantasy there. And so was his response to her reply. It clearly showed no tendency to wish to continue the dialogue. Was pride here a major factor? It was something they both had in unfortunate excess. Oh, Cory's feelings had changed, she reassured herself; she could not remain sane and doubt that, but the reason underlying it may turn out to be more complicated than first thought. Her anguish would not be mollified without more information, and Scorch would be the one best likely to provide it. She wrote him to acknowledge receipt of the crushing news and to express the strong desire to see him as soon as the good Lord saw fit to bring the *Hudson* home.

On the heels of her letter came the electrifying news. On

August 6, a bomb of cataclysmic force, an atom-splitting bomb, was dropped on Hiroshima, on the west end of Honshu, which obliterated over half of the city and eighty thousand of its people. Three days later a second atomic bomb was dropped on Nagasaki with similar annihilation. The Japanese warlords met in emergency sessions, and several days afterward, Emperor Hirohito announced on the radio the unconditional surrender of Japan. In dramatic suddenness the most violent war the human race has ever known was over. People danced in the streets, kissed strangers, and threw victory parties till dawn. Troops overseas could think of nothing but coming home.

The U.S.S. *Hudson* joyously steamed into Long Beach in late September to signs of well done raised in the harbor. Scorch at once contacted Tally and made plans for a visit much earlier than either of them had dreamed possible. She drove up from San Diego, her pregnancy not yet visible, to have dinner with him.

She parked her car, and as she saw his dapper figure moving toward the end of the dock, she dashed out to meet him. They hugged warmly. Tally then made him pose at arms-length while she eyed him critically from head to foot. With a twinkle in her eye, she said, "You've changed. Where is the boy?"

Scorch smiled. "War shortchanges adolescence. But you're exactly as I remembered. The same beautiful doll."

She laughed. "Begorra, Cory has passed to you his chip of the Blarney Stone! Get in the car, war hero, and direct me to your favorite eatery. And in case all those beach landings have left you brain damaged, requiring everything to be said twice to register, let me repeat that you are my date tonight and all the tabs are on me. Now, should you find that intolerable, speak up at once so I can dump you here at the dock and pick me up another war hero."

He threw up his hands. "Adjusting to civilian life isn't going to be the snap I thought. Okay, Rosie the Riveter, drive on. My preferred chophouse happens to be just a couple of short miles down the pike."

Tally engaged in small talk on the way as it was her intent to keep the conversation light whenever possible, anticipating the evening would have more than its quota of heavy moments. She was determined to squeeze as much truth as she could out of Scorch whatever the emotional cost.

Scorch had done well in his restaurant selection. It was quiet, soft lighted, and tastefully decorated. With the house specialty a seafood dish, Tally ordered a bottle of chardonnay. Scorch noticed that she poured herself just a half glass. He grinned. "Light on the grape, I see. Obviously, you war workers have been overdoing the victory celebrations. Finally catching up with you."

The twinkle returned to her eye. "I'll come clean, sir. My plan is to get you a mite pie-eyed so when the inhibitions dissipate, all your dark secrets will come tumbling out." She had made up her mind not to mention her pregnancy or many of the details about the changes that had taken place in her life.

Scorch took a long sip and smacked his lips. "Excellent. Must have come from Burgundy country. If I'm going to get looped on the grape, I say let it be from the French vines." He raised his glass for a toast. "To the bomb: Sadly to the lives it took and happily to the more lives it saved."

"To the bomb," Tally echoed. They touched glasses.

Scorch turned more sober. "As it is, a third of Goat Castle is not coming back. Without the bomb, the toll surely would've been higher. We were set to hit the beaches of Kyushu, and the scuttlebutt was saying a half-million body bags would be needed. Yes, thank God for the bomb."

Tally changed the subject to lighten the tone. "By the way, Scorch, Gash wrote me about his twin who ran off with the skipper's daughter, and how the skipper took his vendetta out on him. I was wondering if ol' Stoneface ever mellowed."

Scorch laughed. "You won't believe the final act. Gash ended up the captain's fair-haired boy. All due to America's favorite pastime. After each invasion, units regroup on some remote, godforsaken island to drink warm beer and play baseball. Each ship had its ball team and some of the rivalries got intense. The admiral of the flagship and the skipper were close friends and the admiral, gloating because he had a pro for a pitcher, gave odds that his team would give ours a royal shellacking. Gash, a heckuva ballplayer, got the game's winning hit. Stoneface walked off with big bucks and thereafter Gash could do no wrong."

How ironic, Tally thought. What Hawk couldn't accomplish going to bat for Cory at all those dinners with the captain, Cory achieved with one swing of the bat on the playing field. "Leave it to Cory," Tally laughed, "to find a way out of the doghouse."

Scorch grinned. "Speaking of Gash, since I know he always avoided sharing with you any aspects of the war itself, I brought along something I found when cleaning out his effects that might be of interest to you." He extended his glass for a refill.

He took a long sip and then removed from his pocket a sheaf of legal-size sheets. "I expropriated these since they were not addressed to anyone in particular. They were some random thoughts Gash had jotted down on the eve of Iwo Jima. Would you like to see them?"

Tally leaned forward. "Yes, indeed. I have wondered what Cory's reflections might be during such terrible moments, the calm before a storm. Would you mind reading them to me?" Tally closed her eyes both to avoid seeing his handwriting and to avoid any distractions while listening.

Would to God I could sleep! Such a small request. But the butterflies refuse to be still. Nothing works. Counting sheep won't quiet them. Nor staring at white caps. Would a little free association do it? Doubt it. The heart pounds too hard and the mind races too fast for the sandman to show up. But, doodling may help pass the time as the minutes tick slowly in waiting.

I command myself: write what comes to mind for who cares and what matters! Write about the miserable day. How we joked and wisecracked! Everybody about as phony as a three-dollar bill. The old story of playing it cool. Fear drives everyone to be a carbon copy of everybody else. Much safer to look, say, and do alike. Would take real guts to stand up and yell: Knock it off, guys, this is bullshit! Who's kidding who? Everybody's scared pissless. Who wouldn't give an arm and a leg to be once again that little boy clutching mother's apron strings, knowing she'd keep him away from the bad boys outside. But that won't do. That's hardly the stuff heroes are made of! But then I for one never much aspired to be a hero.

How mysterious the mind works. It is now D-Day, the day we've rehearsed for what seems forever in poring over charts and in memorizing reports. Yet, until now the island never seemed real. More like something out of science fiction. In truth, Iwo does remind me more of a crater on Mars than anything I've ever seen on our planet. From what I'm told, it's little more than a stinky slab of hardened lava, vile to all flora and fauna. The odor comes from sulphur, the cruddy stuff with the smell of rotten eggs. Yet, a few hours from now, thousands will storm the stinking caves as if they contained all the riches of the Orient. How uncivilized to enter the Pearly Gates smelling like rotten eggs!

No stars above. The heavens, I guess, ordered a black out, anticipating the fireworks. Another irony was our colossal effort to engage camouflage. The invasion was drafted in highest secrecy with only a select few in the know. Even the troops below remain in the dark. Most think we're hitting Formosa. They never heard of Iwo. Air strikes are going on right now over other nearby islands to confuse the enemy. The heavy bombardment from sea and sky began but three days ago to keep from tipping our hand in advance. The massive convoy sneaked out of Saipan on a zig-zag course to mislead enemy reconnaissance. We will silently drop anchor in predawn darkness. Organized deception, all to guarantee the element of surprise when we strike. So what happens? Tokyo Rose fills the airwaves announcing the full cast of characters for the play: the Marine Divisions, the Landing Units, the Task Force. She also announced curtain time and the size of the audience. She played up the wisdom in postponing the performance. So much for codes and censorship. Now that the cat's out of the bag, there's not an artery topside that's not throbbing a notch or two faster.

It makes sense for the young to answer the call of arms because they cling to the illusion of immortality. Sure, the bells will toll, but for the other guy. My illusion is a bit tarnished. True, death doesn't worry me, it's fear of losing parts. The quality of life is what counts and war knows how to put the kaput on that.

I have raised the question: Why do we have war? I think it's the wrong question. It implies that war is unnatural. Think again. Peace is the anomaly. History is a succession of wars with brief interludes between them. Once in a while the interludes are long. Wouldn't the better question be: Why are some of the interludes long?

Isn't it a bit perverse how we see ourselves? We call ourselves the noble beast and God's other creatures the savage beast. Yet, the beasts fight only when starved, attacked, or defending turf—never for greed, power, or trumped-up ideals. Dad took up arms to save the world for democracy. I took up arms to save the world from madness. So what grand purpose, do you suppose, will have my son take up arms? If we could only be a little less noble and a little more savage!

Killing, in our culture, is highly esteemed. He who kills against the odds gets the prized medals. The hero is the one who singlehandedly wipes out a machine-gun nest. The coward's the one who studies the odds, bows to the numbers, raises the white flag. He gets the Bronx cheer.

The butterflies still refuse to be still. Philosophizing on the irrationality of human nature hasn't slowed their flutterings. The peace of sleep is not to be. The nerves are too much on edge.

Nerves kick up badly at the D-Day breakfast. What a total waste! Fresh eggs, real milk, thick steaks, and we haven't the stomach to down a cup of coffee. Then away to the boats where minds get locked on details. I check the engine, the pumps: fuel pump, sump pump, the hand bilge pump. I test the emergency tiller, the ramp mechanisms, the gyro compasses. I inspect the lines: the anchor line, the broaching lines, the bow and stern lines. I examine the guns: the tommy gun, the Springfield rifle, the ammunition box. I make sure we have a thermos jug, two buckets, five gallons of fresh water, ten gallons of lube oil, broom and swab, $CO_2$ extinguisher, boat hooks, tool kit, gun kit—all standard items. I check for life jackets, blankets, foul weather gear, lantern, K-rations, candy bars, and the flags: semaphore flags, Victor and Love flags. I've already double and triple checked these things, so why again? It keeps me seeing the trees instead of the forest, which keeps my diastolic under control.

Then we load the marines and it's off and away to the line of departure. I busy myself going over personal gear. Do I have my helmet (of course, it's on my head), watch, life belt, knife, binoculars, sun glasses, ear wardens, gas mask, pistol, megaphone, flashlight, radio, radio code, beach charts? Then as the ticks of the countdown begin, my thoughts shift to the first-aid kit. Are there bandages, morphine, sulfamilamide? I review procedures for tending the wounded: keep the man lying down and warmly covered; control rapid bleeding, inject morphine, dress wounds, give only small sips of water if screamed for.

When the throttle opens for shore, I obsess on the narrow beach rising before my binoculars, mind dwelling on one thought: get the marines in. Never think of the next assignment: salvage-boat duties to clear sunken boats to let in supplies, medicine, ammunition, reinforcements. The trick to stay composed is to keep the mind on one track at a time.

A handy tip for a hot beach. Ease the boat toward, not away, the nearest exploding shell. The gunner who has a bead on your boat is fast making an adjustment to his last splash. Getting ashore amounts to keeping those near splashes coming.

We're now piping up the cooks and bakers. The day is beginning. The invasion wheels are now in motion. No turning back.


Scorch quietly refolded the sheets and asked if Tally would like to have them.

She added more wine to his glass. "They are yours, Scorch. Keep them. They're the last memento of your best friend. Someday when time has distanced you from the war, I'm sure you'll wish to review them." She could tell he, too, was close to tears as he returned the papers to his pocket.

Tally gingerly pursued her probing. "In your letter, Scorch, you complimented my ability to cage a free spirit of the likes of Cory. Surely, you're not suggesting that I was the first girl to accomplish that."

"Indeed, fair princess, you were. Oh, Gash had an eye for the chicks, but whenever one threatened to get serious, he'd hightail for cover. He was from the old school in one respect. He didn't want to commit before he had his career ducks all lined up. That's what made you so special. You blew him out of the saddle even though he thought he had a tight grip on the reins. Yep, he was smitten."

"You may have jumped the gun a bit, Scorch. He never really committed, you know. There were no strings attached in our relationship."

"Maybe nothing was on the dotted line, but the result was the same. You were the only girl he talked about and yours was the only picture on his desk. He also handed me his little black book. No footloose bachelor ever does that."

Tally suppressed the pang felt in her heart and forced on a smile. "One of the lovable things about Cory was his upbeat manner. He was always full of bounce and cheery humor. So you can imagine my surprise when I got a letter written in early February which was dreadfully different. There was no optimism, totally unCorylike. He despaired of the war ending soon and cast doubt in a caring God. What do you make of that?"

Scorch pondered for a moment. "That must have been written about the time we knew we'd be invading Iwo Jima. Something I didn't know until much later was that Gash always got advanced tips on the campaigns from his bridge partner Hawk. As Gash probably told you, Hawk had spent years in the Pacific before the war and knew most of the islands. Gash considered all that Hawk told him as confidential and never divulged any of it to anyone, even me. So he had a pretty grim picture of what to expect at Iwo. As usual, Hawk was dead right. It was the bloodiest battle yet fought in the Pacific. The amtracks and the first couple of waves got in fine, but thereafter it was Katy bar the door! By midafternoon the beach was littered with the dead and dying." Scorch stopped and took a long swallow of wine.

He continued. "There's a special stress seldom talked about. The many hours that the guys in the boat division spend together in those diesel-fumed boats foster an intimacy rarely achieved in most units. Fears get vented, dreams shared, secrets disclosed. Then, on the eve of battle, those with a premonition of bells tolling will drop by Goat Castle to slip a card with a name and address because telegrams are so cold. Light banter is made to soften the morbid overtones, but deep down we all know there will be some letters to write. Then comes the dreaded moment after the invasion is over when one has to put together the right sounding words to a mother, a wife, or a sweetheart to inform her, a total stranger to you, that her loved one will not be coming back. Gash had a number to write after Iwo. His assigned beach, Red Beach I, was caught in a cross-fire between Mount Suribachi and a ridge of concrete pillboxes. Several of his boats took direct hits. Of the casualties, perhaps, the saddest of all was his coxswain, Rob Roy, who caught a burst and died within seconds after the ramp was lowered."

The tears welled in Tally's eyes as crowding her mind came the thought of Jeanie Mae, the frail frightened girl, too young to have a baby, who Cory said embraced him in San Francisco and whispered take care of all that we have. What a wrenching letter to write! It had to drain the strength out of him. And in the midst of all this, Tally was now realizing, her last letter was winging its way to him.

"Oh, Scorch," Tally weakly cried out, "how war does test the limits of human endurance. Yet, in the face of all this bearing down on him, Cory still volunteers to join the froggies. Why would he do it?"

"I've asked myself that question a million times since I never got a straight answer out of Gash. For a guy with no ambitions to be a hero, he sure did some dumb things. If any group had to be singled out for heroic duty, I can't think of a more deserving bunch than the frogmen." A tear wetted his eye. "The irony of this whole damn thing is that Gash had faced the worst the war had to offer. The landing at Okinawa was a breeze compared to Iwo. The enemy had changed tactics and retreated to the hills to wait for the troops to move inland. Then, the landing at Kyushu never materialized. I had a long talk with Hawk. Next to me, I think he took Gash's death the hardest on ship. So neither of us could be very objective. Over a couple of his stiff restoratives, he took blame. On the day he informed Gash we're hitting Okinawa, he also brought up Operation Olympic, the code name for the invasion of Kyushu, set on the planning board for November first. Hawk felt that gruesome news added to the trauma of Iwo put Gash into a downward spiral that culminated in his volunteering. I disagreed, contending Gash was not the depressive type. I stuck to my theory of the Boy Scout complex, but, hell, who knows!"

Tally kept outward sang-froid, but the pain inside tore at the fibers in her heart. She had to quickly change topics. She emptied the rest of the wine into his glass. "All this, I know, has been very hard on you, Scorch, and you've been a dear to put up with me. I do hope there's been some catharsis in it for you. But, let's now talk about you. What are your plans?"

He still had his boyish laugh. "Have a bit of duty still left on the tub. We head next to San Francisco to discharge the old goats, the married guys with kids who top the point system, and have the long-awaited blowout on the bridge winnings of Hawk and Gash. Then we take the tub through the canal and put her in mothballs in Norfolk." He sighed with joy. "Then I'm out."

"Then what?"

"Finish up the year of college still left, find a job, and gain respectability. Attire myself in a gray flannel suit and wing-tip shoes and sell advertising on Fifth Avenue. . . ." He gave Tally a wry look. "I've given you all evening to say something, and since you haven't, I will. I think it's great to see that sparkler on your finger, and I know Gash would think so, too. He would be delighted to know that your life is going forward in a positive direction. That would be his style. Now, my gorgeous colleen, I suggest you get me back to the dock where you can turn the wheel south and get on with your primary obligations."

"Aye, aye, sir. Regarding the sparkler, I was very fortunate to find a fine man, a person who was a good friend during the war and who turned lover near its end."

As Tally pulled up at the pier, Scorch paused before taking leave. "Just one more thing, Tally. I'm not too good at this sort of thing but I would still like to say it. I look upon you and Gash as being very lucky. Brief though the time was that was in the cards, something like two ships passing in the night, you touched each other's souls in a way that most people never do in a lifetime. Maybe it takes a war for this to happen. We know that the Middle Ages, with all of its violence, was the setting for Dante's love of Beatrice. I'd rib Gash that his emotional collapse was due to too much time in the sun, but deep down I envied him and hoped someday I should be so lucky. Well, that's about it."

Tally squeezed his hand to keep from choking up. She steadied her voice. "For one supposedly so unpolished in smooth talk, Scorch, I'd say you did well, very well. I'm also sure a great life's ahead of you." She watched him stride toward the ship and hop onto the gangplank. He was still quite nimble on his feet.

A strange force gripped Tally. It drew her out of the car and toward the ship, stopping her near the bow to let her have her first glimpse of the U.S.S. *Hudson.* Her eyes moved up to the bridge where Cory stood watch for those many long silent nights, the ocean his only companion. Suddenly, breaking into consciousness came images of the homecoming that once dominated her dreams: the ship steaming into dock, bells ringing, whistles blowing, wild bearhugging on the pier, the world at peace, Sundays together at last. The vision abruptly vanished. A sea of resistance drowned the images. The invisible force released her and let her return to the car.

It was a lonely drive back to San Diego. Scorch would never know the devastation he left in his wake. Tally began to put together the final pieces of the picture, a picture that she now realized had been so grossly distorted by her insecurity and instability as to allow her to draw conclusions to betray her deepest love. There had been no other woman. She was a myth, a figment of the imagination. Cory had no change of heart. He was steadfast and loyal to the very end. He wrote the fateful letter overwhelmed in a deluge of ugliness yet to be matched in the war, the anticipation of the bloodiest invasion in the Pacific, the conquest of Iwo Jima. For the first time that he let his anguish surface to the pages of a letter, it cost him her desertion. Then, when he lost Rob Roy and was breaking the news to Jeanie Mae, he got the letter of ambivalence. He had to reply with no iron left in his blood. And, finally, when her letter that ended the relationship arrived, he was confronted with the knowledge of the invasion of Japan itself. Now alone in his dreams, no girl to come home to, the decision to volunteer for the high-risk mission had to have come from the depths of despondency. Waves of guilt tore at the core of Tally's soul. She was the fickle one, the traitor. Yes, she drove him to join the froggies. She was his true executioner. Tally had to pull the car over to the side of the road. The rain of tears had blinded her. She leaned over the steering wheel and let them run unimpeded down her cheeks. How could she have been so insensitive! So shallow! If she had not been so mired in self-pity, the unthinkable would never have happened. She felt dark forces closing in. She wanted to crawl into a hole and sleep forever. Randy, the young marine with the big brown eyes, flashed before her. She could understand the oppression of his crushing guilt and his craving for eternal rest. How easy, she thought, it would be to miss a curve, plunge over a cliff, and have her pain disintegrate in the rocks below. But, then, tormenting questions bobbed up. If she stopped living would it bring Cory back? No. Would it exonerate guilt? No, it would double it. She'd be deserting Robert and a newborn on the way. Weren't enough sins committed, enough lives ruined?

As her tears dried a new light shined through. Self-pity is a prong of centripetal love. Cory would have me move my life forward, direct my energies outward, enhance the lives of those I can touch, beginning with Robert and the children to follow. The answer is to focus on self-growth, reject the lure of narcissism, turn to painting, the arts, humanitarian interests. Yes, this would be her memorial to Cory.

I vow to God, she swore to herself, to never again let such dark thoughts dominate my feelings, and I shall never let Robert know the exposed truth. He shall be spared the ordeal of having to glue together, which he has so often done, the fragments of a shattered emotion. With her resolve firmly in place, Tally had regained her composure by the time she reached home. She threw herself lovingly into Robert's waiting arms.

A week later Tally received a letter from Hawk. This one she was prepared for as Scorch had reminded her of the upcoming victory celebration on the bridge earnings. It would still not be an easy read.

September 30, 1945

Dear Natalia,

I received your address from Lt. Haskell (Scorch) of the Boat Division. He referred to you in the most glowing terms. Cory, of course, always did, but Scorch, a bit more objective, has fully convinced me that you must be a lovely and charming young lady, making me keenly regret not having the opportunity of meeting you. Fate dealt us all a bad hand. Cory was exceptional. Having three daughters but no sons, I rather adopted him. We shared many good talks and weathered out more than one tough storm.

As you most likely know, we were bridge partners. I once took the game quite seriously and devised a system that proved tournament sound. I taught it to Cory, an apt student, and we played well together. We agreed to sink our winnings into a victory party when our ship dropped anchor in San Francisco, which happened a couple of days ago. I reserved a large suite in the Fairmount Hotel and the entire ship's personnel shuttled back and forth, ship to suite so to speak, for a weekend of unbridled celebration. The rafters rocked but the congenial management never complained. The one important ingredient missing was one of the dual hosts. Toasts to him constituted the only sobering moments.

Cory had dropped by my stateroom to bid a temporary farewell on the eve of joining the froggies. I noticed his mood was somber, almost detached, a condition increasing since Iwo Jima. His wave took a hard shelling on the Iwo shores, which I believe he took too personally, although I could never get him to open up. He seemed to take on a fatalistic mode, which greatly disturbed me because it puts the locus of control outside of the self. It generates a what-will-be-will-be, regardless of what one does in the situation. I'm sure this state of mind influenced his decision to be a froggie.

I regret I cannot be more sanguine about war. The only clear winners are the career chaps. Promotions speed up during combat. Even those who avoid the casualty list don't go entirely unscathed. In my case, lucky throughout, I still lost not only four good years of programmed retirement but at least a decade from my life span, a good hunk of time. But Cory's tragedy can't be measured in years. Its effect on those with a special relationship to him is unmeasurable. I have never been able to find adequate words of consolation for a life sacrificed before its time. My best effort is to say that in the loss we all do become more aware of our own mortality and some of us may be motivated to do a better job with what time is left in our own lives. I share, Natalia, in your grief.

Sincerely,
L. C. "Hawk" Hawkins
Commander, USNR

What a wonderful man you must be, Tally thought, as she dabbed away the tears. You should not take any part of the blame. It rests here. Tally drew a deep breath, stood, and approached her full-length mirror. No more tears, she spoke out, you have a heap of living to do in the years ahead, and tears don't help. She dabbed on some makeup.

Having destroyed enough from a love that had always been constant, Tally assembled the letters, her entire batch, the several remaining from Cory, the ones from Scorch, Cory's mother, and Hawk, and put them in private safekeeping with the intent to put them to the flame on her deathbed. Her heart could not have it any other way.

*Fifty-seven years later*

# The Discovery

Natalia Dorn could feel her toes stretch and tighten, a compulsion invariably triggered by a sudden surge of tension, like when sitting down at the piano to give a recital or standing up before a group to give a speech or reaching out in class for a copy of an exam. This time it was watching Tally—who hated being called grandmother—put the last of her personal belongings, a packet of old letters bound with a red ribbon, into a small vanity case. Natalia saw a faraway look briefly cloud those lovely turquoise eyes, but said nothing. She was too caught up in the meaning of the moment, the closing out of a wonderful era. Tally was about to leave forever the house on the bluff overlooking San Diego Bay, the house that was Gramp's marvelous surprise on their first anniversary, the house that was from Natalia's earliest memories a magical castle.

The turn-of-the-century hacienda, oozing warmth and charm, was the persona of Tally. Their years together had formed such a bonding, such a holy alliance, that the thought of one without the other bordered on sacrilege. Yet, deep in her bones, Natalia knew with Gramp's recent passing a parting of the ways was but a matter of time. The house was entirely too big for Tally to rattle about in alone. She had found a modish apartment near the bay ideally suited for her modest needs. With adaptability her forte, she had accepted the inevitable with much more equanimity than her sentimental granddaughter.

Natalia regarded it a gift from the gods that she, Tally's namesake and pick of the grandbaby litter, to be the one to have the most free time to help in the move. She had a month of vacation left before her final year of college. But as the jet taxied in to its gate from its long cross-country flight, she had no inkling of the great surprise that lay in store for her. The gods seldom show their full hand.

Tally, waiting at the incoming gate, rushed forward on seeing her granddaughter and warmly embraced her. "Darling, so glad you could come."

"Wouldn't have had it any other way," Natalia replied with a big hug back.

"How was the flight?"

"Perfect. Everything was right on schedule and there were no air bumps. A lovely trip on a beautiful August day—a good omen."

Tally smiled. "We'll need all the good omens we can get. We've got piles to wade through. I hope you know what you've got yourself into."

Natalia laughed. "Don't you give it a second thought. I've got thirty days at your disposal. We should be able to clean out the house and have you settled in your new haunts with time to spare."

It turned out to be grubby work going through boxes, crates, and crammed closets, a lifetime of accumulations, sorting out what was to stay and what was to go. Natalia looked like a messy camper by each nightfall, but Tally, in contrast, could have stepped out of Vogue. It was as if some invisible shield had protected her from the day's dust and grime. As they sat side by side on the floor, Tally often let her hair down and told anecdotes on the family that had Natalia in stitches. Like the night Floppy, the family mutt, out on his regular prowl, met an unfriendly skunk who reacted hostilely to his invitation to play. He slinked back to the house drenched and crawled between the sheets next to Uncle Matt, who was five at the time. Uncle Matt, known as the quiet one, was such a sound sleeper that he never twitched a nostril. In the morning, fully adapted, he sauntered into the crowded kitchen and everyone, including Prissy, the imperious and unflappable Persian feline, bolted for the exit. The quiet one sat and nonchalantly munched on his breakfast, quite perplexed over all the commotion his presence seemingly had caused.

It was mystical how much Tally and Natalia were alike. They saw humor and sadness in the same things and shared an identical list of likes and dislikes. Natalia traced her talent in art to Tally, who said she saw so much of herself in Natalia when she was her age. Natalia took this as a high compliment, especially if it also included looks, because the early snaps of Tally in the family album showed her a rare beauty. Although the dark auburn hair had grayed and wisdom lines had deepened the eyes, Tally could still zip in and out of a size-six dress. Natalia prayed the years would wear that kindly on her.

The work accomplished, the house bared, they stepped onto the flagstone terrace for their farewell look far down at the distant bay. Flitting before Natalia came summer scenes of childhood watching the sails of boats like tiny triangles floating on a bluish mist. So dreamily romantic! She wondered what images might be tugging on Tally's heartstrings, but she'd never know. Her brief comment was vintage Tally: "How wonderful if the new owners, too, would have a great love of the sea." There was not a selfish bone in her body.

They wound their way down the moss-stained steppingstones to the parked car. Tally held the vanity case as though it contained a Dresden antique. Natalia was the chauffeur. They rode in silence down the narrow drive snaking from the heights. Neither was in the mood for talk. Tally kept her eyes rigidly ahead, never once looking back. For some reason Natalia glanced down and saw Tally's toes wiggle. Oh, my God, she thought, we're alike right down to our compulsions.

There was little left to do. The furnished apartment was fully set up for occupancy. Natalia's return flight wasn't booked until the following night, which put them in a relaxed state. After freshening up they microwaved a small souffle since neither expressed much of an appetite. Afterward, Tally emptied the last of the boxes, then opened the vanity case and gently placed the ribboned letters in the drawer of her nightstand. How very special, Natalia observed. They were the last item packed, the last item put away, and no item given more care in handling.

Tally insisted that Natalia decide how they should spend their last evening together. They could take in a concert, see a movie, browse in a gallery, or simply mosey about in the new mall. Whatever struck her granddaughter's fancy would be "hunky-dory" with her.

Natalia said she was in the perfect mood for a quiet evening at home sipping coffee and chit-chatting. She had an ulterior motive. Her curiosity had finally got the better of her; she was dying to know what those letters were all about.

Tally raised an eyebrow, but said nothing. She began busying herself in the kitchenette getting a pot brewing. Natalia sought to broach the subject discreetly.

"The letters, Tally, the ones so neatly tied with the red ribbon, sure do look old."

After a pause, Tally replied, "They go all the way back to World War II."

"I've never seen them before."

Tally ignored the comment as she continued her piddling, rearranging a shelf in a cupboard until the last perk croaked. She then poured two cups, added a measured spoonful of cognac to each, and nodded for Natalia to join her on the living-room sofa. With a twinkle in her eye, she said, "The brandy braces the bean and cuts the caffeine." Then those expressive eyes took on a pensive look. "About the letters, darling. No one's seen them because I've kept them under lock and key. Indeed, it's safe to say that you're the first to know they even exist."

"Not even Gramp?"

"Especially not Gramp."

The inflection did not escape Natalia. Thoughts raced through her mind. They were not for his eyes? What was she hinting? That she had a clandestine lover? Was carrying on behind Gramp's back! No! What could she possibly be thinking! Tally, straight as an arrow, the paragon of virtue, indulging in an illicit affair! Yet, could there be a side to her unknown to the rest of us? I've heard it said how little we really know about those we love the most.

It occurred to Natalia that no one had pinned Tally down for a full accounting of her life during the war years. Everybody knew she came to San Diego to be near her brother, a marine badly wounded in the war and in need of major surgeries. She found a job in an aircraft company and lived with several of the other female workers until Gramp ringed her finger near the end of the war. It was a sketchy overview, covering a time frame that could allow many other intriguing events to have happened. There was only one sure way to find out. She gave a roll of the eyes. "Tally, it's not what I'm thinking, is it?"

Tally's pretty head cocked to the side. "An *affaire de coeur?* How can it be denied? The letters incriminate me." Her toes wiggled. "It was intense, wrenching, leaving scars that I shall take to the grave." The strain on her face lightened, as if the words themselves had opened a valve and released bottled-up pressure. "I resolved to tell no one and planned to destroy the letters on my deathbed. But with the passing of Gramp, whose well-being always came first, and now with the pressure from a most inquisitive granddaughter, who somehow always seems to find a way with me, I fear the resolve is facing its stiffest test."

Natalia swore sealed lips, vowing not to utter a word to a living soul. Tally protested that although the affair was short, the telling of it, to be fair, would be long. Natalia persuasively reminded her that they had no commitments before her scheduled flight, and that they had on hand an ample supply of coffee and cognac. Her persistence finally won out. Tally squeezed her hand and retrieved the letters. They curled up on opposite ends of the sofa, shoes off, ready to settle in for a long session.

While removing the ribbon, Tally casually dropped the aside that the letters included all of hers but only several of his. She lifted a hand to halt the question forming on Natalia's lips, assuring her all will become clear in due course.

Natalia picked up the hint that Tally would prefer her to be an inconspicuous little mouse, not exactly her favorite animal.

# *Reminiscence*

Tally took a long deep breath and a sip of fortified coffee. "The romance," she said, "began at a St. Patrick's Day dance in 1944 at the Coronado Hotel. I had left Denver several months before, a girl of twenty-one, to be in San Diego with my brother Ted during his extended hospitalization. His world had crashed down on him. He was facing a series of surgeries from severe wounds received at Guadalcanal, and he was struggling with a rocky marriage now on the precipice. His wife, Jenny, had returned to Denver to contemplate divorce. I was his sole support.

"I landed a job at Convair, an aircraft company that made training planes and bombers. We put out over ten thousand B-24's by war's end. At work I met two wonderful girls, Cindy and Debbie, who invited me to live with them in their recently rented house. Because there was a stable in the rear for Debbie's prize-winning horse, we referred to the place as the ranch. Two other workers, Susan and Avis, became fast friends. The five of us, all on the swing shift, called ourselves the Inner Circle. We did everything together from tennis to theater. Cindy and I, sharing a big bedroom at the ranch, became as close as sisters.

"Bubbling over with patriotism, all of us volunteered to be hostesses at dances for the boys preparing to go overseas. I and the other two of Irish descent, Cindy Gilligan and Susan Rafferty, rigged out in kelly green, took the ferry on this seventeenth day of March across the bay to a limo shuttling to the historic hotel.

"After gyrating acrobatically from partner to partner doing the jitterbug, the new dance rage, I limped exhaustedly back to our table. I was hardly seated when I heard a voice with a trace of the brogue ask if the colleen would care to dance with a Timothy O'Reilly. I glanced back to see a young naval officer with black curly hair, clear blue eyes, and a smile that could melt butter. Every fiber in my weary body came alive. Faith and begorra, I gushed out, indeed she might."

Natalia became mesmerized at the sudden transformation that took place in her grandmother. The lines in her face faded, the tone of her voice lightened, and the coloring of her skin brightened. The clock had dramatically turned back. Tally was radiantly young again. "He must have been a dream," Natalia said breathily.

"Starry-eyed Cindy, who saw a movie star in every male, said he was a cross between Rory Calhoun and Tyrone Power. He was, indeed, quite dashing and marvelously light on his feet. As the band was into playing a slow number, we did the Dip, a popular ballroom step of the day. It goes one, two, bend; one, two, bend; double backward, bend; double twirl, double forward, bend. Oh, how my skirt would swing on the twirls." Tally's eyes sparkled, and they both laughed at her burst of effervescence.

"I could have danced all night long, so easy was he to follow, but intermission broke the spell. Then, instead of escorting me back to the table, he eased me toward the exit and, flashing that wonderful smile of his, said if he had to share the Rose of Erin let it be with the biggest Dipper of all. I disintegrated. Turned to milk toast. I committed the high crime of war: I abandoned my post. I sprightly bounced off with the roguish Timothy O'Reilly to find the stars.

"I would suppose," Natalia interrupted, "the price of desertion was the loss of your hostess badge."

"Cindy and Susan, who had taken care of my purse, again came to the rescue. They covered up for me, convincing the head hostess I left feeling ill.

"As we reached the shoreline, my strolling minstrel, in a tenor voice that rose softly above the sound of the breakers, sang several phrases of 'The Rose of Tralee,' charmingly subbing Tally for Mary in the lyrics. Shades of Dennis Day. I loved it.

"Oh, the energy we did have! We walked a million miles over

sand and rock, oblivious to the world about us. The war seemed light years away. When we did notice the time, we could hardly believe the hour. We snacked at an all-night cafe and then boarded the ferry. As we were crossing the bay, I shall never forget, my philosopher-poet asked if I had ever noticed the narcissism of the stars—how they shine so much brighter on seeing their reflection in the water. I had never met anyone quite like him. He ran his fingers through my wind-blown tresses and called me Mopsy. He then teasingly questioned that with vanity the soul of woman, how could it be that he could not find a single narcissistic hair. I snuggled closer to him.

"We made plans for our next get-together, which had to be the following Sunday because of our work schedules. At the back door of the ranch, which we always kept unlocked, the streets quite safe those days, we exchanged phone numbers and addresses. He gave me a quick kiss and then told me his real name was Cory Zigler. Timothy O'Reilly was borrowed for St. Pat's Day. But, I should know that his mother did come from a prime stock of potato pickers off the Irish Sea. Then, with an agile leap he was off the porch and sprinting toward the landing, to catch the last ferry.

"I joined Cindy and Debbie in the living area, not a too surprising an hour to be up for those on the swing shift. They were busily writing to their steadies but on seeing Cindy impishly waving my purse as I entered the room, I suspected they were delaying bedtime until hearing my report. After bubbling on the glorious time I had, I joined them in letter writing to let Cory, too, know how much I enjoyed the evening."

She handed the top letter to Natalia, whose eyes sparkled on reading it. "The chemistry's already forming," she said.

Tally continued. "How slowly the week dragged on. I chided myself for having him take up so much of my thoughts. I told myself to climb out of the clouds, get control of my emotions, and be the practical girl who understands that war romances have two strikes against them from the start. Protect the heart and stop thinking about him, bonny lass. There's a war going on and before you can say Humpty Dumpty, he'll be on the high seas never to be heard from again. Then I received a letter from him. Witty and romantic, it recaptured the magic of our first night. It wasn't fair. The protective wall I was so painstakingly erecting crumbled like so much sand!"

Tally handed her granddaughter Cory's letter written the day after they first met, the first of his three letters that she had saved. Natalia read transfixed. "Oh, Tally," she bubbled, "so wonderfully romantic. I can tell he's special already. The chemistry is sure flowing in him, too. The week had to have dragged on very slowly for both of you."

"Sunday was divine. Our first true date, we took in a concert in the park, fed popcorn to the pigeons, cooed at the lovable animals in the zoo as they made funny faces at us, then dined on French food and skylarked on the beach. How the time did fly by. More of his grand philosophy of life seeped out. I asked how did he come by it, and he made it all seem so simple. I can hear his voice. He said we have two choices: We can see the world as a beautiful place with spots of ugliness or we can see the world as an ugly place with spots of beauty. One view has us seeing roses in the rain; the other has us seeing the mud. Then, smiling, he asked how would we have it!

"Cory's exuberance for life was contagious. He could make me laugh, forget tomorrow, believe in the impossible. By the end of the day, he was no stranger at all. I nestled in his arms, and as he kissed me good night, much longer this time, I looked up at the stars and saw them grow ever larger. I was at one with the universe.

"He no sooner took off again on a wild dash to catch the last ferry than I grabbed my writing material to open my heart to him, a heart that had never been so open before."

"He was your first love?"

Tally smiled. "My love fantasies began with the childhood readings of King Arthur and the knights of the Round Table. I believed when Sir Galahad came into my life, I'd know at once. It would be love at first sight. But real life failed to live out fantasy. My first big pash was in high school. He was the captain of the football team. We dated exclusively our senior year and in the minds of all, would marry after graduation. But when he popped the question, a little voice inside of me raised a doubt, and in good conscience I could not accept. Happily, his misery did not last long. He soon found a most charming substitute.

"A year or so later, I began going out with one of the town's leading bachelors. Several years older, Ivy-League educated, and set up in his father's business, he was a dream catch for any girl seeking security. He wined and dined me, and one night over flowers and champagne presented me with a beautiful diamond. Once again that little voice rose in doubt, leaving me dumbfounded. I had no option but to decline.

"I was now seriously wondering if I might be constitutionally incapable of forming a lasting relationship. One destined to go it alone through life, depending on good samaritans for help over the big hurdles along the way. A frightening thought for one so young and naive in matters of the world. Then along came Cory and after but two times together, I felt I could go to the ends of the earth with him. So much for all my fears and doubts."

Tally handed her granddaughter the soul-baring letter she wrote on that special Sunday night. A look of incredulity spread across Natalia's face as she read. "M'gosh!" she gasped. "How fast can Cupid's arrow fly?"

A twinkle came into Tally's eye. "In times of war, darling, the bow ever draws tighter. Everything is on an accelerated pace. . . . Cory and I now faced our first separation. He was in the Amphibious Corps and his unit, in its final phase of training, had boarded a training transport to spend more than two weeks honing the skills so much needed for later on. It was this separation that made me fully aware of how much he had become part of my life. Never thinking of myself as much of a correspondent, I, nevertheless, wrote to him daily. The wait for his return seemed an eternity, and I stayed chronically anxious over his safety. While I knew he was in top physical condition, I also knew that serious accidents were not uncommon in those hazardous amphibious exercises, especially when the sea was rough and rising.

"To ease the pain of loneliness, he sent me his portrait and a peace dove pin. The photo, taken of him in his dress blues, accented the blue in his eyes and the warmth of his smile. I placed it on my nightstand so it would be the first thing I saw on awakening and the last thing I saw before closing out the day. I wore the peace dove daily to work."

Tally handed over the letters she wrote during the sea maneuvers. Natalia was now fully enraptured with the letters. She pored slowly over each one, absorbing every line. When she returned them, there was a slight crack in her voice. "One can only be deeply in love to open the heart so freely."

"The high-water mark of the war years," Tally said, "were those precious few days Cory and I had together between the end of his training and his assignment to a ship about to be commissioned in San Francisco. I can say without hesitating that the heart was now the main conduit of my being. My every emotion was routed through it. I could not imagine life without Cory. His beautiful letters warmed every fiber in my body. From the moment he was back at the base, all that mattered was to see him, to nuzzle up in his arms.

"After fervently presenting my case to the boss, I got my first Saturday off from work, so Cory and I could have the full weekend together. I was dressed, coiffured, and pacing when I saw his figure through the window make the turn toward the house. I never gave him a chance to reach the door. I bounded out the house and he braced himself in his tracks to take my rush into his arms. We hugged until we were breathless and kissed as only young passion dares, not caring what eyebrows it may have raised. The world disappeared about us.

"You'd never guess what his first words—indelible in my memory—were: 'You smell like freshly mowed hay.' I tweaked his nose and said something like I never knew he worked on a farm. He replied that although the career was brief, the aroma lasted long. I laughed, loving the quickness of his repartee.

"He met the rest of the Inner Circle as Debbie, Avis, and Susan had returned from the tennis courts. They were charmed by his light banter and social ease. I punched him in the ribs on our way to dinner, saying my mother warned me about dashing men about town. He responded that it's good she's not with us because in a weak moment he had promised his cronies we'd show up later at their favorite hideaway. The sight of these moral degenerates in a den of iniquity would leave no doubt in her mind that her daughter had plumb lost her wits in judging character.

"After a candlelight dinner, we joined his fun-loving mates and their perky dates at Paul's Passion Pit, a nightspot not nearly as raunchy as the name implied. It did have the soft lights and the scantily clad waitresses, but its popularity came mostly from furnishing live combos.

"Everybody had a nickname. Cory's was Gash. His best friend's was Scorch. I made a special effort to know him, figuring he'd have the best stories to report on my sailor.

"When dancing with Cory, I kidded him, calling him a man of a thousand names. Thus far I've met Timothy O'Reilly, Cory Zigler, Sinbad the Sailor, and now Gash. I asked him how that one came into being and he mumbled it was the result of a freak accident. He and a boat propeller got slightly tangled up one day in a boating drill and he ended up with a few nicks. The name followed. I had a hunch there might be a little more to it, which was later confirmed when dancing with Scorch.

"Scorch talked freely about his buddy. They became friends in midshipman school. My poet-philosopher, being a math and physics major in college, had a head start in the academics. Since he finished near the top of the class, he got a choice of duty. Scorch shook his head and said he blew it and elected to go with the rest of the class, which was to the amphibs. Anyone with the sense of a jackrabbit would have jumped at the chance of duty aboard a battlewagon or carrier, but Gash, bogged down with a Boy Scout complex, preferred to go where the need was greatest. Scorch then went on to say that Cory, although acing the tests, was no bookworm. He excelled in sports, loved to party, and had talents to burn. He soloed in 'Holy Night' at a Christmas service and had even the infidels sneaking a look at the Nativity scene.

"I inquired how he got nicknamed Gash, and Scorch supplied the missing parts to the story. In an early day of maneuvers, in a very rough sea, his coxswain overshot his approach to the ship and in reversing the engine to correct, sent a boathand standing on the stern flying off the boat into the hull of the ship, knocking himself unconscious. As the boat swerved toward the ship, Cory dived in the narrow space and after pulling the man away from the boat propeller, brought them both to the surface. Cory looked like he'd come out of a meat grinder, but his cuts were only superficial. On seeing the mess, the gang called him Gash and it's stuck since. Scorch, suddenly sensing I was beginning to put Cory on a pedestal, said that before I sainted him I should ask him how life was in Mexico and has he heard lately from the mermaid. I couldn't draw any more out of him.

"On dancing again with Cory, I asked how Scorch got his nickname. He stalled saying that when the band heats up, I'll get a clue. On discovering that I was not adverse to a little jitterbugging, he smiled when the band hit the boogie-woogie beat, turned me over to Scorch, and wished me luck. Wow! He put my body through contortions I never knew humanly possible. People pulled back to give us room to fly. My curiosity was fully satisfied. Yes, Scorch could melt the wax right off the floor!

"The last waltz was one of the favorites of the day: "Always."

As I rested my head on Cory's shoulder, he sang the chorus in a voice just loud enough for my ears." Tally lilted the words:

> I'll be loving you always
> With a love that's true always . . .
> Not for just an hour
> Not for just a day
> Not for just a year
> But always

"I felt warm all over. This was our song.

"We left the party. It would be the only time I'd see the entire group together. I recall how virile and boyishly good-looking they were, and the sudden sadness I felt in the fleeting thought all too soon they would be on their way to seeing death in its most violent form.

"Cory and I strolled, arms around waists, to the bay and along the shoreline. We frolicked as only silly lovers would do. We'd stop, kiss, and he'd chastise me for my indiscretion under the eyes of heaven. Then I'd break away from him and dash up the beach until his longer strides overtook me. Whereupon I would accuse him a monster on the loose, a meance to women and children. We'd kiss again and solemnly swear never to publicly divulge the awful truth about the other.

"Back at the ranch, with the living area to ourselves, we snuggled up on the sofa and talked and smooched until it was time for another of his mad dashes to the ferry landing.

"The next day he returned in casual attire, a dress uniform over an arm for the *Porgy and Bess* musical which I got tickets for that night. We hiked to the countryside and spread out a blanket. After a wine and cheese lunch, I thought the timing was right to hear the stories Scorch had coyly hinted. It took a little romp and horseplay, not beyond either of us, to get him to oblige. He had me laughing to tears.

"The mermaid was Esther Williams, the popular Hollywood

bathing beauty queen. She had come to the pool at the Coronado with her troupe to give an exhibition for the boys. Cory and Scorch missed her show but arrived later for the regular dance held in the ballroom. Scorch, who was an autograph buff, immediately spotted her at a back table surrounded with several well-muscled escorts. The two differed on who they were. Scorch bet they were bodyguards and Cory laid odds they were PR men. To settle the matter, Cory agreed to ask the mermaid for a dance and if it turned out they were not bouncers, and if she consented, Scorch could break in on signal and have the pleasure of dancing as well as acquiring her autograph. Cory approached the actress, who graciously accepted his request. The jokester in him then took over. He pretended not to know her, which was so unexpected given her popularity that it momentarily flustered her into raising the question. Still playing the devil, Cory played up the coincidence of two attractive strangers ending up in the same boat because he was quite certain that she didn't know who he was. She quickly regained her composure and graciously introduced herself. He, in turn, said that he was Henry Ford the Third. She gasped that he didn't believe her, and he countered that it was she who apparently did not believe him. He then offered to swap a car for a swimsuit. At this point getting cues that she was on to his silly game and was about to clobber him, he confessed to his tomfoolery and told her how she could make his friend, Scorch, the happiest sailor in the navy. A true trooper, she finished the dance with Scorch, and wrote to his delight: To Scorch, a fantastic dancer. Love, Esther Williams. Cory said Scorch picked up the tabs for the rest of the week.

"The Mexican incident was hilarious. During training exercises, the unit experimented with the night invasion. Its element of charm, Cory pointed out, lay in the thought of routing out the enemy in his long johns. Of course, it required learning a whole new batch of signals, but the senior officers never seemed overtroubled in making more work for the junior ranks.

"Cory was selected to land a wave of marines in full battle dress on a beach at the southern tip of California at midnight. He and the troops debarked from the ship quite some distance at sea in a blinding rainstorm and dense fog. They moved shoreward looking for a pair of red blinking lights that had been set up earlier in the day to indicate the boundaries of the beach. All Cory had to do was to spot the lights and land the marines between them. The trouble was that the blowing rain kept splashing the lens of his binoculars, making them useless. The rain and the heavy fog also made visibility near zero. As he sensed they were approaching the shore, Cory told the coxswain to idle the engine until they spotted the lights. While this prevented the boat from running aground, it caused it to drift downward with the current. Cory suddenly saw two weakly blinking red lights rising out of the soup, and ordered full speed ahead. They hit shore and the marines with fixed bayonets stormed the beach. Cory somehow got his wave of boats regrouped and swung seaward with the happy feeling of a difficult mission accomplished. It took him nearly to dawn to find his fog-enshrouded ship. He climbed aboard dead tired only to be piped to the bridge to face an infuriated captain using language most unbecoming an officer and gentleman to let Cory know that he had invaded neutral Mexico, a fiasco requiring a formal apology from the State Department. The blinking lights Cory saw came from the red-light district of Tijuana!

"When I later told the story to the girls, we went slightly hysterical picturing marines with pointed bayonets charging the bordellos of Mexico."

"I can see that Cory can turn humor on himself as well as others," Natalia said after she stopped laughing.

"Cory was also clever at satire. I'll let you read a skit he wrote lampooning the navy caste system. He and Scorch put it on for the ship's officers on Christmas Eve." Tally dug it out of the stack and after handing it to Natalia, she refilled their cups, adding the usual spoonful of cognac.

Natalia giggled from beginning to end. "Cory has a neat way," she said, "of getting in jabs without making anyone too mad."

Tally smiled. "When I first read it, the thought came to me that only one in an American uniform would dare write such a skit. Can you imagine a German or a Japanese officer doing it! It seems to support the belief that what our military may lack in discipline, they make up for in innovation.

"To go on with the romance, Cory and I had only one more time together before he headed north to the Barbary Coast. We arranged a foursome to include Scorch and Susan for an evening of dinner and dancing. Cory and Scorch were a riot. They put on a vaudeville routine that had Susan and me holding our sides. I thought Scorch and Susan had the makings of a great pair, but the war prevented anything further from developing between them. Scorch took Susan home; and once again back at the ranch, Cory and I had the living area to ourselves.

"My favorite spot when he sat on the sofa was to sit on the floor, shoes off, rest my head on his knee and let his gentle fingers knead my neck and shoulders. This time he sensed my mood and asked why the long face. I conceded I was into self-pity knowing that he would soon be back into the clutches of the navy, which would keep us apart until the end of the shakedown cruise. In his usual upbeat fashion, he told me of his plans to take me home from work on his last night in town and give me a kiss for every star I counted in the sky until it was time for him to catch the last ferry. And he insisted I be well rested when the two of them paint the old mission town a torrid red before the ship heads out to sea.

"He saw the tears come to my eyes on the word *out*, ran his fingers through my hair, and said how glad we should feel to be Americans. I remember him saying wars are no longer won by men but by technology. It is not who is best at swordplay, but who can make the most guns and tanks. Out where he's going, the sea and sky are patrolled by American ships and planes because we're the greatest industrial nation in the world. He then pictured a pretty Japanese girl kissing her sweetheart farewell, knowing full well he's on a one-way ticket. How easily we could have been born in Tokyo. The thought of the poor Japanese girl made me feel ashamed of myself. So I snapped out of my funk, jumped on his lap, and thrilled to his saying the three most beautiful words in our language.

"We did some pretty heavy petting but nothing further. Cory, from the old school, honored the sanctity of marriage, which meant not to desecrate its sanctions. Strong though our passions, we bore the same morality. He was also opposed to war marriages, saying that separation was an ill-boding way to start off a life together. Rationally, we were on the same wave lengths, but emotionally, if he had said let's fly to Vegas, I'd have been by his side on the plane. He insisted on no strings attached to our relationship since a commitment curtails freedom. That fate decreed upon him a monastic existence should in no way impose on me the vows of the convent. He wanted me to have a normal social life. With such broadmindedness, I had no desire to stretch or test its limits.

"What a letdown it was when Cory called to say plans had changed, which would keep us from seeing each other before his departure. The officers had drawn straws to determine who'd be in charge of the boat crews scheduled for an earlier train to San Francisco, and Cory was the unlucky one. The trip was a story in itself!

"Cory was convinced that no matter how thorough the inspection at the depot, the American sailor would somehow find a way to smuggle liquor aboard. So, he concocted a daring plan. After final inspection, he informed the men that he had complied with naval regulations. Therefore, once on the train he would confine himself to his compartment for the night. He then read off a list of names, men who were former carpenters and plumbers, to be the cleanup detail in case a party should develop during the night, all spoken with tongue-in-cheek. The men whooped and boarded the train. True to his word, Cory locked himself in his compartment and shuddered at the thought that this would be the men's last ride stateside. But even prepared as he was, he still underestimated how rambunctious things could get. The racket got deafening. After midnight a redfaced conductor pounded on his door screaming that his train was in shambles and he was going to wire the commandant of the Naval District. Cory persuaded him to hold off action until they made a dawn inspection. He was beginning to fear he might be spending the rest of the war in a military prison. The conductor was flabbergasted at the morning inspection. The seats, the aisles, the toilets were in spic-and-span order. The cleanup detail came through with flying colors."

"The more I hear about Cory," Natalia enthused, "the more I love him."

"There was a most touching incident in San Francisco while Cory was waiting on the commissioning of his ship. He met his coxswain Rob Roy, Rob's wife, Jeanie Mae, and their year-old baby for dinner. The two came from Georgia to see Rob Roy off. As Cory rose to leave, Jeanie Mae, a teenager, fragile as a porcelain doll, grabbed his arm and whispered to him to take care of Rob Roy because he was all they had. Cory, the wordsmith, was unable to forge a word. All he could do was press her hand, and lightly, for fear it might burst into a million pieces.

"Out of sensitivity to my loneliness and perhaps even more to make up for his lapse in writing that occurred during the early days in working out the kinks in the ship, the purpose of the shakedown cruise, Cory had a photo taken in his navy whites and mailed it to me. It complemented perfectly his other photo in navy blues. With his black curly hair, he looked absolutely smashing in whites. I placed it on the night table opposite my nightstand so no matter which side I rolled out of bed, I'd be greeted with a smile.

"The disappointment of missing Cory on his leaving San

Diego was softened in the anticipation of getting together at the end of the shakedown cruise. The clock was ticking down. I knew it would be our final days together before he went overseas. I was ready to make every moment count, jeopardize my job if need be. He would call from shore phones as the Hudson slowly wound its way down the coast. The sound of his voice had a wonderful way of lifting my spirits. Then came the call from Long Beach. The ship received sudden orders, superseding all others, to cancel all shore leaves and make preparations to head out. Departure date was set for the morning. I was devastated. I would be deprived once more of seeing my love, this time for even a hug and a bon-voyage kiss. Cory kept a positive tone, reminding me that quality not quantity was what counted most. With only a minute to talk, he repeated the words of our song. Reduced to monosyllables, I could only say, 'me too.'"

Tally handed Natalia the letters written between the end of training and the end of the shakedown cruise. Natalia's eyes misted again in reading them, sentimentally reflecting on the openness in their expression of love in times so fraught with uncertainty. Another wonderment had been slowly growing inside of her. She spoke to it. "Tally, knowing out of deference to Gramp you have not so much as peeked at these letters or told anyone their story, how is it possible that the events of over fifty years ago can come so clearly into your mind? And seemingly with so little effort."

"Bear in mind, my darling, that memories of the heart never age. They have escaped the tyranny of time." A twinkle lit up Tally's eyes. "And in staying forever fresh, they keep love forever young." Natalia squeezed her grandmother's hand.

Tally took a long sip of coffee before resuming. "The stress level was now reaching new highs at home and abroad. At the ranch, it was largely over job insecurity. Those of us who were hired during the war were all temporary workers. Our pay came from military contracts and when the contracts were not renewed or reduced, layoffs occurred. As war supplies approached war demands, more and more pink slips followed. Since there was no senority—we were all hired within the same time frame—it was guesswork who might be next. Since I was in the Research and Development Division, which had less turnover, I was a bit safer than the rest of the Inner Circle, who worked on the production line, but that didn't slow down the rumors.

"Then my concerns over my brother Ted never lessened. While his physical condition slowly improved, his mental state did not. His self-esteem remained low and his self-confidence stayed shaky. He could only see a bleak future ahead of him. This was a drastic change from the brother I knew before the war. The day he received the Purple Heart wrenched my heart. Afterward, he handed it to me, saying he had no desire to look at it. I took it on the condition it was for safekeeping only, and would be returned the moment he asked. It never left my possession.

"Now that Cory had moved into the battle zones, my anxieties over him escalated. The intervals of no correspondence were excruciating because when censorship caused these blackouts, I knew he was into an invasion. The island-hopping campaigns were in full swing. What comes to most people's minds when they think of the Pacific War are the historic moments: the bombing of Pearl Harbor, the flag-raising on Iwo Jima, the MacArthur declaration that 'I have returned' on stepping ashore in the Philippines, and the atomic-bomb explosion on Hiroshima. Only those with a personal stake are likely to be aware of the high price of the torturous island route to Tokyo. The trail began in the Solomons, then through the Carolinas, the Gilberts, the Marshalls, the Marianas, the Philippines, the Vocanos, and finally the Ryukyus. The fighting was fierce and gruesome at each stop because the enemy, fanatical to their cause, refused to surrender, choosing to take a life for a life.

"How was I so aware of this? It was one of the ironies perpetuated during the war. Cory was so obsessed in protecting me against the ugliness of war that he avoided any reference to the invasions in his letters. All the while, as a candy striper at the naval hospital, whenever a rash of wounded arrived, generally coinciding with a period of no correspondence from him, I knew exactly where he was. I would never, of course, make this known to him.

"Working as a volunteer rapidly removed whatever glamour a war might have stirred up in a romantic lass. All I can say is that it tugged at the heartstrings to write for someone without arms or walk for someone without legs or read for someone without eyes.

"One of the boys who will never leave my memory was a marine named Randy, shot up in the landing at Tarawa. Although he survived massive surgery, his mind went amnesic. The staff hoped if special attention was given him before he was transferred to the neuropsychiatric ward, he might open up, something that the truth serum had failed to do. It would be a big help to the psychiatrists. They warned me not to touch him in any fashion or to mention any facet of the war or to press him in any way. They considered him potentially violent and doing any of these things might trigger a rage.

"I saw Randy daily and never saw him violent. All I saw were wonderfully large brown eyes, sometimes soft, sometimes intense. When intense he would withdraw into his psychotic world, tremble all over, and babble incoherently. Talking in a quiet voice often had a calming effect. As trust built up, a breakthrough occurred. He opened up one day and talked of his boyhood days on a farm in Indiana, of his love of working the fields and feeding the livestock. When Pearl Harbor was attacked, he lied about his age to join the marines. He then lapsed into silence, but the staff was excited as they saw his repressions beginning to lift.

"The dam broke loose the next day. He relived his nightmare at Betio Island, the enemy stronghold in the Tarawa Atolls. His landing craft stalled on the coral reefs. Enemy fire commenced the moment the ramp lowered, and they had to wade several hundred yards to shore. His closest buddy was instantly hit and sank into the reef. He was forbidden to stop and assist. Orders were to move forward. Randy, too, was badly hit, somehow made it ashore, and lying near a pile of decaying corpses, passed out. As soon as Randy told that part of his story, he could talk no more. His body went into convulsions and I called a nurse who injected him with morphine. I wept and felt lightheaded, but the staff exulted, declaring Randy had taken the first step toward recovery.

"The next evening Randy dropped the water glass on his dinner tray. He helped clean up the fragments. I stopped by briefly to say hello and promised him a longer visit on the morrow. He waved good night and said he had a letter to write. That was the last I would see of him. He had concealed a sliver of glass and slashed his wrist during the night. The nurse found his sheets soaked in blood and his lips curved in a peaceful smile. He left a note for me saying he was sure I would understand. The smell of rotting flesh tainted his blood and would have to be purged before he could take his place in the family cemetery near the farm. He thanked me for helping him. The official report simply stated that Corporal Randall Scott died of wounds suffered at Tarawa. I cried all the way home.

"It was the tragedy of Ted and Randy and of the many others that I saw moving in and out of the hospital that made it necessary for me to block out the ugliness I knew Cory would be repeatedly facing. Cindy and I began to regularly attend Sunday services to defer our anxieties to a higher being."

"How can anyone," Natalia exclaimed, "who has not actually experienced the terror of war, comprehend the depth of these anxieties? In my college history course, our instructor gave statistics too overwhelming to translate into feelings. She said the numbers killed in World War II included forty million Russians alone, and more millions in China. How can one picture such numbers? The blood of over one million Americans, she said, stained three continents and two oceans and yet our casualties were the fewest among the major powers."

"How can we picture such numbers?" Tally repeated. "I'm reminded of something Cory once said. He was talking about the size of his midshipman class, commenting that they were two thousand strong. When they lined up four abreast for a dress parade, they covered five football fields. Can you picture the number of football fields it would take to accommodate a dress parade of the war dead!

"Returning to Cory's letters, since war experiences were taboo, he would frequently write amusing vignettes on the ship officers. One in particular that I thought was a riot was on his skittish captain. He was a navy man to his bones, having come up through the ranks to be finally awarded with a ship of his own. So imagine his shock and horror in looking over the papers of the officers under his first command: one upon another a ninety-day-wonder, an epithet for those who were pinned officer's bars after only ninety days of training. To make matters even worse for Cory, the captain saw him as a dead ringer of the ninety-day-wonder who had eloped with his only daughter, his one pride and joy. So he took out his vendetta on Cory, swamping him with duties at every turn. He appointed him summary court-martial officer even though he lacked legal training, a gunnery officer even though he had no weaponry training, a communications officer even though he had no coding training. Yet Cory held him in high respect because of his competence. Cory did, however, request the grave-yard watch to keep as low a profile as possible. Those were the only hours the captain slept. But it turned out to be the favorite watch for Cory as he found life most pleasant when most bodies were asleep. During those many quiet nights, he could absorb without distraction the many wonders of the ocean, which were the source for several beautiful poems. In the end, in an amazing turnabout, Cory became the captain's fair-haired boy. In a baseball game after a campaign, Cory got the game's winning hit against the flagship's team, winning for the captain his wager with the admiral. Thereafter, Cory could do no wrong.

"Another fascinating person was Commander Hawkins, the beachmaster. He had developed a system of bridge for tournament play before the war, taught it to Cory, and the pair won regularly from officers in transit. Hawk kept the winnings in his safe for a victory party after the war. Hawk knew the islands well. He had retired a rich man from Wall Street in predicting the Crash of '29 and spent the following years leisurely yachting in the Pacific. Consequently, he had bargaining power with the navy, the one he prided most, exemption from room inspection. The reason: He kept his closet stocked with premium whiskey, which he euphemistically called medicinal restoratives. He only filled prescriptions for a select few; Cory, of course, being one. Hawk kept Cory informed of all the campaigns in advance.

"The poet in Cory came out in his expressions of love and in his deep feelings toward nature—her starlit seas, her raging storms, her crimson sunsets. I would reread his poetry like evensongs before sleep, some so special as not to be shared even with the Inner Circle. His love of the ocean was profound, Coleridge's *Ancient Mariner* and Debussy's *La mer* among his favorites.

"Sometimes he used verse to express humor. I remember when Susan plied me with wine and got me to pose in swimsuit and heels a la Betty Grable, whose pin-up boosted male morale overseas. We sent the cheesecake photo to him. He responded facetiously, oohing and aahing over my measurements but insisting I had other qualities surpassing in importance, best expressed in immortal verse. The final line went something like, while I had a figure which had him impressed, he liked the shape of my bank account best." Tally laughed. "Cory, of course, was fully aware that my spendthrift ways had me constantly living from paycheck to paycheck. He once feigned outrage that civilian workers have salaries far exceeding the doughboys in the trenches. When I read his poem to Susan, she laughed and said she always knew he was three-parts devil and was now fairly certain about the fourth part.

"The philosopher in Cory seeped out in several letters. What influenced me the most, and some of the other girls too, were his thoughts on the paradox of love, its strange duality, its power to produce opposite effects. Love can depress or uplift, zap or energize, ruffle or soothe, degrade or ennoble.

"Starting out with the premise that love spins the head, he turned to the physics of spinning objects for the answer. Two opposing forces act on a spinning object. One force, centripetal, draws the object toward its center, while the other force, centrifugal, thrusts the object away. The centripetal force in love draws the person inward, making one self-centered and narcissistic. The centrifugal force in love thrusts the person outward, making one outgoing and altruistic. The relative strength of the forces determines the person's pattern. Hitler is a case of extreme centripetal love; Francis of Assisi, a case of extreme centrifugal love. Cory then warns that if we don't strive to make our love more centrifugal, we'll be drawn into the vortex of the very evils we're at war to destroy.

"I felt his thoughts contained a beautiful truth. Who doesn't struggle between the forces of selfish and selfless love? Who doesn't vacillate between the urge on one hand to withdraw and be self-serving and on the other hand to reach out and respond to the needs of others. I fear we live in a society in which the centripetal forces dominate because we see so few St. Francises of Assisi.

"The reason the shakedown cruise was aborted, I later found out, was that the *Hudson* was being rushed into the Mariana campaign. Cory, of course, knew this but gave no hint of it in our last phone conversation. To soften the pang of what he knew would be a long separation, he spent a king's ransom to buy me a pearl necklace at the first friendly island on route."

Tally opened an envelope and handed the necklace to Natalia.

"Oh, they're beautiful," she cried. "Such quiet elegance."

"Natural pearls," Tally said, "would be Cory's overwhelming choice. Anything else would be too ostentatious. As usual, the attached card reflected his wit: 'Mopsy, it's an optical illusion. The pearls look strung but there are no strings attached.' I wore them everywhere, but when I married Gramp I put them away. They shall be yours someday, for you can now appreciate their sentiment.

"I, in turn, wanted so much to give something special of myself to him, something that would lessen the miles between us. I finally ended up going to a photo studio and having a portrait taken for him alone. To have it come out as I wanted, I saw Cory, not the photographer, when the camera clicked. The result pleased me, but more important, it seemed to delight Cory, as it gave rise to one of his best poems. The photographer wished to make an enlargement for his showcase and offered to cancel the fee in exchange, but I would have none of that. I took home the negative and put the match to it."

Tally withdrew an envelope and removed a desk-size photo. The moment Natalia looked at it, she could only dumbly stare. Of all the photos she had seen of Tally, none moved her more. It captured her essence. Her soft, lustrous hair flowed off the shoulders and rested on a scoop neckline of frothy lace, bringing out the ultimate of alluring femininity. Her turquoise eyes sparkled in a rare brilliance. "Only a great love could make one this beautiful," Natalia gushed.

Tally, as was her wont, diffused the compliment. "The summer of 1944," she continued, "brought on the conquest of the Marianas—Saipan, Tinian, and Guam—but not without the cost of many more lives. Also considerable changes had taken place at the ranch. Cindy married her beau, Dave, an officer on the *Colorado*, a battleship badly shelled at Tinian, which had returned to stateside for repairs. Cindy returned to live with her folks in Illinois. We kept up, of course, an active correspondence but I missed her dearly. Avis, too, married her navy man. They rushed one weekend to the popular marriage bureau in Vegas. She went to live with her family in Fresno. Debbie and Susan were transferred to days, leaving me the only one on the swing shift. I would see them on weekends. Changes on the homefront moved as dizzyingly fast as changes in the war zones."

Tally handed Natalia the letters she wrote that summer and early fall. "You may read these, darling, while I put on a fresh pot of coffee." Natalia again found herself totally absorbed.

"I can't imagine," she said when she returned the batch to Tally, "the terror of silence, knowing that the longer the battle rages, the worse the odds become because it means the enemy is again committed to fighting to the last man. Did any of you at any time begin to question the wisdom of the war?"

"The Inner Circle never wavered in supporting the country's response to Pearl Harbor. Terrible as separation was, we remained firm that Hitler and Tojo were evils that had to go if civilization as we know it were to endure. Now, how it became possible for these evils to have taken root and flourished was a question for which I could never find a good answer.

"Returning to the theme of change, a happy and normalizing event in my life was my transfer to the day shift and the five-day week. It was wonderful returning to a routine of work, play, and sleep that fitted in with most others. And it was a glorious feeling to have free weekends.

"The military, in the meantime, focused on retaking the Philippines, which was its major accomplishment in the fall of 1944. While the landing was not fiercely contested, the fleet was soon to engage in a sea battle that turned out to be the largest sea battle with respect to amount of tonnage sunk that the world has ever seen. The Japanese, in a do-or-die effort, threw every warship they could muster into the Battle of Leyte Bay. It was a tremendous American victory. The Japanese navy for all practical purposes was at last destroyed.

"But an ominous development was taking place at the same time. With our increasing control of the sea and sky, the enemy countered with the *kamikaze*, or suicide plane. As more evidence of their fanaticism, they had more volunteers than planes. The pilot, requiring minimum training, took off loaded with explosives and just enough fuel to reach the target area. He then set his sights on a ship, most often a destroyer or a transport with devastating results. Many ships were sunk or heavily crippled. Gun crews on ships spent sleepless nights firing at everything in the sky. The kamikaze continued to play havoc for the remainder of the war.

"Cory, in his humorous way, wrote about it in a letter in which he lampooned the proliferation of admirals in wartime. He bemoaned that the surplus get often siphoned into think tanks, a mighty cause for alarm because a thinking admiral is a sure ticket to disaster. He made his point with Operation Smokeboat. A think tank was given the task of finding a solution to the kamikaze. The admirals came up with the idea of a smokeboat, on the reasoning that invisible targets are difficult to hit. Consequently, each transport was ordered to equip a boat with a fog generator capable of producing a massive cloud of black smoke. The moment the general alarm was sounded the boats were to be lowered into the water and begin laying smoke at all possible speed.

"The captain, still on his vendetta, appointed Cory smokeboat officer. The plan was tested. Cory wrote that it was the most harrowing experience of his life. Not only did all the ships on the area become invisible but so did everything else. He couldn't see the coxswain in front of him, and the coxswain couldn't see the compass in front of him. When the signal was given to return to the ship, nobody had any idea where they were. They sweated out the night hoping they wouldn't run into the path of a circling destroyer or drift off lost into the open sea. Cory suggested in his report they sell the plan cheap to the Japanese. The project wasn't abandoned, he wryly added, until the psychiatric cases topped the casualties from kaze hits.

"More of Cory's humor came out in describing the ritual in crossing the equator. An old navy tradition is to initiate those making the crossing for the first time, the polliwogs. Those having crossed before, the shellbacks, are in charge of the hazing. Spirits run high for the occasion and often things get well out of hand. As Cory penned, when this happens the toll of the wounded can be as great as the casualties from a torpedo hit. He had one of those experiences.

"It all began, he said, when several polliwogs the night before sneaked into the sleeping quarters of the chief electrician, a shellback called Fisheyes, and shaved off his handlebar mustache. What could be a worse beginning, Cory asked, than to separate an electrician from his proud symbol of masculinity? Fisheyes spent the entire morning perfecting a phallic symbol that gave maximum shock with minimum fatality. He then spent the afternoon gleefully jabbing polliwogs as they went through a series of torturous activities, ending by having to crawl through the spread legs of shillalah-wielding shellbacks to kiss the greased belly of King Neptune for their Certificate of the Deep. Cory, one of the lucky few who escaped ending up in sick bay, said the skipper watched the entire proceedings with a deadpan, obviously vicariously revenging the SOB who stole his only daughter. I know it had to have been gruesome but Cory's way of telling it hit my funny bone and I couldn't help but laugh. He ended the letter saying that his wounds did heal, all two hundred bones X-rayed showed no breaks, and Hawk came through with his patented restorative."

"Oh, Tally," Natalia gushed. "I can see why you fell head over heels. Cory stays upbeat no matter what. Tell me, what is a person like that doing in the military?"

"Cory never fitted the mold, that's for sure. I don't think he ever dehumanized the enemy. He hated Tojo and Hirohito, but not the men conscripted to fight. In spite of all the brainwashing, he never lost sight that the other side, too, was part of the human race. I often reflected how painful it had to be for him to carry out the mandates of war.

"In late fall of forty-four I took leave and went back to Denver. The workload had slowed down and we were between contracts. My worry index zoomed as letters stopped coming from Cory, meaning that he was into another invasion, which, of course, was the Philippines. It helped to get my mind on other concerns. My father was in failing health and wished to see me. I intended on staying only two weeks but it was about a month, catching up with family and old friends. While I was glad to see Dad and the other sibs, I knew for sure that I was the maverick in the family and could never resettle in Denver. I felt truly I had no home, and Cory was the only real anchor in my life. Wartime makes good friends but they are continually changing addresses and beginning new careers. The word 'goodbye,' became the ugliest word in the dictionary. I was so happy to return to San Diego and reenter into the life of the man I loved.

"It was difficult getting into the spirit of Christmas that year, normally my favorite holiday. How can one enthusiastically celebrate the birth of the Prince of Peace with a war growing in violence? Also many of the sentimental elements were missing. I was used to a roaring fire and snow. Oh, there were parties galore and people were hugging and giving toasts, which only made me ache all the more for Cory. I had to keep reminding myself that I was not alone. The land was full of wives and sweethearts who had to face the most festive time of the year with their loved ones overseas.

"And so we moved into the new year. It was now nine months since I had felt Cory's arms around me, yet how deeply had my love grown. How could this be, you may ask, when in actuality we had been together so few times? Is it explainable? I can only say that a heart in love keeps a different record of time. A chronological minute translates into a hundred minutes of heart time. His beautiful letters kept adding to heart time.

"While Cory had warmed my heart to a depth that neither time nor oceans could cool, could it be entirely the same for him?

That was the tormenting question that separation raised. Could my letters keep the fires going that began in such a high blaze? While I saw love shining in his eyes and express itself in moving poetry, was it too much to expect it to sustain itself through a war that could go on and on? I even wrote in a letter that should his ardor ever cool, my only request was to be so informed. I could not bear to express a love unreciprocated.

"My letters were hardly documents of profundity. His tenderness had opened my heart, dissolved my inhibitions, let the love flow out. That was all they offered: genuine, untrammeled love. If they could provide just a morsel of morale, I would be contented. I had reason to think they did. In one letter he expounded on mail call, which he called the sailor's greatest joy at sea. The moment a ship drops anchor, a boat is dispatched to pick up mail and the cheers ring out when it returns full of mail sacks. Once the mail is passed out, the ship quiets down with the reverence of D-Day devotionals, as men read and reread the words from home."

Tally gave her granddaughter the letters she had written Cory through the late fall and early winter, and refilled their cups during the long interval.

"They may not be treasured for their profundity," Natalia said on returning the letters to the stack, "but they're priceless in their outpouring of love. Cory had to be deeply moved by them. I would say if there's a positive side to war, it would have to be in the incredible production of letters. The number you wrote to Cory in these nine months is twice the number I've written in my entire life. I wonder how many millions of letters were posted in World War II alone? With modern technology we have so many other ways to communicate in peacetime which are easier and quicker. Letter writing has become a lost art. History, as a result, is the big loser."

Tally took a long pause, her face twisting in pain, her toes twitching. "We now come, darling, to the hardest part of the story. It is February 1945. Ted has been finally discharged from the hospital and has returned to Denver to his old job and working to get his marriage back on track. His leaving, confirming his long ordeal was over, which was my reason for coming here, opened a void in my heart. Next to Cory, he was the most important person in my life, and I knew I would not see much of him anymore. He needed all of his energy to make a go of his marriage, and his health was still a big question mark. A piece of shrapnel had lodged too close to the heart to remove. Should it ever shift, which was now in the laps of the gods, it would all be over. And, as I have said, my last visit home made it all too clear I no longer had roots or belonged in Denver.

"Notwithstanding Cory's sweetness and thoughtfulness, I did have qualms, moments of critical reflection, which I guess is the downside of hanging one on the moon. Could I give to the one I loved the happiness I so much wanted him to have? All of my weaknesses I perceived to be his strengths. He came from a stable background, a harmonious family with a high value on education and broad cultural experiences. In contrast, I came from a broken home, a family more inclined to fragment than hang together, a family more concerned with surviving than self-improving. I saw Cory as my prince charming but sometimes I feared I might wake up like Cinderella in rags but with no prince searching for the foot to fit the golden slipper. I needed to have Cory hold me tight and reasssure me all will work out right. I knew I would feel safe in his arms, but it was a luxury not granted me.

"It was out of this context that a letter, which I have come to call the fatal letter, arrived from Cory." Tally pulled it from the stack. "I would like you to read it carefully, Natalia, before I say another word."

Tally slowly sipped coffee until she received it back, and then she began a cerebral dissection. "Notice how it began with a restrained Dear Mopsy, not an effusive Dearest or Darling. Then in the opening paragraph, Cory, with the glass always half full, predicts the war might last till fifty-five, pooh-poohing any thoughts of a quick end. Then he is the prophet of doom for his unit, saying they'll always be ordered to lead in the assaults because the top brass, in cold objectivity, will fall back on the most experienced. This crushed the fragile hope of having Cory home for Christmas, the only present I wanted. It was the one fantasy I clung to most to ease the pain of separation.

"The gloom in the letter continued. He questioned God's protection in war, noting that the good do not fare any better than the bad. The sheer magnitude of man's folly has Providence washing his hands of the whole affair. This sabotaged the comfort I received in putting my trust into the hands of a higher power for his safe return.

"Finally, most painful of all, Cory suggested the truer measure of love is not in how well we laugh together but in how well we cry together. He knew our love dazzled on fun and frolic. In essence, he took out from under me all the props I had erected to endure the unendurable: the agony of long separation and the anxieties of horrible invasions. Those in the knowledge of landings knew why wave commanders were called the expendables. This was the only letter I ever received from Cory absent of crazy verse, funny stories, knight errantry, winking leprechauns, or a tender poem. Why? I flung myself in tears across my bed. There had to be a reason, and it couldn't be good.

"I went into shock. My body felt the dagger before my mind could comprehend. Cory sought to distance the relationship. His ardor had cooled. My heart struggled to beat. My hands and feet turned cold, then numb. My body shook. Then I became feverishly hot. It warmed my brain, bringing some life to it. I wish it hadn't. It, too, agreed the ardor had cooled. Cory would never have written such a letter driven by passion. I felt a desperate need to be outside, alone, in fresh air. I always found renewal of spirit at Coronado Beach where I could draw on Cory's strength. I changed into the white-and-red dress of our first date, put on a sweater, and caught the ferry.

THE RED-RIBBONED LETTERS

"It was not a night for strollers. I had the chilly shoreline pretty much to myself. I buttoned up my sweater as the wind stung my face and messed my hair. As I strided the beach, I sobbed and vented my fury at a war hostile to young love and to a God unmoved to do anything about it. Cory was still unblemished integrity in my eyes. He loved me until the forces of a higher fate intervened.

"As more thoughts started to sift through my slowly reviving brain, a doubt began to rise that fate may not have been the sole perpetrator. For the first time, the possibility of a rival crept into mind. How foolish that I had never considered it before. Only the abnormal times could account for it. As I pondered more on the idea, the argument grew stronger. Cory had to have a life in the prewar days. A disturbing scenerio was taking shape. A woman of the world, chic and most beautiful, was weaving her web even while Cory and I were meeting. This is not to imply that his love for me was ever insincere. I could not have been misled on that. I do recall a letter in which Cory expressed the belief that one could have more than one great love. I took on reading it as a point of theory, but I now wondered if he was not reflecting on himself. His love for my rival would also have to be genuine. It would not be in his nature to condone deception.

"The triangle theory went along with his insistence on no commitments, no long-range promises, no social limitations. He must have had the same arrangements with the other woman. At first the scales were balanced but then they tipped in her favor. What would cause that, I puzzled, since he was out at sea, away from each of us? My heart then sank. It had to be our letters. How drab mine must have been, a working girl rambling on about the mundane affairs of everyday life, compared to hers, a world traveler recounting exotic adventures. Misery now engulfed me. I had cried my eyes out. The hour was late. I returned home and slept fitfully till noon, thankful it was Sunday. I told Debbie and Laura my washed-out look was due to a virus, not yet wishing to get them caught up in my misery. I may have failed to mention that Laura, a long-standing friend of Debbie's, married to a navy officer, had replaced Cindy at the ranch. She fitted right in and was fully accepted by the Inner Circle. . . .

"On Sunday afternoon, I returned to Coronado and sat on the rock that was so special to Cory and me. My mind was fresher and my emotions more under control. Looking out at the ocean waves I could almost sense Cory's anguish radiating toward me. How difficult it must have been for him to have written the fatal letter. I felt I had now bareboned his plan. He hoped in breaking down my defenses, the emergence of despair would influence my practical side to see the futility of a romance founded largely on a fantasy linked to an endless war. In the painful reassessment, I would suppress the sentiment and learn to disconnect. This would be Cory's sensitive way of resolving conflict. In creating the conditions to have me the instigator, he would preserve my pride.

"Oh, how he had misjudged the strength of my love! I would have endured a thousand wars and a million tortures! But he must never know I had divined his strategem. He must be led to believe the ploy had worked. I could not forget the fulfillment he had brought into my life, awakening feelings I never dreamed possible. But had I the cleverness to cover the grief now drowning my heart? At least in turning my mind to what I believed would lighten his pain, it had the effect of somewhat lessening my own.

"I spent the afternoon starting a dozen letters. None satisfied me. My weary mind needed rest. Perhaps a new day might inspire a better effort. As I rose to leave, I could not help but take another long lingering look at the white caps and ask why this had to be. If leaping to the rocks below would solve anything, I had the courage, but even my tormented soul understood that would only make matters worse."

Tally heaved a deep sigh to rally her composure before continuing. "I shall now introduce a new person, who up to now had played no significant role in the story. We had crossed paths several times before I met Cory. Rather on the reserved side, he did little more than smile and exchange brief greetings. He was deferred from the service because he worked in a critical war industry. Cindy, with her penchant for movie stars, likened him to Spencer Tracy, a cozy teddy bear who keeps growing on you with time. His squarish, rugged features meet more of a man's definition of handsomeness than a woman's, but his easiness of manner and attentiveness made him attractive to women.

"I ran into him again after Cory went overseas. Over a cocktail he said his duties as an executive often demanded his appearance at cocktail parties and dinners, a role that was not his cup of tea. He was looking for a congenial female companion to make these events less of a drudgery and wondered if I might consider the part. I, of course, told him of my involvement with Cory, which only sparked more of his interest as he said it would lower the chances of either misinterpreting the motives of the other. He clarified the remark, saying that he had no intention of pursuing a serious relationship until after the war. With Cory's strong insistence that I have a balanced social life, his offer took on an appeal. It would allow me the pleasure of fraternizing with the coat-and-tie set with no compromises required. So I accepted on the stipulation that either party could voluntarily withdraw at any time without question. The pact was made. Thereafter, my social calendar included events that allowed me to wear my prettiest dresses." Tally laughed.

"I became his regular lady companion and he, true to his word, was the perfect escort and gentleman. He often asked about Cory, never impatient with my babblings, always sensitive to my mood when a new invasion was reported in the Pacific. He was adept at pleasant conversation, was courteous and refined and, like Cory, had a good sense of humor and a nice way of touching a woman's vanity. He lacked Cory's dashing good looks, quick wit, and range of talent. His forte was an astute business mind. Already well up the corporate ladder for one not yet out of his twenties, he was examining what opportunities may lay in the postwar era. He frequently left on business trips and I always looked forward to his companionship on his returns.

"He was now on one such trip. Before leaving, he called and suggested we have dinner together the night he was back. While this was a deviation from the usual protocol, I suspected no hidden agenda or anything improper in the offer. I cheerfully accepted. It suddenly occurred to me riding back on the ferry that this was the day of his return. My first impulse was to call and cancel the dinner, but then reconsidered. Wallowing in self-pity would do no good and moping about in solitude would only increase the concerns already beginning to surface at the ranch.

"Another reason for keeping the appointment was that I had come to fully trust my friend and value his judgment. If the conversation should drift to my heartache, I felt certain that he would keep everything in strict confidence and might even offer wise advice.

"In spite of my efforts to be buoyant, chatting gaily all the way to the restaurant, he read me terribly well. Our cocktails had no sooner arrived than he gently asked me what was wrong. I denied any problem but once into my cocktail, I dropped all pretenses and bared the situation, keeping myself mostly composed, dabbing up the occasional tear with my handkerchief. His reaction, so typical of him, was to admire my desire to take the path of least pain for all, saying most people under similar circumstances would tend to think entirely of themselves. Already I was feeling some relief in that he seemed to understand where I was and where I wished to go.

"After a long pause, he suggested that in responding to Cory I admit to certain troubled feelings which good conscience could no longer leave unaddressed. Tell him of the existence of our relationship, the pact we made, and the good faith on which we entered it. Then tell him of the sudden flip-flop that happened this one night when he confessed to amorous feelings, something totally off the wall and out of character. Say he followed this with a proposal of marriage. Tell him you were stunned speechless and shocked more in finding you were not able to automatically reject the proposal.

"I was deeply affected. I told him it was a gracious gesture on his part to be willing to embroil himself in my plight, but I was certain Cory would see through the guise.

"Then he really threw me into a loop. He said he had spoken the truth. In spite of his honest intentions of seeking no romantic involvement, he found himself more and more out of control of his feelings. I increasingly dominated his thoughts, became an obsession, destroying his every effort to think rationally. The feelings continued to persist knowing full well if they ever were revealed, our relationship would be over.

"My eyes must have grown wide as saucers. I had never fantasized us romantically, or even thought he was so inclined, and he was right in that I surely would have dissolved the pact had I any inkling of his changed feelings. I wouldn't have given myself the liberty of even contemplating the possibility.

"He intervened, seeing my struggle to collect my wits, saying he chose this moment to make his feelings known with the hope they might help in fashioning a reply to Cory, who should be my entire focus. Only after that issue is resolved should I give any thought to what he had admitted. That I didn't instantly revoke the pact on learning of his feelings was sufficient comfort. But, to avoid adding more complications, he advised we not engage in further contacts with each other until I had resolved the more pressing matter.

"And so it was, with a bursting heart, I wrote a letter to Cory the next day containing the strategy of an ambivalence arising out of this new development, a window for him to advance more easily the strategem he had set in motion. I wrote as I believed truth would dictate, straightforward and with no frills. My eyes teared up as I posted the letter."

Tally gave the letter to Natalia. She watched Natalia's face twist in pain on reading it. She then gave her Cory's letter in reply. Natalia's eyes now brimmed with tears. She refrained from making any comment.

"As you can see," Tally said softly, "his reply ended further speculations. I took it as a sensitively crafted letter full of tenderness and acceptance. I fought back the tears, capped all my emotions that were straining to burst out, and summoned every ounce of my remaining strength to write what I knew would be my last letter to Cory." Her toes twitched as she handed it to her granddaughter.

Natalia felt a lump rising in her throat in knowing this was the letter that would close out a beautiful romance that began in the magic of a St. Patrick's Day and ended in the gloom of an Ides of March, two days shy of one year. She became aware that the Tally she and the family knew was taking form in the content of this letter: a woman of outward serenity but guarded emotionality; a woman of dignified reserve, but deep caring; a woman who found love more rewarding in giving than in taking. The letter formally ended Tally's sentimental period. Natalia could not help but notice that Tally could not bring herself to say goodbye to Cory. It was still good night.

Tally paused long before continuing. "I was now ready to look afresh at what started out as a simple friendship. He was so patient. He did not force his feelings on me. He was gentle, thoughtful, and undemanding. He understood that wounds of the heart are slow to mend. I found his love to be good and unselfish. His steadfast devotion was bringing a stability back into my life, instilling in me a confidence that I could be a good wife, that I could meet his wants and needs. I became more energized.

"One day I had an impulse to return to the rock in Coronado. I scaled it and told Cory I loved him and would always have a place in my heart for him and hoped that the woman of his choice would bring him the happiness he so deserved. I then told him I was going to get married, and I was not on the rebound. I could not tolerate that because that would be egocentric love. If that were the case my little voice would cry out, and it has remained silent. It is also silent, I told him, because it was seeing that my love was flowing outward, for which I shall be always grateful to my first great love. I left the rock sensing the beginnings of a new inner peace.

"I informed the Inner Circle, now a round half-dozen with the addition of Laura, to mark their calendar for an Easter marriage. Dumbfounded was the general reaction. While they had been aware of strange goings on, they were not prepared for a major change in the making. Rather than opening up old wounds, I chose only to fill them in on the developments in the new relationship. While they professed outward joy, I sensed an undercurrent of disappointment; and in Cindy and Susan, who had placed Cory next in line after the Holy Trinity, the added feeling of betrayal. I'm sure they felt I had compromised my principles, caught up in the security of choosing a bird in hand. They all, however, attended the wedding, with Cindy my matron of honor. So now, my darling, you have for the first time the complete story of how Gramp—since you have undoubtedly identified my good friend—came permanently into my life.

"To get the marriage off to its best possible start, I destroyed Cory's pictures and all his letters except those at the beginning and end of the affair, those not laced with words of passion. I was determined to avoid flights into the past, a self-defeating indulgence. I could not bear to depart with the necklace and the peace dove pin, so I put them away with the vow never to wear them as long as Gramp lived. If at the time I had the foresight that someday I'd be telling the romance to an incurably curious granddaughter, I might have stored all the love letters and photos in a secluded place. Their loss makes it more difficult to give a proper balance to the story."

"Oh, Tally," Natalia said with warmth, "I understand fully why you did what you did, and while I would have dearly loved to have read all of Cory's letters, especially the poetry and his storytelling that meant so much to you, he has come very much alive to me through your wonderful letters and your remarkable memory. He is more than a distant image. I see him in flesh and blood."

"I cannot overstate how much of a godsend Gramp was during that turbulent period. I don't know how I would have survived without his calming influence and tenderness, which had me loving him without reservation. Knowing my nostalgia for snow, he thoughtfully arranged to have our honeymoon in a cabin high in the Sierras. The snow and isolation was a balm for my beleaguered nerves. I ran like a child in the snow, made huge snowmen, and gleefully tossed snowballs at an agilely ducking husband. We would sit on the hearth before a blazing fire in the evenings and sip champagne while he fed my vanity. It was a perfect honeymoon, and we returned to a cozy apartment he had found, no small feat in those days of severe housing shortage.

"His flow of loving attention never ceased. I was very lucky, with so many exposed vulnerabilities, to have put my fate in the hands of such a good man. He made me feel loved and wanted, and I, in turn, fully reciprocated. Since he knew so much about Cory, I was careful about bringing up his name or suggest comparisons. It was perhaps an unwarranted sensitivity because the two were cut from such different cloths. Cory was Don Quixote; Gramp, Sancho Panza. Cory had the Pegasus touch; Gramp, the Midas touch. Cory was spontaneous; Gramp was cautious and more predictable. In a way it was good that Gramp knew about Cory. It had him putting up better with my moods. 'Now, Tally,' he would say, 'it's going to be all right.' His voice was so reassuring. He made it easy for me to be a good and loving wife. I never once rejected his advances.

"We were about two weeks in our new apartment when a letter from Scorch arrived, which had been forwarded from the ranch. It took away my breath." Without further ado, Tally passed it to her granddaughter.

"Oh, my God," Natalia gasped after taking in the first paragraph, "I never dreamed it would end this way." She finished reading the letter and simply handed it back, too choked up to say more.

"I thought my heart would explode," Tally said. "I lost all feeling and had to down a strong brandy to jump-start the nervous system. It slowly began to sink in that Cory's beautiful heart would beat no more, that his beautiful eyes would open no more, that his beautiful lips would smile no more. The overwhelming sadness was now less personal in that his love had been spoken for, but more universal in the reflection of the magnitude of the loss. Its depth can never be measured because no one knows what beauty he might have contributed to a world in sore need of a liberal dose. Cory was right. God deserts his watch in wartime, leaving randomness to run its ugly course. Once again Robert was called upon to glue together the pieces of my shattered emotions. . . .

"It deeply bothered me that Scorch, his closest friend, seemed uninformed of our breakup, even though he was with Cory when my last letter arrived. I finally reasoned that he probably knew but out of discretion pretended otherwise. I wrote the other members of the Inner Circle of the tragedy, who poured out their grief in phone calls and letters.

"I had about returned to an even keel when a package arrived from Cory's mother. Ironic, the one woman who would have warmed my heart the most to have heard from just several short months before, now raised goose bumps in seeing her name on the package. I opened it. A letter from her was on top of the stack of my letters to Cory." Tally handed over her letter.

"What a lovely woman," Natalia exclaimed on reading it. "What a terrible loss this had to be to her."

"My heart bled for her," Tally replied. "How can we put a figure on the emotional cost of war? Her letter, too, deeply disturbed me in several ways. First, she said only my letters were saved. What about my rival's? Second, she said Cory planned to introduce us after the war. Why would he say that when at this time his heart belonged to another? What would be Cory's purpose in dissembling his choice of women to his own mother? For the first time, seeds of doubt crept into my mind. Could I have misinterpreted the fateful letter? Had my imagination run away with me? I couldn't have been that unstable. Cory's feelings had changed, I could not remain sane and doubt that, but the reason for it may be less clear than I first thought. I could not let the issue die. I needed to get more information to settle my troubled mind. Scorch seemed the most likely source. I wrote him and, taking advantage of his kind offer, told him I would like very much to visit with him whenever the good Lord saw fit to return him stateside.

"His return was much quicker than any of us dared dream as the atomic bomb, a shock to the entire world, was dropped in August, and Japan, reeling under the impact, quickly sued for peace. The long, horrible war was over and the Hudson arrived soon after in Long Beach. I drove up there, carrying child but not visibly, to have dinner with Scorch."

"You were pregnant!" Natalia's eyebrows arched in surprise.

"I had received the good news just a few days before I received the letter from Cory's mother. I did not feel right about sharing the news with Scorch and, in fact, thought it best to say as little as possible about any of the changes in my personal life.

"He was waiting for me at the dock. How much just one year of war had changed him! The boyish look was gone. How war subverts adolescence! We went to a quiet restaurant. Painful as it was for him to relive the tail end of the war, he gallantly strived to fill in the gaps haunting me. I hoped it had some cathartic value for him.

"The fateful letter was written just before the invasion of Iwo Jima. Cory had just returned from Commander Hawkin's room with the dismaying news that the island was a natural fortress capable of withstanding the heaviest bombardment. The landing promised to be the worst yet in the Pacific. My heart palpitated. Cory was writing the letter at the moment he knew he was in for the bloodiest action of the war. He chose for the first time to share his honest feelings. I, who should have given succor when his beautiful world was bracing for its worst onslaught of ugliness, totally failed him. I fell apart, personalized the message, and imploded in my own misery.

"The landing was as devastating as feared. Bodies were violently dismembered, piled up on the beaches, some never getting off the landing ramps. Rob Roy, Cory's coxswain, caught an early shell. It was Cory's wish to write his wife to soften the blow of the telegram, which is so cold.

"My eyes filled with tears as Scorch related this. Before them rose an image of a frail, frightened girl, too young to have a baby, embracing Cory in San Francisco and whispering to him to take care of all that they have. To write this letter had to take the iron out of his blood. And to think, in the midst of all this, my last letter was on its way to him.

"The new truth was dawning on me, but I had to hear it all, no matter how painful. My final letter, the one formally ending our relationship, arrived amidst preparations for the landing at Okinawa. Hawk had given Cory the added information that plans were completed for Operation Olympic, the invasion of Japan proper. It was set for November 1, 1945, and the *Hudson* was to land marines on the southern tip of Kyushu. Casualties were expected to run into the hundreds of thousands. Scorch stopped at this point to give a toast to the atomic bomb, which brought an end to all this madness. A tear escaped from his eye. What Cory was to never know, he said, was that he had seen the worst. The landing at Okinawa was much different from Iwo. The Japs changed tactics and concentrated back in the hills to slow the advances. The biggest worry for the amphibs was the damn kamikazes, which kept coming night and day. But Cory was not to benefit from these changes. His Boy Scout complex had him responding to the call for froggies.

"I took Scorch back to the dock and watched him nimbly manipulate the gangplank. I then stepped out of the car to take my first and last look at the U.S.S. *Hudson.* I let my eyes drift upward to the bridge where Cory stood watch those many silent nights, gazing out at the ocean, the inspiration for several of his poems. Then I got a flashback of my dream of homecoming: the ship docking, whistles blowing, wild bearhugging on the pier, the insane joy that the world was at peace and our Sundays would be together again. Then the image vanished. A void engulfed me. I returned to the car, feeling terribly alone.

"Scorch would never know the devastation he wreaked in what he probably thought was a cathartic healing. On the drive back to San Diego, the full impact hit me. My insecurity and instability had tunneled my perception, keeping me from seeing the big picture, permitting me to betray my deepest love. There had been no change of heart, no loss of ardor, no rival. Cory was steadfast and true-blue to the end. In anticipation of over-whelming ugliness, he shared his angst, and the cost was my desertion. He could only conclude that I was the fickle one. Alone in his dreams, no girl to come home to, he would have no strong reason to shy away from high risk. His Boy Scout complex was not the issue. I was his true killer. The word executioner seared on my brain. Guilt tore apart my soul.

"Tears blurred my vision. How easy, I thought, to miss a curve and plunge off a cliff. Randy, the marine with the big brown eyes, loomed before me. I could empathize with his crushing guilt and the appeal of eternal relief. But, this would not be Cory's way. He would have my life move forward. I saw what I was doing. I had regressed to centripetal love. My energies had turned inward, thinking only of myself. I must turn them outward and think of others, those whose lives I can touch and enhance, beginning with

Gramp and the children to follow. I must emphasize self-growth, reject narcissism; explore painting, the arts, humanitarian interests. I must cap my guilt and never expose it to others for it would solve nothing and only become a shared torture. The crime has been committed and the punishment, I decreed, should be a silent bearing of its pain. Gramp especially should be spared of the agony. Keeping my love centrifugal would be my memorial to Cory.

"There is a postscript to the story. The *Hudson* steamed into San Francisco a couple of weeks later and Commander Hawkins threw the victory party financed on the bridge winnings. He graciously wrote to me of the event, expressed his fondess of Cory, and his assessment of the tragedy, which only deepened my sense of guilt." Tally passed on his letter, the final one in the stack, as she dabbed away the stray tears.

Like the others, Natalia read it slowly and carefully. "So," she said, softly, "Gramp had no glimmer of the guilt you carried, did he?"

"I had regained my composure by the time I reached home from my visit with Scorch. Yes, Gramp was spared the ordeal of putting together more shattered pieces. But to prevent a relapse, I had to make some painful decisions. I had to separate myself from the parts of my past connected in any way with Cory. Most excruciating, this meant a break from the Inner Circle. Too many of our gab sessions at the ranch involved Cory. I began a gradual withdrawal process, gave excuses to avoid get-togethers, dropped Christmas and birthday cards, and by the arrival of my last child had lost all contact with them. The last card I received from Cindy was an announcement of her move to Boston where Dave was beginning a new career in the insurance business.

"The thin ties I had with Denver soon evaporated. Dad was too ill to attend my wedding and died shortly afterward. Ted gave me away, returned to Denver, and managed to save his marriage only to fall victim to that piece of shrapnel which moved into his heart. I never was close to mother, who stayed chronically bitter after her divorce, or with my other sibs, who had too many of her negative traits.

"On the happy side, Gramp, anticipating the postwar population boom in San Diego, went into real estate and made a tidy fortune. The city more than quadrupled before he retired. And, as you know, on our first anniversary Gramp slipped me the key to the dream house that overlooked the bay, which has been my joy for a lifetime.

"As for the ranch, in the spirit of progress, it has been razed and the area is now part of the city's business district. Anything more you need, my darling, I suspect can be found in the family album.

"Now, I must insist you honor your pledge of keeping all that I've said to yourself. What I've told you is to remain a secret between us until I have gone."

Natalia watched her grandmother carefully retie the stack of letters. It was now very late. Much coffee had been drunk. Tally looked very tired. The patina of age returned to fade the radiance that had so dominated the reliving of the romance. Natalia gazed in awe at her grandmother, wondering how it was possible for her to have been the bundle of vivaciousness all these years with such heavy guilt weighing on her heart. She never faltered in her love and devotion to Gramp. Natalia poignantly remembered Gramp telling her on his death bed that Tally was the best thing that ever happened to him. She now fully comprehended why Tally could never destroy her letters to Cory. Her love could flow only if it was reciprocated. The letters are the one remaining conduit to keep her love flowing now that she knew his was always there. She edged over on the sofa and silently embraced Tally, her way of thanking her for sharing a love, a beautiful love born and bred in an age of violence, but at a time when love itself still flourished in the sweetness of innocence.

# New Contacts

The love story had an extraordinary effect on Natalia. It awakened a psychic power she never knew existed in her. In the wink of an eye, she could enter a trance, regress in time, and be the Tally of the 1940s. She could feel with her passions, hurt with her pain, introject her fantasies. Although she had never seen a picture of Cory, while in this altered state she just knew she could pick him out of a crowd.

Equally remarkable was that she had full control of the phenomenon. It was like pressing a magic button and, presto, she would be in Tally's shoes. Press the button again and she would be back in her own. It both fascinated and frightened her. Was it a gift or a curse? Is the power latent in everyone or does it exist only in the few mystically linked to the occult? Perhaps this is the core element defining the pathology of a Virgin Mary or a Napoleon who have roamed the halls in our mental institutions. Drawing from her case, Natalia concluded the power is potential in everyone, its release only requiring the sharing of an intense and prolonged emotional experience with a highly admired person. This causes the bonding process to exceed its normal limits. The basic difference between herself and a Napoleon is that she has control of the button. She can switch back to herself at any time but poor Nap is stuck for keeps in his armor. Nevertheless, Natalia decided it would be wise to keep these beliefs to herself.

The metamorphosis, however, was limited to the emotions. Natalia was still able to think independently and form her own conclusions. Thus, while she suffered all of Tally's pain over the fateful letter, she was not ready to accept Tally's self-flagellatory theory that it was a gross misread because of an unstable, runaway imagination. To be sure, the triangle proposition became discredited as more information was gathered, but that only meant the real motive stayed unknown.

Most baffling to Natalia was Cory's posture of resignation in the last exchange of letters. It was the last response Tally had hoped her feigned ambivalence would elicit. Why would he do that? Could other forces have been acting on him? Forces unrelated to the relationship? Forces that would have him join the froggies even if there had been no rift? Such vexing thoughts made Natalia feel it premature for Tally to have branded herself with the mark of executioner.

Her toes wiggled during the flight home in the exasperation of trying to make sense as to why a man would let a woman he loved so deeply slip away so easily. If one element stood out in her assessment of Cory's makeup, it would be his competitive spirit. What happened to it? To have him behave this much out of form, the ugliness of war notwithstanding, gave Natalia the hopeless feeling that she was trying to put together a jigsaw puzzle with a key part missing.

She returned to college and sought to bury herself in her studies, but it was no use. The puzzle became an obsession. Perpetuating it, of course, was the outside chance that the missing part would free her beloved Tally of the albatross weighting her down through the years. What she desperately needed were new clues. Where might they come from? Cindy, Tally's wartime confidante, came to mind. From their many girl chats at the ranch, perhaps she might open the door to fresh leads. It would be a long shot after so long a time, but if she was still in the Boston area, still another long shot, its short distance from Northampton would make a visit a snap. Even if nothing came of it, it would be fascinating to meet in the flesh a member of the Inner Circle. In fact, it would be exciting.

☆ ☆ ☆

Natalia found the house, classic Georgian architecture—symmetrical, hipped roof, double-story pilasters—in an old historic suburb. It set well back from the street on the crest of a knoll. Sugar maples, in flaming autumn colors, formed a canopy over the cobblestone walkway leading to the main entrance. The perfect balm, Natalia agreed, for tight nerves. She pressed the doorbell. A petite elderly lady with tinted hair, in chic clothes and smart high heels, opened the oversized oak door.

"Might you," Natalia asked, "be the Cindy who married a Dave Hertnik, navy officer in World War II?"

She smiled prettily. "Indeed I might. And who might I ask be raising such a question?"

Natalia smiled back. "The granddaughter of your crazy roomie during the big war. My name is Natalia."

Cindy caught her breath, recoiled for a moment, then stepped forward and took stock. Her lovely smile broadened and her eyes danced. "The saints be praised! Yes, indeed, you have her coloring, her bone structure; yes, even her Maureen O'Hara looks. I can't believe it! After all of these years! A page from a book I thought forever closed. I think I just might cry." She clasped Natalia's hand. "Come inside, come inside, my dear."

Cindy led her into a living area crowned with a high beamed ceiling. Natalia glanced about. It was a cheerful room. The furniture, tastefully arranged, was elegant but not forbidding. Lush oriental rugs were strategically scattered on a polished hardwood floor. Sunlight filtered through the upper windows and brightened the colors in the impressionistic paintings hanging on paneled walls. But the main eye-catcher was the massive stone fireplace that pulled everything together and cast a warm, cozy ambiance.

Cindy, in her ebullience, practically wrestled Natalia into a chair as she called out to Dave to come in at once and see the big surprise. A tall, erect man with a shock of gray hair and long slender hands appeared.

"What do you see before you?" Cindy asked unfairly.

After a sweeping look-see, without a cue, he rallied gallantly. "How could anyone think otherwise, a most lovely bloom of a rose."

Cindy ended her tease. "This is Natalia, granddaughter of Tally; you know, my roommate during the war."

This time he peered more intently. "Of course. The resemblance is remarkable. Hair's a bit shorter, eyes a mite less green yet full of the same sparkle." He rose to the occasion. "This calls for a pop of the cork. So happens I have on board just the right stuff." He moved spryly out of the room to fetch the champagne.

While Dave was doing the honors, Cindy asked how they were found. Natalia reminded her that her last note to Tally told of their move to Boston. It was thus a simple matter, as she was a student in Northampton, to get access to a Boston directory. Only one Hertnik was listed, their son, who gave her their address. So, since it was a delightful Sunday day, she hopped in the car and took the chance of catching them at home. Dave laughingly piped up that Hertnik was not a common Brahmin name.

"You came at the right time," Cindy said. "We have a condo in Florida and now that Dave has retired, we go to the gulf after the first cold spell and return with the first bloom of the jonquils. We'll soon be heading south."

Dave suggested first things first and had them clink their glasses in a toast to Tally. Natalia found them such a charming couple. While they sipped, she updated them: told of Gramp's fatal heart attack in the spring, the selling of the house on the bay, and Tally's move into smaller quarters. She then gave them a brief rundown on the family, including where they all currently live and their main activities. Cindy reciprocated and brought forth pictures of her children and grandchildren.

With the perliminaries over, Natalia switched the conversation to the issue prompting her visit. She told them of her last night with Tally and hearing for the first time the fascinating story of her life in the war years. She reminisced on her days at the ranch and the wonderful times with the Inner Circle, freeing memories that had been dammed up for more than a half century. She spellbindingly told the story of her love affair with Cory, but only gave sketchy details of its breakup. Natalia said the star-crossed romance so engrossed her that one of the reasons for her visit was the hope Cindy could shed more light as to how and why it ended.

Cindy sighed. "I was hoping you might fill me in. Tally never told any of us exactly what happened and we respected her privacy. But I will tell you what I think." She waved her glass for a refill.

"First, about the Inner Circle. There was Debbie, Susan, Avis, Tally, and myself. A girl named Laura took my spot at the ranch when I moved. The war brought us together and the war scattered us. We all worked at Convair, an aircraft company, became fast friends, shared everything together, weathering out the thick and the thin. All of us married before the war was over except Susan, who, although smart and attractive, never found whatever she was looking for. Tally and I were inseparable. We could be silly and we could be serious; on reflection, more often silly. I missed her terribly when I moved home as jobs were petering out, but we kept in close touch until after she married Robert. Then, after writing each of us of Cory's death, she slowly drifted out of circulation, finally corresponding with no one, which was crushing to us.

"I still exchange Christmas letters with the other girls and we have a reunion every ten years. All are doing fine. Debbie and Jack share a ranch with Laura and Chad outside of St. Louis and breed champion horses. Susan owns and operates a boutique in Seattle. Avis got divorced shortly after the war, remarried Mr. General Motors, and now spends her time between a penthouse in Manhattan and a villa in Spain."

Cindy's face took on a pensive look. "I've always blamed

myself for what happened between Tally and me. I must have hurt her very much in the way I reacted to her marriage. When she called and asked me to be her matron of honor, I, knowing it was Robert, your grandfather, not Cory, broke down and cried. She reminded me it was a wedding, not a funeral, and asked how many girls did I know lucky enough to marry a Spencer Tracy? This was a private joke between us. I was always comparing people to movie stars and Robert, cuddly as a teddy bear, was my Spencer Tracy. I got to know him fairly well. He came frequently to the house to pick up Tally and escort her to social functions. He was the perfect gentleman. Now, don't misunderstand me, dear, I was fond of Robert, never doubted he would take good care of Tally, and knew he would provide well for her, but when in your twenties, Spencer Tracy is no substitute for Tyrone Power. I could never imagine Tally without Cory. If a match ever gained the smiles of the angels, this was the one. It was love at first sight. Susan and I were with Tally when they first met at a dance and saw what a dashing couple they made. Sometimes when we chatted into the wee hours, Tally would read parts of his letters. They were beautiful. And how her eyes would sparkle! I cried again just before she walked down the aisle and asked if she was certain of what she was doing. It was my hangup. She seemed fully at peace. Yes, it was my messy sentimentality that ruined things between us."

Natalia had to interrupt as a tear formed in Cindy's eye. "When Tally wrote you of Cory's death, did she go into the details?"

"Very little. She only said that he was badly wounded in the Okinawa invasion, died aboard ship, and was buried with honors at sea."

Both she and Dave looked shocked when Natalia told them Cory had volunteered for underwater demolition duty and suffered his fatal wound as a frogman. She added that Tally personally took the blame for his decision, and it was out of intense guilt and a desire not to embroil Gramp in her emotional distress that she pulled herself away from all associations which would remind her of Cory, which, of course, included her beloved Inner Circle. That was the most heart-rending separation of all.

Dave let out an audible sigh. "Thank you so much, Natalia. You've just removed a monkey that had been on Cindy's back all these years."

Cindy, with the look of a prisoner given reprieve, paused to let the full meaning sink in before going on with her theory of the failed romance. "I think," she said, "it was several things. First and foremost, there was Cory's adamant refusal to make a commitment. As much as Tally loved him and he her, it had to mess up her mind. Why Cory refused was beyond me. Shooting from the hip, one of my lesser social graces, I asked Cory one day why he didn't up and marry her before his ship sailed, and he replied that he loved her too much to do a thing like that to her. Although Tally never protested, I always felt it gnawed at an insecurity, which had its taproot, as you know, in a broken home.

"A second thing was the crazy, helter-skelter times. Each day brought on big changes and kept everybody wildly guessing what would be coming next. We all stared into a scary future. As a result there was a lot of leaping and little looking. War breeds impulsivity and a strong craving for a security blanket.

"And then, of course, there was Robert himself, a no small factor. Easy going but solid as an iron gate, he was the soul of stability. When the love bug nipped him—which nobody saw coming—Tally realized she had to fish or cut bait. It was not in her bones to play one against the other. Knowing her like I did, I would say she wrote a completely honest letter to Cory, stated the facts, and expected a clear and unequivocal declaration of intent. What then actually happened still has me buffaloed. I'm guessing stubborn pride intervened and caused misunderstandings that remained uncorrected. All I know for sure is that Cory lost his love and I lost my dearest friend."

Oh, Natalia thought, how I wish I could tell her of the fateful letter, but I am bound to confidentiality.

Cindy continued. "When I first became aware of the altar plans—her phone call setting the date—I sat right down and wrote Cory a long letter, imploring him to act, and to act swiftly, as time was running out. I never mailed it. I decided after three drinks it was not my proper place. And what would it accomplish? Meddling would only stir up waters already over the dam. I cried in frustration."

Natalia stayed on for dinner. She assured Cindy that Gramp was wonderful to Tally, loving her with great tenderness and spoiling her with all the good things in life. He let her develop her talents. He was never possessive but was always there when needed.

In hugging Cindy goodbye, Natalia had to comment that for a group of girls scared stiff about the future, the Inner Circle did right proudly of themselves.

Cindy laughed. "None of us dreamed of the prosperity that peace would bring. We all were depression babies and feared we'd be back to the soup lines when the war was over. We needed a heavy dose of Cory's philosophy."

As Natalia shook Dave's hand, she couldn't resist asking what movie star was his double. Before he could reply, Cindy burst in. "Why, can't you tell? Gary Cooper, of course. But, then, I guess Gary was a little before your time."

Although the visit with Cindy failed to provide any fresh insights, Natalia was happy she made the trip. Cindy had met all of her expectations: bubbly, friendly, genuine, delightful. It was clear the years had not diminished her affection for Tally. She also could tell her visit meant much to Cindy, beyond the relief of no longer shouldering the blame for the separation between the two wartime roommates. She did not write Tally of the visit for fear it might exacerbate her guilt, the last thing in the world she would want to do.

One thing Cindy said stuck with her. It was Cory's reply to

Cindy's inquiry of why he didn't marry her: "I love her too much to do a thing like that to her." What did he mean? Had it some special meaning or was it only another of his clever rejoinders? She felt her little brain was at a loss to analyze further.

Natalia continued to agonize. She felt she was in a blind alley. Fixated as she was to dissolve Tally's guilt, she was running out of leads. Where could she go? Who was left to turn the tide? Starting to haunt her was the disturbing thought she might be on a will-o'-the-wisp venture. In identifying so strongly with Tally, could she be deluding herself? Was the reason she was unable to find exoneration simply because there was none? But, surely, she told herself, there must be more to her obsession than misguided devotion.

☆ ☆ ☆

Shortly after the charming visit with Cindy, a thought hit Natalia out of the blue. What about Cory's sister, Kathleen? Tally had referred to his close-knit family, but having never met Kathleen, made no attempt to ever contact her. Was it possible she could be holding the missing pieces to the puzzle? Nothing lost in exploring it. Stranger things have been known to happen. Natalia's heart jumped at the remote chance. But, then, was the lady even still alive? She raised her eyes to the heavens and asked for that little favor.

How to locate her? That created a big problem. She did not know her married name nor anyone who might have a clue to her whereabouts. Then her sleuthing talents bubbled to the surface and she thought of the High School Alumni Association. These organizations keep current addresses of all graduates. Tally had mentioned Cory's hometown, and Natalia could guess the approximate year of Kathleen's graduation. She wrote and the heavens honored her little favor. Kathleen Zigler Malone was indeed alive and was now living in a retirement village in Arizona. Natalia penned a letter to her, taking great care in composing it, aware that she had come to her last hope. She introduced herself, briefly explained her grandmother's close connection with her brother, and expressed her vital interest in getting more information about Cory, especially his thoughts and feelings in the final stages of the war. She told her she'd be infinitely grateful for whatever she might provide. With breathless anticipation, a thick letter arrived.

November 12, 2002

Dear Natalia,

How strange it was to hear Cory's name mentioned after all these years. He was my only brother, we were extremely close, and the shock of his death at such a young age, especially with the war so close to its end, still lingers heavily on me. The thought of the terrible waste mists up my eyes. He was such a very special person.

I am the doyenne of the clan, but with my heart irregularity becoming increasingly more so, I may not hold that distinction for long. You did well to write when you did.

It was with a warm feeling that I read the words on your grandmother. Cory, as you know, affectionately referred to her as Mopsy. I never met her, but I imagine her most lovely and charming, for how otherwise could she have stolen his heart so completely! How devastating his loss must have been to her. I contemplated writing her, anguished over it, but never did, not knowing really what to say, being such a total stranger in her life. In my distraught state at the time, I likely would have been more upsetting than comforting to her.

You asked about Cory's state of mind near the end. Odd that you should raise such a question. The last letter I was to receive from him came in early February of 1945. It was not his usual buoyant letter. It left me floundering a bit as to how to respond to it, but fate sadly resolved the issue. In the letter he brought up personal feelings that he had obviously carried within himself for a long time, which was so typical of Cory. Despite his out-goingness, he was a very private person. It was his wont to keep controversy or any general form of unpleasantness out of conversation. Perhaps he was inclined to make this disclosure because he had a premonition of things to come and thought it might in some way help lessen the burden for others. Who knows. Sometimes Cory's mind worked in ways that completely mystified me. I was strongly tempted to destroy the letter after his death because it had lost its currency but, being his last written words to me, I could not bring myself to do it. And now perhaps, these many years later, it may serve some useful end. With that possibility, I am copying it in its entirety for you.

Dearest Kathleen,

As the war lengthens, its horror deepens. The peak will come in the battle of Japan itself, for the enemy will defend his home soil to the last drop of his blood. The die is cast in the samurai code: Loyalty is heavier than a mountain; life is lighter than a feather. Thus, there will be few prisoners. How much of this can the mind absorb? Will it snap without warning? Surely before its sun blots out, it will have a premonition of rising black clouds.

For a long time I've held back feelings about Uncle Brian that I'd now like to share with you—while the sun, *compos mentis,* still shines.
(Uncle Brian, I need to insert, returned from World War I a shellshock victim who never recovered. He lived with family members who took turns caring for him. He spent four months of each year in our home, mostly alone in his room. He died of causes unclear while we were still children.)

It may surprise you, Kathleen, to learn that I've always felt a close affinity toward him, always considered us two peas in a pod, always believed our destinies were guided by the same star.

As you know, I was twelve when he died. I kept my silence at that time while others spoke of his total break from reality, although I wanted to shout out: wrong, wrong, wrong. Uncle Brian and I had many moments together, brief though they were, when his mask was off. The earliest memory—I couldn't have been more than three or four—was when he had an art book open on his bed. I leafed through several pages and pointed excitedly to a print of the *Duchess of Alba.* "Very pretty," I said. He suddenly smiled, his eyes brightened, and he said, "Goya," the first word I ever heard him speak. The mask immediately returned. Another time I showed him a print of the *Luncheon on the Boating Party.* Again, a brief moment of lucidity. "Renoir," he said. He patted my hand. "Such beauty is rare." I could cite a number of other such occasions and, perhaps, the most impressive one was the night when we were alone in the house and he led me to the piano. He sat down and played flawlessly Chopin's Étude in E Major. His eyes turning soft and thoughtful, he said, "Chopin," and then the protective mask slipped back into place. It was a one-time keyboard performance. I would guess he had a repertoire of Chopin's études. On several different nights he took me to the window, pointed out and named a prominent constellation. The relevance of all this, Kathleen, is that he was communicating with me. And he was communicating with me at a level he intuitively understood we had in common—a deep appreciation of beauty. Thus, I came to believe early that we were cut out of the same cloth; his dominant genes were passed on to me. I raised the issue once to mother and she was quick to see strong similarities, rating us both much alike in empathy. She related an incident when I was only two. I ran into the house to ask for two cookies as a little boy had joined me in the yard. By the time I returned with the cookies, another tyke had joined us. I looked at the two of them, then looked at the two cookies, hesitated, and gave a cookie to each one. I stood with my hands behind my back and watched my little friends eat. The scene reminded mother of an almost identical story her mother had told on Brian when he was about the same age. Yes, mother agreed, the two of us were born with remarkably similar sensitivities.

Uncle Brian has been on my mind very much of late. His world fell apart in Belleau Wood and he could never reassemble it. Is my Belleau Wood ahead of me? Is it in the empire of the rising sun? I fear that more than death itself. Uncle Brian could endure only brief moments of lucidity because he could not bear the dinosaur he had become. Oh, how well I can understand that! He willed his death but it was painfully slow in coming. How much more humane if Belleau Wood had properly finished the job it had ruthlessly begun. Were I ever in such plight, I'd do all in my power to assist our heavenly Father to complete the job that was bungled. I could not face becoming a human shell to those I love.

I assure you, Kathleen, I'll never bring this subject up again. . . .

Cory.

Well, my dear Natalia, as you know, the crisis never came. Cory died in the line of duty with all his faculties fully intact. But, nevertheless, this concern must have affected his mood during his last days. I hope I have been of some help to you.

Sincerely,
Kathleen Malone

P.S. I did keep one other letter as it was the only one in which he shared a battle experience. But since it happened earlier in the war, it would not likely have much direct bearing on your request. I regret I had not kept all his letters, but when young we have so little of the sense of history in the making.

# Final Reunion

Joy seasoned with sadness is bittersweet, which was how Natalia Dorn felt after reading Kathleen Malone's letter. The joy was in finding the missing part of the puzzle but the sadness was in what it exposed. It brought to light the poignant motivation underlying Cory's response to Tally's letter of feigned ambivalence. But, overshadowing the anguish of that discovery was the exultation in knowing that Tally at last would be free of the guilt pressing on her heart all of these years. The evidence that clearly pointed to forces outside herself for affecting the outcome of her ill-fated love affair, would let her be able to grant to herself, in a long overdue act of justice, a pardon for a tragedy, for which she had assumed full culpability. The timing could not have been better. Thanksgiving was approaching and Tally had chosen among her many invitations to join the Dorn table in New England— the perfect holiday to have the epiphany.

Natalia decided to savor the grand moment of truth at lunch on the return trip to the airport. There would be just the two of them, and immediately afterward Tally would have the privacy of the long flight home to slowly digest its full meaning.

Tally's visit was pure delight. Everyone reveled in her company. The venting of her long suppressed guilt was showing its cathartic effect, most notably in her spirits. The family detected more spring to her step. They also noticed, equally baffling, more bounce in Natalia's.

Finally the day and hour for the exciting disclosure arrived. Natalia and Tally stopped on the way to the airport to snack at a quiet roadside cafe, and while capping it off with a cup of espresso, Natalia drew the letter from her purse. With a burst of narrative flourish, she hyperbolized the drama of finding Cory's sister to heighten the suspense before slipping the envelope into Tally's hand. She watched intently the changing expression as Tally read. Thunderstruck best described the look when she finally put the letter down. The whipsaw conversation between them began.

"Dear Lord, it was not all my doings."

"It was his doings. He did want to distance the relationship, but only to protect you."

"If I had only known."

"That would've been the last thing he'd want."

"I really didn't give the death sentence?"

"Uncle Brian did."

"I'm not fully to blame?"

"You are free, Tally, of a sin you never committed."

"If Kathleen had only written."

"She never even knew he volunteered."

"Of course. How could she?"

"Cory slipped up on that one."

"He loved me always."

"As you loved him."

"He died knowing I loved him."

"I can't imagine otherwise."

"He was a saint."

"St. Francis of Assisi."

Natalia cried when Tally boarded the plane.

☆　☆　☆

The annual reunion of the Robert Graham family was always held at Christmas, Tally's favorite holiday. All would gather at the big house. Tally and Robert made a big production of it with a spectacular splash of lights and decorations. There was always a tree, the singing of carols, homemade candies, punch, champagne, storytelling, wholsesale frivolity. Christmas of 2002 was the first to break the long-standing pattern. Robert, of course, was gone and the big house had sold. The clan met at the home of the oldest sibling, Robert Jr., who lived in a rather staid mansion in a San Diego suburb. He and his wife went all out to carry on the spirit of the tradition, seeing that there was an abundance of everything, but all felt it wasn't quite the same. Conspicuously absent was Tally's vivaciousness, which had been spiraling downhill since Thanksgiving. It was all too evident that the family rallied round her for its cohesiveness: her light, infectious mood getting everyone into the festive holiday spirit. How keenly they missed her sparkle this day. After the sumptuous dinner, in which she only dabbled at her food, she mentioned being a bit tired and begged indulgence to be dismissed. She declined offers of assistance home and, not wishing to disrupt family activities, insisted on driving alone to her cottage. The moment she left, she became the chief conversation piece. Natalia's mother began it.

"I'm very worried. Mother looks so pale and run-down."

Her sister chimed in. "I agree. Although she recently had a physical and the doctor could find nothing wrong with her, I'm going to make an appointment with a specialist. She's definitely losing ground."

Natalia's Uncle Robert, an advertising executive, was more sanguine. "There you two doomsayers go again, making a mountain out of a molehill. Mother's only a bit depressed, still working through the loss of Dad and the giving up of the big house. After all, when you're entering into the octogenarian years, it takes a little longer to adjust. But she's a tough ol' bird and should have good years left. She'll start perking up when the days start getting longer."

Natalia's Uncle Matt, the taciturn one and her favorite, a marine biologist, did not venture an opinion. Instead, he said: "Natalia, you've been the one closest to Mother of late. What do you think?"

Natalia suddenly felt all eyes focusing on her. She spoke

hesitantly. "I doubt if a specialist can do much for her. It's beyond medicine. Nor do I think that time is the cure. I fear it's more than just the loss of Gramp and the selling of the big house."

"Why do you say that?" a voice cried out.

"She has fulfilled her goals. She brought up her children in a loving and caring home and saw to it that they and their children were given advantages never given her, a college education at the best schools and annual trips to the world's cultural centers. She involved herself in community affairs, worked unselfishly, did cheerfully whatever was asked of her. She nursed Gramp through his final days. Most people in her shoes would be content to rest on their laurels, but Grandmother is not of that mettle. Above all, she doesn't ever want to be a burden on anyone. In fact, if she were the slightest bit aware of the direction this conversation has turned, she would get red-cheeked with embarrassment."

"Well then," someone gravely asked, "how much longer do you think she'll be with us?"

It was a question that caught Natalia unprepared. She thought of hedging, reconsidered, and decided to answer candidly. "Not very long, I fear. St. Patrick's Day has a special meaning for her. I cannot see much beyond that."

With her little spiel over, a pall fell over the room. The family looked rather funny at her. She could not blame them. They had no inkling of what she knew—that Tally had finally found an inner peace which had eluded her for a lifetime. The cycle of self-recrimination, guilt, and need for atonement, originating in the chaos of war, was finally broken. The grief of the heart, which time can never fully heal, was free at last of festering, a relief that seems to have brought on the desire for final rest.

Natalia bit her tongue. She knew she had said too much and wished she had been less candid. She had spoiled the day and knew not how to make amends. She began to feel lightheaded, could feel her pulse weaken. She, too, excused herself.

☆ ☆ ☆

Natalia's premonition heartbreakingly came to pass. Tally did not wake up on the morning of St. Patrick's Day. She missed an unusually beautiful sunrise, one that would have warmed the cockles of her colleen heart. The family had gathered the day before on the advice of the attending physician who said she was fading fast and was now in God's hands. She spoke to each one alone, inquiring in her vintage fashion about their hopes and ambitions. She exhorted them to stay with their dreams and, above all, to never lose their sense of humor. She called Natalia back to her bedside as day moved into twilight and had her play on her antique record player, still in remarkable working order, her favorite Chopin, "Étude in E Major," made popular in the ballad "No Other Love."

"Cory once told me," she said, "that no composer does to an étude what Chopin does. As usual, he was so right. I often played them while painting."

She then calmly and dispassionately went over final instructions with Natalia. She was to be immediately cremated, no matter how much the family may fuss for her to rest in the natural form next to Gramp. Natalia was to then take her ashes without delay to the "rock" under the full stars and fling them out to sea.

She was wearing the peace pin and the pearl necklace, the inhibitions at last removed. Natalia commented on how lovely they looked on her. She took them off, pressed them into Natalia's hand, and told her they were hers to have, to wear, to love. She pointed to the bedside stand and said the letters were now also hers to do with whatever she wished since her guardianship had come to its end.

Natalia thought the moment was ripe to tell Tally of her visit with Cindy and Dave. A warm smile spread across Tally's face as she heard the kind reception Natalia received and the love rendered to her on hearing the reason for her withdrawal. The smile

lingered on as she was given the good news on the lives and for-
tunes of the rest of the Inner Circle.

"I'm so happy," she murmured. "They deserve life's fullest."

Natalia had two more surprises to spring on her. She had rum-
maged about in old shops until she found a recording of "Always."
She placed it on the turntable and slyly glanced at her grandmother. "You'll never guess, Tally, what caught my eye in the window of an antique shop the other day. I simply had to snatch it
up."

Tally's eyes, which were dimming, slowly brightened as the
song filled the room, and by the time the record ended, they had
regained their former luster. "Our song. Thank you, darling," she
breathed.

Natalia was down to her last surprise. In her thank-you note
to Kathleen Malone, she commented that Cory had assiduously
avoided making any reference to his combat experiences to Tally,
and she has come to regret knowing nothing of this special side
of his life. The sweet lady promptly sent a copy of the one other
letter she had saved. Natalia pulled it from her purse. She told
Tally of this latest communication received from Cory's sister and
asked if she would like to have it read. Tally smiled and gave a
strong vertical nod of the head.

> My Favorite of Sisters,
>    It's come to mind that you may be wondering why I've said
> little about the nails we've hammered into Tojo's coffin. I'm
> meaning, of course, how the stars got to be on our ribbons. I
> shall confess. My ruse was to stay mum until the day I visit your
> teepee, beat the bongos and stir the little papooses up into a war
> dance to get stories from Big Chief Uncle Cory. By then I'd have
> ballooned them up into such whoppers that their eyes will pop
> out of their sockets. I have one tale, however, because of your
> long-standing *amor* with physics, that's plain too pressing to
> hold out of circulation. (I should insert that physics was the one
> school subject giving me the most fits.)
>    We had made a good landing. By that I mean we hit the right

beach on the right island on the right day. We hung about until the beachhead was secure, the cue we're no longer wanted, a snub we always take gracefully since Jap-infested beaches have a way of robbing us of sleep, getting us off our feed, festering old ulcers. Orders were to weigh anchor, deposit a shipload of wounded, and head for a resort island where gallons of warm beer were on tap to drown the fading sorrows of parting. So far, SOP.

Then on the morn of sailing tragedy struck. Our communications officer on routine business ashore caught a sniper's sight. Our skipper, still on his vendetta, flashed a diabolical grin and appointed me temporary replacement. You understand, I am one who had never seen the inside of a communications shack, having respectfully heeded the warning posted above the door: HIGH VOLTAGE, KEEP OUT. I pleaded incompetence. The captain humorlessly reminded me there was a manual of instructions and presumed I had mastered the rudiments of reading. What he ignored was: (1) The manual was as thick as the New York City phone book; and (2) My mind after these beach encounters is brain dead. With great effort it might muster up a blip on an EEG graph. My one and only hope lay in a quiet, uneventful voyage to our destination.

It took but a few miles at sea to know that fate had other plans. The hint first came in the form of a coded message. In a comedy of errors unworthy of re-hashing, I finally decoded it. We were approaching a submarine net area, meaning we were entering hostile waters where enemy sub activity was recently reported. All ships went on the alert and doubled the watches. Since convoy vessels are defenseless against "cigars," all we could do was tighten ranks and pray that the escorting destroyers do their job. The devil at this point intervened and his perverted sense of humor created tension too thick for a bowie knife to cut. He broke key bolts in the ship's engine, resulting in that fine piece of machinery, purring quietly since the day of commission, to go wheezy and die. Our competent engineer, doubling up the work crew, estimated at least an hour to complete the repairs. The captain instructed me to so inform the flagship and request protection. By the time I bumbled out the message, the convoy was fast disappearing over the horizon. So efficient was I that a message from the flag beat mine to tell us a sub was detected off our port bow and a destroyer was on its way.

Our skipper moved with surprising alacrity. He sounded general alarm to prepare to abandon ship. Bedlam ensued as bodies frantically scurried to load the wounded into lifeboats. I pell-melled to the manual to find what the communications officer does at such perilous moments. I located the paragraph. My job was to bind and weight down the top-secret documents, drag them to my battle station on the bridge, and heave them overboard when the abandon-ship order booms out. Then I jump into the nearby lifeboat and lower myself into the ocean blue.

Even my enfeebled brain could spot the glaring fundamental flaw. My battle station was next to the smokestack. Any seasoned sub commander—and who wasn't at this stage of the war!—periscoping a sitting duck would level his torpedo at midship, which would blow up the engine room and split the ship in half. The explosion would shoot debris up the smokestack. Only a totally dysfunctional idiot could believe one would have the time to toss the documents into the sea, climb into a lifeboat, lower himself three decks, and paddle off before a ton of flying steel fell on top of him. My course of action was clear. I'd jump with the documents into the sea and swim a la Tarzan to anything floating.

Another insight hit me, amazing myself at my prolonged acuity. When I jumped, I would have to land on a wave moving away from the ship. Riding one toward the ship would draw me under the falling debris, a sure way for an early date with St. Pete. The situation called for the application of the law of falling bodies, no big deal for one majoring in physics. Suddenly, my mental juices went bone dry. For the life of me I couldn't recall the formula, vaguely remembering it had nothing to do with mass and everything to do with acceleration. A coin would land about the same time as a falling man. But was acceleration at 16 or 32 feet per sec.? Oh, me! I despaired. Then, strangely, I thought of you, dear Kathleen, the one who never adjusted to the thought of reducing nature to sterile mathematical expressions. What would you do in my shoes? Of course, of course! You would be empirical. And holding a pocketful of change, that I could be.

I stood on the bridge staring down the lower decks, dropping coins on the moving groundswells, timing their landings to coordinate the jump. Several dollars' worth of change were donated to Neptune's coffer before I was convinced I had it all figured out.

I can happily say the derived calculations were never tested. After what seemed endless minutes of near panic waiting, but probably no more than twenty, a mighty roar went up. Black oil was spotted on the sea off our distant bow. The can had zapped the sub before the sub could zap us. The skipper took one look at me and in a moment of temporary amnesia, suggested I repair to the wardroom for a reviving cup of coffee. I took one swallow and a funny thing happened. I heard it thud somewhere in the lower part of the thoracic cavity, missing everything on its way down. I knew with a second swallow it would be all over. I'd be hanging over the rail joining the big crowd that had already gathered.

We reached port without further mishap and my short, undistinguished career with the coding machines was over. An expert in the area was waiting to relieve me. And now as I laze under the palms sipping warm beer, I hoist a toast to my precious sister whose substandard approach to solving the problems of physics might well have saved the day if a certain sub commander had been a mite faster on his patrol.

Your most appreciative brother

"Oh," Tally exclaimed, "that is so much the Cory I know. Even humor in bedlam." There was an extended pause in which she struggled with her breathing. Natalia put a finger to her lips to suggest she not talk, but she wanted to say something more. She briefly rallied and her voice steadied. "Cory, you know, really wasn't down on admirals; he was indicting war and he used them as the necessary foil. Cory cried through satire. I love satire. So we do cry well together." Her breathing was now anxiously labored.

Natalia hugged her, pressed her wet cheeks on hers. It was the only way she could say: I know, I know. "Happy St. Patrick's Day," she did whisper.

Tally's beautiful turquoise eyes closed, a peaceful smile softened her face as she slipped into her final slumber.

☆ ☆ ☆

Natalia walked alone along the Coronado shoreline. She touched the magic button and was suddenly Tally in the year 1945. She was dressed sentimentally in red and white, his peace dove decorating her bosom, his pearl necklace embracing her neck. She was drawn like a magnet to their rock, feeling the sweetness of his presence. She climbed to the top, her mop of hair blowing in the wind, and listened enthralled to the sublime sounds of the surf below. The night air was mild, the stars uncommonly bright, the ocean utterly majestic. She called out gently to Cory:

"Oh, my dear heart, my foolish heart, if only you had known! If you had gambled with life, you would have won. There was no Operation Olympic, no palace moat to cross. A miracle which lit up the sky of New Mexico would end the war and have you in my arms for Christmas, the wish that always ended my nightly prayers.

"Oh, my dear heart, my foolish heart, you chose instead to gamble with death and lost. I now know why. It was the vision of Belleau Wood. In your zeal to protect your love you forgot how the gods were protecting you. They gave to you, which they never gave to Uncle Brian, the gift of humor to blunt the insanity of war.

"Oh, my dear heart, my foolish heart, I now know your love never wavered or strayed, even though tested to the extreme by my frailities. In protecting me instead of informing me, you went in loneliness to your death. If there is a less selfish sacrifice I know not what it could be.

"Oh, my dear heart, my foolish heart, what might have been,

what should have been, what would have been if only the roses had not vanished in the rain."

She pressed the magic button and the clock whirled forward to 2003 and Natalia, now the granddaughter of Tally, stood poised on the edge of a flat-topped boulder and cocked an ear toward the soothing sounds of the sea. Her hand clutched a small urn of ashes. She spoke above the whispering waves:

"Cory 'Timothy O'Reilly' Zigler, many years ago at a festive St. Patrick's ball, you met and fell in love with a beautiful Irish colleen and she with you. You sallied forth to fight a war and she took upon herself a pledge. She said as long as you loved her and wanted her, she would be there waiting for you. Twas not a lightly taken pledge. Time neither weakened nor corrupted it. Finding out at long last, after a most confusing and balled up exchange of signals that you really still love her and want her, she hastened preparations to have that reunion, long overdue, take place on anniversary day. We Natalias, you know, are incorrigibly sentimental."

Natalia looked up at the Great Bear bright in the heavens. "This time, Gash and Mopsy, there is no war or perverted power in the universe that can keep the two of you from continuing on with the magical journey begun many years ago on these very shores."

With her toes crushing in pain, she flung the urn with all of her strength. She watched it strike a tiny wave, raise a little bubble, suspend momentarily as though it were defying gravity, and then disappear. Tears that had been welling up all day began oozing out, making tiny puddles on her cheeks. But they were tears of centrifugal love as a tiny rainbow appeared in the mist before her eyes, a sign that Tally was now among the stars. As Natalia began her slow descent, she touched her dove of peace. Her toes relaxed, her pain subsided because she now knew all was right in the world. God was back on his watch.